JEFFERSON

REBELLION TO TYRANTS IS OBEDIENCE TO GOD

JEFFERSON

REBELLION TO TYRANTS IS OBEDIENCE TO GOD

A Novel

MAX BYRD

BANTAM BOOKS

New York Toronto London Sydney Auckland

JEFFERSON

A Bantam Book / November 1993

Thomas Jefferson insignia courtesy of Thomas Jefferson Memorial Foundation

Book design by Carol Malcolm-Russo / Signet M. Design, Inc.

Library of Congress Cataloging-in-Publication Data

Byrd, Max.
    Jefferson : a novel / Max Byrd.
      p.   cm.
    ISBN 0-553-09470-X
    1. Jefferson, Thomas, 1743–1826—Fiction.   I. Title.
PS3552.Y675J44   1993
813'.54—dc20   93-15243
                                         CIP

JEFFERSON

REBELLION TO TYRANTS IS OBEDIENCE TO GOD

PROLOGUE

There were two facts about Jefferson that I never could reconcile.

Fact one: When he first spoke to someone he invariably stood with his arms folded tightly across his chest. The day I arrived in Paris, twenty-six years old, so naive and enthusiastic I blush at the memory now, four wretched weeks beating across the wet Atlantic to rejoin him—that November morning I leapt out of my carriage and rushed through the house on rue Taitbout, calling his name at every room and finding him at last in the innermost study, seated with a book in a wing-backed chair; or slouched in the chair Virginia-fashion rather, with his knees higher than his head, like a half-open knife. He stood up at once to greet me—all six feet and more of him, always taller than anyone he met—but in the same motion the arms and the book came mechanically up and crossed over his chest. Even after he had taken my hand and shaken it, the arms sprang back to his chest, crossed, and stayed there, clasped. I was to see him do it a thousand times, I suppose, in the same way exactly, no matter whether in Paris with little French counts and countesses bobbing up and down like dolls, or in New York with brusque Federalist men of business or even with his own poor bullied daughters. In the end, observing the ritual from my discreet corner of the room by the secretary's desk, I came to think of it as a gesture of keeping something away, instinctive fence-building for a shy and reserved man.

His French architect Clérisseau said I was exactly wrong, of course: It was the instinctive gesture of a cold man locking something in.

The other fact was his singing. He sang *constantly*—in my old age now I turn over the myriad accounts of him stacked on my table, reminiscences of friends, enemies, comrades, and I never see it mentioned anywhere, but sing he did. Snatches hummed or more often actually sung in that soft, reedy voice that made him such a bad public speaker. He sang while he rode—more than once I rode with him from the *hôtel* he had rented on the Champs-Élysées to the palace at Versailles and heard not a word from his lips all morning except those quiet little songs. He sang when he wrote (and he never stopped writing). Italian songs most often, or French ones. Nothing could have been more serene in effect, or truer to the impression of cheerful imperturbability he always gave his friends (and enemies). Nothing could have been less like the rigidity of those folded arms.

Having written this much of these little memoirs of Jefferson, I am reminded of a third trait. He was a superb rider all his life, even for a Virginian, and we are born to horses. But before he rode, every time, he performed a strange personal ritual, such as I've never seen another man do. While the groom held the bridle, Jefferson always wiped off the horse's back and neck meticulously with a clean white handkerchief. More than once I watched him then put away the kerchief and moments later take the whip to his poor wiped horse—and as the miserable animal wheeled round and round, rearing and shying and kicking, he would grip the reins short in one hand and smash the leather thongs down furiously again and again till the flesh bled in buckets. I never saw a more *violent* horseman.

Why did he do it? Was he teaching the horse who was master? Was he venting some internal anger—or guilt—hidden from everyone else, kept locked away in that remote, unapproachable, fenced-away center of Jeffersonian privacy?

Did the great democrat whip his black slaves that way? Clérisseau would ask with an ugly grin.

—William Short
Philadelphia, July 4, 1826

PART

REBELLION TO TYRANTS IS OBEDIENCE TO GOD

O n e

CHAPTER

One

JUNE 4, 1781 — CHARLOTTESVILLE, DAWN. The Lord Cornwallis's troops menacing Virginia once more, not six months after Benedict Arnold had stormed by surprise through Richmond, burning half the ramshackle wooden city to the ground and tossing the governor's own private books and papers — the governor who lived by ink — into the silky brown James River. That same governor, Thomas Jefferson, still sleeping now at dawn in a dark unpainted room at Monticello or else beginning to stir and think about his houseguests and their breakfast.

Seven hours earlier, thirty miles away, a huge young man, small-faced as a bear but taller even than Governor Jefferson, had suddenly put down his glass of whiskey and cocked his ear to listen. His father owned a tavern in Charlottesville, and filial Jack Jouett had just stopped in at the Cuckoo, opposite the Louisa Courthouse, for a last drink at midnight and then a dirty bunk upstairs. Even in the warm June night Jack still wore his long scarlet militia coat of the Virginia Guard and his new captain's bars, which he meant to show his father tomorrow. If there was anyone else in the room besides the sleepy bartender, legend has utterly lost him.

Jack Jouett put down his drink and cocked his ear and finally crossed the floor to the window. On the other side of the square, fifty yards distant, he heard harnesses clinking, spurs, the rattle of swords, the unmistakable rub and thump of horses. There was a quarter moon blanketed off and on by clouds that night. Through the Cuckoo's shutters he could see only indistinct figures and shadows; then a candle came down the steps of the courthouse and plumed caps sprang into silhouette.

If he had waited another ten minutes, Jack Jouett could have seen the red-coated foot soldiers coming uphill at a quick march, bayonets flashing, to join the green-jacketed mounted dragoons at the Louisa Courthouse, wheeling and backing now as they re-formed their columns. And in their midst, holding the candle over a map on his saddle, he would have seen Colonel Banastre Tarleton himself. *Tarleton!*—in London, Sir Joshua Reynolds had painted his famous full-length portrait, a beautiful baby-faced English dandy in skintight trousers, with a girl's red lips and blond spit curls turned delicately up in place of sideburns. But in Virginia, after they had found the five heads in a Williamsburg farmhouse, severed crudely from the bodies and lined neatly along the mantel, after they had buried the pregnant housewife, stabbed in the belly, the bloody words "No more Rebels" smeared on her homespun sheets, after Tarleton had ordered his troops to charge full speed into Abraham Buford's surrendered army—in Virginia after that Colonel Banastre Tarleton was known simply as the Butcher, the man who gave "Tarleton's quarter."

Jack Jouett never saw him. He was on his horse and thundering through the shadowed backwoods before the first foot soldiers ever reached the courthouse, backwoods and paths and alleys Jack Jouett had ridden all his life, night and day, sober and drunk, man and boy. Because whiskey or not, he was still clear-headed enough to guess that a troop of British cavalry mounted and armed at midnight was planning no harmless bivouac stop-over at Louisa but was heading north toward Charlottesville to do what the furious Arnold had only just missed doing—capture the sleeping governor and all the rebel legislators with him.

Jack Jouett rode till his horse's heart nearly burst—down black tunnels of overarched catalpa and pine, parallel to the highway but far inland, gaining a mile an hour over Tarleton's emerald-coated dragoons even before they stopped again at Thomas Walker's estate called Castle Hill—father of that John Walker whose beautiful wife the governor had watched too closely years before—stopped and for the sheer malice of it burned half a dozen wagons and sheds.

By the time Jack Jouett pounded into Charlottesville, the sun was rising behind him and his face was whipped bloody with cuts from branches and tree limbs (scarred all his life, his family said). He paused long enough to hammer at doors along Locust Street, rousing some of his militia cohorts, then he kicked his horse again, more sweat and lather than horse by now, and started uphill to the mountaintop where Jefferson had been building his mansion off and on for the past ten years.

Down the unfinished steps of the east portico—he would trip and break his left wrist on the same steps forty years later, making it *both* wrists that he oddly broke in falls—down these steps Jefferson came in shirt-sleeves, hugging his torso. Afterward, Jack Jouett would swear that Jefferson made him sit down and drink not one but two leisurely glasses of Madeira wine before he even listened to his message, but the legislators who had been his houseguests (Patrick Henry's friends, to be sure) swore just as hard that Jefferson had turned instantly pale as milk and raced over the lawn to the telescope he kept mounted by a wall. When he trained it downhill on Charlottesville and saw nobody in the streets yet, nothing but spokes of pure white sunlight crowning a blue-green Virginia haze, the governor raised his voice for his servants and disappeared running toward the stables.

This was the moment, Patrick Henry afterward declared, when the great god Panic laid his hand on Jefferson. His shouts woke all the slaves, who came piling out of their shacks on Mulberry Row. Upstairs in the half-finished house, the sleepy lawmakers stumbled to the windows and looked down on a scene of amazing hysteria. Jefferson—Jefferson the sworn governor—was dashing back and forth in a mob of screaming blacks, gathering his arm-loads of silver, his gold-framed paintings, and his fine English bone china, and the slaves were shoving it all helter-skelter, as fast as it came, under the mansion floor.

The lawmakers, of course, when they could pry the news out of him, took to their horses and scattered down the hill to warn the city. Jefferson meanwhile—with no thought for the rest of the government, no dispatches off to General Steuben, not a word—stayed frantically wrapping his goods in yellow oilcloth (what other leader in all the Revolution was ever so *fastidious*?) till he heard the slaves out by the garden beginning to call.

"They's started up the hill!"

It was black Martin Hemings (yes!) who saw them first, a squadron of green-backed wasps swarming up from Charlottes-ville toward the governor's lonely hilltop. And it was Martin Hem-ings who led the governor's huge bay stallion Caractacus up to the steps and boosted the governor into the saddle. Even then Jeffer-son kept one arm filled with treasures and galloped off to the west clutching his silver.

Say what you will about the Declaration of Independence, the years in the Continental Congress, the double terms as governor—by universal consent (Virginia consent), this *fiasco* undid it all—it was the nadir of Jefferson's political career, the absolute low black point of his reputation as a leader and a man, and in Vir-ginia, despite everything that followed, he never recovered from it.

"Our illustrious, *scampering*, governor," said Betsy Ambler with her sweetest irony, "took neither rest nor food for man or horse till he passed over Carter's Mountain and rode to safety twenty good miles from Monticello." Once hidden from the green-coats he promptly fell off his bay horse and broke his arm, so he had to stay in the woods for six weeks, until the Virginia legislature met to impeach him for cowardice.

"Caractacus who unseated him," Betsy would add with wither-ing scorn, "was of course the name of a British king."

Even in retrospect I pause and sigh.

Because this is the *first* version of the story I heard, a tale told by Jefferson's political enemies but corroborated, it was said, by half a dozen more-or-less neutral witnesses at Monticello. And when he became president twenty years later, the Federalist press would resurrect it, outrageously embellished: "Jefferson's Great Shame." "Jefferson in Flight." "Jefferson the Horseback Governor, Galloping Away."

But who that knew Jefferson could really believe it? In fact, as I soon discovered, it is only one of two completely contradictory versions. (The Federalists never printed the other.) The truth is—the enduring riddle of Jefferson's character is—if you ask another (smaller) set of more-or-less neutral witnesses what happened that day at Monticello, then *this* is the story you get.

JUNE 4, 1781—CHARLOTTESVILLE, DAWN. The Lord Cornwallis's troops menacing Virginia once more, raiding inland as far as Richmond and swinging a torch against every rebel building and field in reach. The sun rising like a torch itself through the blue-green haze of the eastern mountains, a blazing white disk balanced ominously on a finger-ridge of shadow. . . .

At Monticello when the slaves started to shout, Jack Jouett was crashing on his horse through the dense undergrowth near their cabins. With a huge whoop and a yell he burst free of the last bushes and charged uphill over the lawn and out of his saddle. And Jefferson, who never slept late a day in his life, was already coming down the steps to catch his arm as he staggered, leading him into the north cabinet that would later become the tea room, sitting him down in a fine chair, and calmly saying his name. He knew Jack Jouett and he knew his father, and before he let the boy talk, he called for strong wine—Madeira was what they had by—and poured him two large glasses. Afterward they would say in New England that Paul Revere had got his poet and so his fame —Virginia always long of horses, short of poets—but the truth was, inept, unlucky Paul Revere had been stopped and captured by the British before he even reached Concord (who remembers that now?), while Jack Jouett had out-ridden and out-lasted seventy of George III's finest cavalry over thirty miles of tar-black wilderness and thereby saved the life of the author of the Declaration of Independence.

What that author did first was walk to the end of the lawn and carefully study the horizon. Seeing no troops, he came back to the house and brought his guests calmly down to breakfast. Then, although he had legally stopped being governor two days before, he gathered together all the official papers he still had in his possession and started to burn or hide them—no secret would ever fall into enemy hands if he could help it. Meanwhile, on his instructions the houseguests hurried down the mountain to warn Charlottesville and the outlying settlements (when they woke a boozy Patrick Henry at Cismont, he disappeared so fast that he forgot one shoe). The state's papers safely hidden, Jefferson sent his family west to a friendly plantation, and he himself rode halfway down the mountain to a lookout point. Legend says he looked through his telescope and saw nothing, so started back; then he realized that he had dropped his sword at the lookout point, and when he returned and stopped a second time, he saw Tarleton's soldiers winding uphill like a green-backed snake.

Indisputably, he rode back to the house and warned the servants. By the time the British horsemen reached the first roundabout, he was gone again and Martin Hemings (twenty-six and known to everyone as the "sullen" Hemings) was handing the last pieces of family silver to a slave named Caesar, who was hiding them under the floorboards. As the British tore over the lawn, Martin slammed the plank down, trapping Caesar under the floor. The first officer through the door shoved a pistol against his chest and threatened to fire if he didn't say where Thomas Jefferson was, and sullen Martin Hemings put his hands in his pockets and scowled and muttered, "Fire away then."

Not ten days later, such was the disreputable state of partisan politics in Virginia, a fat-faced young henchman of Patrick Henry forced the legislature to investigate Jefferson's conduct—*never* to *impeach* him, as the Federalists afterward said. In early December, after brooding in silence for five months, Jefferson walked into the Assembly at Richmond with a sheaf of papers in his hand. Neither Henry nor his henchman had the nerve to be there. Eyes straight ahead, Jefferson strode up the center aisle to the speaker's rostrum and from his great height looked down on a sea of lowered and embarrassed heads. Methodically, one by one, in that reedy-soft voice of his that was never any good for public speaking, he began to answer the charges. As drama, it was a brilliant performance, revealing his character perfectly, revealing . . . revealing—what?

In perfect fact, like all his performances, Jefferson's speech in Richmond that day revealed nothing whatsoever, nothing at all— his friends believed him, his enemies laughed; the Virginia Assembly voted him a grudging resolution of thanks. And the real truth of the whole subtle, notorious Tarleton episode remained just as ambiguous, as elusive, as *un-self-evident* as before.

If you ask my unbiased opinion . . .

☆   ☆   ☆

William Short opened his gold watch. The spidery hands showed ten minutes to three in the afternoon. At the window, Parisian rain drummed with Parisian impatience against the glass.

"Sir, you'll be late. And sir, the carriage is here."

Short looked up and worked his jaw in a gesture of irritation he had recently perfected in order to look older. He let his hand hover above the stacks of correspondence he had just finished sorting across Jefferson's desk. Next to the desk, arranged on a polished shelf, lay three new pedometers Jefferson had purchased to measure his walks around town. Short's hand stopped just above them. One of the pedometers was so complicated that it apparently had to be strapped to the knee like a pony's harness and attached to the waist through a hole you cut in your trousers.

"And it starts to rain," the footman said from where he stood by the door, then added helpfully in infantile French, *"pleurer,"* and pointed toward the window.

Short dropped his hand and stood back, tugging at his vest. It was in fact raining like twenty demons, he decided when he peered at the window, and he was going to be seriously late getting to Auteuil. At the door the footman coughed and stretched his cuffs expressively. Despite himself Short felt the beginnings of a smile. The truth was, he couldn't be irritated long at anything French, not even the weather. From wig to calf the footman was beautifully dressed in Jefferson's red livery, with gold buttons, gold epaulets, and even an inch of too-expensive, dandified white lace at the collar and cuffs, but in place of shoes this sophisticated Gallic being had strapped on his feet—a pair of huge white soapy scrub brushes. He looked exactly as if he were standing, in all his glory, barefoot on two melting cakes of snow. Lace and epaulets aside, however, he was merely Jefferson's official *frotteur*, the servant assigned to polish and wax the wood floors, which with inimitable French gaiety he did by putting on his brushes and gliding up and down the hallways, hands behind his back like a skater on a pond.

Short made his way cautiously down one side of the newly waxed hall, checked his powdered hair in the mirror, then allowed himself to be bundled into his coat by yet another servant and handed down the steps to the carriage.

"You're late," David Humphreys grumbled, pulling the door shut himself and rapping on the window for the driver to start. "And this filthy rain is going to make us later."

"À Paris on est toujours de bonne heure et en beau temps," Short replied, knowing very well that Humphreys understood not three words of French in a row.

"Shut up," Humphreys said, and rapped again.

Short settled back and grinned at him. The further truth was, not only did he love the French, but his heart quickened at the thought of the dinner they would shortly attend, more precisely at the thought of French bosoms heaving in their décolletage under John Adams's fat candles. To think of white, round cakes of snow—

The carriage bounced around the corner of the Cul-de-sac Taitbout and turned right into the rue Taitbout itself. This was a stretch of alternating new three- and four-story houses and vacant lots, treeless and largely unpaved, ending at the muddy broad promenade known so far simply as the Boulevard. Only at the Boulevard, in front of the Théâtre des Italiens, did you enter the elegant bubble of style that Short had already come to think of as *his* Paris.

"January," Humphreys muttered, wiping the clouded window with his sleeve. "Four more months of rain and sleet. Then rain and heat."

Short shook his head in mock sympathy. Humphreys was a New Englander and had grown up in the foulest climate on this planet. Even Jefferson, always courteous and positive, could be made to agree that Humphreys had an ounce too much spleen in his makeup. Miss Adams made the astonishing claim that he wrote poetry upstairs in his room, but Short refused to believe it.

They clattered through a squadron of other carriages and horses, and Short leaned forward to glimpse the stubby brown columns rising out of the mud where a crew was building, with excruciating slowness, a new church to be called the Madeleine, which would face majestically south toward the vast, fashionable Place Louis XV. The rain now was the color of cold steam, the pavements a carpet of mud and straw and horse ordure, flung up in a disgusting spray whenever the little four-wheeler rocked sideways into the center gutter.

"Now I want to remind you," Humphreys said, putting up a gloved hand like a warning signal. "He will be there already. He left before noon for his appointments, and he went on in the fiacre."

Short pulled his head back from the window and nodded. Who did Humphreys think had arranged every appointment, hour by hour, down to the very horses and tack for the fiacre?

"And I want you to let him stay till the end," Humphreys said. "No fussing, no significant remarks about the weather and the time." He let his gloved forefinger tap in stern rhythm on Short's knee. "No mother-henning."

Short tested his gesture of irritation again, but the collar of his greatcoat, he saw, made it invisible to Humphreys, who would in any case ignore it. Humphreys was a military man—he still used his title of Colonel—he had been at Washington's side in Annapolis the day Washington resigned his commission in 1783. Short suspected he regarded them all, including Jefferson, as nonmilitary and hence not quite serious.

"He is still not well," Short said. "His health is not good." They lurched right and onto the rue du Faubourg Saint-Honoré.

"He is perfectly well."

If you wished to become a diplomat, as Short intended, he believed there was no better place to practice than with the stiff, dogmatic, permanently belligerent Humphreys. Jefferson—the "he" of all their conversations—had left home today for the first time in six weeks, after being confined virtually every moment to his bedroom with a whole series of debilitating ailments—the headaches that came from nowhere and twisted his face in pain, the diarrhea that also afflicted him periodically, the general "seasoning," as everyone called the natural period of adjustment to foreign water and air. By great good luck, Short himself had escaped all serious "seasoning." Humphreys was constitutionally immune.

"Well, I will be sweet reason itself," Short said.

Humphreys snorted. "You're a Virginian. You wouldn't know sweet reason if it bit you."

The carriage lurched again suddenly and bounced one wheel hard against a wooden street post. Hanging on, peering through his window, Short could see beggars or peasants fighting in front of a bread stall. Fists, caps, furious wet faces. He gripped his leather strap and twisted to watch as the coach tilted away and turned. Arms flew. A man crashed backward into the stall. This was Paris, too, he had to admit, violent, brutal, riotous as a kennel. But here at least (his mind rushed to its defense) the violence was predictable, comprehensible—here they fought over food, they scrapped fiercely for the right-of-way in a crowded street. By contrast, in Virginia the violence was of another order of mystery altogether. The day he had begun to practice law, Short remembered, a Tidewater farmer had come in with a shriveled black *thing* in his hand: a slave's *ear* he had cut off and for some reason wanted to register in court. The young William Byrd of Westover, they said, fearing for his daughter during an epidemic, had the slaves dig up his father's corpse, six years buried, so he could study death.

"A Virginian," Humphreys repeated as they hit smoother pavement and began to pick up speed toward Auteuil. He spoke with the abstracted, single-minded tenacity that no doubt won battles. "All Virginians are bloody strange."

CHAPTER

Two

In January 1785, William Short was twenty-six years old. At William and Mary College, where he studied Latin and French, he had intended to become a poet, but turned out instead (by a familiar declension, Jefferson said) to be a lawyer. He was related to Jefferson in a cousinly Virginia way through a minor branch of the Skipwith family, and at home—but Short tried not to think of home.

Farmerlike, John Adams opened the door for them himself, blinking and peering.

"Late enough, young men," he told them brusquely.

"The rain," Humphreys said, almost as brusquely, shedding his wet coat with an exasperated shrug. Mud and water covered the red tile floor of the hallway. "We thought about coming in an ark."

Beyond Adams's stumpy figure Short could just see Jefferson moving through a crowd of brightly dressed guests.

"An ark," Adams repeated dourly. He was a short, pigeon-breasted little man with protruding eyes and an air of permanent, hard-earned impatience. He cocked his head, listening to the rain. "Maybe wash away Paris," he said, closing the door. According to Adams's own frequent declarations, he rented the huge Palladian house and garden in Auteuil simply to be out of Paris, which he hated, and into the French countryside, which he tolerated.

"We're the last?" Short's instinct (mother-henning) was to push past and make his way to Jefferson—now turning, a crown of sandy red hair, his back to the other guests—but politeness (a Virginian's constant guardian angel) and a rational fear of Adams's sharp tongue kept him in the cold hallway next to Humphreys.

"The very last. That would be in the French mode, I suppose. Arrive just when the food is ready." Adams waved their coats into a servant's hands, jammed his own hands into his pockets, and appeared to think his hostly duties done. "In fact, there's plenty of time left. The doctor"—he tilted his head to indicate Benjamin Franklin's round figure following Jefferson's tall one—"the doctor has been exceedingly *informative* as usual, with the result that we three are still in high conference despite our little *social* pause." Adams sniffed. His dislike for Franklin was so fixed and so great that the invitation for dinner had unsettled and fascinated every American in Paris.

"Wipe your shoes and wait in there with the congregation." The hallway opened to double doors on each side. Adams pointed to the crowded drawing room on the left but stared disconcertingly hard at Short. "We'll make our grand appearance when he's finished in the study."

Humphreys, as official secretary to the American commissioners, had been to Adams's house a hundred times, but for Short it was only the third visit. He hesitated for a moment in the hallway as if to study the bright paintings and the ornate gold trellis paper that, uncharacteristically, Adams had bought to decorate his walls. New England Puritan though he might be, Short thought, there was an undeniable sensuousness in John Adams's makeup; granite streaked with sugar. Humphreys was already striding through the guests, bowing every few feet like a mechanical doll.

"Franklin," Adams said in a tone of disgust, reappearing somehow beside Short, "drinks only mineral water. Try the punch"— he pronounced it *poonch*. "Mrs. Adams made it." Then he too was gone.

Short nodded obediently to empty space and took a tentative step toward the room. In front of him two dozen or more people appeared to be frozen in a typical French tableau. The men stood in small, tight circles, their tricorne hats tucked firmly under their arms to show off their powdered wigs, their ceremonial swords poking from under their coats like silver rats' tails; for their part, the women, equally powdered but bare-shouldered and dazzlingly colorful, sat in chairs or sofas as close to the single fireplace as they dared, hoping to catch whatever warmth the men had not managed to block with their legs.

"Monsieur Short, *viens ici,* come favor us."

The great Madame Brillon, growing stout, growing gray, was at forty (and more) accustomed to having her way. She sat in a stuffed chair next to the fireplace holding a cup of Mrs. Adams's *poonch* and smiling in invitation. Short made his way over the vast carpet (Persian, expensive, like strolling through a sunburst— nobody put carpets on floors in horse-foul Virginia). There were two younger French ladies flanking her, their powdered white hair piled and shaped as high above their brows as their bosoms were cut and scooped below (Short bowed low himself, thinking of cakes of snow); around them stood a ring of five or six be-powdered and be-wigged French gentlemen, hats jammed under their arms, dressed, Short thought, like celestial beetles.

"We awaited our translator," Madame Brillon said in beautifully accented English.

Short bowed again, acknowledging his reputation as a student of French. When a French garrison had billeted at Williamsburg in the war, he had haunted their officers' tents to practice the language. When he had first arrived in Paris two months ago, he had taken a room in the sleepy village of Saint-Germain just to perfect his accent.

"But we wondered if you would be willing to cross so much water tonight to join us." The speaker was a man Short had seen at twenty parties—the French had a maddening habit of never introducing anyone to anyone else. He was in his late fifties, faultlessly dressed in sapphire-blue coat and white lace, possessed of two bulging Gallic eyes, a nose like a flattened horn, and a sardonic, anti-American wit.

"Monsieur Short has an aversion to ocean travel," Madame Brillon explained serenely to the satin-clad woman on her right. "He vows never to return home by sea."

"Monsieur Jefferson will have to part the waters for him," the blue man murmured (but when Short looked up he affected not to have spoken).

"Ah, but Monsieur Jefferson is a monk, not a prophet. A woman looks at those cool gray eyes and knows that." Madame Brillon placed a warm, plump hand on Short's. "Now. Has he told *you* why we are all summoned here? Franklinet brought us our invitation"—she glanced toward a tall young man in a curled wig who stood by the fireplace ladling punch. William Temple Franklin, the illegitimate son of Franklin's own illegitimate son, known universally as Franklinet. A brainless, harmless, perpetually slack-jawed person. It was rumored that he had proposed marriage to Madame Brillon's daughter, just as Franklin himself had once proposed something less (or more) to Madame Brillon.

"Not a word. There were letters from home on Tuesday, and he skipped his usual Thursday evening here."

"Unwell," said one of the beetles significantly, and the others nodded. Jefferson's poor health had not gone unnoticed. Which one—or three—of these encircling dandies would be the court spy? Short wondered. In the midst of all its virtues, French life suffered from a chronic, circular preoccupation with spying. The police spied on the citizens, the citizens spied on foreigners and each other, the court spied obsessively on everyone. Any unconsidered remark or gesture, however harmless, seemed to have a second life at Versailles, where Short imagined the stout-bottomed young king standing perpetual guard in a tower, a huge white-powdered ear turned suspiciously toward Paris.

"Letters from America? Letters perhaps from the Marquis de Lafayette?" The blue man was interested enough to drop his shield of irony for a moment.

"Lafayette," Short told him, "we understand is en route. If the winds are good, we expect him to arrive next week, with satchels of letters and news, of course. He's been touring in America six months at least—I saw him there myself."

"The Marquis de Lafayette," said Madame Brillon thoughtfully. Her fingers tapped the back of Short's hand. "A very odd man. He has a head shaped exactly like a pineapple."

"Well—" he blushed. He knew he blushed. Both French and English deserted him like court spies.

"Well." Madame Brillon mocked with a smile. She was no longer young, but she was still shapely, still flirtatious, with an indefinable vivacity that Short had decided was the birthright of Parisian females alone. Her dress was cut as low as those of the younger women beside her, so low that—Short fashioned a complicated sentence in French—"le moindre mouvement faisait sortir du corsage le bout des seins." He had been told it was of her, dressed in a generous morning chemise, that the withered old poet Fontenelle exclaimed, "Oh, to be seventy again!"

"I want you to tell me about Monsieur Jefferson," she demanded, rising.

Across the muddy hallway the dining-room doors were swinging open. Against the candles Short could see the bustling angular figure of Abigail Adams pushing the last chairs into place herself.

"He is the author—" Short said (pompously, he knew; he blushed all the harder).

"Of the famous Declaration of Independence that changed the world. All men—but not women—are created equal. Yes, yes. It's been translated over and over in Paris, everyone's read it."

Madame Brillon held his sleeve with two fingers. John and Abigail Adams notoriously ignored the French practice of formally leading guests, according to their social rank, in to the table. Pell mell was the rule here, Adams liked to say. People were beginning to drift now in small chattering groups toward the hall and the dining room on the other side. "He's a great statesman," she said. "He was a governor. Chastellux visited him at his house on a little mountain and tells everyone he lives like an ancient philosopher."

"Well . . ."

"Well. Does he like music?" Madame Brillon was considered a gifted musician—for a woman a genuine prodigy. A young genius named Boccherini had dedicated six wonderful sonatas to her.

"Mr. Jefferson loves music. He plays the violin an hour every day. He buys *volumes* of music at the Quai des Grands Augustins."

"He has a child but no wife."

"Mrs. Jefferson died two years ago."

"So. He is not as fierce as Monsieur Adams, obviously, or as . . . what should we call it? As *free* as Franklin?"

"Votre chèr papa," Short said, risking the freedom himself.

Madame Brillon was celebrated for having sat in Franklin's lap during a court dinner at Versailles (scandalizing the two Adamses, whose eyes had almost popped). She called the good doctor *"mon chèr papa"* and stroked his bald head, but then, so apparently did half the titled ladies in Paris.

"No, not at all. Monsieur Jefferson is not 'papa' material, however much you young men worship him."

She released his sleeve and smiled again. Her own gray eyes, Short thought, were absolutely gorgeous—pools of smoke.

"He really must find a position for you," she added, with the same abrupt thoughtfulness she had used in speaking of Lafayette, "before all your lovely money vanishes."

The door to the study swung open again, and behind them the triumvirate of American commissioners was passing to the dining room: Franklin first, waddling slowly, using his cane and bowing; Adams, with a face like a pasty white ball, working his narrow mouth up and down in impatient expressions of greeting; and Jefferson last, hesitating at the threshold as if he might change his mind and retreat back to the shelves of books. At the door to the dining room his arms folded across his chest like a cross.

☆   ☆   ☆

"I shall demonstrate," Franklin announced to the table at large, "how to flirt."

Smiling benignly, he turned in his chair and reached for the ornamental fan that the woman on his left hand placed beside her plate. Still beaming, Franklin picked up the fan between two fingers and opened it with a snap. Then, grinning, he began to turn it rapidly back and forth in front of his face—at each turn simpering like a girl or stopping the fan in midflutter and peeping over the top with huge coy eyes at one of the men.

"Oh, lord." Madame Brillon laughed until she began to choke.

Franklin peered over his fan in a moony way at sour John Adams all the way down the table.

"To flirt," Franklin said. "A splendid old English word meaning a quick jerking motion. I *flirt* this fan."

In the general laughter Short found himself thinking that two rules had been broken at once—first, the French custom of speaking at a meal only to one's neighbor; and second, Franklin's own rule of never starting a topic of conversation. Poor Richard was famous for sitting quietly in his chair and speaking only when spoken to.

"But why does she have a fan in January?" whispered the young woman to Short's left. An Adams voice of fascinated disapproval. The pell mell of the table had thrown Short leeward, toward his host and, as it turned out, the nineteen-year-old Miss Nabby Adams, who was a softer and prettier version of her mother Abigail.

"It's warm where she is, by the fireplace," he said, noting that up and down the table each Frenchman had, true to form, placed his hat beside his plate. Rumor had Miss Adams recovering from an improper romantic attachment to a Harvard wastrel with the implausible (and very un-Adams) name of "Royall" Tyler. Had the canny Abigail steered her toward Short tonight for a reason? "Even the flowers in your centerpiece are melting," Short told her.

Miss Adams was studying doubtfully the plate a maid had just slipped in front of her, but she raised her head quickly. "The centerpiece. We went to a dinner in the Louvre Palace, Mr. Short, where the centerpiece was a huge model winter landscape made out of artificial frost. *It* was by the fireplace, too, and during the meal the frost slowly began to melt, and underneath it you suddenly saw miniature trees and houses and little flowing streams, and just as dessert was served, hundreds of tiny blossoms sprang up on wires to symbolize spring!"

She was actually a charming girl, Short thought, if too serious.

"This is a new dish someone has invented in Paris," she said, toying with the dark mass on her plate. "Mama and I weren't sure —it's called pâté de foie gras. The liver of a fat goose. Don't ask how it's made. Dr. Franklin loves it."

At the middle of the table, liberally spreading his pâté on toast, Franklin was now telling a joke. One of the French gentlemen, speaking English with a slow syrupy accent, asked Franklin if he really intended to ascend in a hot-air balloon that summer, as rumor had it. Franklin beamed again and squinted through his spectacles down the table.

"Mr. Jefferson," he said, finding him almost in the corner, next to Abigail Adams, a tall, tranquil figure, dressed in the latest French tailoring but unmistakably, in his clear skin and long, slouched frame, American. "Mr. Jefferson is the very man to ascend in a balloon. I am too old—"

A little clatter of disagreement, led by Madame Brillon. But Franklin was eighty if a day, Short thought.

"—and not much given to travel anymore. As you know."

Everyone nodded in more or less solemn sympathy. Franklin's constant battle with the bladder stone was widely known. He moved about in great torment, usually drank only mineral water, and sometimes had himself carried in a litter like an Oriental sage to this or that noble lady's house. In fact, Short considered, the cult of Franklin in Paris was astounding—Jefferson had warned him: down to the servants in a house, everyone knew about him, his bons mots were quoted and reprinted everywhere, there were paintings and engravings of him in shops and on mantelpieces, even on paper fans. At a gallery near the Palais Royal a woman sold plaster dolls of him, complete with famous wire spectacles and tiny fur hat.

"But you should go," the Frenchman persisted. "You should fly your wonderful kite from a balloon."

Franklin nodded. "Somebody will," he said. "Eventually." He turned and smiled genially in the direction of Adams, who was stabbing the pâté with his fork. "I've seen every balloon, you know. The first was two years ago—before you arrived, Brother Adams. The Montgolfier brothers sent up an unmanned balloon made out of red silk from the Champ de Mars, even though it was raining torrents. It flew for nearly an hour and came down ten miles away in a village."

"Where the villagers," said Madame Brillon, "promptly destroyed it with their pitchforks."

"They thought it was the devil," Franklin agreed.

"But the next—"

"The next balloon," he said, "had a wicker basket hanging below the hot-air stove, and in it the Montgolfiers put a sheep, a duck, and a rooster, all of which returned unharmed after a tour over the Faubourg Saint-Antoine. Then at the end of the year—it was '83—they launched from the Tuileries, and this time one of the brothers rode in the basket where the sheep had been, far above Paris. Later he told me his first thought when he cleared the rooftops was 'What a wonderful sight!' " Franklin peered over the tops of his spectacles, toward Colonel Humphreys, it seemed. "And does anyone know what his *second* thought was?"

Humphreys shook his head.

" 'How priceless this would be in a battle!' "

At which moment the servants arrived, noisily passing out courses of fish and game, and the conversation broke apart into tête-à-tête. Short strained for a moment to catch a glimpse of Jefferson, but against the flickering candlelight and the mountainous, not to say snowy landscape of powdered wigs ranged down the table, he could hardly make out the commissioner's face. But pale, melancholy, Short thought; not well, even at a distance.

Miss Adams entertained him with a long, breathlessly indignant description of Franklin's particular friend whom they did *not* invite to dinner—a Madame Helvétius, who lived with two young priests and a bachelor philosopher (respectively ten, twenty, and thirty years younger than herself) and who, her papa swore, had used her chemise to wipe the floor when her lap dog had wet it. By the time dessert had arrived—the wilting flowers in the centerpiece stayed just as they were, failing to metamorphose into anything at all—the entire party was light-headed and gay. In the midst of it, reverting to his customary silence, Franklin seemed to watch benevolently, like a small pink-faced balloon, but as the servants began to remove the cloth and bring the wine, he nodded expectantly toward Adams.

There was an inevitable delay while Adams stood and rapped on the table with his knuckles. The French misunderstood his signal and talked more loudly, Abigail Adams bustled dishes and bottles herself to the kitchen in a whirl of aprons, but then Adams's cool New England twang began to bore through the hubbub. He was delighted so many of them would brave the rain that day to come to his home—he remembered a poem in a single verse written by a newcomer to describe the Paris climate: rain and wind, and wind and rain. But the Baron de Grimm had complained it was too long by half: "Wind and rain would have said it all."

Adams wiped his lips, put down his napkin, and laced his fingers behind his back.

"Now. The other two American commissioners wish me to make an announcement tonight, of general interest. As all of you know, we arrived in France originally to sign our treaty with Great Britain—that was the doctor, Mr. Jay, and your humble servant. Mr. Jay has long since returned to America, and while the doctor and I have stayed on to negotiate other, *commercial* treaties, and Mr. Jefferson has joined us—nonetheless Fortune turns her wheel."

He stopped and repeated everything in slow, correct French (as stiff as buckram, Short thought; not one to board in Saint-Germain, John Adams studied French in a ponderously formal way at home—he had shown Short the copy of Bossuet's *Funeral Orations* that was his text).

"Fortune turns her wheel," Adams said once more. "The doctor observes that he travels very little now, but he has authorized me to announce to you that in the spring of this year he means to relinquish permanently his post here and travel back to Pennsylvania."

The outburst was all that Franklin would have wished. The ladies groaned, the French gentlemen sprang from their chairs, a general bilingual lament rose from the length of the table. Adams remained standing, hands still clasped behind him. "I guessed," Miss Adams whispered to Short. "All those letters and meetings. He wants to go home to die."

In the drawing room afterward, while servants passed around bits of orange and nuts and sweet red wine, a trio of musicians played Scottish and Irish melodies—Franklin's favorite kind of music—and he himself gave a brief demonstration on his own glass-and-finger instrument, the famous and briefly fashionable "armonica," which he had invented twenty years ago in London. And then, before Short was at all prepared for it, the party was ending. John and Abigail Adams handed guests into coats and cloaks, carriages ran up through the interminable rain, and footmen splashed in and out of the hallway with their boots and umbrellas. In the confusion Short found himself face to face with Franklin as they waited for a carriage to move.

"Mr. Short."

"I saw your likeness yesterday, sir, in the shop at the Palais Royal and was amazed at the resemblance."

Franklin chuckled, like a great elf, Short thought. "Yes." He leaned on his cane, smiling. "I like to say that I have been i-*doll*-ized in this kingdom."

"Your popularity, sir—"

Franklin had the old man's habit of finishing young men's thoughts. "My popularity is a source of great amusement to me. Do you know that when I first arrived in Paris and was being made much of, the king grew so prickly about it that he presented the Countess de Polignac with a Sèvres porcelain chamber pot, and my portrait at the bottom of it."

Franklin chuckled again and looked around. From the drawing room Adams and Jefferson were slowly advancing, heads down in conference. "You're serving him as secretary?" Franklin asked.

"Informally. There's no salary or title—"

"So you don't know how long it can last. He's a very deep man, very deep. Mr. Jefferson doesn't wear his heart on his sleeve." Madame Brillon was two steps away, holding up Franklin's gray hooded cloak and chattering over her shoulder in rapid French. Franklin patted Short's wrist in an unexpected gesture. His hand was as soft and skittering as a mouse. "Now, of course, you're thinking what my departure means politically for him—and you."

"My plans—"

Franklin bent forward confidentially. Short expected him to warn against Adams, or to recommend "Poor Richard"-fashion some sly mixture of prudence and horse sense. Instead, he cocked his elfish head and looked past Short's arm and into the darkness of the hallway, nodding as if he were seeing a familiar, harmless ghost. "France will change him," he said quietly. "It changes everyone. Whatever he was, he will turn out different. Whatever *you* are"—the old man straightened and grinned—"flirt like the devil," he said.

CHAPTER

Three

I n Virginia, Short reminded himself, the beds were very small
and people slept more or less sitting up, propped on cushions and
pillows. In France, however, the fashion now was to sleep "lying
flat," stretched out full length over the whole bed.

He rocked his chair back on its legs, looked over the desk to the
odd, extra long, very comfortable French bed, and yawned. In the
tall frame of his window the afternoon rain had slowed to a fine
gray curtain of drizzle. Jefferson had left hours ago to visit his
daughter Patsy at the convent across the Seine, where she
boarded as a student; Humphreys had mounted his horse at noon
and ridden out to John Adams once more at Auteuil. As for his
own duties—Short lowered his eyes to frown at the portfolio of
letters he was supposed to translate or copy for Jefferson, just as if
he were a real secretary and this would all last, Paris, and Paris
beds, and Paris winters.

He stood up abruptly, poked once at the little pyramid of sea-
coal burning in his fireplace, and then crossed the room to the
window. From his third-floor apartment he could see the rooftops
of the neighboring Chaussée d'Antin, bright sloping quadrangles
and chimneys of wet tile and soaked gray stone, and beyond them
the distant black horizon of Auteuil. With another, briefer yawn

he thought of the dinner party the day before. If *he* were to fly in a hot-air balloon, floating high over rooftops and gardens and carriages, there would be no speculation about how to use it in a battle. Leave that to Colonel Humphreys. In a balloon you would be able to comprehend all Paris at once, take it all in at once. In his mind's eye he saw the rooftops themselves coming away like little lids on boxes, himself peering down into every room, every secret. An odd question occurred to him. No one had ever flown in the sky like that before: What would the old poets have written — what would Virgil or Horace or Spenser have said if they could have seen the world *from three thousand feet*?

Below the windowsill, on the street, a thoroughly earth-bound water carrier was staggering under the weight of his two wooden buckets, which he had carried up from the river to deliver somewhere. Short watched the stocky little man disappear around a corner. The other day Jefferson, standing at his own study window, had characteristically worked out for Short that a strong porter beginning at nine o'clock in the morning could complete thirty round trips a day, coming as far up the Boulevards as the rue Taitbout.

Short made a wry face. No dreamy questions about dead poets and balloons. Jefferson's mind worked in its own way. Never — not in a thousand years — would anybody else have thought to calculate such a fact.

Memoirs of Jefferson — 2

 THE TARLETON AFFAIR COULD ONLY BE understood in the light of what came after . . . and before.

It is no disgrace, certainly, for a man to fall into a period of despair or even a kind of paralysis in his own affairs. So vital and energetic a person as John Adams confessed that more than once in his life his "demons" (good Puritan word) had brought on fevers, headaches, "anxiety" (his own word too), and general collapse. In the spring of 1781, two months before Banastre Tarleton thundered into Charlottesville, Governor Jefferson received another of those blows that hammered him throughout the Revolution. His wife, a widow when he married her, had brought to their marriage a young son, who died soon after. Their own first child, Martha, also known as Patsy, was healthy and even robust (inheriting, it was clear at a glance, Jefferson's big, lanky frame); but a daughter and a son had subsequently died; a second daughter, Mary, also survived, but in April yet another infant daughter, Lucy Elizabeth, succumbed. The governor was sufficiently battered by this loss, but his wife—his wife now entered a period of melancholy and paralysis all her own.

"I mean to retire," Jefferson wrote a friend. "Public service is private misery." He watched in despair as his young wife more or less ceased to function in the household. She sat for hours in her room or wandered the big unfinished house (all that Southern *clutter*) without speaking. The house slaves took over the purchases and records for the kitchen, the garden and laundry came to a halt, and the governor galloped helplessly back and forth between Richmond and Monticello as often as he could break away from those swaggering, ineffective, whiskey-stained legislators. But Tarleton's raid and the flight to Carter's Mountain, if they shook Martha Wayles Jefferson back into a semblance of life, had just the opposite effect on him.

Those who visited the small cabin called Poplar Forest, where he kept his family in retreat for two or three months, say that the tumble from Caractacus broke Jefferson's spirit more than his bones. Now Melancholy took him for its own. Now it was *his* turn to be confined to his room and nursed—"I am reduced," he wrote General Washington, "to a state of perpetual decrepitude" (he was thirty-eight!). Even though Tarleton's troops had raged over his property in a spirit of total extermination, sparing the house at Monticello but destroying virtually all of his crops, all of his Elk Hill plantation, driving off slaves, cattle, horses (they slashed the throats of the colts too young for riding)—even with so much work to do (and doctor bills, in that inflated currency, of £600), Jefferson stayed whole days silent in bed, writing steadily on a board he held across his knees. Toward the end of the summer he would leave his bed and sit propped by a mountain of cushions at his desk, writing for hours at a time, barely eating, rarely speaking. Yet strangely enough, during this whole period he wrote almost no letters at all, just two or three like the one to Washington.

The worst moments, the slough of despondence so to speak, came when Jefferson finally put down his pen and returned with his wife and daughters to Monticello. There he received first the news of the inquiry into his conduct (his supposed cowardice) and a few months afterward the notice of his election once again to the state Assembly at Richmond.

He refused to serve.

He wrote a letter of resignation. He raged in his house. He exchanged decrepitude for a chill, bitter, month-long anger, and when poor young James Monroe came to Monticello to urge him to serve (James Madison was more perceptive, as always, and simply kept his distance), Jefferson told him bluntly that no man was obliged to "everlasting servitude" for the sake of the public. "In thirteen years of service I have sought nothing except the affection of my countrymen," he told Monroe—they were pacing back and forth (Monroe remembers) on the lush green lawn of the west portico, looking toward Carter's Mountain. Jefferson would reach the end of the grass, stare at the mountain, and turn abruptly, like the lash of a tail. "I have stood arraigned in my own country for incompetence and cowardice," he said (Monroe wrote down every word later), "for treason of the heart. With this investigation the Commonwealth has inflicted on me an injury that will be cured only by the all-healing grave."

The reference to the grave must have shocked the twenty-four-year-old Monroe far more than Jefferson's anger. Anyone who came to Monticello in the spring of 1782 could see that Mrs. Jefferson was about to deliver again, this about one year after the death of the little girl that had plunged her into such depression, and her features were gaunt to the point of exhaustion. She was always a small, frail woman—odd to see next to the tall, indefatigable Jefferson—and she ought not to have been having children at all (Monroe thought, daringly), let alone seven of them. The grave indeed. A fine and private place. Jefferson's thoughts were clearly running to his wife's health and the ordeal she was about to undergo. But as he paced back and forth with Monroe, he justified his refusal solely on legal grounds. With cold eloquence he cited cases where other men had been elected to office and declined to serve. He invoked English common law. He weighed at length the duties of public service against the duties of home and the cost of neglecting his farm. But he made no reference or mention of his wife's condition. And it was not merely (Monroe thought) that in Virginia a gentleman doesn't speak of such things in public. It was (stiff, unimaginative Monroe attempted a rare flight of image) as if, with all his marvelous power of language, the former governor were building a fence of precedents and theory to keep out a wolf.

"They may take this in Richmond," Jefferson said ironically, turning on his heel and citing his own ultimate precedent, "as *my* declaration of independence."

On May 8, two days after Monroe's visit to Monticello, Mrs. Jefferson gave birth to another daughter, whom they named Lucy Elizabeth, the same name as that of the child who had died the year before, a common Virginia custom. Now there were three daughters in the household, plus the six children of Jefferson's widowed sister: plenty of life for a man in search of affection.

But summer came relentlessly on, as Virginia summers do. And in Albemarle County the summer of 1782 was long and hot and parching dry. The new baby, Lucy Elizabeth, thrived. She had red hair like her father and her sister Patsy and fierce good lungs that she put to use in the service of an early colic; a delightful child, likely to live. But Martha Wayles Jefferson saw little of her baby, or any of the other children. Through the whole long miserable season she was too weak to nurse and too weak to rise. She simply stayed in the narrow bed where she had given birth, her eyes growing larger and larger as her face wasted. Two women attended her constantly—Jefferson's sister Martha Carr and Martha Jefferson's own sister—but it was Jefferson himself who gave the sick woman her medicine, poured her the water, pressed the wet handkerchiefs to her temple. A few days after the birth he wrote to Monroe, repeating almost word for word what he had said in defense of his resignation—the reaction in Richmond was scornful, he was taking a sulky "revenge" out of spite—but thereafter he wrote no letters at all, none to anybody. For four full months he was never out of her calling. And yet just as at Poplar Forest, when he wasn't directly at his wife's side he was writing constantly—he had a small room that opened directly at the head of her bed. Writing what? More fences against the wolf?

For the wolf had come clear, teeth, claws, and all. One day late in August, Martha Wayles Jefferson sat up in bed, supported by bolsters and cushions, and penned a few lines:

> Time wastes too fast: every letter I trace tells me with what rapidity life follows my pen. The days and hours of it are flying over our heads like clouds of a windy day, never to return more—everything presses on . . .

Her hand faltered and stopped. The passage was from Sterne's *Tristram Shandy*, a novel that Jefferson had read over and over; read aloud to her often in the days of their courtship. He took the pen from her hand and finished the quotation:

> . . . and every time I kiss thy hand to bid adieu, every absence which follows it, are preludes to that eternal separation which we are shortly to make.

In Virginia, with its swampy malarial climate, they call late summer and early fall "the dying time." By the first day of September, Martha had begun to weep uncontrollably when she saw her children. The servants remember that on the fourth Jefferson stood by the bed, holding her frail hand in his, while she asked him to promise that he would never marry again, never, never bring a stepmother in over her children. On the morning of the sixth, Dr. Gilmer, who would accept no payment except the loan of some salt, called all the family and servants in. They stood in silent rows around the bed. A moment before the final scene, Jefferson, unable to stand or sit, was led from the room by his sister Mrs. Carr. She took him to his library, where he fainted and collapsed on the bare floor and remained insensible so long that they feared he would never revive.

For three weeks he kept to this room, walking incessantly day and night, lying down only when he was completely exhausted, and then only in the thin little straw pallet that had been brought in when he fainted. The *violence* of his emotion was what everyone remarked on—his neighbor Colonel Randolph, who was a hard, violent man himself, but violent in another direction, wrote Madison contemptuously that even a month after his wife's death,

Jefferson still swooned like a woman whenever he saw their three children. Madison wrote back with precise indignation that his story was "incredible."

Somehow Jefferson managed to write in his account book for September 6: *"My dear wife died this day at 11:45 a.m."* Then in an act of extreme—not violence but privacy, he gathered all her letters, all the notes and letters that had ever passed between them, every slip, and burned the whole mass in the fireplace. He ordered an inscription in Greek for her tombstone. Five days after her death, he picked up his pen again for the first time and wrote in his garden book (I have seen it and checked the dates):

September 11, 1792

W. Hornsby's method of preserving birds.

Make a small incision between the legs of the bird; take out the entrails & eyes, wipe the inside & with a quill force a passage through the throat into the body that the ingredients may find a way into the stomach & so pass off through the mouth. fill the bird with a composition of ⅔ common salt & ⅓ nitre pounded in a mortar with two tablespoonfuls of black or Indian pepper to a pound. hang it up by it's legs 8 or 10 weeks, & if the bird be small it will be sufficiently preserved in that time. if it be large, the process is the same, but greater attention will be necessary.

A fence indeed. Who could get past *that*? Was he thinking of his wife's body and its inevitable dissolution in the grave? Or was it an example—spectacular—of that precise, objective scientific curiosity that his enemies claim made him so cool? Or is this really a recipe for preserving something beautiful and dead that you cannot bring yourself even to *name*? Virginians are strange. In the five years I lived with him in Paris, I never once heard Jefferson refer to his wife.

☆   ☆   ☆

Abigail Adams, energetic as a hurricane, sent over by messenger that evening a prescription to cure Jefferson's "seasoning" once and for all.

"I made the mistake last night," Jefferson explained, lifting his head and smiling at Short, "of describing my symptoms to her."

"You mentioned the dreaded grippe?" Short asked. They had each taken a chair near the coal fire in the library, the tea table spread between them, Jefferson in his mildest, most expansive mood. Short thought they were like two English dukes stretching their legs in their manor.

"I gave it full credit, the grippe, the headaches, the fever—all of them *ad seriatim.* I was the ideal dinner guest, presenting a new and fascinating symptom for each course. It was a shameful appeal for sympathy. I only neglected to expire completely when dessert was served. Now. She writes, 'Dear Sir, I once found great benefit in treating the same disorders by taking an ounce of Castile soap and a pint of Bristol beer, dividing it into three portions, and taking it three mornings in a row, fasting.' "

Short groaned. Jefferson smiled again and folded the note away.

"You won't take it," Short said firmly.

"She's a wonderful woman." Jefferson placed his teacup on the silver tray. "John Adams's greatest asset. But no, this is only the New England way of making certain they drink beer somehow or other, and at the same time making sure they suffer a little for the pleasure. Franklin once told me he never drank so much beer as in Puritan Boston. 'Conscience,' he said, 'makes you thirsty.' "

"You seem well in any case, almost cured."

Jefferson stood—unfolded himself in stages—and began to walk in front of his shelves of books, humming snatches of an Italian song. He was forty-one years old, Short reminded himself —forty-two in less than three months, on April thirteenth—and in fact he did not look well at all, not cured at all.

"You show great self-control." Jefferson broke off his song and looked back with an expression still mild and ironic. "I had assumed that you would be filled with questions about Franklin's departure—what it means, why he does it, what the future of the delegation is to be. But you seem content to analyze la grippe."

"Dr. Franklin is an old man," Short said tentatively.

"Dr. Franklin wants to go home to die," Jefferson replied. "He has a horror of dying in a foreign country. He keeps young Temple Franklin with him, he says, because he wants to know that a blood relation is on hand to close his eyes and bury him."

Short stirred uncomfortably. There was altogether too much dying in this conversation.

"And of course—" Jefferson moved farther along the shelves, humming, running his hands across the spines of his books. A born sensualist, Short thought, the hands of a great painter, a great artist. He strokes the bindings of his books (an unworthy simile) the way another man would stroke a woman. And a sensualist is sensitive, will collapse when coarser men are unbothered. Jefferson had the frame and body of a Virginia mountaineer, he should have effortlessly knocked aside Paris's effete headaches and grippes—John Adams had, Humphreys had, Short himself— instead Jefferson looked pale and fragile. With his red hair and feverish skin he looked like a burning stick.

"Of course," Jefferson said. He looked at a title, frowned, pushed the book back. Then he crossed and sat down in another chair farther from the fire. "Of course, there is no business for our delegation. That discourages Franklin and makes him willing to leave. That discourages everyone. No country will negotiate with us—"

"They think our government is unstable."

"They think our Articles of Confederation leave us without a central power, and they may be right. The Comte de Vergennes insists that he sees thirteen separate governments, not one United States. He frankly doubts we can make commercial treaties that will *bind*."

"So they stall and wait to see how stable we prove."

Jefferson made a tall steeple of his fingers. He wore no rings, no jewelry of any kind. According to the old Virginia custom he had only one first name—*Thomas* Jefferson—while the northerners liked to have two at least (John Quincy Adams, Short thought, remembering the Adams son), and the French positively rioted in them: Marie Joseph Paul Yves Roch Gilbert du Moher de Lafayette. When he spoke again, Jefferson's voice took on the rich visionary energy it always did if he spoke of the future.

"Whale oil, tobacco, timber." He ticked them off on his long fingers. "Rice, fish, lumber, fur—the wealth of our United States, the potential wealth is astonishing. If the barriers of trade would go down *here*, our ships and farms could feed—Europe!" He cocked his head and smiled wryly, as if conscious of the criticism his political enemies always made, that Mr. Jefferson was greatly addicted to hyperbole. "When Lafayette returns next week, we mean to make an all-out assault on the tobacco monopoly here at least."

"I think," Short said, venturing an opinion that he had over-heard John Adams give, "that the French resent our continuing trade with England. We still trade three-fourths of our goods with our former enemy."

Jefferson nodded absently and rubbed his face with one hand, suddenly, obviously tired. "Politics in Europe is the systematic organization of hatreds. It should never come to that in America."

He stood up and seemed to sag for a moment.

"You've tired yourself out," Short said, rising quickly.

"I'm fine, I'm well." Jefferson turned and walked in his rather shambling, loose-limbed way to the door. He rested one hand on the handle. "I have an invitation for you from Patsy," he said, "by the way."

"Ah." Short clicked his heels. Patsy was Martha, Jefferson's twelve-year-old daughter, fashionably immured in Panthemont, the Catholic convent school across the Seine, a tall, rangy, big-footed girl with sandy red hair—Jefferson's daughter!—and Short made a game of treating her with mock-French gallantry.

"She reports," Jefferson said with something like renewed energy, "that the drawing master is less severe than the one in Virginia, she does *not* like reading Livy, and the other girls call her 'Jeff.' "

Short grinned, Jefferson smiled. Jefferson had once told him that domestic happiness was the highest good in life. Without a wife, he now lavished all his affection on the three girls; Lucy and Mary in Virginia, Patsy in Paris. Patsy most of all. To Short, given to erotic rather than domestic reverie, it was wonderful to see how the mention of any one of the girls could brighten Jefferson's face.

"Tomorrow morning," Jefferson said, "we are to assemble early at Panthemont to witness a ceremony—two French girls take the veil: they call it 'dying to life.' "

Short's grin faded. Jefferson appeared not to notice. Humming, he pulled at the brass handle of the door and opened it. At the end of the hallway his black servant James could be seen, backlit by the candles in their scalloped holders along the stairs. He carried a small flat tray with Jefferson's glass and crystal water bottle.

"I may send for Castile soap after all," Jefferson said, a gravelly weariness coming back to his voice. In an uncharacteristic gesture —Short remembered it afterward as a premonition—he touched the younger man's arm for an instant before turning away.

CHAPTER

Four

"'France alters everybody,'" Miss Adams said with Adams decision and an Adams lift of her chin. "That is Dr. Franklin's favorite saying. But I think it has metamorphosed our family most in their *heads*."

Involuntarily Short glanced ahead to young eighteen-year-old John Quincy Adams, marching resolutely if unsteadily beside his mother Abigail, with his left foot on the street and his right foot on the curb. For the honor of the ceremony at Panthemont, Johnny's dark brown hair had been "frizzled" (Abigail's impatient term) into a state of unnatural, even luminous, curliness.

"Not *hair*," said Miss Adams, showing the unnerving family ability to read thoughts. "I meant our *thinking*. But it is certainly true that everyone's hair is metamorphosed here."

"Not your mother's."

"No." Miss Adams shook her own very slightly frizzled head in agreement. Abigail Adams was notorious for insisting that she could not be seen in public without her head covered—she had mysteriously lost four of her five caps on the ocean voyage over and replaced them only with enormous difficulty in Paris. In the fashionable company proceeding now along the street, her tall white mobcap bounced up and down like a runaway cake.

"Mama permitted Esther and John to go to the hairdresser last week—the other servants were ridiculing them for being unpowdered, but Esther wept because it took so long and her hair looked so strange afterward. Now," Miss Adams added with her father's tartness, "she seems happy as a lark."

Short touched the edges of his own immaculately curled and powdered hair and squinted to see where the party was turning. Rue de Grenelle was new territory for him, so narrow and clogged with carriages and people this morning that they had all gotten out two hundred yards from the convent entrance and started to walk.

"Mother says—" Miss Adams began. They came to a halt at the end of the line filing into the convent. Thirty, forty people or more had now converged—Abigail and Johnny were lost in a sea of wigs and billowing skirts. An elderly French couple smelling of gallons of rosewater pushed ahead of them. Short cupped his hands and blew into them for warmth and then fumbled for his ticket of admission. "Mother says," Miss Adams resumed, "that to be out of fashion is more criminal in Paris than to be seen in a state of nature, to which the Parisians are not averse."

She darted a glance at Short, conscious perhaps that she had gone rather far.

Short smiled and led her forward. "Mr. Jefferson," he said, quoting authority back to her, "says it's all show and parade."

"I know. He told Papa that since he didn't expect to live more than a dozen years, he was loath to give up one of them to the hairdresser."

"Mr. Jefferson," Short said, holding up his ticket—

"—is greatly given to hyperbole." With a snap of her own ticket, Miss Adams stepped through the wicket and grinned back at him.

The wicket opened into a cobblestone alley that ran between two tall buildings. They hurried along with the crowd, turned right through another small black door, another, a final turn to the left, and entered the chapel. So crowded was this room that they were ushered along with dozens of other guests up to the very altar platform itself and there shown to seats. Not certain what to do as he took his chair, Short made a vague gesture of pious respect toward the altar—Miss Adams looked at him sharply—and tried to locate Jefferson.

"The convent," she whispered. She pointed to an iron grille on the far side of the altar, open to a courtyard and a brown January garden. To their right the main floor was covered with a great elegant carpet like the one in John Adams's house; on it, in rows of stiff, slender wooden chairs, nuns were murmuring prayers and chants. Behind them, like a wall of wine—or blood, Short thought—hung two curtains of rich crimson velvet, fringed with gold.

"I've found your parents." On the other side of the altar Short could just make out, behind an Alpine range of wigs, John Adams's apple-round face, Abigail's pristine cap, Jefferson's powdered red hair. "But not Patsy."

"The boarders and students come in together," Miss Adams informed him. Their shoulders touched. "Watch the curtains."

At the moment she spoke the velvet curtains parted, and a procession of nuns began to file two by two down the center aisle. Each nun held a candle and a missal; the young girls following them, all dressed in a school ensemble of crimson and white, clutched gilt-edged prayer books or sheets of music, and scrambled whispering to benches set up behind the chairs. Short shifted his legs, inhaled perfume, pomade, rosewater, incense, a thousand alien smells. In Virginia he had sat for a lifetime of Sundays in a dusty wood-frame Anglican church at the crossroads of the Staunton highway, where the windows were clear glass—the congregation looked out on sloping pine forests, not Parisian courtyards—and the minister judged impromptu horse races after the service. To Jefferson's left sat an elderly Frenchman with a gaunt face and sunken, unhealthy eyes. The younger woman next to him wore a dark gauze veil from her hat to her throat, impenetrable. She looked directly at Short.

The audience rose, then sat. The two girls who were to take their vows came through the crimson curtains, escorted by two pensioners of the convent, one at each side. They were pale blond and English in feature, beautifully dressed in full-length gowns of yellow and blue, glittering with jewels on their hands, their hair, their scooped bodices. Representing, Short thought an instant before Miss Adams whispered it, the vanities of the world.

At the altar the abbess waited with a priest. When the girls knelt and dropped their hoods, the crowd made a little gasp. Their heads had been completely shaved. (Beside him it was Miss Adams's turn to touch her hair.)

Before the crowd's murmur could subside, the abbess had moved briskly forward and the Vanities had lifted their skirts to climb the platform. The priest stepped between them, swished his own black robe, and began to deliver a sermon in the slow, incantatory rhythm (like a sad Kentucky mule, Jefferson said) that Short had come to expect whenever a Frenchman spoke in public. In a low voice, he translated for Miss Adams: the king was good, the French people, every class of them from throne to footstool, were good; the great city outside these walls held pleasures, beauty, opportunity for virtue. The world itself was good to live in; when God had finished His work of Creation, He looked upon it and saw that it was good. It was wrong therefore to quit this beautiful world and live apart from it. (In Jefferson's row the veiled woman had lowered her head.)

"He wants them to change their minds," Miss Adams whispered. "He's warning them."

But the priest had abruptly changed his logic. The truth was, he continued, this beautiful world was now losing its excellence; a false spirit of self-interest guided everything, they were right to turn their backs on such greed and pride. And yet their decision brought many difficulties. They would be confined in this place year after year, season after season, till the last day of their lives. Their actions would be misconstrued. If they should be gay, their superiors would say they had not really quit the world. If they should be grave, others would say they were unhappy and repented their vows. Holding both hands high over his head, he chanted a psalm in Latin, and from the back of the chapel eight pensioners approached in a double line, carrying spread out between them a huge black pall, like the flag of a ship, crossed with brilliant white.

"This is the dying to life," Miss Adams told him as the pensioners spread the black cloth over the two girls, now prostrate before the altar. "When they lift it off again, the girls are resurrected as nuns."

To his amazement, Short found that his eyes had filled with

tears. The candles, the chants, the dark quivering air of the ancient chapel all worked on him like charms. His heart went out in a rush to the young girls lying on the cold floor, covered by the pall—eighteen, nineteen: near enough to his own age. His mind seemed to roll and rise with the sheer idea of it, of dying to life, sacrifice, a church, a city, a lineage that went back in time toward a dim Gothic dawn. A show and a parade, but utterly, utterly moving. When he turned to Miss Adams, he found her weeping quietly. Around them the French spectators sobbed or stood in attitudes of deep affliction. The girls' parents had come almost to the edge of the platform. At their feet the pensioners lowered the pall until it completely covered the two still forms. Short listened to the anthems, sung in a beautiful sweeping Latin, and felt a deep sense of—what? How had Europe metamorphosed *him?* He watched Jefferson rising with the rest of the audience. As the girls' soft voices sang and the candles drifted around them in the scented darkness, he let his eyes move to the veiled woman.

"For Wednesday next, *mercredi demain,*" Jefferson said in answer to a question that Short had missed. A scarlet carriage clattered by, drowning the next few words as well, then Jefferson bowed, made a little salute with one hand, and turned back. "I never know what I say or what I agree to in French." He tucked his hat under his arm, smiling wryly. "At my age any new language is Greek. Can you ride back with me in John Adams's carriage? The ladies will shift around and go to Auteuil together, and we can talk."

Short glanced quickly over his shoulder. In the crowd still pouring out into the sunlit rue de Grenelle, the elderly Frenchman and his veiled wife—companion? mistress? daughter?—had returned Jefferson's bow and already vanished behind the bustling line of voitures. "That was—" he began hopefully, but Jefferson had absorbed the French habit of never introducing. He took Short's arm for support and guided them both along the edge of the kennel, through a trail of horses' rumps, cobblestones, curbs, debris, skirts, curses—the normal French chaos that made every excursion into streets a festival of flying bodies. Belatedly, Short registered Jefferson's words: talk about *what?* At the end of the carriages the black figure of John Adams could just be seen, round and squat as a tree stump.

"Horror, abomination, blasphemy!" Adams growled as they burst through a ring of liveried footmen and reached him. They clambered into his carriage, and he barked an order through the window in appalling French and continued his catalogue: "Paganism, sorcery, witchcraft—take the whole caste of priests and line them up against the walls and shoot their livers out. Do I err by way of caution, brother Jefferson?"

Jefferson was laughing and holding the strap on the side of the carriage, Short was bouncing forward and back, trying to avoid Adams's bony knees.

"No, you have three daughters, Jefferson—we turn left, *gauche*, there at the rue du Bac, *idiot*—three daughters. You couldn't stand to see them in such a masked ball and pantomime, I know it."

The carriage rattled into another narrow street, crisscrossed by swinging signboards, and plunged abruptly toward the river like a stone down a hill. "My Patsy tells me that the nuns leave all the Protestant girls to their own beliefs, and very few of the French girls ever take orders. All the same—"

"All the same," Adams grumbled, "you agree with me. You worry. I know you do." Adams leaned toward Short with a confidential scowl. "My wife claims she never saw a more *motherly* father than Mr. Jefferson, by which she means a great compliment. You must have seen in Virginia how he dotes on his daughters?"

But before Short could answer, Adams had changed the subject. "He says you're a wonderful writer."

"No, sir." Short felt his face warming to a blush.

"Yes, sir. He tells me he gives you work to do in a private capacity and you do it beautifully. He says you're always writing."

For the first time Jefferson spoke. "Mr. Short is also gifted in languages. At William and Mary he founded a new scholarly society called Phi Beta Kappa. George Wythe says he was a superb student of Greek and Latin."

"And he speaks French," Adams said, nodding. "My daughter Nabby believes you have perfect pitch." Adams cocked his head and confided to Jefferson, "She speaks it well herself, if a father says so—but you and I, sir, are too old to make much progress. And Franklin . . . Franklin mumbles some private mixture of tongues never heard before, the Ambassador of Babel."

No one, Short thought, was ever so sensitive to atmosphere as Jefferson. Seeming to agree, saying, in fact, nothing concrete, he leaned gently forward and steered them out of the shoals of Franklin. "Mr. Adams and I have had many other chances to speak of writing."

Adams laughed and sat back in the jolting carriage. "Your friend here," he said to Short, "will have told you about writing the Declaration."

"No, sir."

Adams spread his fingers across his waistcoat, thumb to thumb. "In Philadelphia," he said. The carriage swerved; through a space between buildings Short could see one of the round towers of the Church of Saint-Sulpice, like municipal inkwells, bright in the sunshine, and for a dizzy instant he felt himself on the wrong stage, with the wrong backdrop. "In Philadelphia in '76 our learned friend was made chairman of the committee instructed to write a declaration of separation," Adams told him. "Franklin was on it too"—Jefferson leaned forward again—"but Franklin declined to draft anything, he only writes in almanacs. I told Jefferson he should write the draft and we would sign it. He demurred. He said *I* should write it, being senior to him. I said, 'No, I have reasons enough not to write.'

" 'What reasons?'

" 'Reason first: You're a Virginian, and a Virginian ought to appear at the head of this business. Reason second: I am obnoxious, suspected, and unpopular. Reason third: You can write *ten* times better than I can!' "

Before their laughter had died away, Adams was peering through his window at the traffic of wagons and carriages come to a dead halt on the rue de l'Université. A hundred yards ahead of them the Pont Royal began its white arch across the Seine.

"Business," Adams said, turning back. "Franklin is leaving for America. You must now know, Mr. Short, in total confidence, that I mean to leave too."

Jefferson was wedged against the padded side of the carriage, his eyes closed in fatigue, but now he opened them. He said, "In total confidence, our friend expects within a few months to become American ambassador to London."

"To bait John Bull," Adams muttered.

"And therefore—" Jefferson continued in his deliberate fashion.

But Adams's nature was blunt, impatient. He interrupted, "And therefore Mr. Jefferson is to be left here, in this sink of noise and pleasure, and therefore he needs an assistant."

"A secretary."

"He needs a private confidential secretary who can write well and speak French."

Short held his breath.

"Colonel Humphreys has received a thousand pounds a year in that capacity." Jefferson spoke with his eyes closed, his shoulders pressed back as the carriage jerked and rocked forward again. "Since he goes with the ambassador to London, I have written Mr. Jay to say that, if you accept the post, I expect Congress to pay you the same salary."

Short exhaled with a pop.

"Not enough," Adams said firmly. "You need *twice* that amount. Why, food alone—"

Swiveling from one to the other, Short began to say yes, it was enough, more than enough, to thank them, to trip and splutter over his tongue—Virginia was gone, Paris was his; but his effusiveness was suddenly undercut by Jefferson's low voice, at once dreamy and ironic, quickly putting his new secretary back in his youthful place. "Well, brother Adams, our friend is vigorous and handsome. Paris no doubt has its own coin to pay him with."

At the *pont tournant,* the rotating wooden footbridge that connected the Place Louis XV and the Jardin des Tuileries, Jefferson asked for the carriage to be halted so that he and Short could walk home through the garden. Adams protested briefly, but set them down. Jefferson, he told Short in a whispered aside, was still too feeble for much exertion. Watch him, guard him, his spirits more than his body had undergone seasoning. And as Short pulled away to rejoin Jefferson's tall figure at the garden entrance, Adams motioned him back for one last word.

"You know, he never complains or rages, as I do perpetually." For a moment Adams looked neither choleric nor impatient but shrewd. "You polite Virginians bottle up all your anger. *Dum in dubio est animus, paulo momento huc illuc impellitur.* There's Latin for you."

☆   ☆   ☆

"Terence," Jefferson said, shaking his head, showing a quick, faint half-smile. "The greatest Roman playwright. 'While the mind hangs in balance a straw will upset it.' My hearing at least is still acute."

Short, still bouncing, emboldened by his appointment, asked the question he had held back for half an hour. "Is he right—did you think the ceremony in the church just now was all sorcery and witchcraft?"

They had reached the riverside edge of the gardens. Over the balustrade, across the sparkling brown barge-littered river, they could discern an enormous clearing along the Quai d'Orsay and scattered piles of bricks and timbers. As always, Jefferson brightened at any sign of building. "Brother Adams puts things forcefully," he said, waving the question away with the same half-smile.

"In Virginia your enemies call you atheist." Short held his breath at his own boldness. Jefferson turned with a look of mild surprise.

"In Virginia my enemies are much given to hyperbole." His smile faded. "You are serious. Let me be too. In my view there is nothing in life more important than a man's religion, unless it is his marriage or family. Nothing more important—nothing more private. Every religious idea and act should be free of the state, free of coercion. John Adams wouldn't agree—though Franklin would—but in fact it does me no injury at all for my neighbors to say there are twenty gods or no god. It neither picks my pocket nor breaks my leg."

He placed his elbows on the stone balustrade, as if to study the construction across the river, but kept his head turned toward Short. Behind them, on a gravel path between bare trees, passersby looked up curiously. Short thought that he knew Jefferson's face well enough to paint it—the long symmetrical features, the pointed nose, the pale blue eyes that gave away nothing; thin, sensitive lips, prominent chin tilted up. Even in its present weariness a Frenchman coming by would instantly recognize the face of an aristocrat, refined, delicate, used to luxury, used to command.

In point of fact, the aristocratic Jefferson was now speaking with something like his old radical, democratic energy. "Bill eighty-two," he continued, giving the modest legislative name to the Virginia declaration of religious freedom that he had written and labored bitterly for seven years to pass. "Bill eighty-two was intended to break the stranglehold on privacy that the state enjoyed."

Short nodded and moved his lips silently; he could recite whole portions of the preamble: *"Almighty God hath created the mind free . . . Truth is great and will prevail if left to herself. . . ."*

"In Virginia," Jefferson said, "before we presented our bill, heresy was still a capital offense. Denial of the Trinity could be punished by three years' imprisonment, children could be snatched away from their parents. These were dead laws, William, but dead laws can be revived. In any case every landholder in the state was compelled to support the Anglican Church with his taxes. The tyranny in Massachusetts was worse. I hear it said that our settlers came from England seeking religious freedom, but that is an untruth of great malignity. They came seeking *uniformity* of religion, a thing there never can be and never should be."

The energy died away from his voice, and he rubbed his face with his hands. His smile returned cautiously, not to his eyes. "As for the ceremony we have just witnessed," he said, straightening, "to you, on this day of confidences, I will admit that I take no consolation from superstition."

On the long walk back to rue Taitbout—"the sun is my almighty physician," Jefferson said—Short listened to a recital of the duties they would jointly undertake, when and if a lumbering Congress, now settled in New York, completed the appointments.

There were sixteen treaties in all that they were authorized to pursue, commercial trade agreements with every European nation. So far only Prussia had shown interest. In addition, Congress chafed—to be precise, Jefferson and Adams chafed—under the yearly tributes they paid to the pirates of the Barbary Coast to ransom the sailors they routinely abducted from American ships. (Defiance and a large navy, Jefferson said, were his idea of tributes.) And sale of three specific American commodities—tobacco, rice, whale oil—needed to be negotiated directly with the Farmers-General of France. Jefferson laid out the problem with laconic clarity: In return for an annual payment of cash, which he badly needed, Louis XVI had granted to a group of wealthy individuals, the Farmers-General, the sole right to purchase these three crops; they collected indirect taxes on every sale and used the full power of the government to enforce their monopoly. What Congress wanted was a market for American goods. What the Farmers-General wanted was the highest possible taxes. What the king wanted was any agreement that would damage British trade.

"You're not daunted, William," Jefferson asked a little mischievously, "by the prospect of writing a brief on whale oil?"

Short had never encountered a subject that didn't interest Jefferson. "I will master the whale," he declared.

"We will shake the poetry from him."

"Whale—hail!"

But Jefferson's moment of playfulness was over. As they ascended the six stone steps to the door, he rubbed his face again wearily. James Hemings pulled the door open and took his hat, and in a matter of moments Short stood alone in the hallway, listening to his vanishing footsteps.

The next day was Sunday, ordinarily the most festive day of the Parisian week, when cartloads of shut-in city dwellers flocked to the Bois de Boulogne. But the rain had returned, there was a bleak hint of January snow. Jefferson kept to his room, and the others passed quietly through a gray tunnel of twenty-four hours.

On Monday Lafayette arrived from Philadelphia, as expected, and went directly to Auteuil for conferences with Franklin and Adams. At midday, still in rain, he stopped for half an hour at the rue Taitbout. (Short glimpsed the extraordinary gilded carriage from his third-floor window, the swift pineapplish top of the marquis's head.) He spoke privately with Jefferson, presented a great leather pouch of mail, and left with a flourish. When one of the manservants came rapping wildly on the door, Short had just opened the first of his letters.

"Le maître—venez-le-voir! Le maître est mort!"

Short ran down the stairs two at a time, shouting for Humphreys. At the study door he collided with James Hemings, shoved him aside, and bolted through.

Jefferson sat, legs akimbo, sprawled backward in a chair by the fire. As Short reached him he struggled upward and started to stand, then simply held out a sheaf of letters and fell back.

"Lucy," he said.

"Sir?"

His face had lost every tint of color. Short seemed to peer straight through it, a transparent shadow. He caught Jefferson's wrist; the older man shook him away. Then Humphreys was beside him speaking loudly and going to his knees on the floor. Servants darted behind the chair and hurried forward with linen and bowls of water, but Jefferson motioned them all toward the door, as if an impassable zone surrounded him.

Humphreys thrust the sheaf of letters at Short. The first was from Francis Eppes, Jefferson's brother-in-law in Richmond. Short scanned it, seeing the names of Jefferson's two younger daughters, the words *illness—Hooping Cough—fears*. The second was from Dr. James Currie:

> I am sincerely sorry my dear friend now to acquaint you of the demise of poor Miss Lucy Jefferson, who fell a Martyr to the complicated Evils of teething, Worms, and Hooping Cough.

Short glanced at the date—October 14, 1784. Three months ago. The last letter was from Jefferson's sister:

> It is impossible to paint the anguish of my heart. A most unfortunate Hooping cough has deprived you, and us of two sweet Lucys, within a week. Ours was the first that fell a sacrifice. . . . Your dear angel was confined a week to her bed, her sufferings were great though nothing like a fit. She retained her senses perfectly, called me a few moments before she died, and asked distinctly for water. Dear Mary has had it and is now recovered.

When Short looked up again, Jefferson was on his feet, swaying, supported by Humphreys's strong arms. We are all in our shirt-sleeves, Short thought irrelevantly.

"My daughter," Jefferson said with a ghastly smile, "is dead to life."

CHAPTER

Five

Tea first, pastry second, brought crisp out of a "slow" oven while the tea cooled. James Hemings knew the prescribed order the way he knew everything else about Jefferson's habits, automatically, completely, precisely, a great rock of fact that sat perpetually in the center of his brain.

He bent, placed the silver teapot on the table, and stood back. To his right, Jefferson. To his left, Mr. Short, Mr. Adams, his wife, and the daughter they called Nabby. Behind Adams, none too effectively warming the room, the coal fire that one of the other servants had let fall dangerously low. Jefferson hated to be cold.

"Thank you," Short said to him, reaching for the teapot. Always polite. Always natural. The only person in Jefferson's house, James believed, who really noticed he was there.

"The pastry now," Jefferson said.

James nodded but walked to the fireplace first, where he tossed in a little brass shovel-load of coal. In the kitchen, Marc, the foul-tongued maître d'hôtel, sat by the oven door drinking Jefferson's red wine straight from a bottle.

"Monsieur le Noir," Marc said.

James knelt and slid the macaroons out of the oven. You get the proper heat for baking pastry, Jefferson had instructed him—he had written it out on one of his slips for James to keep—by holding a bit of white paper in the oven. If it burns, it will scorch your macaroons; if it just browns the paper it is exact.

"Black man," Marc repeated in slurred French, then waved the bottle. "But you're not black, you're *mulâtre*. Mu-lat-to. So who was the black man's papa?"

When James returned to the study Patsy was perched on a stool at her father's side, her nose buried in a teacup. Two weeks after his letters from Virginia, Jefferson still had the stiff, dried-out face—the *mask*, James thought—of a man in grief, but Patsy, Patsy was the Jefferson this time who could hardly speak or move. Her sister's death seemed to have turned the girl to stone. Mrs. Adams had been trying to make conversation while the men debated their business, and now she looked up at James first with relief, then anxiety. Like most northern ladies, Abigail Adams always tried to think of something to say to him and invariably struck the wrong note.

"You must write down this recipe for me, James. Or . . ."

James handed a plate of warm macaroons to Patsy.

"James can write," Patsy said.

"Well. Well, of course. I was just thinking—I've heard he was very sick."

Short turned around in his chair and stabbed at a macaroon. "It's true. James had a violent seasoning, just like his master."

"Well. I have a remedy. You need to take some Castile soap, James—"

"Oh, he's been fine for weeks," Short said quickly. "He's back in school, aren't you, James, studying French cuisine?"

"Yes, sir."

Patsy leaned forward with the same awkward long-boned motion her father had. She was twelve years old and already five and a half feet tall. "Is Marc drunk again, James?" She cocked her head at Abigail Adams. "Daddy has got to dismiss Marc, *I* think. He steals and he drinks."

"French servants," Mrs. Adams said, pleased with the topic. "I have seven in our house and two more, Esther and John, that came with us from Braintree, and none of the French will do any work that's out of their station—the *coiffeuse* won't sew, the *femme de chambre* won't wash. *Nothing* gets cleaned."

On the other side of the room John Adams was pacing, declaiming, while Jefferson slouched with his long knees higher than his shoulders. When he bit into a macaroon, Adams bobbed his head up and down and made a gratified jack-o'-lantern smile.

"James, you're a genius."

"He's started with pâtisserie." Jefferson straightened to take his own plate from James's hands. Six feet two-and-a-half inches tall, James thought, and whenever he sits in a chair, he folds up in sections like a carpenter's rule.

"From pâtisserie," Jefferson said, who loved any kind of system, "his school progresses to sauces—six months on sauces—then soups, game, meat. Fish they reserve for very late in the training."

"I'd give anything for some Massachusetts cod," Adams said, his mouth full. "Tell James to fix you some cod."

In the hallway James looked at the coin Adams had given him —on every visit Adams slipped him something—hitched his shoulders, and went down the hall, down the grooved stone steps, into the glowing red kitchen. Now two of the French servants had joined Marc by the oven (but only Marc dared to drink Jefferson's wine), warming their hands.

"Terminé?" the taller one asked with a jerk of his head toward the door. The kitchen was small and crowded and hot, and his long French face was nearly as red as his coat.

"Une demi-heure," James said. "Faut préparer."

"Merde." Marc rolled the bottle neck between his fat palms; lurched to his feet; spat on the floor. The tall footman simply stretched his shoe over the place and rubbed. In Paris, James thought, stacking the plates from his tray, they all spit wherever they want, even the well-bred lords and ladies with their wigs and ruffles and little gold swords. He had seen a diamond-covered duchesse at Dr. Franklin's house put one hand to her throat, make a loud hawking sound like a Virginia field hand, and spit right on Franklin's polished parquet floor. Her husband had done just what the footman did—while Franklin kept on talking—and rubbed the spot out with his soft leather shoe. *Nobody* ever spat on the floor at Monticello.

"You wait, and I show you some sights tonight," Marc said, squeezing past, squeezing his arm. "French girls adore *les noirs*."

By the oven the footmen were chattering in French and waving their hands one last time over the charcoal. In another two minutes they would have to lead the horses and carriage around to the street and wait in the freezing cold until the Adamses finished their tea. Then Jefferson would go upstairs, Patsy would sulk to her lessons, and Short . . . James thought that Short had fallen in love with a girl in Saint-Germain and would be calling for his horse as soon as they left.

"They love a black man's hair." Marc squeezed past in the other direction now and ran his hand across James's head. James bared his teeth and shoved it away. "Curly as a cunt," Marc whispered, staggering drunkenly.

James reached for the heavy sheepskin coat he kept on a peg, bought with the money Jefferson paid him. On the street outside, where the footmen were struggling with the horses, he paused to look up at the stars—*French* stars—then started to walk as fast as he could toward the lights that glowed on the horizon, just above the Boulevard.

Rue Taitbout, the Boulevard, rue de Grammont—he could go left at that point and wind his way up to the Café Montpelier, where all the English-speaking visitors gathered nightly. Or he could push straight ahead from the rue de Grammont and down toward the Palais Royal, which turned into an open brothel at sundown. He could go, he thought, and suddenly grinned at the stars like a wolf, *anywhere.*

James Hemings was nineteen years old, or possibly twenty—nobody knew for sure—and "bright" in the peculiar Virginia sense of the word, meaning a Negro who was extremely light-skinned, nearly white. He was also quick-tempered, intelligent, and after four months, completely at home in Paris. He came by his brightness on the male side. His father, as all of eastern Virginia knew, having been the planter John Wayles, Martha Wayles Jefferson's own father, Jefferson's father-in-law. By the laws of descent, that made him Martha's half-brother, but by the laws of Virginia, because his mother was a slave (and his grandmother too), James Hemings was Jefferson's servant.

Servant.

In *Paris* he was a man with money in his pocket, hair powdered and scented, a warm coat in the latest fashion.

He turned left, decisively, along the Boulevard. This was the road to Clichy and Saint-Denis, his favorite stretch in the whole city when the mood he called the "trembles" seized him. For nearly two miles you walked past rich men's glowing *hôtels*, the enormous new Opéra building with its hundreds of candle boxes and canopies and colored placards, *cafés turcs*, where turbaned waiters served sweet coffee, Swiss theaters, *jeux de paume*, red and green Chinese bathing houses—a wild boiling soup of Parisians, foreigners, horses—prostitutes, beggars, milords; blacks. At the Théâtre des Italiens the speeding carriages, trapped in the masses of playgoers, wheeled and turned like bugs.

He dug his chin into his collar and slowed to watch an egg-and-rope man do his trick on the narrow sidewalk of the theater's colonnade, inches away from a roaring bonfire somebody had started in the gutter. A little Parisian *fille* in a fur bonnet bumped sideways out of the crowd, smiled, and ran her fingers down his leg, and James, inhaling perfume, smoke, the icy edges of a February night, pushed her away. While he patted his pocket with one hand, the whore laughed and called him a name in French. On Sunday night they were wilder than ever, he thought, grinning. He touched himself on the leg where the girl had touched him and shoved off into the crowd again, a black boat bobbing in the current.

Past the theaters the sidewalks turned into ribbons of silk and mud. Bathing houses and cafés took over. The Cabinet des Littéraires had English newspapers for its patrons, James had been there a dozen times. He put his face to the window and watched for a moment—he could read and write just as Patsy had said, because he was a house slave and a Hemings (no other slaves at Monticello had last names), but he had heard Jefferson say more than once that a slave should be taught only to read; when they could write, too, he said, they could forge their papers and run away from their masters. Inside, by an oak-paneled wall, a huge white-haired Alsatian waiter with a mountain slide of double and triple chins recognized him and motioned toward the door—in Paris a black could go in, sit down, order coffee, the whores would flock and settle on his shoulder like sparrows—but James shook his head, made a vague French gesture of regret, moved on.

In another two minutes he pushed his way through a door, to a bar. Two quick cognacs—the girl who had rubbed against him (hard whalebone stays, soft bubbles of flesh) had raised the trembling from his knees, where it always started, to his crotch, where it always ended.

There were whores in the bar too. He looked around. He smiled, he rolled French words off his tongue like candy drops, and the *filles* bent to whisper clove-scented propositions. He kept one hand tight on his money, the other on his glass, filled again; refilled again.

At nine o'clock when the theater crowds had thinned and the streets grown even darker, he twisted sinuously down the rue de Richelieu, sweating cognac. The wind had knocked out all the glass panes and most of the candles in the streetlamps here. He stepped and tripped around a pyramid of new bricks—they were building Paris all over again, he thought, on every block and corner. Just like Monticello. He fumbled at last for the door. A loose metal handle shaped like a horn. A curtain of beads and cloth. The overpowering smell of cooked red meat.

"Jim-mee! Jim-mee—regardez notre américain, c'est dimanche encore!"

The cognac had made him hot. In front of the coal fire James stripped off his heavy coat and shook his sleeves loose.

"Jim-mee, you visit a little early. We're going to make you wait."

The smiling face came in and out of focus through a film of cognac: eyes, lips, greasy black hair falling down to his neck. In the markets James had noticed that the French vendors looked like the animals they sold—beaked nose, neck like a little string for the chickens; shaggy old bearded peasants for the goats. The woman who drove her pigs up the rue Taitbout lumbered under cascading rolls of fat, on hips like wagon wheels; her flat white snout, Short had told James, was for devouring her young. Denis Bretelle had a girl's slender figure, no beard at all, and he dressed in a long, belted robe that reached to his feet.

"Jim-mee, both of them are busy, *tous les deux*."

Slow, exaggerated French, palms spread wide in apology; if you concentrated you could follow every word. James took the brass cup of cognac that Denis brought him from out of the darkness.

"It's Sunday, Jim-mee, you don't have to supervise the house? You can stay a long time?"

"All night, all night." He nodded, lifting the cup. In Paris—one of the things James did in Paris was invent new identities for himself. If he went into a shop, he liked to practice his French, change his history. Sometimes he said he had worked for General Lafayette as an orderly and his mother was a Portuguese Creole drowned at sea; sometimes he had lived free in New York and passed for white, and his mother had died, shot in the streets by her lover, and he had come to Paris to study art. For Denis . . . he struggled to remember. For Denis he veered closer to the truth: He was Jefferson's aide in Paris, he personally knew Ben Franklin; he was a freed mulatto.

"Elisabeth," the little Frenchman said, kneeling. A confidential breath, an invisible cloud of garlic, saffron, and vinegar-wine. Under his pimp's robe Denis had no shoulders at all. In the dark his arms seemed to grow out of his hips, like sticks. "Elisabeth says she wants you this time herself."

James shook his head. Denis had two girls, one of them dark and mongrel, much darker than James, and she was the one he chose every time; the other, Elisabeth, was pure white and French, and that was a line he wasn't prepared to cross. Not yet.

Denis was bustling back and forth—another brass cup, stirring a pot—voices on the staircase. The fire sounded like rain, the meat smelled like flowers. He wasn't drunk, James thought; he needed the cognac to slow him down and draw out the pleasure. Seventy francs could squirt away, just like that, right in her hand, first touch. And then Denis was back, kneeling again, talking politics.

"Now you've heard at the American *hôtel*," he said, "about the Petit Trianon?"

James nodded. He didn't care.

"At the Petit Trianon the queen is building a *hameau rustique*—you know the word?"

"Hamlet. Yes. A little village."

"Hamlet. The queen has had a hamlet built behind the palace at Versailles, she wears a shepherd's dress, no tops—" ludicrously he grabbed the robe where his breasts would be and fluttered the cloth. "All the cows have blue silk ribbons in their ears. She milks them in a silver bucket."

"This is the queen?"

"She sleeps with her little boy." Denis had practically fallen across James's lap. His breath, his *smell* was overpowering. He pumped one hand at the robe under his belt. "She teaches him like this."

At the other end of the room the shadows were waving like dark fronds, big rippling black leaves that moved with the fire. The girl leaned against the doorjamb, calling his name.

"But it's much worse in America." Denis struggled to his feet. "Riots, murders. In New Orleans they brand their slaves with hot irons, right on the cheek, they feed the slave children to dogs."

"You shut up!" James shouted. He swung at the little Frenchman, once, twice, sending him flying, the cup flying. On the fire a pot overturned, and Denis rolled through a stream of hot grease.

"It's true!" Denis bleated, dodging another blow. He staggered, twisted and fell, upending a chair. "La vérité, Jim-mee—je l'ai lu dans les journaux!"

Cursing, James kicked blindly into the shadows. The pimp backed into a corner, squatting on his haunches like an Arab, and held up his hands. "No, I read it all in the papers, from England— they stoned General Washington, Jim-mee, it's *true!*"

Upstairs, his legs were still trembling. The girl tugged him through a doorway, more beads and curtains, and into the cramped little room she used. From the stairwell they could hear Denis muttering in strangled French, calling aloud a word or two in English as he straightened the parlor. Across the stairs, through the swinging lacework of beads, James saw another candle, an arc of white skin.

"Jim-mee, Jim-mee," the girl crooned, pushing close, working her fingers over his shirt. She called herself Marcella and claimed to be half-Italian, but there was full-blooded African not far back, not any farther back, James thought, than his own grandmother.

"Last time, too," she scolded, "you fought somebody else downstairs." Fingers, now lips, nibbling. "Always politics, Jim-mee."

"I don't care about politics," he said. She had short, stubby legs, and she straddled his right thigh as her hands worked, moving her belly voluptuously up and down his leg. James swayed and reached, tugging at her cotton shift.

"It's cold," she protested. "Your hands are cold. Every time they say something about America—swing, fists!" Now she was riding his thigh faster, and her fingers had pulled his shirt completely open. He closed his eyes and groaned when her breasts touched his skin. The shift bunched at her hips. His hands dug, kneading. In the flickering light of the candle she had left on the table he saw creamy brown flesh and his own hands, lighter in color, like ghostly prints. When the trembling spread from his legs to his center, *there,* he backed away a step, breathing hard, and whispered for cognac.

"Lie down, wait." Marcella's bed was a coarse mattress covered with blankets. He sprawled and rolled. The white girl was in the hallway, passing from her room. Looking in? The glass Marcella handed him was fat like a sherbet bowl. He propped himself on one elbow and watched her shift rise, snag on her breasts, then float away in the drunken, wavelike darkness. *Tea first, pastry second. If your white skin browns, it is exact.*

He lifted the glass and swallowed. Warm cognac crawled down his throat like a snake.

"Jim-mee," Marcella whispered, settling on top of him, sighing, a soft, distant sensation of warmth. "Jim-mee *hates* to be cold."

CHAPTER

Six

"One of the most elegant ladies at the entire table," John Adams said. He paused and looked around the study impressively. In his chair Franklin cocked his egglike head, clasped both hands over his cane, and pursed his lips into an indefinably impish smile. In the other chair Jefferson made a steeple with his fingers and smiled as well.

"Elegant," Adams repeated. He was wearing a new black suit of quite beautiful silk. À la mode, he carried a new tricorne hat under his arm. He paused happily in front of Jefferson's fireplace, showing off his clothes, enjoying his story.

"This was in Bordeaux," Adams said to Short, who had entered the room carrying an armload of papers. "I am explaining to Dr. Franklin the wanton dissipation of the French, whom we are both fortunate to be leaving."

"I am eager to learn," Franklin said drolly.

Adams, thought Short, not ironic in himself, was the cause of irony in other men. He placed the papers on the table beside Jefferson and stepped back. Adams resumed his pacing.

"This was in Bordeaux, in '78, when I had first arrived as part of the peace commission and was making my way north to Paris. Mrs. Adams was not with me. My French hosts set out one of their grand dinners and seated me as the guest of honor next to a very elegant young lady. Young and handsome and elegant," he added. "Even though she was married to one of the French gentlemen there, she ignored him utterly, spoke not a word to him, and addressed all her discourse to me."

"Very wanton," Franklin said.

" 'Mr. Adams,' she said." Adams paused, lifted his chin, and superbly imitated a woman's high-pitched French accent. " 'Mr. Adams, by your name I conclude you are descended from the first man and woman, and probably in your family may be preserved the tradition that will resolve a difficulty I could never explain.' "

Adams cleared his throat and looked at each of them in turn. "She then said, 'I never could understand how the first couple, Adam and Eve, found out the art of lying together.' "

Franklin guffawed. Jefferson closed his eyes and raised one hand to his brow.

"Never having heard a woman speak in this way," Adams said, "I found the question—I will be frank—I found it scandalous. I believe at first I blushed."

"The spirit of scientific inquiry runs deep in this nation," Franklin said with a straight face. "Does it not, Mr. Short?"

"I told her"—Adams turned his back to the fire and flipped up the tails of his coat with one hand to warm himself—"I told her that there was a physical quality in us resembling the power of electricity or the magnet, by which when a pair of men and women approach within striking distance they fly together like the needle to the pole, or like two objects in electric experiments."

"I like your image of the needle." Franklin winked at Short.

"She replied," Adams continued, "that whatever its origins in history, she thought it was a very *happy shock!*"

As they laughed again, he turned to Short. "I would not have repeated such things before young ears, Mr. Short, had not our gifted friend here assured me you have made great progress in French manners."

"Mr. Short," Jefferson said, rising, "has been living for weeks at a time in Saint-Germain-en-Laye, perfecting his French. I understand there is a young lady in the household."

"Mr. Short is a very handsome young man," Franklin said tolerantly.

"But he returned the day before yesterday to help me here with
. . . certain 'projects.' " For a moment Jefferson seemed about to
say more. Then he shook his cuff and changed the subject. "More
to our purpose, gentlemen, he has assembled and brought into
order—this great pile here on the table—all of my correspondence
with the House of Burgesses in Virginia." Jefferson's voice, Short
thought, was stronger. His face, caught in a slant of the morning
sun, had regained much of its natural color and lost the stiff, brittle
quality of the past two months. In conversation he made no reference—ever—to the dead child Lucy. She had simply vanished
into that completely private core of independence (Short considered his word), of independence and reserve where Martha
Wayles Jefferson's name and memory were also fiercely guarded.

"With the most recent letter"—Jefferson held it up—"we are
fully authorized to commission a statue of General Washington,
and at Monsieur Houdon's price of twenty-five thousand livres."

"That is," Adams said doubtfully, "more than a thousand English guineas."

Jefferson nodded. By this time they were all at the door, James
Hemings holding it wide, and following Franklin as he hobbled
toward the hallway and the carriage entrance at the cul-de-sac.
"Monsieur Houdon expects us this morning to discuss the arrangements for payment and also our preference for design."

"I favor an equestrian statue," Adams announced as they all
climbed into Jefferson's personal brougham, a black four-
wheeler, newly purchased, furnished with a smooth, leather-cov-
ered interior and a gilt eagle on the door. "A statue of the general
mounted on his horse would be appropriate, artistic."

Franklin settled into his seat opposite Short, facing the horses,
and smiled weakly through the pain of his stone. "Mr. Jefferson is
going to take us to Houdon's studio, I surmise, by way of a short,
educational tour of Parisian statues. That way he can instruct us a
little in our true preference." He tilted his head toward Short as
the carriage began to roll. "The world missed a great professor
when Mr. Jefferson took to politics instead."

Adams stroked his round little belly with both hands, as if it
were a cat in his lap. "I pride myself on knowing a bit about
statues," he said.

"There is only one statue, in fact, that I hoped you would see."

Jefferson balanced his letters on his lap and looked diplomatically from one to the other.

"Well," Franklin said, closing his eyes. "Let me guess. Monsieur Houdon's studio is on the rue du Faubourg Saint-Honoré, correct?"

"Nearby. The rue du Fondary." The carriage had reached the corner of the Boulevard and with noisy shudderings begun to wade into traffic. "But I've asked the driver to go by way of the Place Louis XV."

"Ah." Franklin nodded, eyes closed. Humpty Dumpty sat on a wall, Short thought. "Thomas, you outdo yourself. The king's statue as a model for our great democrat. Subtler and subtler."

The statue of the great king, when they came in sight of it, stood at the center of a vast gray-green cobblestone square, laid out between the Tuileries Gardens and the beginning of the grandiose new development called the Champs-Élysées. At Jefferson's command the carriage rocked and swayed into a clockwise stream of horses and wheels. Jefferson leaned eagerly forward.

"This I propose as a general model," he said over the noise.

Short squinted. Adams jostled impatiently against him. Jefferson, Short was convinced, would never need glasses; he had the serene, crinkled expression of an old Shenandoah hunter, and in fact his legendary father had been just that.

Adams found fault. "I don't see anything remarkable. And what's more, I can tell you Houdon didn't carve it. It's too old."

They slowed, tilted, eddied near the statue. "No," Jefferson agreed. "It was carved by Edme Bouchardon. And it is old. But what is remarkable to me is the size."

Adams frowned, shook his head.

"It's life size," Franklin said suddenly, apparently opening his eyes for the first time. "By God, it's life size, not oversize. I never saw that before."

"Not quite," Jefferson said. They were all crowding forward now, cranking the window down and peering at the statue. "I took its measurements one morning. Of all the equestrian statues in Paris, this is the only one that approaches human proportions. Even so, it's impossible to find a point of view from which it doesn't appear too large, even monstrous, unless you come back as far as we are, and then you lose sight of the actual features on the head. A statue is not made, like a mountain, to be seen at a great distance."

"You took its measures, tape and pencil in hand, I suppose." Franklin was nodding and winking at Short, as if to say the man will fall into a lecture on *any* subject. Adams, who had no artistic interest whatsoever, was rubbing his jaw in an effort to find something to say.

"So I want to propose to Houdon," Jefferson said, "a statue of General Washington on this scale, perhaps even smaller; and I need your support to persuade the Burgesses. What's more, I want it to show him standing, not on a horse, simply standing alone on a marble base."

The carriage bumped and plunged into a narrow street at the top of the square. "Well," Adams said gravely, at last able to contribute something, "that will at least be cheaper."

☆   ☆   ☆

Like every middle-aged Frenchman Short knew, Jean-Antoine Houdon had a pretty young wife.

She received them at the door, curtsying, smiling, chirping like a bird, and they followed her through the hallway, through the kitchen, across the garden, and into a two-story detached building that served the great man as a studio. There Houdon himself greeted them, without a servant, standing cheerfully in the midst of an enormous (truly southern, Short thought) clutter.

He bowed first and formally to Franklin, whose bust he had done in 1778 and so fixed forever, in Short's opinion, the old man's image in American iconography. Then he wiped his hands on his white sculptor's smock and shook hands with them each in turn, waving them forward one by one, in pantomime and broken English, toward a row of dusty chairs along one wall.

Wheezing, Franklin sat down. Jefferson, still in the middle of the room, gestured for Short to come forward as translator. Behind them Adams had begun to stroll among the statues, head cocked at a disapproving angle, his round belly, in the French expression, two steps ahead of the rest of him.

"You discover me," Houdon said in slow, careful French, "at work on another foreign commission." He raised one hand—the longest, whitest hand Short thought he had ever seen, like the flipper of a huge fish—and indicated a boy posing on a foot-high wooden box. Short had actually not seen the model as they entered, so jammed was the studio with plaster and marble figures, blocks, torsos, busts, casting furnaces, tools, paintings. Now he and Jefferson both turned to examine the boy, who was naked except for a small linen cloth tossed strategically across his thigh. He sat on another box, arms wrapped around a wooden staff, gazing unconcernedly at the ceiling. In the manner of all French salons, Houdon had decorated every square foot of wall space with shelves of busts or triple or quadruple rows of frames and paintings. So many eyes gazed down on him that, for an instant, Short stiffened to address the jury.

"A Spartan lad," Houdon was saying wistfully. "Sitting naked in the temple. Commissioned for the King of Prussia."

"These are *our* official commissions," Jefferson said. The King of Prussia's explosive sexual habits were a subject all diplomats avoided. Jefferson presented Houdon with the bundle of papers and letters that Short had arranged and translated last night. The little sculptor motioned to another boy, this one fully clothed, who appeared to come suddenly to life like Pygmalion's dream and step forward from yet another wall of statues.

Without even glancing down, Houdon extended the papers to him. The boy opened his mouth in a vast snaggle-toothed yawn, no longer mythological, but human, and looked squarely at Short, one attendant to another. Then he winked and ran from the room.

When Short turned back from him, Jefferson had already begun in his halting French to explain his ideas. The statue should be life size or a little larger. To take Washington's exact measurements, it would be necessary for Houdon to travel, at Virginia's expense, all the way to Mount Vernon. Jefferson himself preferred a pedestrian pose, with Washington either walking forward or his knee otherwise bent at an angle to the pedestal. Modern dress he thought much better than the usual Roman toga or indeterminate robe; the general should be depicted in his uniform, with epaulets visible but not distracting from his countenance.

Houdon listened attentively. They were an odd pair, Short thought, scribbling notes: the stocky little Frenchman with the thinning gray hair and square, bourgeois forehead, and the towering, aristocratic Jefferson, whose face, as always when he talked about ideas, seemed animated like a girl's. Short glanced at Adams. Franklin, old as he was, shared the same extraordinary capacity to be *interested*. It was the mark of the genuinely great; the two of them could discuss electricity, statuary, architectural design, printing types, the geometry of wigs—any subject whatsoever that touched on the material world. John Adams had nothing of their intellectual range. He had bought yards of landscape paintings for Auteuil, but simply to please Abigail, he grumbled— you can see the sky and the hills anytime you want, he had informed Short; you just open your door and look outside. Adams had no interest in science. His mind was emotional and unpredictable and really quite limited. Out of the corner of his eye Short saw him now scowling at a small nude Diana made of bronze. As Houdon's beautiful young wife came through the door bearing a tray of wine and glasses, Short found himself first glancing at the plump, tremulous figure she casually revealed; then thinking with something like horror: of the two of them, Adams and Jefferson, his own mind was far more like Adams's.

The "certain project" Jefferson had mentioned was in fact a secret.

Three hours after they had entered Houdon's studio, Short found himself on the other side of Paris, alone in the printing shop of a stub-necked, square-jawed Frenchman named Philippe-Denys Pierres, whose window looked squarely out on the rue Saint-Jacques, in plain sight of the two black towers of Notre-Dame.

"You are too late," Pierres said rudely, taking up a position behind his table and studying Short's coat and trousers. By contrast with Houdon's cluttered atelier, this room was a model of Jeffersonian neatness. Presses, tables, cabinets, box after wooden box of inky types: everything had a place, every possible flat space was cleared for work. By contrast with Houdon's serious friendliness, Pierres's rudeness was—French, Short thought.

"And you are too well-dressed by far to do this business, Monsieur Short."

Short placed his hat on a stool and pulled out his watch. Pierres unfolded Jefferson's letter and read it again. "He says you are to correct the first twenty sheets here in my shop." He turned the letter over and then turned it face up again, scowling.

"Queries one through five," Short told him in what he knew was impeccable French. "I can work at one of your excellent tables or"—he pointed toward the door to an inner room from which the heavy thump of a press could be heard—"I can stand directly beside the pressman."

"Written in English," Pierres muttered, shaking his head. "Is he coming, too, the author?"

Short flipped up the gold hunter's disk on his watch and rationed out one crisp, ingratiating smile to the printer. "Ambassador Jefferson will call for me in his carriage at five, exactly two hours from now."

"Much too soon," Pierres snapped, and reached under his table for a wrapped bundle.

The first printed page was simple: *Notes on the state of Virginia*, without the author's name or the date. Short checked the spelling, drew three lines under the "s" of *state* to indicate a capital, and turned to the next sheet, the table of contents. Why Jefferson must be so secretive about the book Short had no idea—not a word had he breathed to Adams, or even to Franklin—but then, Jefferson's motives often remained mysterious to him, no matter how innocent the "project." He is the most approachable and the most impenetrable of men, Franklin had told him, smiling (himself, Short thought, not always the soul of penetrability).

He picked up the third sheet.

Query I

An exact description of the limits and boundaries of the state of Virginia?

Below it Jefferson's answer began in straightforward, fact-laden prose: "Virginia is bounded on the East by the Atlantic: on the North by a line of latitude, crossing the Eastern Shore through Watkins's Point. . . ." So far as Short could see, *Notes on Virginia* amounted to nothing more than a two-hundred-page anatomy of Virginia's geography and natural history. A modest questionnaire, Jefferson had called it two days ago, when he had spread the manuscript across his desk, to arrange for the printer. On one side the twenty-three precise queries that the Marquis de Barbé-

Marbois, secretary of the French Legation, had sent Jefferson from Philadelphia, during the last months he was Governor of Virginia. On the other side, clipped in order, Jefferson's neat handwritten answers. Short paused at a paragraph giving the exact latitude and longitude of Mason and Dixon's Line and made a mental calculation. Marbois had returned to France in early 1781. So Jefferson must have written out his answers while he sat all summer in the long, miserable retreat at Poplar Forest, after the disastrous flight over Carter's Mountain.

He ran his pencil to the bottom of the page: "These boundaries include an area somewhat triangular, of 121525 square miles, whereof 79650 lie westward of the Allegany mountains." Short pinched the bridge of his nose hard with two fingers. Square miles. Longitude. Where were Jefferson's *feelings*? To write like this—calm, meaningless fact after fact—when up and down the state your enemies were laughing at the "horseback governor." Short twisted his mouth in irritation. Obviously feelings would sink out of sight, crushed by the sheer leaden weight of *facts*. Was that Jefferson's motive? To build a cairn of numbers over his feelings? Short reached for sheet number five, spotted a long smudge of ink like a lizard along its margin, and read Query II with a sinking heart.

A notice of its rivers, rivulets, and how far they are navigable?

How far navigable. He rubbed his eyes and looked up. Outside the shop, wagons, voitures, horses clattered by in their own perpetual river of noise and life. A trio of laughing *grisettes*, young shopgirls in gray dresses, peered in through a pane and waved at Pierres, who grumpily turned his back. They drifted away, giggling.

No one actually crushes his feelings, Short thought. The best you can do is disguise them. His mind flickered back to the entry in Jefferson's journal five days after his wife's death, the grotesquely factual account of how to stuff a dead bird. Feelings rebounded. Feelings came out at an angle sometimes, like a ricocheting bullet.

He smoothed the proof sheet over the counter.

The *Mississippi* will be one of the principal channels of future commerce for the country westward of the Alleghaney. From the mouth of this river to where it receives the Ohio, is 1000 miles by water, but only 500 by land . . . What was the Eastern Channel has now become a lake, 9 miles in length . . . which yields turtle of a peculiar kind, perch, trout, gar, pike, mullets, herrings, carp, spatula fish of 50 lb. weight, cat fish of an hundred pounds weight . . .

This was better, Short told himself, rubbing his face. You would need an ear of stone to miss the note of patriotism here. You wrote this way if you loved the land like a suitor, every dimple, rivulet, and spatula fish in it. But when had Jefferson ever made a secret of *that*? How many times had he said that the longer he stayed in Paris, the more beautiful Virginia became?

Short flipped ahead. Ports. Mountains. Caverns. He picked up a poorly inked sketch of Madison's Cave, on the north side of the Blue Ridge Mountains. After it an indented title, "The Natural Bridge."

The *Natural bridge*, the most sublime of Nature's works, though not comprehended under the present head, must not be pretermitted.

Short frowned and drew his finger down a battery of numbers. Then:

Its breadth in the middle, is about 60 feet, but more at the ends, and the thickness of the mass at the summit of the arch, about 40 feet. A part of this thickness is constituted by a coat of earth, which gives growth to many large trees. The residue, with the hill on both sides, is one solid rock of lime-stone. . . . Though the sides of this bridge are provided in some parts with a parapet of fixed rocks, yet few men have resolution to walk to them and look over into the abyss. You involuntarily fall on your hands and feet, creep to the parapet and peep over it. Looking down from this height about a minute, gave me a violent head ach.

"I use the word *sublime* in its technical aesthetic sense," Jefferson said behind him. Short whirled around, blushing. "I take it from Edmund Burke. The 'sublime' is what gives us a feeling of danger or violence, but without real risk."

"I have seen the Natural Bridge." It was all Short could think of to say.

Jefferson took the proof sheet from him and smiled. "People compare it, you know, to the great falls at Niagara—a tremendous, terrifying roar and spectacle, but you watch it from below, on a rock shelf, in perfect shivering safety."

"And the 'beautiful'?"

Jefferson bowed in greeting to Pierres, who had that moment entered from the thumping press room. "The beautiful," he said, "is harmonious, orderly, regular—much inferior to the torrential sublime, Burke claims." With an exaggerated gesture Jefferson presented to the scowling Pierres a new bundle of manuscript for printing. "Our friend here, for example," he said mischievously in English, "is clearly a 'sublime' man."

Short laughed and picked up his hat from the stool. "Homer is sublime," he said.

"And Pope is beautiful."

Jefferson turned away to study a sheet of figures that Pierres had silently presented, and Short felt a quick rush of disappointment. But after a moment Jefferson lifted his long aristocratic chin and added in the same mischievous tone, "Now which are you actually, William, a sublime man or a beautiful?"

"Is it necessary to choose, sir?"

"Well, I suppose I have found it a condition of life always to be choosing one thing and losing another." The smile never faltered, but melancholy suddenly ran silver-thin through his voice. Short raised his hand in involuntary protest.

Jefferson pushed away the sheet of figures. "I've dismissed my carriage. Come outside and walk with me a bit. Our friend Pierres can send all this home by messenger."

There was no gainsaying such an invitation. Short tucked his hat under his arm, like a Frenchman, and turned toward the door.

On the street he expected that they would proceed along the river, in the shadow of Notre-Dame, toward the Quai des Grands

Augustins, where all the antique booksellers' shops were clustered and Jefferson was well known as a customer. Instead, Jefferson chose an odd, many-angled side street, apparently unnamed, and began to lead him in the other direction, uphill toward the Sorbonne.

"I like these little out-of-the-way bric-a-brac shops. You never know what you'll discover." He halted to indicate a dusty display window at street level. "The owner of this one told me the other day he was at work on a perpetual motion machine that would astound the world."

"Just like America. Half the artisans I knew at home were trying to make a machine like that." Short peered into the window, but thanks to the sun's glare saw only Jefferson's reflection. It was a tall, calm, reassuring presence against the ever-present tumult of Parisian wagons and horses. The haunting oddities of *Notes on Virginia* had vanished from his mind, and inwardly Short was relishing, not for the first time, the idea that he could now spend day after day like this in Jefferson's company, in perpetual motion, perpetual friendship.

"Exactly like America." Jefferson beamed at the thought. "It appeals to the optimistic temperament, the American temperament. You meet it rarely here. But when I was practicing law in Williamsburg, I must have seen at least two dozen inventors who had put together some unheard-of combination of springs, weights, and balances and claimed it was a machine that would run forever."

In the case of anything mechanical, Short was on uncertain ground. "Theoretically, I suppose," he said doubtfully, "such a machine is possible."

Jefferson shook his head. "I am, alas, that contradictory thing, a skeptical optimist. Newton's laws of motion show that energy can be released but not created. Friction will eventually stop the parts of any machine. To tell the truth, though I would never want to discourage invention, the Almighty Himself could not construct a machine of perpetual motion while the laws exist that He has prescribed for matter."

Short felt himself at once humbled and instructed. It was true what Franklin had said, that when Jefferson went into politics the world had lost a great professor.

"You were happy as a student at Williamsburg, were you not?" They had started to walk on up the street, but Jefferson paused and waited expectantly for Short's answer.

"I studied far less than I should have done." Short cast his memory back to a scene he could scarcely picture now, standing in the center of Paris. "The war had just begun when I entered William and Mary, you know. There were soldiers marching through every week, making their bivouacs on the campus. We adjourned classes for two whole months in my first year. A French regiment set up camp, and that was a distraction. And then, of course, my father died. I was not quite twenty."

Jefferson nodded. "It was a very different time when I was there." He steered them down a narrow alley, and Short saw with delight that in two minutes more, by a shortcut he didn't know existed, they would be at the gates of the Luxembourg Gardens.

"When I was a student," Jefferson continued, "the only soldiers I saw were the two or three guards at Governor Fauquier's palace, where George Wythe used to take me for evening musicales. We would play chamber music with the governor, then sit and talk at dinner. I heard more good sense, more rational and philosophical conversation with them than in all my life besides." He stopped to let a rumbling coach-and-four go by. "My own father died when I was much younger."

At the turnstile gate Jefferson paid the entrance fee for both of them. "Did Mr. Wythe bring you along as far as Sophocles in the Greek?" he asked.

"The *Antigone*, yes. I still read it sometimes in my college copy. There is no poetry like the Greek, nothing."

Jefferson took his arm and they headed across a gravel path, stones crunching underfoot as they walked. To the left the garden's famous parterres stretched in rigid French formation, covered with squads of yellow blossoms. In the corner of his eye, Short could see the east wing of the old Palais du Luxembourg, home of the king's brother; beyond the palais the flags and pennants fluttered atop the new Théâtre Français. Jefferson ignored the view. "In earlier life," he said, bending closer, "I was fond of poetry, too. But as years and cares advance, the powers of fancy have declined." He looked at Short with undisguised affection. "It is a great pleasure to see you with all those powers in full vigor, to bring you along a little way, if not in the Greek exactly, then in Paris, the world. I never had a son, you know, William."

Short's face blazed like a torch. His tongue could manage nothing more than, "Sir. Yes, sir."

"Tell me now," Jefferson said, releasing his arm and altering his tone from solemn to playful. "We are to go tomorrow to assist John Adams at his house-closing ceremony at Auteuil. After my little lesson on aesthetics, which is that likely to be, young scholar —the sublime or beautiful?"

CHAPTER

Seven

It depended, Short thought, on the sublimity of manure.

They arrived at Auteuil the next day just after noon, coming on horseback for the exercise and cantering up the hillside from the Bois de Boulogne almost to the doors of the house. Jefferson had barely swung out of the stirrup before John Adams had him by the arm, dragging him out through the central hallway and into his prized five acres of garden.

"Look at this," he was saying as Short caught up. Between his stone fountain and his summer gazebo Adams had heaped up a row of chest-high brown pyramids, crusty and odiferous as a barnyard. "Look at this—dry! lumpy! half of it straw! By the great gods of a cow's rear end," he said fiercely, glaring left and right, kicking suddenly at a clod, "won't you agree, Thomas, that *American* manure is better?"

At lunch they talked of Mesmerism.

Franklin had come over in his litter—a trial run, the little doctor said cheerfully, for the journey to Le Havre he was shortly to make—and the ladies settled him in a great throne of cushions and bolsters on the terrace, where they all faced the twin rows of orange trees in tubs that Abigail had contributed to the garden.

"I have forty beds in this awful house," she told Short with a confidential groan. "Forty! In Braintree we had six. And the only part I've ever liked here is the garden!"

Short looked where she pointed, down a lovely alley of trees laid out amidst oblongs, octagons, and circles of brilliant flowers. Fifty feet from them a gray-green bronze statue showed a boy robbing a bird's nest, one finger caught in exquisite surprise by the bird's beak. Beyond it rose yet another mountain of very brown, very inferior (he must believe) manure.

"These are your letters that came in the pacquet to Mr. Adams," Abigail said, pulling two or three folded envelopes from her apron. "Pretty illegible handwriting, yes?"

"Mesmer," Franklin said behind them with a loud sigh, evidently answering a question. He held up his empty glass, and Madame Brillon, sprawling next to him, dressed in a dirty blue chemise, a straw hat with gauze around it, and a black scarf, languidly reached for the pitcher of mineral water to refill it.

"Dr. Anton Mesmer is absolutely—"

"Mesmerizing?" Nabby Adams had taken her place in a chaise longue beside Short, smiling sweetly and raising her voice to tease Franklin, another Adams family trait.

"The very word." Franklin tipped an imaginary hat to her. "Monsieur Short brings out the minx in your daughter, my dear Abigail."

"It's the prospect of leaving France that does it," Adams said from deep in his own chair. "Not that going to England will be better," he added gloomily. To Adams's left Jefferson lounged against the wall of the house and held his face up to the sky like a six-foot sunflower.

"Mesmerism," Franklin continued, "reached its peak, I believe, one year ago exactly. In fact, it was our own *chère* Madame Brillon who first suggested I join the king's investigation."

"Anton Mesmer," John Adams told Jefferson. "Viennese quack."

"Faith healer," Abigail added, carrying in a tray, Short guessed at once, of James Hemings's patented macaroons. "In the last century we would have hanged him for a witch in Massachusetts."

"Well, he likes to play my 'armonica,'" Franklin said pleasantly. He folded the tails of his coat neatly over his breeches and lifted his head, like Jefferson, to the spring sunshine. "He uses it as background music for his séances, so I was quite well disposed to like him."

"You are disposed to like everyone, Franklin."

"I am told," Abigail Adams said, "that he chiefly uses his tricks to prey on young women."

"He is," Madame Brillon said in emphatic French, "a very handsome man. He is as tall as Chefferson and very forceful. He cures every kind of illness."

"You would enjoy his scientific pretensions, my learned friend," Franklin said to Jefferson. "At Mesmer's séances you sit, about thirty of you altogether, around a long oaken case a foot or so high, specially carried in from Vienna."

"*Le baquet*," Madame Brillon translated.

"This *baquet* is filled with a layer of powdered glass and iron filings, then with dozens of bottles arranged symmetrically. Then he places a lid on the trough. Each patient takes an iron rod supplied by an assistant, and he inserts the rod through one of the holes in the lid. Meanwhile Mesmer walks around the trough tying every one to each other with a cord at the waist. Now they are linked to 'the magnetic fluid' of the atmosphere."

"He always wears a coat of lilac silk." Madame Brillon pulled her black scarf aside and revealed more dirty gauze and an impressive bosom. A kitten appeared at the edge of Franklin's mound of cushions, and Madame Brillon dangled the end of the scarf on its pale triangular nose. "Dr. Mesmer carries another, very long iron wand himself," she added.

"With which he touches the diseased parts of your body." Franklin looked frequently to Jefferson as they talked, not anxiously, Short thought, but with an affectionate curiosity that he himself had yet to understand. The two had met over a decade before at the Second Continental Congress in 1775, that legendary gathering of immortals, as Short thought of it, and apparently from that moment had been mutually devoted. No two men could be more different—plump, earthy Franklin, with his liking for sweet food, flirtatious women, constant joking; Jefferson, as tall and thin as Franklin was short and stout, reserved, serious, sternly unattached to women of any stripe. All that they shared were politics and scientific ideas, and even there Franklin tended to joke and tinker while Jefferson studied systematically and gravely. "In an election," Franklin had told Short once, "I always think the tallest candidate should win. I took one look at our Virginian and said, 'What *he* writes, I will sign.' " In his mind's eye Short drew an imaginary family tree—Franklin the father to Jefferson the son; Jefferson the father to Short the son.

"Now, he also touched other parts, I am reliably told." This was Colonel Humphreys, passing onto the terrace from the house and carrying—incongruously—an armload of cut flowers.

"The military mind at work." Franklin smiled at Humphreys as he smiled at everyone else. The secret of so much smiling eluded Short. Franklin simply never quarreled or criticized. Jefferson said that he had learned from Franklin the one great lesson of his life: always to nod and walk away when another man disagreed angrily with him.

"Colonel Humphreys," Franklin told them, "refers to the *titillations délicieuses* of the famous doctor. From time to time, it is true, Mesmer will place himself *en rapport* with a patient by seating himself opposite him—or her—and pressing foot against foot. Even, ladies, knee against knee. They all go off into a kind of trance."

Jefferson stirred and folded his long arms across his chest. "But as I recall, sir, your official investigation determined Mesmerism to be a fraud."

"Ah. Our skeptical committee did indeed say that. The language struck me as strong—the benevolent Dr. Guillotin wrote it —you should ask him about his ideas on humane execution, by the way, learned Thomas. He has a new machine—ghoulish. But yes, we all concluded that Mesmer's magnetic fluid is a hoax—he's since taken to Mesmerizing trees and animals. Patients are cured —if they *are* cured—by their own imaginations, which are far more powerful than a *baquet* of bottles." Franklin leaned to one side and patted the sulking Madame Brillon on her shoulder. "If I thought Dr. Mesmer could make vanish the little gravel quarry in this old stony body, my dear, I would roll naked in his trough like a baby."

At the great front doorway of the house Abigail and Nabby kept Short to one side while Jefferson, Franklin, and Adams stood by the old man's litter. The three commissioners talked in low, businesslike voices. Abigail was concerned for Jefferson's health. Nabby stood cradling a single long-stem rose and remarked archly that if reports were true, Mr. Short's health should be their real worry.

"The poor man must be exhausted. I hear," she said, "of the 'Pomona' of Saint-Germain, who is your tutor in French; the 'little opera girl'; the 'fair Grecian,' who is Madame de Tott—"

"Stop," Short said, both hands high in protest.

"The Ace of Spades—"

"Good heavens!"

"Mr. Short will have need of Dr. Mesmer himself," Nabby told her mother. "C'est la vie sportive de Paris."

"Nabby, go in the house." Abigail studied the huge bay mare that the footman had led from the stables for Jefferson. "You know, Mr. Short, we part for London in three days."

"We shall miss you." Short never knew quite what tack to take with the formidable Abigail. In her New England mob bonnet, with her unfrizzled brown hair, her sharp nose and sharper voice, she seemed the most hopelessly provincial woman in Paris; like all the Adamses, however, she specialized in surprises.

"And we you," she said briskly. "Mr. Adams, of course, will miss the politics, but he despises Paris. Do you know what *I* shall really miss, Mr. Short?"

Short began a halfhearted gesture toward the massive house and its forty beds.

"The ballet," she said firmly.

Short opened and closed his mouth.

John Adams's raised voice drifted over the grass. *"Hic autem perturbationibus . . ."*

"It is astonishing to me," Abigail said, ignoring it. "The first dance I ever saw in my life—dragged to it by Madame Brillon, as you might guess—it absolutely shocked me. In Boston—well, my delicacy was wounded. Girls clothed in the thinnest silk and gauze, petticoats short, springing in the air and showing their garters and *drawers*."

Short felt his face warming.

"The truth is," she said, "their motions are light as air; I go every week now, and when you watch for a while, the spectacle becomes astonishingly beautiful, and you begin to think of it all as a charming, innocent art."

"We attend the concerts," Short said, stupidly.

The white cap bobbed. The brown eyes turned liquid. For an instant Short saw past her dry middle-aged face to the softer face of a young girl, as young as Nabby. "Now I find myself asking," she said slowly, "have I been wrong all along? Is it really innocent? Or is daily example merely the most subtle of poisons?"

"Well—"

"Well, I wanted to say before the men break off." She glanced toward Franklin, now easing himself backward, with the help of two servants, into his Roman litter. "I have brought six children into the world, Mr. Short, and followed two of them to an open grave. I know what it is." She nodded once, sharply, at Jefferson. "Mr. Jefferson," she said, "is one of the choice ones of the earth."

"Yes, ma'am."

"You watch him."

"Mr. Short," John Adams said, breaking away early from the sight of Franklin's struggles. Thumbs in his vest, head cocked, he walked toward them like a Braintree farmer out to inspect his manure. *"Quicquid erit, melius quam nunc erit."*

"Horace?" Short guessed.

"Ovid." Adams grinned with a schoolmaster's pleasure. "'Whatever happens will be better than what's now.' Come to see us in England, Mr. Short."

☆   ☆   ☆

"The Ace of Spades," Jefferson said when they entered into the Bois. He stretched his long torso forward and adjusted the headstall of the bay.

This time Short's face genuinely burned.

"I have acute hearing," Jefferson reminded him. His expression was as mild and smiling as Franklin could have wished, but to Short's ears his tone was icy thin in disapproval.

"Sir—"

"I also see that you receive more letters from Preeson Bowdoin."

Short automatically touched the pocket where he had placed Abigail Adams's packet of letters. "Yes, sir."

"Brother Adams will tell you that French life offers more than enough temptations to a young, agreeable gentleman," Jefferson said, "without actually seeking a guide to them. Preeson Bowdoin comes from a good Virginia family; he has parts. For the sake of your old friendship I was glad to entertain him at the rue Taitbout. But he is led about by the strongest of all human passions. He has an uncontrollable voluptuary streak. I trust we agree that in his grand tour of Europe so far he lacks serious application. Time spent in his company is time pretty well lost."

"Yes, sir." Short spurred his horse to keep up with the energetic prance of Jefferson's great bay. In his mind's theater Preeson Bowdoin was being hanged and slowly quartered.

"It is only," Jefferson said, lifting his chin, looking straight ahead, "that I have such high hopes for you."

At Neuilly they threaded between the numerous and chaotic sites of new construction that dotted the riverbank as far downstream as the Isle of Swans—Jefferson leaning far out of his saddle, peering critically at foundations and casements—and finally came to a halt by the bridge. He would cross here, Jefferson explained, and deliver certain messages from Franklin and Adams to Lafayette on the Left Bank. Short, on the other hand . . . Short hastily assured him that he was heading home, straight to business. Jefferson nodded somberly. They parted with a quick, flat-palmed wave Virginia-fashion, and Short wheeled his horse around with both spurs digging.

His route took him parallel to the river, and then by a northward turn up to the newest avenue in Paris, the broad, dusty Champs-Élysées, where Jefferson had recently talked of moving.

At the corner of the very property Jefferson had in mind, by the rue de Berri, Short paused to rest his horse. Along the riverbank they were building houses. On the Right Bank the government was just completing a long enormous wall, twelve feet high, made of thick masonry and iron spikes, which would serve as a customs barrier around the city. Here, on the Champs-Élysées itself, the Farmers-General had erected a fortified toll gate, likewise built of masonry and iron, that spanned the entire road between the ends of the wall.

Short backed his horse to one side. Even at this late hour in the afternoon a line of carts and wagons stood in front of the central turnstile, the only one open, and the drivers waited stoically, arms folded, while the tax collectors, the hated *gabelous*, unpacked their loads, examined each bundle, and calculated the tax. The hands — or pockets — of the Farmers-General were everywhere, Jefferson liked to say. To enter Paris with merchandise of any kind — milk, eggs, silk, salt — you had to pay a duty; there were similar gates and collectors all around the city, at every gate in the wall. In Virginia, Short thought, the collectors would have been lynched, the walls long ago blasted into democratic rubble. Here, he knew from observation, by dawn all four turnstiles in the gate would be open and the lines of patient carts would stretch miles down the road.

He glanced at his gold watch. Five o'clock, the dinner hour.

He would keep Preeson Bowdoin's damnable letter in his pocket unopened. He would place it sealed on the mantel in his room. Look at it every day, morning and night, as a memento moriae. A reminder of Folly.

He spurred his horse viciously back into the road. How the *devil* did Jefferson, of all men, know about the Ace of Spades?

☆   ☆   ☆

"Colonel Humphreys sent a message he wouldn't be in tonight, sir. Mr. Williamos gone to stay in Versailles."

James Hemings closed the door and decided against practicing his French on Short this night. You gauge them like a strange horse, he thought, no matter how many times you've seen them. Horse you've known all your life still can kick. Short the politest man on earth, but he walks in flushed like a field hand, chewing his mouth, cords in his neck tight as a whip. James watched him scrape his boots hard on the floor. Woman trouble, one thousand — one million to one.

"Williamos gone *again*?"

James nodded and took Short's hat and his light outer riding coat, mentally noting that the hat should be brushed for dust and that the coat smelled of manure.

"Not back till when?"

James shrugged. "Didn't say, sir." Williamos was another of

Jefferson's unofficial boarders, a n'er-do-well drifter with nothing to recommend him but a hangdog look and a fund of stories about the Revolutionary War. They would come for a week, stay for months. The young men keep me young, Jefferson would say.

"Nobody called then?" Short asked, looking into the study.

"Nobody did." Dropping the *sir* out of sheer piss.

"No messages, letters?" Short was tapping the pockets of his neat silk jacket. Fine white powder shook from the curls of his hair like a little cloud of snow.

James shook his head slowly. No powder, no snow.

"I'll be upstairs tonight. I don't need dinner. If somebody does call—anybody—I'm not in."

Not in. Working. Showing SERIOUS APPLICATION.

Short crossed the room to adjust his curtains. Even in April the light lasted longer here than in Virginia. Across the horizon the sun still cast a low orange glow; the houses on the next street held a tenuous silhouette. If they moved to the Champs-Élysées, they would look out on the wall, soldiers, tax collectors. From his present window he could see only the occasional spark of horseshoe against stone. Not even a light in the arching *réverbères* over the rue Taitbout. Vandals stole the oil and candles so often that the city lit them now only on completely moonless nights, four or five times a month. In western Virginia, Short thought, beyond the Chesapeake plantations you could stand by a window every night for years on end and see no *réverbères*, no carriages, no buildings at all, only the endless oceanic forest along whose black bottom you seemed to crawl like some warped species of fish, deaf or blind.

Mesmerism and manure.

Abruptly he let the curtain drop and turned to his desk. Across the length of it, between two new candles, he had arranged stacks of letters to file or else to copy in diplomatic code (Jefferson loved to write in code); printer's proofs of the book, six well-sharpened pens in a row. By the time Jefferson returned, Short would have done a week's worth of work, disciplined his mind to a fine, hard edge. He rubbed his hands together briskly and sat down.

Memoirs of Jefferson — 3

IN THE RUGGED WESTERN FRONTIER OF Virginia, no man ever achieved a more spectacular reputation for physical strength than Peter Jefferson, Thomas Jefferson's father.

Our Jefferson, then a boy of nine or ten, remembered his father once striding out into the barnyard of the old Tuckahoe plantation, in the fierce heat of a July noon, and waving aside the party of slaves who were struggling to lift upright a spilled shipment of tobacco barrels. Peter Jefferson was well over six feet tall and muscular even beyond his extraordinary height. While the admiring blacks squatted in a circle and looked on, this Virginia Samson gripped one hogshead of tobacco in his right hand, a second hogshead in his left, and started to pull. His face turned red, the veins sprang out on his neck and forehead; the left barrel rose, then the right, and with a final grunt he pulled them both straight up on their ends. His son later weighed a similar set of barrels and found that each one came to more than five hundred pounds.

On another occasion, when Jefferson was twelve or so (with his father's height but never his bulk — "Tall Tom," the slaves called him), his father came upon three timberjacks trying to pull down a ruined shed near the James River. After watching them heave fruitlessly for five minutes at their girdle of ropes, Peter Jefferson pushed them away, seized one end of a rope himself, and dragged the whole shed down in an instant.

Years later, visitors to Monticello would be surprised to find the great statesman tinkering with a machine (of his own invention), made of levers and weights, that measured strength. It was Jefferson's habit, in fact, even after he retired from the presidency in 1809, to challenge the younger men to strong-arm contests on it. Thomas Mann Randolph, his luckless son-in-law, was never able to beat the old man. I was still in my forties, Jefferson in his sixties when I came to Monticello to inspect some neighboring property. Should I say how uncomfortable and embarrassed I was when, after being shown a prize copy of *Piers Plowman* more than two hundred and fifty years old, I was led back into the entrance hall and had my hand and forearm slapped into the machine's main lever, this to pull with all my strength while a marker rose up the wall? Should I add that Jefferson beat me?

Odd thought: Jefferson's cool, measured, amazingly lucid prose, likewise impossible to match, has often struck me as made of levers and weights, like his machine. He can lift an idea higher than anyone else.

☆ ☆ ☆

Short drew an inky line across the blotter on his desk. The first letter on his stack was addressed to John Jay, the secretary for foreign affairs in Philadelphia. It concerned the enthralling matter of the Comte de Vergennes and tobacco duties. Jefferson's code consisted of a little booklet of ciphers for which Jay had the key, and it was Short's task to encode all proper names and whatever words he thought important. He glanced at the open booklet. For the word *by* Jefferson had devised the symbol "1461." Short dutifully dipped his pen in the inkwell again. A bead of ink formed at the tip, like a drop of blood.

He was clearly not in the mood to write. It would be far easier to read. The next installment of printer's proofs lay in the halo of his candle, Queries VIII–XVIII of *Notes on Virginia*. At random he chose a page from the middle and in less than a minute saw exactly why Jefferson had kept them a secret.

CHAPTER

Eight

N ot in a better mood, James Hemings thought.

He stood by the window fiddling with the string on the curtain and watched William Short take his seat at the long dining table opposite Jefferson. It was eight o'clock, early for Short, late for Jefferson, who had already gone through his invariable morning routine of washing his feet in a basin of cold water and writing for twenty minutes in his letterbook. Then he had played his violin in his room for an hour. *Then* sat down to have breakfast and open his mail. Now Short comes in carrying a stack of long printed papers and staring pop-eyed like a frog at *him*.

James gave the string one last twist and left the room.

In Virginia by unspoken rule, Short remembered, watching the young black man go, a gentleman always refers to "my servants," never "my slaves."

He murmured his morning greetings to Jefferson, tucked his serviette into his collar, and waited. Two minutes later, James returned from the kitchen and began to spread out in front of him a dish of butter, a wicker basket filled with warm bread, and a wooden-handled pewter jug of coffee that Jefferson had bought on one of his excursions to the Palais Royal. While James worked, Short sat very stiff, chin back. He was acutely aware, as if for the first time in his life, of the mulatto's bright skin, his curly brown hair like an Englishman's, his absolutely impassive and impenetrable face.

"Yes," Jefferson said from the other end of the table, sliding his cup forward and smiling, "thank you, James."

Pour. Bow. Neaten the mail and papers. Where did James go after he served them each morning? Short looked at his gold pocket watch. Eight-six. James went to his culinary school in the Faubourg Saint-Honoré from nine till dusk, then returned to the house to cook and clean. He was light enough, almost, to pass for white; but anyone who looked could see the unmistakable Negroid flare to his nostrils, the sullen flat yellow of his eyes. You met blacks and mulattoes everywhere in Paris. Here they were legal French citizens, free as anybody else; in fact, if rumor could be believed, they were highly prized as sexual partners by certain ladies (and not only ladies) of the nobility. What did James Hemings think when he ran across them in the streets?

"Well, I've just received a mysterious note from John Paul Jones," Jefferson said. He held up a handwritten card for Short's inspection. "He asks me to meet him tomorrow at the Hôtel d'Orléans and inquire, if you can credit it, for 'the gentleman just arrived.'"

"Meet him in a hotel, and not by name?" Short pulled his mind away from James Hemings. The heroic admiral John Paul Jones, short, muscular, and possessed of the most musical Welsh accent in the world, was much given to intrigue with French ladies; he understands their toilette better than a ship's rigging, Abigail Adams had sniffed—but in matters of masculine business the admiral was usually candor itself.

"I will hazard a guess," Jefferson said, laying the note aside, "that he means to tell me—in confidence—what the Russian ambassador has said about a war against the Turks. The Empress Catherine is a restless person. For months she's been making bellicose noises, but her navy, as everyone knows, lacks experienced officers."

"Then she means to hire Jones as a mercenary to lead her fleet."

"In which case, since Jones's loyalty is entirely American, we may want to ask him to report on the state of her preparations."

"Spy for us?"

"Well, travel for us." Jefferson slid his cup forward, and James stepped from his post by the window to refill it. Breakfast, Short had found, was the only time of day when Jefferson was willing to be leisurely and inefficient; as soon as he rose to go to his study, concentration went up around him like a wall.

"The Empress Catherine," he continued musingly, "much covets the Black Sea, which she thinks of as a Russian lake, and she wants Constantinople as well, for its port." He leaned back in his usual boneless, slouching way; his sandy hair caught the light from the window and seemed to turn pure white. "In 1774 she made the old Tartar Khan declare the Crimea independent. Now she clearly means to drive the Turks out of that 'independent' zone and push as far south as she can. But so far, her Black Sea fleet is no more than a scratch collection of ships, manned by serfs and Cossacks. *She* wants someone to mold a navy. Paul Jones wants a navy to mold."

Short glanced impatiently at his stack of page proofs, then at James, who was just leaving the room.

"Sir—"

Like the musician he was, Jefferson possessed an exquisite sensibility to tones of voice. The *undertones* of voice, Short thought. Jefferson put down his cup and leaned forward.

"Sir, these proofs of your book . . ."

"They present a problem."

"Yes, sir." Short selected one page from the six or seven he had set apart. Silently he carried it to Jefferson's end of the table. The sunlight fell squarely on the paragraph he had marked with his pen; the paper seemed to shimmer and burn under it like an unbodied flame.

In the very first session held under the republican government, the assembly passed a law for the perpetual prohibition of the importation of slaves. This will in some measure stop the increase of the great political and moral evil, while the minds of our citizens may be ripening for a complete emancipation of human nature.

"Query eight," Jefferson said dryly. " 'What is the number of inhabitants in Virginia?' I went beyond the strict terms of the question, I suppose, but I wanted to make the point that Virginians recognize slavery for an evil." He pushed the sheet away. "Many of them do," he said.

Short started to speak, but instead chose another proof sheet.

It will probably be asked, Why not retain and incorporate the blacks into the state, and thus save the expence of supplying, by importation of white settlers, the vacancies they will leave? Deep rooted prejudices entertained by the whites; ten thousand recollections, by the blacks, of the injuries they have sustained; new provocations; the real distinctions which nature has made; and many other circumstances, will divide us into parties, and produce convulsions which will probably never end but in the extermination of the one or the other race.

" 'Extermination of the one or the other race,' " Short repeated. He rubbed his mouth, then looked down at Jefferson's calm face. "This is apocalyptic. This is terrifying. 'Deep rooted prejudices—' "

Jefferson picked up the sheet of paper. "It may also be true. You grew up among blacks, Mr. Short. You own slaves, if I'm not mistaken."

Short rubbed his mouth again. "When my father died, my brother and I inherited twenty slaves. My brother controls them."

Jefferson smiled ironically but said nothing.

Short felt his face grow warm. He sat down slowly beside Jefferson, folded a sheet of paper, and began again. "You are for abolition."

"I am for emancipation," Jefferson said. It was a lawyer's distinction. "I am for emancipation and then colonization. What I want to see is every slave, every black and mulatto in America, placed in ships and returned wholesale, all of them, every one to the African coast."

"But—" Short spread his hands at the impossibility of it.

"The great unanswered question of our times," Jefferson said. He stopped, turned his spoon in the cup of tepid coffee, then placed it neatly on the saucer. "The great question is the nature of 'human nature'—I used the phrase quite deliberately in the passage you marked. What *is* a human being? What *is* human nature?

Tiny, insignificant, trivial, like Gulliver's Lilliputians? Or irrational and squalid and bestial like his Yahoos? Or even noble, capable of growth? What does the phrase actually mean?"

He stood and walked to the window, where he appeared to be staring out at passing carriages and walkers.

"I think the black is inferior to us," he said finally, still staring at the street. "I would willingly be proved wrong, but I do think it. Inferior in reason. Inferior in body. On the great scale of being that runs from angels to insects, I am not even certain where, as an object of science, the black man fits—are they really human like us? They have less hair on the face and body. They secrete less by the kidneys, more by the glands in the skin. Their smell is disagreeable. They bear heat better, cold worse than we do. Given a choice the black male always declares in favor of the superior beauty of the white female—"

"But to *say* these things in a book?"

Jefferson turned back. He folded his arms. "Well, I wanted you to see them because I ask your advice. Once the book is printed, what should I do with it? A few copies I've already decided to distribute here in Paris."

Short nodded. The most enlightened Parisians spoke openly for the abolition of slavery everywhere.

"But the other copies . . . I've written Madison to ask his opinion as well. My plan at the moment is to send a hundred copies to the students at William and Mary to place the question of emancipation rationally before them. Perhaps a new generation may yet succeed where all others have failed."

Short leaned back in the chair and ran his fingers through his hair; when he looked, his hand was flecked all over with sparkling white "frizzle" powder. What could be more unreal than to sit in a gilt-papered room in Paris, three thousand miles from Virginia, from William and Mary—automatically he checked himself by glancing at the unmistakably French building across the street, with its strange gray mansards and its carved Normandy clock over the door. Last night he had dreamed he would stay in the rue Taitbout forever.

"Because whether or not the black is inferior to the white," Jefferson said slowly, "does not bear on the right or wrong of slavery." He chose another sheet of paper, from far down in the stack, and handed it to Short, then returned to the window. From there he added, as if to himself, "It is a matter of human nature. When you hold absolute power over another person, you are yourself corrupted. Despotism is degradation. The slave cringes. The master rots."

Short looked down at the page Jefferson had given him. To avoid reading it, he calculated the useless fact that if Jefferson had begun to write his book in the months after Tarleton's raid, he must have still been writing it during the long summer weeks that his wife lay dying.

> Indeed I tremble for my country when I reflect that God is just: that his justice cannot sleep for ever: that considering numbers, nature and natural means only, a revolution of the wheel of fortune, an exchange of situation, is among possible events: that it may become probable by supernatural interference! The Almighty has no attribute which can take side with us in such a contest.

Short replaced the sheet on the table and stood up himself. In the cavity of his stomach, where he always felt fear strongest, a chill, blank, palpable space had opened.

"To possess a living soul," Jefferson murmured from the window.

"This will infuriate the slaveowners and the planters."

Jefferson crossed his arms.

"They will see it as encouraging rebellion."

Jefferson said nothing.

"It is a very brave thing, sir, to publish this."

But Jefferson seemed to be slipping further and further away. Any reference to his personal qualities had that effect, always. Was it coldness? Or pride? Or reserve? What was the nature of Jefferson's nature?

Below them on the street James Hemings descended the steps. He paused on the cobblestone and lifted his face to the warm morning sun. Although it was now May, he still wore the heavy sheepskin coat he had worn throughout the winter. He flapped his arms once or twice, feeling the air and weather and pulse of the morning as a human being does.

Short, who recognized in himself more and more a man driven by emotion and impulse rather than logic, spoke daringly: "By the laws of France, James is now legally a free man, is he not, sir?"

Jefferson watched him turn the corner of the street and disappear, but made no answer.

CHAPTER

Nine

The Ace of Spades had completely white hair on her head.

Short drummed his fingers on the wooden counter of Pierres's print shop and wondered why on earth he had thought of that.

The association of ideas? He glanced from the counter to the long cylindrical rolls of white printing paper stacked along the back wall. Pierres himself rose like an inky Neptune from the lower shelves where he had been grappling with string and scissors and slapped a package ungraciously onto the counter, but Short ignored it. He had read in John Locke's philosophy that our minds work by association of ideas, one idea pushing into the next like a chain of falling dominoes. What could he have just been thinking of? Women? A good bet, always—Jefferson's favorite novelist Laurence Sterne was full of jokes about men's risqué associations. Or white printer's paper? Hardly. Frowning, Short paid out coins into Pierres's palm. White rolls of paper had no logical meaning at all.

And then as he turned away, thanking Pierres and clutching his package, he saw—for the second time, he realized—the frizzled white hair of John Adams's wig, marching past the printer's window.

When Short reached the door, Adams had come to a halt

twenty feet away, back turned, hands on the hips of his black
frock coat, white wig perched like a snowball on a stump. At
Short's call he spun around.

"I thought you were in London!"

"I'm not," Adams said, spreading his hands. "I'm lost."

Short turned automatically to look at the street sign—rue Saint-
Jacques; beneath it the usual midday chaos of wagons, horses,
pedestrians: *life* exploding from the paddock. He grabbed Adams's
sleeve and pulled him back out of the crowd.

"But you left three days ago!"

Adams was unfolding a sheet of paper and shaking his head.
"No, no. Delayed again. Miserable business with the miserable
treaty. I sent a note to Jefferson—*two* notes—you've probably
been gallivanting with the ladies in Saint-Germain." Short opened
his mouth to protest, but Adams pressed on in his usual brusque
fashion. "I came to town an hour ago and had the fiacre let me off
here"—he gestured downhill toward Notre-Dame—"now I can't
find the *street*." He pursed his lips and pronounced his strongest
New England expletive: *"Firecrackers."*

Short squinted at the paper. "Sir, you're on the wrong side of
the river."

"I want Verrières's store. That's off the Quai des Grands
Augustins, yes?"

Short shook his head. Seven months had made him a complete
Parisian. "It's in the Palais Royal, on the *Right* Bank, one mile and
two bridges from here."

Adams groaned. Under the white wig his face blazed red with
exertion and heat. He looked up at the sun, down at the crumpled
note. "It's the store where all the prices are already set," he muttered, half to himself. "The man pins a card with the price on every
item. The newest thing. Don't have to bargain. Mrs. Adams wants
bolts of silk for London."

"Palais Royal," Short said firmly.

"Walk me there, to the bridge at least."

Short took his arm and started up the rue Saint-Jacques, winding left in the direction of the Pont Neuf, the "New Bridge,"
which everybody made a point of saying was in fact the oldest
bridge in Paris. As they pushed through the crowds, Adams raised
his voice to explain the disaster of the treaty. Of all the European

rulers, he said, only Frederick of Prussia had faith enough to sign a trade agreement with the thirteen squabbling, undeveloped American states. But the post crept at a French snail's pace; the text had to be approved in two languages; all three American commissioners must sign—and Franklin and Adams would both be gone in a matter of days.

"Hopeless," Adams declared, and came to one of his sudden, inexplicable halts. In front of them red-and-white-printed posters fluttered up a brick wall like a patchwork paper tree, two stories high (all commercial posters were actually illegal—"défense d'afficher," the *official* posters announced at every corner—but no Parisian building escaped them). " 'Come see the puppet show,' " Adams said, reading the nearest one. "They must mean Versailles." Then he poked a stubby finger at the package under Short's arm.

"Mr. Jefferson's printing work?"

"Yes, sir. New calling cards." Adams bobbed his head knowingly; two weeks ago, on May 2, Jefferson's official appointment as minister plenipotentiary had finally arrived from Congress. "And his book." Short pulled aside the waxy green paper that was Pierres's trademark to reveal a half-dozen little octavo volumes.

"Ah!" Adams seized the first volume and cracked it open, greedy for print, indifferent to the stream of jostling passersby. He had Jefferson's addiction to books, Short thought, trying to block the crowd for him. (All of them did, he corrected himself: Franklin, Adams, Madison; even the soldier Washington would quote *Cato* by the yard to his lieutenants.) On the cobblestone, peering, grumbling, Adams flipped the pages with one hand, read, flipped again. Abruptly he snapped it shut and handed it back.

"Now you know, *I* think of writing a book myself," he said as they resumed walking. In sight of the river now, they had to battle for every inch. A herd of oxen was rounding the corner in an armada of horns and dust. Along the walls on either side of the street, like sentinels, the licensed beggars of the quartier had set themselves up in double lines, holding their green permits to beg in one hand, gesturing and snatching at sleeves with the other. Shopgirls and matrons squeezed by Short, giggling; a ragman tilted his cart. Every few yards a chanteur stood singing—different songs—and rattling a tin cup. Over the din of voices and cattle

Adams pushed his thought. "I would make it a comment on democratic government," he said, scowling at the beggars, "on the
theories of democracy, starting with the ancients." They retreated
to let a barrel-laden wagon, big as a ship, scrape through. "Jefferson has his pedantic streak, you know." Short put a hand to his
ear. "All right, all right," Adams said impatiently, allowing himself
to be dragged into the nearest doorway. "You worship him, he's a
statesman, he's written a book. Well, I remember in the Confederation Congress, one day Robert Morris delivered his proposal for
the national currency—it had got to the place one state wouldn't
accept another state's money—and Morris came up with a new
national unit, calculated down to the 1,440th part. He said it was
the most mathematically perfect coin in the world. Jefferson took
one look, came back himself three days later with a proposal that
the national currency be called a 'dollar' and be divided by
decimals—pennies and dimes."

"Extremely practical," Short said.

"Practical enough. Jefferson said in that calm way of his, 'the
bulk of mankind are schoolboys through life—how can they calculate to the 1,440th part?' And that's one side of him. Man of
business. We used his coin. And of course he wanted to go on and
reform the weights and measures, too, and make *them* decimal; but
that was too much and we voted it down. Now here's my point.
Before we knew it, Jefferson had put away his sensible coins and
got out his maps and was making another proposal, this time for
the names of the new states when we admitted them—below
where the Michigan Indians live, he wanted that to be Cherronesus!"

"Cherronesus?"

"Break your jaw, wouldn't it? Below that, just north of the
Kentucky territory, he wanted Metropotamia, Polypotamia, and
Pelisipia!"

The wagon lurched on, and they stepped back over the muddy
kennel that ran down the middle of the street; a moment later they
emerged on the rue Saint-André-des-Arts, a murky stretch of slick
cobblestone and mud that ran downhill like a drain. From under
their feet the stench of filthy water and rotting food rose everywhere, a thick miasma of smells. A beggar squatted over the mud,
pants down. Adams made a face and pinched his nostrils. Short

took his arm and steered him down a new passageway, hardly wider than their shoulders. At a corner they stopped again, and Adams wiped his red face with a handkerchief.

"Now Mr. Francophile-Parisian," he demanded, jerking his head, "did you ever notice *that* before?"

Short followed his pointing finger. A slanted doorway, cracked open like a gloomy mouth. Windows, drains, an iron grillwork balcony; three or four boys of indeterminate age helped an old woman stack trays of lettuce.

"The *bird*." Adams shook his hand at a tiny bamboo-slat cage hanging in the nearest window, where a wretched gray sparrow huddled like a ball of rags. "Have you never noticed that every French family, no matter how poor they are, keeps some animal in a cage? Birds, rabbits, little puppies—I've looked in half the windows in Paris. They all cage up something."

Short stood with him in the alley feeling doubly foolish—he had never noticed; Adams was absolutely right. "Why?" he began— "for food?"

But Adams was already hurrying on. "Because they have a *king*," he growled, spitting out the word. "Because if you live under somebody's thumb—king, noble, priest—you want to keep something or somebody under *your* thumb. It's *human nature*." At the end of the passage he stopped and jammed his hands on his hips, staring. Before them stretched the greenish-brown river, the chimney-pecked silhouette of the Louvre, and just to the left, a quarter of a mile away, the roaring, boiling, permanent carnival of the Pont Neuf, where crowds of pedestrians and wagons converged from three directions and poured into a tilting, poster-white mass of buildings and scaffolds and shops that covered the actual bridge from bank to bank. As always, Short felt his mind leap—the great city crested here like a bursting wave.

Beside him Adams mopped his brow and shuddered. "I *hate* Paris," he said. And with the abrupt change of subject that was his confusing singularity, he jabbed a thumb at Short's package and added, "Does he say anything about slavery in the book?"

Short looked down at his package. "He's sending you a copy, of course, as soon as the binder finishes."

"Because that is the great contradiction in you Virginians, you know."

"Mr. Jefferson—"

"—proposed in the very same Confederation Congress a bill that would prohibit slavery in any new state admitted to the union, Cherronesus, Michigan, Polypotamia—*any* new state."

"It failed."

"It failed by one vote. Beatty of New Jersey was too ill to come. It took seven states to carry; Jefferson got six. Only two southerners voted for it—Williamson of North Carolina and Jefferson. Every other southerner voted no, they *saw* that the result would be eventual emancipation. Confined to a few seaboard states, the whole wicked institution would shrivel and perish. Can you imagine how different the nation would be, thanks to one vote?"

Short readjusted the string on the package, suddenly heavy and warm against his ribs. What inner association of ideas did Adams follow? How was it possible to estimate rightly a man at once so vain and pompous and *shrewd*?

"I go across the bridge." Adams sighed, watching the crowds swirl toward the Pont Neuf. "Then the bridge on the other side. Through the gardens and there I am."

"Yes, sir."

"And you are delivering those books to somebody?"

"The Marquis de Chastellux, who promises to send on a copy to Buffon."

"What horrible names they have. *Buffon.* Like 'Bufo,' the toad in Latin. Buffon's the one who says all American animals and people are smaller than Europeans, yes? Because of the climates?" For a moment Short expected another flare of the Adams temper, always triggered by criticism of America. But the older man simply nodded to himself, uninterested in Jefferson's scholarly debates with the great naturalist. He placed a friendly hand on Short's arm. "Good-bye again, Mr. Short. I have reason to think you'll turn up in London one of these days. Meanwhile, distrust the cunning French."

"I will. I do."

"John Jay's wife Sally," Adams said, "was so attractive and looked so much like Marie-Antoinette that when we all walked into the theater one night—it was '81—the crowd mistook her for the queen and rose in applause."

Short twisted the string, uncertain of the point.

"Another bird in a cage," Adams told him flatly. "The crowd will turn on her one of these fine French days."

And with that he was gone.

Pont Neuf to Saint-Germain, crowds to mansions. Hat under his arm, Short bowed politely to the Marquis de Chastellux's major-domo, a remote, gilded being who bowed back a calibrated quarter of an inch and waited impassively in the doorway. Short traced an Adams-like association of ideas: masters, servants, *liberty.* In rapid colloquial French (bringing an eyebrow of surprise to the majordomo's face) he presented the copies of *Notes on Virginia,* explained that one was for Buffon, and reminded the man to check the letters inserted in each volume. Mr. Jefferson wished the letters and books delivered at once, as soon as the marquis was free. Bowing, backing, he regained the street, hefted his remaining books and papers and looked about.

Free. At liberty. He snapped the cover of his gold watch. When they finished their work that morning, Jefferson had quickly retired to his study to assemble the new copying machine just arrived from Philadelphia. Tonight he would attend a concert on the Boulevard—harpsichords, Bach, and boredom—and Short was free, unengaged. Paris lay all before him, where to choose his . . . He watched a trio of brightly dressed ladies step from their carriage onto a makeshift wooden ramp, where the universal mud of Paris lay only an inch or so deep. Laughing, they glided toward the marquis's door. The image of the Ace of Spades rose in his mind like a card from a conjurer's deck. Short smiled crookedly. There was no mystery whatsoever about his association of ideas.

With a brisk kick of his legs he began to walk. He could continue down the rue de Bourbon and drop in unannounced on Lafayette, who relished informality. Since his return from America the pineapple-topped marquis kept a perpetual open house for Americans and French "américains," sweeping them into his parlor with outstretched arms. Or two streets beyond, there was the town house of Madame de Tessé, Lafayette's wife's aunt, whom Short had never met but who likewise kept an open house for political liberals. (He *had* seen her handsome and learned protégée

Sophie-Ernestine, who read Greek and Latin and bowed very low to pour tea.)

Still walking energetically, Short veered away from the great houses that lined the street. Left Bank for books and study, Right Bank for . . . what he wanted. At the first corner, when the Seine could be seen winking in the sunlight, he tucked his books and papers high under his arm and strode toward a boatman's landing.

Twenty minutes later he was lifting the hammer-shaped knocker on a familiar door.

"C'est Monsieur Chort?"

"Oui. Madame est ici?"

"Elle est . . ." The young maid stepped into the hallway and partially closed the door behind her. "Elle est occupée."

"Ah. Et ce soir, peut-être? Occupée encore?"

The maid leaned forward to study Short's gold watch. She was about fifteen, he guessed, with straight black hair only lightly powdered. She wore a short skirt as Parisian women usually did on the streets, to keep the mud and filth from their clothes, but the ankles and calves she showed were farm-girl thick and covered with coarse little hairs. Did Madame hire such a girl as contrast with her own luminous white mane of hair? Or because a peasant girl would work for practically nothing, just to stay in the city?

"You are the Englishman?" the maid said, lifting her eyes from the watch but touching his hand with her fingers.

"American." Or did she keep her as an apprentice, so to speak, to the trade?

"And you are Chort, but in fact you're tall."

Short put away the watch. "Tonight perhaps?" Between the door and the doorjamb he could glimpse plush red velvet and a crystal decanter on a table. Even in the cool hallway he felt suddenly red-faced and warm. The girl pretended to think.

"Eight o'clock," she said at last. "Madame could see you then, for an hour or two."

Memoirs of Jefferson — 4

 JEFFERSON, THE SOPHISTICATED MUSI-cian, author, and statesman of European fame, who served French wine in the White House and spoke four different languages, grew up barefoot along wild and untamed rivers with barbaric Indian names: Pamunkey, Rappahannock, Mattaponi, Potomac.

A European confronting one of these strange-sounding American streams for the first time will be struck even now, after two centuries of settlement, by their desolation. No bridges, no Ponts Neuf, few boats; the traveler in Virginia still fords a river where he can, on foot or on horseback, waist-deep and higher in dangerously fast mud-brown water; or else waits hours on a slippery bank for one of the flat-bottomed ferries that work back and forth near the seaboard, between two dense, silent walls of blue-green forest.

In 1746, when his son was three years old, the Herculean Peter Jefferson set out with a small party of men to survey the so-called "Fairfax Line," an immense grant of land from King George II to Lord Fairfax, reaching from the salty head of the Rapidan all the way up to the first clear springs of the Potomac. For nearly eight weeks, while their families waited in suspense and terror, the explorers tumbled up and down over uncharted rocks and precipices, sleeping in the crevices of pines to stay clear of bears, using their rifles and knives to live off the land like savages. They went over five successive ranges of mountains that Peter Jefferson afterward remembered as endless, vast, dark, crisscrossed and choked with fallen timber and hanging ivy. They lost horses (but no men) in impenetrable swamps of laurel and stump pine. At the top of the Potomac they set up a stone marker (still there, still called the Fairfax Stone), and Peter Jefferson carved his initials deeply on a beech tree. On their return they plunged southeast through a mountainous area so rugged that they labeled it Purgatory on their map; the black, furious, dismal river that rushed through it they named Styx.

The river that Jefferson knew earliest was the less mythological but still dangerous Rivanna. In the midst of some four hundred acres of forest—bought from a friend for a bowl of warm punch in the Raleigh Tavern at Williamsburg—Peter Jefferson built a small wooden house on the sloping north shore of the Rivanna, just two hundred yards from the water. This settlement he called Shadwell, after the London parish where his wife had been born.

Here he also erected some barns, a dairy, and eventually a water mill that was to collapse in a flood.

His son, unable to leave any structure or house or room in its original state, made an early effort to alter even the Rivanna. As a young man he canoed it south to see if a channel could be made navigable all the way to the James, and then on to the Tidewater ports. It *could* be navigated, young Tom Jefferson reported back to his neighbors—and their tobacco carried straight to the waiting ships—all that they needed to do was remove some rocks and boulders six miles down from Charlottesville. He collected the money and workers and moved the rocks. It was his first act of public service (and remodeling).

But long before that, Peter Jefferson had taken him upstream into the wilderness and introduced him to the skills of a pioneer. In camp he brought his son under the watchful, unfriendly gaze of Indians, who sometimes reappeared later at Shadwell to bargain for grain or cloth. By family tradition somewhat Indian-like himself, that is to say, grave and taciturn, solemn, Peter Jefferson spent long hours teaching his boy how to hunt and ride in the rough-and-tumble frontier manner; taught him so well that long after Shadwell, Jefferson scorned all "town" games, especially those played with a ball (a prejudice he kept all his life) and recommended that for building self-reliance boys learn to shoot a rifle instead.

Now to a boy, a father is like a king. . . . For Jefferson the antimonarchist I suppose I had better correct my phrasing. To a boy, a father is like a *hero*. Peter Jefferson could sleep all night in the hollow of a tree, gun across his lap; he could fight off savage animals (or Indians) and lift gigantic hogsheads with one hand. His fastidious son, who never slept in anything but a bed his whole adult life, inherited the physical stamina but not the father's taste for the frontier. If Peter Jefferson was a hero to his son, it was doubtless in the more civilized guise of the skilled surveyor, whose maps imposed measurement and order on an otherwise chaotic Nature. A surveyor, moreover, with the manual laborer's passionate reverence for book-learning. In the house at Shadwell, hundreds of miles from any bookseller's shop, Peter Jefferson somehow managed to accumulate forty-two volumes of books, including Addison, Swift, Pope, and Shakespeare, and his dying

instruction was that the boy should receive a thorough and "classical" education. "If I had had to choose between my father's estate
and a liberal education," Jefferson liked to say years later, "I
would have chosen the latter." No need to choose, of course. On
August 17, 1757, when the boy was fourteen, the father died, in
the dying time, leaving to his care sixty slaves, seven
thousand acres, six sisters, one brother, and a difficult
widow who lived twenty years longer.

☆   ☆   ☆

Short poured champagne and glanced down for the twentieth time
at his open watch. He had chosen a café off the rue Saint-Honoré,
half a mile from the cul-de-sac where, at eight o'clock, his appointment awaited him. On the table the garçon had placed a second
bottle of champagne squarely atop his copies of *Notes on Virginia.*
Short leaned forward and daubed the little ring of moisture the
bottle had left. Then the clatter and noise of the café rose even
higher. A gentleman wearing the huge silver star of an English
lord on his coat crossed the room, scattering good money and bad
French. Short smiled at the fuss, the scene, the easy cosmopolitan
air, the reflection that he was *here,* an ocean away from—everything. He twisted in his chair to watch the milord emerge on the
street, adjust his powdered wig, and disappear. In the windows of
the opposite building, twilight was slowly hardening into darkness. On the street carriages sailed by like golden boats.

He cupped his watch in his palm.

☆   ☆   ☆

The Ace of Spades had white hair above; black hair below.

Short leaned back against the bolsters, stretched his legs under
the silk sheets, and watched her cross the room toward him,
carrying a scented candle on a candlestick.

Not only black below but trimmed neatly into the shape of her
name.

Short sighed and inhaled deeply as she slid into the bed beside
him. French women rarely bathed—Marie-Antoinette was said to
bathe three times a week and was widely regarded as a fanatic—
but his companion kept a small tub in her bedchamber, behind a
translucent gauzy screen, and after each *conversation* she liked to

retire for a few moments there. Short inhaled again and turned on his side to touch soft, damp skin. In the flickering light of the candle and the coal fire, her body was a landscape of black and white shadows.

"So, Guillaume, you brought me a present?" Her English was perfect; one languorous arm dipped to the floor and came up with a copy of—Short blinked: *Notes on Virginia.*

"No. No, I brought you champagne."

But she had already pushed her white shoulders higher and opened the book at random. " 'Cumberland, or Shawanee river intersects the boundary between Virginia and North Carolina 67 miles from the Mississippi, and again 198 miles from the same river . . .' " One part of Short's mind registered the thought that here indeed was the surveyor Peter Jefferson's true son speaking. Another part recoiled from the indecency or comedy (or both) of reading Jefferson's book in such a place. But as always the controlling part stirred and grew at the sight of breasts rising, nipples hard and dark as berries. His hands curved down the valley of belly and thigh, burning.

She flipped to another page. " 'The Comte de Buffon,' " she read incredulously. "This is a book about France?"

Short had begun to pull the sheet away from her hips. She was long-legged, small-breasted. The white hair framed an oval face of slow, sensual intelligence, punctuated by a black beauty patch at the corner of her mouth. Like all Parisian women she was never entirely naked; a gold chain hung around her neck, its triangular diamond medallion flat between her breasts, reflecting the hair above; below.

"Buffon," he told her, "claims that all animals and men in America are physically smaller than in Europe, because the climate is hotter."

"Don't." She stirred.

"And moister."

"Don't."

"The author refutes him." The book closed. The sheet fell. In Williamsburg, of course, Short had known women—upstairs in the Raleigh Tavern you could arrange what you liked—but nothing had prepared him for the exoticism of Paris. He inhaled the smell of cinnamon, peach. Long legs wrapped around him, skin against skin, moving like silk against silk. White hair, soft wide lips; games played with a ball. Two. The candle guttered and the bed creaked as they shifted. Her voice, at once amused and breathless, came first in French, then English. "Buffon a fait une erreur." Short felt her fingers brush the flat, rigid muscles of his stomach.

"Proof in hand," she whispered.

Firecrackers.

PART

REBELLION TO TYRANTS IS OBEDIENCE TO GOD

T w o

CHAPTER

Ten

The king's great palace at Versailles stood as a textbook demonstration of how to control a crowd.

From the highway to Paris, some four hundred yards below the palace gates, a narrow graveled road climbed on a slight uphill slant, bearing to the west, through a grove of trees. In mid-December 1785 the trees were already leafless and black and presented no obstruction to the gaze of soldiers in their scattered wooden sentry boxes. Behind the soldiers the first barricade ran the width of the palace, a twelve-foot high fence of iron bars topped with sharpened spearheads and snow, and it opened at two symmetrical points only, just wide enough for a carriage to pass. Inside, between the two wings of the palace itself, an icy cobblestone courtyard narrowed to a second gate, a second iron barrier. Beyond this, at the very entrance, a third iron gate, watched like all the others by the king's enormously tall Swiss guards. Beyond *this*, still in progressively narrowing enclosures, the king's chambers, the king's rooms, the king's closet, the king himself.

Jefferson walked across the courtyard in lightly falling snow. It was not yet eleven in the morning, but the guards on duty had already begun their afternoon meal, toasting long yellow baguettes on a charcoal brazier, heating wine or punch in a copper kettle sheltered from the snow. The nearest guard squinted at Jefferson's passport, then used one hand to lift the white bar of wood that blocked the door.

In the hall soldiers and courtiers hurried at showy, inefficient speed in all directions. Jefferson displayed his passport again, turned right, proceeded past the chapel, from which music, voices, and hammers could all be heard, and stopped finally at the east staircase to unfold his passport yet again.

In the opposite direction lay the state chambers, in which the king received ambassadors and in which, not seven months before, John Adams had presented him, bowing and kneeling far more than strictly became a Massachusetts rebel, to the great fat-bottomed, slope-browed young despot, whose hands, Adams later complained, were still streaky black with grease from his royal hobby of making miniature locks and keys. When Jefferson had taken his place beside Adams, he had read a prepared speech from a sheet of paper, praising the friendship of France and America and pledging his good will in continuing it. To the sardonic amusement of David Humphreys, who stood in the circle of guards and onlookers, at every mention in his speech of either the king's or the queen's name, Jefferson took off his hat and then replaced it, and the king and all his courtiers did the same.

At the top of the east staircase he paused for a last check of his papers; then a secretary led him through a series of rooms to the small private office of the foreign minister. The Comte de Vergennes rose to greet him with his watch open in his hand.

"You know Monsieur de Reyneval," Vergennes said in French, snapping his watch closed. "Of course."

From a shadowy corner by the window, so white-haired and pale that he gave the impression of stepping in from the snow, Reyneval advanced, bowed, grinned unpleasantly.

It was the special feature of Versailles always to be frigidly cold. Formalities over, Jefferson rubbed his hands together for warmth and took the center of three chairs that the foreign minister had arranged some ten impractical, bone-chilling feet from his tiny fireplace. On his right, Reyneval began to demonstrate at once why, in the diplomatic corps, he was known as the comte's "eyes."

"You have moved your residence," he said, still grinning as he sat down.

Jefferson nodded and stretched his long legs toward the fire. "Yes, to the rue de Berri, on the Champs-Élysées. We moved in September, the whole household."

"A charming location." Reyneval imitated Jefferson's gesture of rubbing his hands together. "The Hôtel de Langeac, correct? With garden, stable, marvelous furnishings—you must have received a generous lease. Or housing allowance." He glanced at Vergennes. The first subject on which the comte had written the new ambassador, months ago, was the American Congress's repeated, embarrassing failure to pay its promised salaries to the French officers who had fought in the Revolution. Reyneval's pleasantries were legendarily unpleasant.

"You feel the cold, Monsieur Jefferson," Vergennes said. "Move closer to the fire."

"And Monsieur Short is well?" Reyneval asked. "We missed him at Versailles during the summer, but now I understand that he was traveling, sightseeing in London and the Hague."

Jefferson smiled and inched his chair politely to the arctic edges of Vergennes's carpet. Most of the American correspondence was written in code—by preference Jefferson even used code in his personal letters—but the "infidelities" (young Short's tactful word) of the French post office were so gross and common that no one in the room, least of all Reyneval, was ignorant of the fact that Short had traveled to the Hague on strictly diplomatic business, to personally convey a treaty with Prussia to the hands of its foreign minister; or that his trip to London involved Jefferson's impatient desire to organize American warships against the marauding Barbary pirates of North Africa.

"Monsieur Short," Jefferson replied conversationally, "has been suffering from jaundice, I'm sorry to say. He stayed in Saint-Germain the whole of November, but last week he came back to the rue de Berri."

Vergennes snapped open his watch again, holding it at arm's length in his lap. "Your letter to me was very forceful," he said.

"I appreciate your willingness to see me."

"But I do not precisely take your point." The foreign minister's smile was unfailingly polite; but Vergennes's eyes were remote and stony, and his brow was almost scarred by a dark comb of deeply notched frown lines. "You wish to improve commercial relations with France—your ally, whose soldiers fought for you—yet the greatest part of American business continues to go to England, your former enemy."

"And not yet your friend," Reyneval added.

"Well, of course, old habits are hard to break," Jefferson said. "Most of our merchants have traded with England all their lives, you know. They sell their goods in England and in the nature of things use their profits to buy where they sell. Now if they could sell in France, they could buy here as well, to everyone's benefit. We could shake our dependencies on England, you could expand your markets."

Vergennes conceded it.

"I have brought a list of American products you might consider importing."

Reyneval stood and crossed to the fire, which he poked ineffectively with a brass shovel.

"Rice," Jefferson said, reading from a paper. "Rice grown in South Carolina, which France now presently buys exclusively from the Mediterranean."

"Egyptian rice," Vergennes said, "is so much superior to American rice that I see no market."

"Indigo," Jefferson continued, "which you now import from your own American colonies."

"Yes," said Vergennes, "because it is so much better than your product."

Flour, fish, and wood products met the same objection. Reyneval stood by the fireplace, turning slightly from time to time as if to examine his coat and wig in the full-length mirror behind him. Jefferson reached into his portfolio and produced a new sheet of paper.

"Whale oil."

"The most romantic of all your products," Vergennes said tolerantly. "Monsieur Adams described it to me in great detail—your heroic New England sailors, the single frail boat, and the vast animal, the solitary harpooner."

"Leviathan to lamp," Reyneval said.

"Well." Jefferson consulted his notes. "At the port of L'Orient an American merchantman named Barrett has just landed with a large cargo of oil, which he proposes to exchange, one-third for money, two-thirds for French merchandise."

Vergennes folded his hands across his lap.

"This is because of a special reduced duty on whale oil for this year only. If the duty continues at the same reduced rate next year, Barrett proposes to exchange his whole cargo for merchandise, to the clear advantage of the French merchants, who will see no coin whatsoever leave the country."

Vergennes wore a brilliant gold insignia of rank, like two linked stars, on the left breast of his coat. Diagonally across his chest, left to right, hung a blue silk ribbon the width of a man's hand, embroidered with delicate white fleurs-de-lys. He used his right hand to tug at the ribbon; then refolded his hands in his lap. It was obvious that he had no intention of committing himself to a continued reduction of the whale-oil duty. After a moment, without changing expression, Jefferson returned to his sheet of paper.

"Tobacco."

"Ah." Reyneval detached himself from the mirror. "We come to the crux."

Jefferson raised his eyes to follow him as he paced to the window. Beyond it thick snow now swirled like the batter of a cake. Reyneval, Lafayette had warned, is no friend to America. As soon as you raise the question of tobacco—and the whole plan of meeting with Vergennes, in Lafayette's view, was a disastrous mistake in the first place—Reyneval will sneer it to death.

"You yourself grow tobacco, I believe," Reyneval said. Insinuation, the ghost of the ghost of a sneer. "On your farm."

Jefferson turned his eyes and blandly addressed Vergennes. "Now, Monsieur, as you know, tobacco arrives here from various sources—Virginia, the Indies, Turkestan—the ships deposit it in barrels at all your river ports, from Bordeaux north. The Farmers-General, who have the monopoly of course, register and seal each barrel and collect a tax in the port; then the tobacco is shipped inland to another set of warehouses, inspected and sealed again; another tax. Then another stage, by wagon; for central France a fourth or fifth stage, for the Jura even more. And at every stage the Farmers-General collect a new tax, issue receipts, allow a local sale or two. It is"—Jefferson paused—"a complicated system."

Vergennes's allegiance to the status quo was automatic. "You must not forget, my dear sir, that the king receives a revenue of twenty-eight million livres a year from this complicated system. If American tobacco is largely excluded, well, it is a very old and ancient arrangement. We don't tamper with it. I might perhaps ask—"

As if drawn by the tiny fire, Jefferson had crossed his legs while Vergennes spoke and slowly slid down the back of the chair, lifting one shoulder and dropping his long right arm almost to the carpet. When he suddenly interrupted, his voice and posture were so casual that the undiplomatic effrontery of it left Vergennes blinking, his open mouth a silent O.

"I wonder if I could make a proposal, Monsieur?"

The mouth closed, the brow frowned. Vergennes sat in stiff vertical blue lines, unmoving, as if he had been slapped. In the abrupt silence of the room, snow brushed against the window in long, soft feathers; a single coal snapped into embers.

"Instead of collecting import taxes over the whole kingdom," Jefferson said, "at five or six or even seven different stages, why not simply restrict the import of tobacco to a few designated port cities? Cherbourg, for example, and Nantes. That way, a single collector in each city could do all the work."

Vergennes opened his mouth again, then closed it. Reyneval stood frozen, equally stiff and vertical, between the chairs and the window, one hand clasping the back of his neck, white eyes staring down at Jefferson.

"You employ some three thousand tobacco tax collectors now," Jefferson said calmly, "and every one of them draws a salary. My plan is radical, of course. But consider. The Farmers-General's monopoly remains, the king's revenues actually *increase*. And American tobacco can be easily included."

"Monsieur Jefferson," Vergennes began, and stopped.

"It would work," Reyneval said in a tone of complete amazement.

☆   ☆   ☆

Twenty minutes later at the entrance to the hallway, in an icy draft from the heart of Versailles, Vergennes bowed formally, tugged at his ribbon, and promised to consider Jefferson's proposal.

"It would actually work," Reyneval repeated, offering his be-jeweled hand. "It is a brilliantly practical idea."

"Monsieur Jefferson is famous for his practical sense," Vergennes said. A courtier in a greatcoat with shaggy epaulets of snow approached, and he waved him away. "You will remember how pleased I was to learn that you would replace Dr. Franklin here."

The mention of Franklin always brought a curiously boyish smile to Jefferson's face. He took his hat and riding coat from a waiting secretary's arm and nodded at the nearest table, where a foot-high ceramic figurine of Franklin, complete with fur cap and gold spectacles, flew a little silk kite on a wire. "I'm afraid, my dear comte," he said in a phrase that would be repeated for weeks at the court, "I only succeed Franklin. Nobody could replace him."

☆   ☆   ☆

"It would work *brilliantly*," Lafayette declared. "Why didn't you tell me what you were going to do? It's *brilliant!*" He clasped Jefferson by both arms and looked as if he were about to burst into tears. Short intervened.

"He used *your* figures, of course," he said, speaking loudly, bowing deeply, and the marquis turned his narrow face eagerly toward Short. Any mention of his role, in anything whatever, made the marquis swing like a magnet toward the speaker. "Those figures you devised for him months ago, the names of the ports you gave us."

"Yes, yes." The marquis was nodding and drinking from his wineglass at the same time.

"Well—" Short had reached a dead end. "Well, only *you* could have discovered them and set them out so perfectly. *You*, with your friendships and connections."

Lafayette swiveled back to Jefferson for confirmation, and Jefferson, on cue, began speaking in his softest voice, repeating Short's assurances. Short exhaled with a sigh and moved a step away from them. When they paid no attention, he retreated even farther, paused at a sideboard laden with food, and then looked about the crowded room.

He had forgotten how far Lafayette's obsession with things American had gone. To visit him now on the rue de Bourbon was to plunge into a fantasy world. At these soirées no French was to be spoken. At some point, sooner or later, the boy George-Washington Lafayette and the girl Virginie would be hauled forward to recite American poems in American English. At the drop of a hat the modest and devoted (and surpassingly dull) *la marquise* Adrienne would guide you through room after room stuffed from floor to ceiling with repellent homespun American souvenirs: woven cane baskets from South Carolina, dried leaves of Virginia tobacco, a stuffed possum shot by Lafayette himself, a brick from Mount Vernon. Tonight—procured who could guess how?—the butler passing wine among them was a full-blooded Indian, dressed for the Parisian winter in a deerskin loincloth and shirt, war paint, and a headband crowned with turkey feathers.

Short sipped his own wine and found that it had a bitter, coppery taste, the aftermath of the bout with jaundice that had driven him to bed (alone) in Saint-Germain for nearly five weeks. He edged around a group of bare-shouldered French ladies, feeling slightly light-headed and unsure if it was the décolletages or the wine. In front of the fireplace he stopped to admire the huge framed and glassed copy of the Declaration of Independence that Lafayette had hung in a place of honor.

"You must know the one by heart," a woman's voice said, "and the other you must think a bizarre French *jeu*."

Short looked down into the formidable, pockmarked face of Lafayette's cousin. The celebrated Madame de Tessé was a woman about Jefferson's age, petite in figure, famously partisan and fiercely liberal in her politics. She pointed her silk fan at the equally huge but empty frame that hung on the wall next to the Declaration. "My cousin says *that* frame is reserved for the French Declaration of Rights, yet to be written, of course."

Short started to reply, but she continued, "The most revealing thing I can tell you about our young Lafayette is this. When he was eight or nine years old, growing up in the dismal forests of the Auvergne, which with luck you will never visit—he dances so badly because he grew up in the provinces, it is why he took so

completely to you Americans—there was a wild dog or animal—
they called it, I think, the 'hyena of the Gevaudan'—that roamed
the countryside devouring livestock. The peasants claimed it de-
voured women and children, too, and naturally it drank their
blood. Little Gilbert used to go out every day into the woods,
determined to see the hyena."

"To kill it?" Short managed to ask.

"Certainly not. To *admire* it. Gilbert sympathizes with any out-
cast or hunted beast. It's how he sees himself. He was nearly
forced to leave the Collège du Plessis when he wrote an essay on
'the perfect horse.' He wrote that the perfect horse would buck
and throw his tyrannical rider as soon as he saw a whip. The
Jesuits flogged him for that, of course—a rare instance of Jesuiti-
cal humor."

"Then—"

"Were you there for General Washington's 'great conversation'? No, I can see you're too young. I want to meet an American
who was there—perhaps Monsieur Clever?" She bent her head to
indicate Jefferson, who stood ten feet away in the center of the
group.

"Monsieur Jefferson was not actually in the Continental
Army . . ."

"Washington," said Madame de Tessé, "is supposed to have put
his arm around our Gilbert and said, 'Please think of me always as
a friend and father.' "

Short raised an eyebrow. The idea of Washington placing his
arm around anyone staggered the imagination. There was a story
about Washington and the one-legged roué Gouverneur Morris—

"From that point on Gilbert was happy." Madame de Tessé was
gathering her skirts and beginning to look around the room. "You
know his real father was killed in the Battle of Minden. Gilbert
was two. Then his uncle, who was his guardian, fell at the siege of
Milan. So to have a general for a father—a *live* general!"

She started to walk away, leaving Short by the fireplace, but
with the casual coquetry of the middle-aged and homely, she
looked over her shoulder as she left. "You are Monsieur Short?"

"Yes."

"You know Madame de Tott?"

"Your protégée, yes. She's very charming."

"Come to see us at my estate in Chaville, both of us. We shall talk politics and revolution."

He nodded to the back of her wig and then pinched the bridge of his nose. A servant had pulled back the curtains, so that the cobblestone courtyard now shone before them, a carpet of snow under a radiant moon. Everyone else was going to a performance at the new Théâtre Français—Racine's *Les Plaideurs*, a play so baroque and boring that Short had instantly pleaded jaundice-inspired weakness; and in fact he meant to go straight back to the new, luxurious quarters on the rue de Berri and fall asleep.

By the opened curtains Lafayette had begun a complicated explanation of their order of departure, his big horse teeth flashing as he spoke, eyes turning greedily from face to face. Short took a moment to study him: the hunter of the hyena, the aristocratic friend of all rebellion. His politics were brave and Jeffersonian, but there was always something about Lafayette that just missed being truly impressive, that turned at the last moment desperate or comical. His appearance worked against him, of course: the huge teeth, the spiky red hair that no coiffeur could tame. But his deeper flaw, as Jefferson had written Madison (in code), was "a canine appetite for popularity." Doglike, puppyish. For a would-be hero, Short could think of no more devastating adjective.

Beside Lafayette now his wife Adrienne was looking up adoringly while the rest of the company were busily throwing on coats and hats as they listened. Which of the various ladies present, Short wondered, was Lafayette's mistress this week? Jefferson, as smooth in movement as Lafayette was awkward, gallantly adjusted the shoulders of Adrienne de Lafayette's cloak. Not immune, not by any means immune to the physical charms of women, but as far as Short knew, absolutely, resolutely chaste, even in Paris.

Even in Paris. Short began to follow the crowd to the doors—held open, he saw, by yet another American Indian in costume. The ladies passed before him, chattering, laughing, *jingling* (he considered the image) like kittens with bells. Jefferson frequently said that domestic happiness constitutes the highest form of human bliss. What did he think of an atmosphere like Paris, where infidelity was so commonplace, the flesh so ripely displayed, where a gentleman, however adoring his wife, would as soon go into society without his sword (a *better* image) as his mistress?

At the door, back to the inevitable draft, shoulders hunched like a scarab, he waited on shifting feet to make his excuses again. Adrienne Lafayette looked grave and mouselike. An Indian brave held out his cloak.

"I think," Jefferson said behind him, "that Vergennes may yet insist that the king's contract with the Farmers-General is already so advanced for the year—he won't reopen the question of tobacco."

Lafayette squeezed his long face into a frown.

"But the king, I believe," Jefferson added as they moved to the door, "also has the right to strike out any single item he chooses from the contract."

"He never uses it," Lafayette muttered.

Outside, Short walked alone across the courtyard. Snow crunched under his boots. Cold moonlight swam on the distant river. The shapes of boats and barges could be dimly seen bumping with the current. At the stables on the far corner of Lafayette's house, he leaned against the iron gate while a grumbling stableboy saddled his horse. Overhead, from this angle, the roof blocked the moon and the whole eastern sky blazed with a long trail of brilliant white stars.

Like God's white beard, Short thought, more light-headed than ever. God would wear a gigantic beard of flickering stars, would He not? and stroke it from time to time with His even more gigantic moonstruck hands? He watched the stableboy curse the leather straps and disappear under the horse's belly. Short could still taste the coppery red wine, of which he had undoubtedly drunk too much. Had God ever been young like him? And then grown old and sad in a foreign country?

In the salon of Lafayette's house the last few guests were awaiting their carriages. By the fireplace Madame de Tessé, muffled from chin to ankle in a wrap of silver fox, stood with the quite beautiful young wife of the decidedly older Duc de La Rochefoucauld.

"So, now, Rosalie," said Madame de Tessé indifferently, "you must come to Chaville and visit me, as soon as the roads are clear again."

Rosalie drank tea from a cup, not wine, and watched the servants bustling around the room. "Who was the young man you were talking with, here?" Shyly, she indicated the fireplace and the two great frames above it.

"Ah. Monsieur Short. Jefferson's personal assistant. You don't know him?"

And then, as she so often did, Madame de Tessé supplied her own answer. "Not yet, you don't."

CHAPTER

Eleven

THERE IS A SECOND EPISODE IN JEFFER-
son's life for which, like the flight from Banastre Tarleton, two contradictory versions exist. In order to approach it,
however, I need to fall back several years and set the scene.

Friends of Jefferson during his student years — and these include his early twenties, when he was still an apprentice lawyer —
all speak of two distinct traits. First, Jefferson could study longer
and harder than any other student who ever entered William and
Mary College. Fifteen hours at a crack, said his friend John Page,
and then he would get up from the books, stretch his long arms
over his head, and disappear for a two-mile run in the forest.
Second, he was most interested in girls.

We have everybody's word for it. We have, in fact (thanks to
Page and another amused friend, William Fleming), a number of
letters that Jefferson wrote, starting around age seventeen, that
dwell on the female question. For that matter, we have (*I* have)
Jefferson's own rather wry memory of certain youthful "turbu-
lences" and his confession that during these years, unable to sleep,

he often lay in his bed formulating "love and murder novels" that he intended to write in his spare time. (*Love and Murder*, by Thomas Jefferson!)

The ambivalence of "love and murder" is nice. And ambivalence is what he felt (I am sometimes tempted in these pages to say that ambivalence was the core of the Jeffersonian character; only there are so many things—democracy, freedom of religion, freedom of speech—about which he felt no ambivalence whatever).

The letters that Page and Fleming saved all have to do with a sixteen-year-old beauty to whom Jefferson refers as R.B., Becca, Belinda, Campana in die, and best of all, Adnileb, which is *Belinda* spelled backward. This Proteus of young womanhood was in reality Rebecca Burwell, whose father served as governor back in the days when Peter Jefferson reported to Williamsburg with his famous map of Virginia; by the time Jefferson met her, she was an orphan, under the care of her uncle William Nelson (one of the horse-racing Nelsons from York, famous for piety and bloodstock), and he, Jefferson, was twenty or so, still studying at Williamsburg and the favorite of Dr. Small, who taught him philosophy and mathematics, and Dr. Wythe, who taught him (it is said) to dislike slavery.

Page claimed that Jefferson wanted to marry her; that he rehearsed long speeches he intended to make to her (stood outside the Apollo Room in the Raleigh Tavern and quoted swaths of poetry to himself); that he told Page he would die if he lost her; that at last he declared he would buy a boat (the *Rebecca*) to sail the world in and cure himself of love. Always the reluctant speaker, he missed asking for her hand once because a mysterious case of "red-eye" kept him at home during a crucial month. He missed winning her (perhaps) anyway when he finally told her that (stammering) he had thought out a life-plan that included her, but before he could ask her, it was absolutely necessary that he go abroad on a trip to England and Europe for a year or so, as part of his education: Rebecca wouldn't wait, would she?

Rebecca wouldn't. While Jefferson was still seesawing between love and study, marriage and freedom, Belinda and Adnileb (his old love of code), she simply married Jack Ambler.

James Monroe has told me that the day he received the news was the first time Jefferson ever suffered one of those terrible "megrim" headaches that attacked him periodically all the rest of his life and left him sprawled in his bed, unable to work for weeks.

Rebecca Burwell rejected him in 1764. From that time on he devoted himself to studying the law and then to building his house at Monticello, where he was finally to bring a bride, Martha Wayles Skelton, on New Year's Day 1772.

But—and now I approach my two contradictory stories – around the year 1768 the man who considered himself Jefferson's "best friend" came to him with a request. John Walker had been at school with Jefferson from the age of fourteen, five boys cooped up in a log cabin on the Reverend James Maury's shabby place in the South-West Mountains, and afterward had gone to William and Mary with him. Their fathers had been close friends: In his will, in fact, Peter Jefferson named Thomas Walker his chief executor. When he married, John and his new wife Betsy had settled at Belvoir, about six miles downriver from Shadwell, where Jefferson still lived. So it was natural enough that John ride over one day and announce that because he was traveling to Fort Stanwix to negotiate a treaty with the Indians, he had made a will himself (the Indian wars, even at that date, were brutal affairs) and in it he named Jefferson chief executor. Jefferson bowed. And therefore, as Jefferson's best friend, John Walker asked him to keep a close eye on the health and safety of Betsy and their little baby daughter while he was away. Doubtless Jefferson bowed again.

All agree that the executor kept too close an eye on Betsy.

Weekly visits became daily. John Walker lingered four months in Indian territory. Jefferson was twenty-five, unmarried, strong, and vigorous. At some point in the four months, he has admitted (but with a lawyer's distancing, indefinite nouns), "I offered love to a handsome woman. I acknowledge its incorrectness."

What happened?

Betsy Walker told her husband her version—but not until many years later, when Jefferson was about to leave the country and set out for France as commissioner. And John Walker in his turn waited to dictate his grievance to Henry Lee (never a friend to Jefferson) until 1802 or 1803, when Jefferson was president and Walker had become his bitter political foe. These are Walker's own words:

In 68 I was called to Fort Stanwix, being secretary or clerk to the Virginia commission at the treaty with the Indians there.

I left my wife and infant daughter at home, relying on Mr. Jefferson as my neighbor & fast friend, having in my will made before my departure named him first among my executors.

I returned in November, having been absent more than four months.

During my absence Mr. Jefferson's conduct to Mrs. Walker was improper, so much so as to have laid the foundation of her constant objection to my leaving Mr. Jefferson my executor, telling me she wondered why I could place such confidence in him.

At Shadwell, his own house, in 69 or 70, on a visit common to us being neighbors & as I felt true friends, he renewed his caresses. He placed in Mrs. Walker's sleeve cuff a paper tending to convince her of the innocence of promiscuous love.

This Mrs. Walker on the first glance tore to pieces.

After this we went on a visit to Colonel Coles, a mutual acquaintance & distant neighbor. Mr. Jefferson was there. On the ladies retiring to bed, he pretended to be sick, complained of a headache & left the gentlemen, among whom I was.

Instead of going to bed he stole into my room where my wife was undressing or in bed.

He was repulsed with indignation & menaces of alarm & ran off.

In 71 Mr. Jefferson was married and yet continued his efforts to destroy my peace until the latter end of the year 79.

One particular instance I remember.

My old house had a passage upstairs with a room on each side & opposite doors.

Mr. Jefferson and wife slept in one. I & my wife in the other. At one end of the passage was a small room used by my wife as her private apartment.

She visited it early & late. On this morning Mr. Jefferson knowing her custom was found in his shirt ready to seize her on her way from her chamber—indecent in manner.

In 83 Mr. Jefferson went to France, his wife died previously.

From 79 Mr. Jefferson desisted in his attempts on my peace. All this time I believed him to be my *best friend* & so felt & acted toward him.

I quote it in full in order to add: What a document! Depending on your state of mind when you read it, Walker's narrative sounds like scenes from an old farce by Molière, full of hallways and nightshirts and slamming doors. Or else, if your mood changes, like the grim stalkings of a professional seducer—a dark-bearded, moustache-stroking Lothario who insinuates notes mysteriously into sleeves and appears without warning in the virtuous woman's chamber. From the lending library of fantasy: Virtue at the Mercy of Priapus. *Beauty and the Virginia Beast:* a tragic novel of love and murder by Samuel Richardson.

Here is the *other* version:

☆   ☆   ☆

". . . I acknowledge its incorrectness."

On a day early in October, when the hills west of Charlottesville had turned into low red mounds of color, soft embers for the summer to expire on, Jefferson drew his horse to a stop outside the door at Belvoir.

Inside, in the living room where the solemn old black servant led him, he found Betsy Walker sitting on a couch and pasting entries into her commonplace book. The baby was asleep. In the warm afternoon air the whole plantation seemed asleep. Jefferson sat down beside her, an expert in commonplace books and literary clippings and a tall, muscular figure as well, fresh from the hard masculine world of horseback and fields. Betsy Walker, buxom, tall herself, placed the book on her lap.

That day they read no further.

In this version of the story Jefferson leans forward and kisses her. "Offers love." The young matron turns swiftly, makes no objections, allows him, in fact, every freedom, every kiss or caress —and then at the crucial instant suddenly pushes him away and hurries from the room, calling hysterically for her baby. The attacks afterward, the notes in her sleeve, the villainous figure waiting in her bedroom with pedantic disquisitions about the legality of promiscuous love, all of those were figments of Betsy Walker's imagination.

Why would she publish them?

Well, what mystery is there about it? I met John Walker once in Williamsburg, when I had just started out on my brief, unsatisfactory career as a lawyer. He was a short, squarish man, florid and patchy of complexion, ineffective, intellectually dim. Walker looked ten years older than Jefferson; rumor whispered that he had lost half his plantation because of poor management and debt; he wandered Duke of Gloucester Street talking compulsively to anyone he saw. By contrast, the month after Walker returned from Fort Stanwix, Jefferson had been elected overwhelmingly, triumphantly, to the House of Burgesses. Shortly thereafter he had gone to the Continental Congress, written pamphlets—*written the Declaration of Independence*—then served two terms as governor, then secretary of state; when the Walker story appeared, he was President. Why *wouldn't* she say those things? In her own (poisonous) way Betsy Walker had made it known to the world that, insignificant as her husband might be, nonetheless one of the great men of Virginia had found her irresistible. Whatever else happened, the celebrated writer and statesman and paragon of virtue Thomas Jefferson had once fallen under her mesmerizing spell. If her husband was a cipher, *she* counted.

Do I defend Jefferson too vigorously? I doubt it. As long as men stand for elections, scandals like this will follow. And as for that *other* Jefferson scandal, *that* one—what can I truly say about *its* "incorrectness"?

☆   ☆   ☆

Light-headed, trembling slightly with fever, Short forced himself to get out of his chair and cross to the window.

When he had left Lafayette's house an hour ago, the moon was just rising over the river. Now it stood directly above the rooftops, bathing the Champs-Élysées in a blue-white glow. From the window of his new bedroom in the Hôtel de Langeac he could see, as he had predicted, every detail of the massive customs wall and the Farmers-General toll gate, called these days by the innocent name Grille de Chaillot, after the little tree-covered hill that sloped away westward behind it.

Short glanced at his watch. Past nine. Jefferson and the others would have just sat down at the theater. A movement below caught his eye, and he snapped the watch lid closed. At the nearest turnstile a peasant was struggling to replace a tottering stack of boxes (chickens?) on a wagon bed. Nearby, a *fille*, holding her skirt high to show her legs, tried to attract the attention of a guard. The wind blew a dusting of snow from the trees. The girl dropped her skirt and disappeared into the darkness.

In Virginia, Short thought . . . His mind swung back to the bare-shouldered ladies at Lafayette's. In Virginia things were at once more open and more Puritanical in matters of the sexes. Black women were available, exotic, *dependent.* Young southern cavaliers were encouraged to be predatory, ruttish. In the free and easy Chesapeake where he had grown up, they used to say that a virgin was a girl who could outrun her uncle. But after marriage everything changed. After marriage Virginians kept to a strict, suffocating, churchly decorum. No mistresses, no infidelities. No French *tolérance.* His mind swung again. Who was the beautiful young woman at Lafayette's house who had stared so intensely at him that night?

By the Grille de Chaillot the prostitute had returned. One of the *gabelous* had built a small fire a few feet from his guardhouse, and she stood close to it now, skirt hiked up to her thighs, warming herself and calling something in a raucous voice that carried all the way to Short's window.

Wearily, Short smiled and turned away. The Old World and the New. Everyone in Paris was aware that for the first years of his marriage the king had been impotent. Despite careful instruction, despite a whole wall of indecently explicit pictures lining the corridor to the queen's bedroom, stout, myopic, butter-brained Louis XVI had got it into his head that you simply inserted yourself in the woman, lay perfectly still for a minute or so, then withdrew and politely took your leave. The queen had raged and complained incessantly—adding to her reputation as a nymphomaniac from whom no footman was safe—until her brother, visiting from Austria, had sat down with Louis in exasperation and examined the royal equipment. A quick surgical cut on an abnormally tight and elongated foreskin, and the king at last experienced pleasure and the queen ceased to complain.

In the corridor leading to Jefferson's study Short passed the silent figure of James Hemings. They each raised their candle in pantomime salute. Their shadows crossed, split. Short entered the study and walked to Jefferson's desk to make his nightly inspection. Pens, ink. The big folio letterbook lay open on the blotter, the letters sent and received that day already noted in its columns and followed by a three-line summary of contents. Beside it was the leather-bound account book in which Jefferson recorded every franc, livre, and sou that he spent, an astonishingly complete tabulation, day by day, that Short tried faithfully to emulate (but the money went so fast).

On the seat of the swivel chair Jefferson had placed six more copies of *Notes on Virginia* to be wrapped and mailed.

Letter files, books of addresses, bank records. Short searched a moment before finding the pocket-size notebook in which, to his complete and abiding amazement, Jefferson wrote down the temperature each morning when he awoke, as well as his notations of the weather generally and his sightings of various plants and flowers, when they first bloomed, when they died.

Finally, he checked the copy-press machine that Jefferson used to duplicate most of the letters he wrote. It was a clumsy drum-shaped contraption the size of a wine cask, which exacted daily tributes of ink and mashed human fingers. Short disliked the machine—Jefferson loved it—but then, Short disliked most machines, most mechanical cleverness. He himself could barely sharpen the points of his pen satisfactorily, while Jefferson kept a little tool box beside his desk and in spare moments amused himself, like Louis XVI, by devising ingenious locks and keys.

Different minds, Short thought. He himself understood politics so poorly; Jefferson's mind analyzed, judged, noted with extraordinary clarity. Why would the king put up with such an obviously clumsy and inefficient tax-collecting system as the Farmers-General? Short had asked. Jefferson had looked up in his mild way and put everything into political perspective. The Farmers-General, he told Short, formed a huge protective shield between the monarch and the people. Their sullen, growing anger about taxes was deflected from the remote figure of the king and onto the ubiquitous *gabelous* and private financiers, who seemed to work for themselves alone.

At the study door he paused, holding his candle shoulder-high, yawning. His mind drifted. Lafayette. Lafayette's mistresses. The shy young woman at Lafayette's house, dark eyes, raven-black hair, staring at him. Why did the French never introduce themselves? In Lafayette's dining room the clubfooted Abbé of Saint-Denis, Charles-Maurice de Talleyrand, had been pointed out to him. Talleyrand had a mistress, Short knew, who lived in an apartment in the Louvre with her very French, very *tolérant* husband. When she had recently given birth, she had named the child, with her husband's bemused approval, Charles.

His candle transformed him into a ghost on the window.

Short inhaled and smelled the tart filament of wick and smoke. After his fever lifted, after he regained his fleshly existence, perhaps he would be Parisian—or Virginian—enough to find out the dark young woman's name.

CHAPTER

Twelve

"In America," said the Comte de Buffon. He paused and looked up and down the long dinner table. An extraordinarily ugly little man, Short thought; big head, stumpy legs and brown and wrinkled as a nut. He had come to Jefferson's dinner party dressed not in the usual lace shirt, jacket, and knee-breeches, but in slippers and a yellow robe with white stripes and blue flowers, excused from ordinary formality by his great age and fame.

"In America," repeated Buffon when he was sure he had everyone's attention, "as I have shown many times, the temperatures are lower on average, the air colder, the climate more moist than in Europe. It stands to reason that animals and men in such a climate grow to a smaller size than here."

"Well." Jefferson had seated himself opposite Buffon in the center of the lavish table. In fact, unusually enough in Short's experience, Jefferson himself had laid out the seating arrangement for the whole table, huddling with his maître d'hôtel Marc and even checking the place cards twice before the guests arrived.

"Now, Monsieur le Comte." This was Nathaniel Barrett, a Boston merchant and sailor whom Jefferson had met somewhere. He carried himself like a bluff farmer but spoke a surprisingly good French. "It's an interesting theory you have. But in the first place, where is the *evidence* that temperatures are colder in America? I've survived some forty-five Massachusetts winters, man and boy, and I can tell you that they were nothing compared to the last few months in France."

Buffon turned his gnomish little head and nodded to the Abbé Raynal, who sat several chairs farther down, toying with his food. "Many studies," Raynal said. Despite his reputed wealth, the abbé wore an unfashionably plain black suit and a blue cloth cap like a turban, instead of a wig. Buffon was rumored to have his hair curled three times a day, like a woman, but the priest Raynal had the blunt, ascetic air of a soldier. "A *great* many studies, some of which I have had the honor of conducting myself, all establish the differences in temperature and moisture. It is indisputably a fact."

"Well," Barrett persisted, scratching his head, "even if it *were* a fact, how precisely does it work, that heat and moisture can change the size of animals?"

"And men," Raynal said.

"And men."

"I sent you a panther skin, Monsieur le Comte," Jefferson said.

"Yes, and also a copy of your interesting study of *Notes on Virginia*. Our friend Chastellux here delivered the book and the skin to me at Montbard. You were quite kind." The old man's eyes twinkled. He refused to be drawn into further comment on the panther skin, which had smelled like moldy blue cheese and which Short had personally watched James Hemings wrap and then had delivered himself to Chastellux. Short thought the old man was enjoying his game with Jefferson immensely.

Jefferson slouched in his chair and smiled. "To tell the truth, I actually hoped that the size of the pelt might convince you that nature, in our part of the world, is no less vigorous than in this."

Buffon spread his tiny hands. Paws, Short thought; from the moment the comte had arrived at the rue de Berri, Short had seen him as a diminutive talking forest creature, complete with curls and spectacles. "My dear sir," Buffon said genially. He turned to include Chastellux in the debate. "One pelt does not a species make."

"No." Jefferson imitated Buffon by gazing up and down the table, fourteen guests, seven on a side, all men for once. In the usual French custom each man had brought his own manservant to stand behind his chair and change plates and glasses, so the effect was more like an overcrowded lecture hall than a dining room. "Well, in any event I've asked some friends in New England to hunt down a few more panthers and also some moose skins and antlers and send them on, for your cabinet of objects. Now the moose, which is native only to America, you will find a gigantic creature, much larger, for example, than your European reindeer."

Buffon nodded cheerfully, reminding Short of a mouse-size Franklin. "It would help your case more, Monsieur, if you would also furnish additional skins of the so-called mammoth." He turned to the Abbé Raynal again. "Monsieur Jefferson believes that the mammoth, whose bones he has examined in America, is in truth a different creature from the elephant. Naturally I don't." He looked directly at Short and, behind the little glass disks of his spectacles, actually seemed to wink.

"What disturbs me most, I suppose, in your theory," Jefferson said, "is the idea that nature in America is somehow less energetic, less active than life in Europe. As if," he added with a tone of controlled sarcasm, "both sides of the earth were not warmed by the same genial sun."

"In America," said the Abbé Raynal, in a tone as lofty as Jefferson's had been sarcastic, "it is the case that even when animals are transplanted from here to there, they in fact degenerate in size."

"And men," Jefferson said, still slouched in his chair and staring up now at the ceiling. "I believe you argue in your books that all races are smaller in America, red, black . . . even white men whose fathers came over as settlers from Europe."

"And men," agreed the abbé.

"I wonder." Jefferson straightened, smiled, looked from one end of the table to the other. "I see that we have by chance arranged ourselves so that all the Frenchmen are on one side, all the Americans on the other. Perhaps we could just stand up and test the theory?"

He slowly rose from his chair, all six feet two inches of him. Barrett rose. Short, a second merchant, William Bingham, the other three American guests. None was smaller than five feet nine or ten.

On the other side of the table, smiling, the gnomish Buffon

stood. Then Raynal, three inches shorter than Barrett. Of the seven Frenchmen only the man opposite Short matched any of the Americans in height or bulk.

Jefferson smiled serenely. Barrett burst into cackling laughter.

☆   ☆   ☆

"Your friend Jefferson has an unfortunate habit of never facing the person he addresses. He looks like a fox."

Short moved a step closer to the fireplace and frowned. Charles-Louis Clérisseau was the Frenchman with the bulging eyes and sardonic voice he had so often encountered but never officially met until tonight, and then thanks only to Jefferson's place cards had he learned his name.

"He always gazes to one side, or up at the ceiling," Clérisseau said. "It makes him appear insincere, or"—he switched from French to English and mouthed the next word with exaggerated delicacy—"*sly.*"

"Ah." Short made a point of looking straight into Clérisseau's great saucer-shaped eyes before twisting his head to locate Jefferson. "He's a reserved, diffident man, really." At the other end of the room Jefferson was displaying some of his books to Buffon.

Clérisseau shook his head. "Diffident like a fox. I believe that trick he played at dinner was first done by Franklin years ago."

"You think—"

"Moreover," Clérisseau said, "I find it suggests another disturbing trait."

"Which is?"

"He makes his defense of America too *personal.* As if, when Buffon and Raynal propose their theories, he himself is being criticized. Look at him—six feet tall, broad-shouldered. What does it matter to him if the moose is large or small? What does it matter to him how big the mammoth is? Is it a personal contest? Your Monsieur Jefferson has a very thin skin."

"He has a very strong sense of place, in fact," Short said, wondering if Clérisseau had just said something painfully insightful. No, he thought. Not at all.

"Ah well, place; setting; atmosphere. The sine qua non of an artist. I am an architect, you know, Monsieur. When he asked me to dinner, I sat down and read the description of his mountaintop house, in Chastellux's *Travels*. Monticello. A marvelous name. A marvelous *idea*—to clear off a whole mountaintop and put up a house."

"He originally meant to call it the Hermitage." Flushing, Short put his wineglass down on a table. *Hermitage* sounded foxlike.

Clérisseau smiled and said nothing.

By the tall French doors, under a handsome crystal chandelier that Jefferson had bought last week at auction, Buffon held up an engraving between his tiny hands, shook his head, and replaced it in the folio Jefferson opened for him.

"No, no, Monsieur Jefferson," he said. He looked up at Short and twinkled a greeting. "There we must agree to disagree too. You think that this so-called science of 'chemistry' is bound to lead to new and brave discoveries, to *unlock the secrets of nature*—your words?" Jefferson nodded. "Whereas I," said Buffon, beaming at all of them, "think chemistry is merely cookery."

As Jefferson, objecting vigorously, reopened the folio and began a second defense, the Abbé Raynal moved back a step from the group and squeezed out a square inch of smile for Short.

"I suppose that you, also, Monsieur Short, grew up among Indians and slaves?" Like all the French abbés whom Short had met, Raynal had an impressive repertoire of pleasures. One hand clutched a large glass of Jefferson's excellent sauternes; the other hand raised a cakey gray mound of snuff to his nose. But the effect of good humor was spoiled by the little dark worms of wax now streaking his cheeks, makeup melted by the heat of the fire.

Short took a new glass of wine from a passing servant and steeled himself to answer diplomatically.

"Slaves, yes. Everybody in Virginia lives among slaves. But I've seen few Indians in my life, and then mostly in the towns along the Chesapeake Bay, rarely in the forests or their own villages. Monsieur Jefferson, however, lived much among them when he was a boy. His father traded with them and took them as guides on his map-making expeditions. He seems at home in Paris, as you see, but his boyhood was spent in the wilderness."

"With savages." Raynal smiled a great deal, like Clérisseau, but Short felt it a cooler, more condescending smile.

"I doubt if he would agree. Monsieur Jefferson has a high regard for the Indians he knew. In his *Notes on Virginia*—"

"I have not seen the book," Raynal said.

"Well. There he quotes a wonderful speech by a Mingo chieftain named Logan, a speech the Indian wrote himself when he was accused of breaking a treaty. Jefferson says the speech is worthy of comparison with Demosthenes and Cicero—"

Raynal's smile became a sneer. With his wineglass he touched Short's sleeve, a polite signal for interruption.

"Not," he said with Gallic precision, "Demosthenes and Cicero. Surely not. Monsieur Jefferson's penchant for exaggeration carries him too far."

"Logan?" Jefferson said behind them.

"Monsieur Short has been quoting your praises of Logan." Raynal looked complacently about him. Barrett drew closer, chewing a stick of bread. Buffon lowered himself into a chair and folded his hands in his lap.

"I was saying," Raynal continued, "that you surely give too much credit when you compare a half-naked savage to Demosthenes."

"I don't accept the word *savage*," Short said doubtfully, shaking his head.

"Logan was a splendid figure," Jefferson said. "But if you are interested in Indian oratory, I remember another great chief." He looked down at the floor, then toward the fireplace. "This was a famous warrior from the Cherokee tribe, named Outasette. He was frequently my father's guest in our house at Shadwell. In about the year '62—I was still a student at William and Mary—Outasette came to Williamsburg to see the governor and to embark on a trip to England, at the invitation as he called it of his 'white Father' the king."

"He had his portrait painted by Joshua Reynolds," Barrett said through his breadstick. "I saw it in London. The damned English made such a fuss about him—they love the brutes. Oliver Goldsmith wrote it up in a book."

"Well, I saw him," Jefferson said, "not in London, but in his camp outside Williamsburg, before he sailed. About two hundred Cherokee braves had marched in to see him off, and the last night he assembled them out in the forest and made a farewell oration. The moon was in full splendor, I remember, and Outasette stood above us on a cliff, in his feathered headdress and buckskin, and made a speech directly to her, as if they understood a common language."

Short's fingers itched for a pen. When the mood was on him Jefferson could speak for hours in absolutely perfect sentences and paragraphs. One needed only write them down, as from dictation.

"His prayers were for his own safety during the voyage, first, and that of his people during his absence. I remember his sounding voice, his distinct, beautiful articulation, the solemn silence of his people sitting at their scattered fires—all that filled me, a boy of twenty or so, with genuine reverence and veneration." Jefferson raised his head to smile wryly at Raynal. "Although, of course, I confess that I didn't understand one word in the language he uttered."

The abbé had sniffed most of his little gray mound of snuff. Now he wiped the back of his hand across his nose and glanced sideways at Buffon.

"Charming, picturesque memories," he said. "The scene—you, Monsieur Jefferson, on your knees beside an Indian campfire, the full moon, the orator in his costume—yes, yes, very good, very *American*. But my dear sir, my dear friend, these impressions have nothing to do with history or science, our previous subjects. They only show how quickly the white man falls under the spell of savages—not Demosthenes—and how quickly the white man will then . . . degenerate."

Jefferson's face had turned faintly red.

"For example," Raynal went on, oblivious, raising one hand, palm open to the company. "For example, one is astonished, really astonished that America has not yet produced a good poet. Or an able mathematician. Or a man of genius in *any* art or science whatever."

Barrett was staring slack-jawed. William Bingham and several others had stiffened. Even Buffon in his chair stirred uncomfortably.

"Well. When we shall have existed as a people," Jefferson said with a casual half-shrug of his shoulders, "as long as the Greeks did before they produced a Homer, or the Romans a Virgil, or the French a Racine, well then, a fairly deserved reproach, I suppose. Though *degenerate* is hard. On the other hand, in the science of physics our little country of three millions has already produced a Franklin, whose discoveries in electricity are second to none in all the forty millions of Europe. I imagine Mr. Rittenhouse the equal of any astronomer living. And of course"—he looked mildly from Raynal to Buffon—"in war we have produced a Washington, whose memory will be adored so long as liberty and freedom have their disciples."

"Ah. Washington. Liberty." Raynal made a pretense of inspecting the color of his wine. Clérisseau began to say something, but Raynal lifted his chin and spoke loudly over him. "We hear reports that General Washington's house has been burned by mobs—"

"Nonsense!" said Barrett.

"—and the general himself hanged in effigy."

"These are reports from British newspapers," Jefferson said.

"Burned his house," Raynal repeated firmly. "To the ground. Attacked him. Chased him from his property. Stoned him as he got into his carriage. The liberty-loving mobs. Here in Paris we are much concerned about what they will do, these Ciceronian democrats, when Dr. Franklin finally arrives home from England."

Jefferson looked over Raynal's shoulder, at the windows opening onto the Grille de Chaillot. For an instant Short thought Jefferson was about to abandon his lifelong policy of walking away from a quarrel. His face had gone from red to dangerous white, his profile under the flickering candles was thin as a blade. But he inhaled deeply and then looked back at Raynal. "When Dr. Franklin reaches home," Jefferson said, turning away as he spoke, "the citizens will undoubtedly salute him with the same invisible stones they used on Washington and Lafayette."

Early the next morning, Jefferson came into the study grinning.

Short looked up from the desk, where he was writing a memorandum to their banker.

"Paul Jones has just left us a parcel of mail from London," Jefferson said. He took his seat at his own desk, swiveled his chair, and held up two sheets of stiff buff-colored paper. "And

John Adams has written me a letter too wonderful to bury in my files. Listen."

Short put down his pen and grinned in return.

"To set the scene he first says he paid a call on the Ambassador of Tripoli one afternoon last month. Two secretaries of legation— this pleases Adams, twice the normal attention—two secretaries— ushered him into a room with a fireplace and a pair of luxurious chammy chairs and ottomans arranged in front of the fireplace. They placed him in one of the chairs but obviously didn't dare sit down themselves. In walks the ambassador five minutes later, a genuine sultan by the name of Abdurrahman, who takes the other chair, crosses his legs, and promptly starts to speak in a combination of Italian and Lingua Franca."

Jefferson ran his fingers through his hair, then stood again, carrying the letter.

"Adams speaks no Italian," Short said, leaning back in his chair. "Not a word."

Jefferson had reached the far wall, on which, hanging to his left, was an oil portrait of Washington meant to give the study an American air; to his right a French *serinette,* a wicker cage holding two small parakeets and a music box on a crank, meant to teach the birds how to sing. He gave his usual glance of bemused irony at the silent birds and shook his head. "Not a word. But let me read. You recall that these Barbary pirates, after capturing who knows how many of our innocent merchantmen, have finally proposed their terms—peace for one year at 12,500 guineas; 'perpetual peace' for 30,000 guineas. The subject of the meeting was to offer our counterterms and see if we could ransom our hostages. But the ambassador insisted on a little ceremony first. Now listen, these are Adams's own words.

" ' "We make tobacco in Tripoli," said his Excellency, "but it is too strong. Your American tobacco is better." By this time, one of his secretaries had brought two pipes ready filled and lighted. The longest was offered me; the other to his Excellency. It is long since I took a pipe, as you know, but as it would be unpardonable to be wanting in politeness, I took the pipe with great complacency, placed the bowl upon the carpet, for the stem was fit for a walking cane, and I believe more than two yards in length.' "

Jefferson stopped and lowered the sheets of paper, still grinning boyishly. "I think I should commission a painting," he said. "For the Annals of Diplomacy."

"He must have turned green—or green and white!"

"No, William, you underestimate the Adams resolve. Listen: 'I smoaked in aweful pomp, reciprocating whiff for whiff with his Excellency, until coffee was brought in. His Excellency took a cup after I had taken one, and alternately sipped at his coffee and whiffed at his tobacco, and I followed the example with such exactness and solemnity that the two secretaries appeared in raptures and the superior of them, who speaks a few words of French, cried out in ecstacy, *"Monsieur, vous êtes un Turk!"* ' "

In the carriage an hour later Jefferson took out the letter and started to read it all over again. "The Puritan Turk. The Sultan of Braintree. I would give much to know what Abigail thought of our John in his awful smoking pomp."

"You miss him, sir," Short ventured. "It's good he's invited you to visit him in London."

Jefferson rubbed his shoulder against the leather upholstery of the carriage and stretched his long legs. "I could do more good here," he said. His smile slowly faded. "Much more good, you know. Vergennes has finally appointed a committee to examine the tobacco duties, and Lafayette is on it. If I stayed to prompt him—"

"But if Adams says the Barbary chiefs are ready to negotiate?"

Jefferson tugged at his ear. "John Adams," he said, "is a remarkable man. It is no secret to you that he has a degree of vanity, that he is, Turkish pipes aside, too attentive to ceremony."

"He is"—Short hesitated—"irritable."

"As the day is long. Vain, irritable, and a bad calculator of human motives. When you have said that, you have said all you can against him. But I expect he is wrong about the pirates. Why should they treat? Why should they not take our money and do as they like? I see no solution to hostages ever, except war, war or an outrageous ransom year after year. If it were up to me, I would send Paul Jones with half a dozen frigates and cut them to pieces one by one."

"Well." Short stirred. Jefferson as war-making general sat uneasily with all the other Jeffersons he knew. The carriage came to a jouncing halt, and he glanced out at a logjam of horses and wheels.

"And in any case," Jefferson said, "when I arrive in London, most likely the king's royal government"—his voice mocked the phrase—"will ensure that I encounter the maximum of delay and humiliation. In his love of ceremony I'm afraid Adams plans to present me at Court."

"The king would ignore *you!*" Short protested, not knowing that he would prove a prophet. Adams strolled about in life wherever he liked, thick-skinned, armored in irritability, but Jefferson was exquisitely sensitive to the slightest affront. Before the war the British Court had frozen out poor Franklin with astonishing rudeness. What would George III do to the author of the infamous Declaration of Independence?

"Look there." Jefferson pointed to a corner house where servants were scattering armloads of straw across the muddy pavement. "They do that when someone in the house is sick, to muffle the noise of wheels."

"Better to be deaf altogether," Short said, turning automatically to look. The carriage lurched forward with a crack of the whip. Their destination that morning was the Institut des Sourds et Muets, the deaf-and-dumb school operated by yet another Parisian abbé, open to visitors on Mondays and Wednesdays. Jefferson's apparently limitless curiosity had produced a special invitation to observe their classes.

"Well, I leave in three days," Jefferson said, "king or no king, count or no count. Adams says he has a young American painter I will like, John Trumbull. And when I return we may have heard at last from Eppes." Short nodded. Jefferson had written twice already to his brother-in-law, requesting that his eight-year-old daughter Mary, now calling herself Polly, be sent to join him and young Patsy. "But all the same"—his smile came back, tighter and smaller—"Washington stoned, Mount Vernon burned—what a nation of liars and villains and fools." He crossed his arms like a bandolier, and his warlike tone suddenly flared. "I wish there were a *sea of flame* between England and America."

At the Institut a gentle abbé, flanked by two Portuguese nuns, led them through a series of rooms where children sat in rows of wooden desks, communicating with their teacher by means of rapid, incomprehensible finger signals. A kind of code, Jefferson murmured, clearly fascinated. Short trailed him with a dim sensation of unease. No sounds except their footsteps or the scrape of chairs, the occasional whispered explanation from the abbé. Silence was un-French, Short thought; it was also unnatural to the condition of children. And yet his mind wheeled back irresistibly to the endless silent green forests of his own childhood, the silent country of Virginia. Clearings of flat red clay, encircled by huge, ominous trees; encroaching walls of silence. What did he miss? What did he hate? When he looked up he saw that, as usual, he had been absorbed in himself, while, as usual, Jefferson had been casting his nets wide for knowledge.

"Have you ever instructed one of the 'wild boys,' Monsieur?"

The abbé frowned, clearly not understanding, and Jefferson turned to Short for translation. "Il fait une allusion aux enfants sauvages, les enfants trouvés dans les forêts, dans les déserts." For months Jefferson had been reading in the *Mercure de France* about the numerous children discovered living alone in the forests of Germany and France—abandoned in most instances because of physical deformity or simple poverty; often the wild boys had no speech at all and appeared to be totally deaf and dumb.

"No." The abbé shook his head and smiled. "Never. All our children are normal; normal human beings."

"I ask," Jefferson said, "because Monsieur Short and I had a debate one morning: What is the nature of human nature? What single quality is essential to the definition *human*?" His gray eyes rested on Short thoughtfully. "Monsieur Short said, 'The power of love.' "

The abbé was pleased. He nodded and placed his palms together at his breast and bowed. "But," Jefferson continued, "I concluded that the nature of human nature demands the power of speech. Of all our faculties, only language is uniquely human—don't you concur?"

The abbé smiled in gentle disagreement. "I am bound to your friend's position, Monsieur," he said softly. "One would fall short of being human if one could not express one's love."

"In language?"

"Somehow."

In the carriage Jefferson shifted his legs restlessly—*restless* was the word for Jefferson that month, Short thought—and stared at the passing gray and brown facades of the rue Saint-Honoré.

"A fascinating school, but I could never learn the hand signals the children use. I'm too old. They made my brain swim to watch them. At the end of the tour," he added ruefully, "I felt as if I were one of Buffon's experiments, a Virginia savage transplanted to the Old World and subtly beginning to 'degenerate.' "

Short grinned at the expert imitation of Raynal's thin voice. "Vous êtes ou un Turk ou un enfant sauvage."

"Un Turk sauvage," Jefferson said. "Trouvé dans les forêts et dans les déserts."

Short smiled again. Jefferson read and wrote French easily, but he spoke it weakly and with, of all things, a slight Scots accent, absorbed from his first teacher in Virginia, the very Scottish and very fierce James Maury.

"When I come back from London," Jefferson said, reading the amusement in Short's eyes, "I will no doubt express myself better."

Short proved himself a second time that day a prophet. "When you come back," he said, "Paris will be wearing a new face."

CHAPTER

Thirteen

In any event, as the London newspapers all recorded, it was not a face that Jefferson saw next.

At the Court of St. James's on the seventeenth of March, as John Adams, coughing and muttering into his fist, led him forward through a phalanx of silk-sleeved British ministers and courtiers, the man Adams sometimes called the Great Hanoverian Ham caught sight of them.

In the best of circumstances George III lacked self-possession. Red of face, small of head, unusually tall and thick-waisted, he presided over his levees and ceremonies with fussy Germanic stiffness. His grandfather, the first George, had known not a word of English when he assumed the throne in 1714 and made no secret of his preference for the large ladies and larger horses of his native Hanover, where he retreated for a full six months of every year. The second George was not much better. The third George, determined to be a good *English* king, had promptly lost half the empire to rebellion and was rumored to suffer intermittent fits of insanity, in which he stood talking loudly to the roses in his garden.

On the morning of the seventeenth, as he caught sight of Adams and Jefferson advancing through the crowd, the monarch crossed his arms, jammed one hand under each armpit, and stared. An aide whispered in his ear. Adams made a round man's attempt at a bow and murmured their names. Jefferson advanced another step. The king turned on his heel, presenting the two Americans with a clear view of the Hanoverian rump, and walked away. After half a moment of contemplation the rest of his courtiers did the same.

☆ ☆ ☆

"In brief," said Clérisseau some months later, after Jefferson's return, "he delivered a typically English insult. Witless and wordless."

Short grunted (witlessly, he realized) and made a feeble swipe with his handkerchief at his sweating brow. It was the first week in August, and outside the window on the rue de Berri, Paris lay breathless in a hot, dry cloud of dust.

"And in any case," Clérisseau persisted, "why didn't John Adams explode on the spot? I always picture John Adams as a round little bomb with a sputtering fuse."

Short let himself grin at the image. "Well. Unlike the rest of us, Adams rather likes the English. Likes *London*. Abigail is happy there. The daughter Nabby is engaged to marry her father's secretary and *she* is happy. It would take more than an insult to make him explode."

"I lived there five years," Clérisseau said, "in my younger days, when I would do a great deal not to starve and the English were fond of hiring French architects. I would *never* go back."

"Nabby is marrying an American, actually," Short said, following his own thought. "William Stephens Smith. Twenty-seven and a half years old, my age exactly. She wrote to ask when *I* would marry."

"Miss Adams thinks you have become a French libertine," Clérisseau said with amusement. He mopped his own brow and neck and blinked his big eyes. Even for August the day was sweltering. "The ladies of the town swarm about you—or vice versa—you leave a sea of broken hearts in your wake, Short. Have I mixed my metaphors?"

"Clérisseau," Short said pleasantly, "shut up."

He turned away from the Frenchman and studied the huge

clutter of packing boxes and wadded tissues that covered Jefferson's study floor. Clérisseau likewise folded his arms and regarded the neat rows of thermometers, microscopes, and drawing instruments extracted from the boxes and lined up across the desk. In the great salon that adjoined the study, under the beautiful sunburst painting that Jefferson had commissioned for the ceiling, stretched a second brigade of identical trunks and boxes, all presumably stuffed with more of Jefferson's London purchases.

"William, thou shouldst be married. How long was he actually in England?"

"Seven weeks altogether."

"Then he didn't have time to buy quite everything on the island. What is this?"

Short squinted at the object in Clérisseau's sweaty hand. Ever since the day they had gone to visit Houdon, he decided, his eyesight had grown steadily more blurred. He moved his head slightly, so that his peripheral vision, which was better, would come into focus. "That is a new kind of mercury thermometer, for use indoors."

"Ah." Clérisseau replaced it on the desk. "To tell us it is hot."

"He wants precise information," Short said defensively. In his journal Short had lately tried to devise code names for Jefferson: the Roman, for those days when diplomatic politics held sway and Jefferson went about his business with a certain stern aloofness; the Rebel, for those moments when he seemed suddenly angry and impatient enough to dismantle *any* established authority (after seeing George III in London he had purchased a seal engraved with the motto *Rebellion to Tyrants is Obedience to God*). But for the restless, unreachable person behind his grid of precise information and books, Short could come up with no satisfactory single word. Sphinx? Poet? Evader?

"Now," Clérisseau said. Despite the heat he observed the rigid French fashion of dressing without regard to elements or weather. Today he wore, as always, a full dress coat and a ruffled shirt and, at the corner of his mouth in the middle of his powdered cheek, a small black beauty patch the size of a coin. He straightened his elegant lace cuffs. "Where have you hidden my model?"

"Upstairs," Short told him, "next to Trumbull's room."

They threaded their way between boxes and trunks and

climbed the stairs to the second landing, where Jefferson had set up a library for overflow volumes. The room looked down on the garden, and as Short pulled open the windows he could see James Hemings—no blurriness about that—walking in shirt-sleeves between rows of shoulder-high Virginia corn.

"Next year he plants a hectare of tobacco, yes," Clérisseau asked, "and the Comte de Vergennes will smoke it?"

"Your model," Short said, and tugged at the linen sheet that covered the library table. Clérisseau helped him draw the sheet to one side, and then fell back into a silent study of the scale-model plaster building before them.

Outside, a wagon passed. A solitary Parisian crow cawed in the garden. Short glanced at his pocket watch; walked to the window; returned with a black-and-white engraving that Jefferson had left on a shelf.

"The Maison Carrée," he said finally, just to be saying something. He propped the engraving on a chair.

Clérisseau glanced at it, then knelt and frowned at the tiny columns that ran across the porch of the plaster model; he penned a series of numbers in his pocket notebook. "At Nîmes, yes. That was the design we started from."

He fell silent again and Short cleared his throat. "And Jefferson has made changes?"

Clérisseau scribbled another entry in his notebook, stood up, and crossed his arms over his chest, looking for all the world, Short thought, like a pop-eyed Jefferson.

"He puzzles me, you know." Clérisseau tapped the front of his nose with his metal architect's pen. "Is he a great universal genius, or simply the most complete mediocrity in history? Look." He aimed the pen at the plaster model. "This is to be the state capitol at the city of Richmond, yes?" Short nodded. "The revolutionary new city, the revolutionary new country. But where does he turn for his inspiration? Not to the new— to the old! To Rome—Rome the unfree, Rome the tyrannical. A Roman *temple*. I show my drawings of the Maison Carrée, purely as a starting point for discussion, and he seizes them out of my hand—the very thing!"

"But he's changed it?"

"Well, he has. But is it a good change?"

Short looked at the black-and-white engraving; then at the model.

"You need spectacles," Clérisseau said sardonically. "Too much wine and women. The columns first—look, look, look; here they're Corinthian; in the model they're Ionic."

"Windows?"

"He's added windows." Clérisseau made an indescribably French sound like the pop of grease on a skillet. "He had to, I suppose. For offices. Even revolutionaries need offices. But there —the portico's reduced from three columns' width to two, and the pilasters are gone. And what is this?"

Short followed the pen. "A monument hall. The statue of Washington goes there."

"By Houdon?" Clérisseau sniffed. "Mathematics. Jefferson draws and alters everything by mathematics—he's like a machine, he applies the numbers and does exactly what they say, so that the effect is austere, severe, pure—"

"Roman," Short said.

Clérisseau shook his head. "Not a bit. My question is, why does such an apostle of freedom bind himself to such arbitrary rules and numbers?"

He sat down on the window bench and fanned himself with one of Jefferson's rolled architectural drawings. "Williamos is gone."

Short nodded once and busied himself with reexamining the model, intending to look brisk and uninterested. It was one of the secrets of the house that Jefferson had written his disreputable boarder Williamos a furious confidential letter and sent him away. What could make Jefferson furious? Disloyalty? Ingratitude? Downstairs he distinctly heard voices now.

"And so Trumbull is here and you don't like him." Clérisseau began to sketch something in his notebook.

"Of course I do. He's a painter, he's an artist."

"I know what he is. A painter of dull historical scenes, come all the way from London just to study Jefferson's head, which he means to include in some vast patriotic tableau."

"The 'Signing of the Declaration of Independence.' "

"Precisely. Yards of canvas, inches of talent. He and Jefferson go everywhere together. And you don't like him. You grind your teeth at his name. Is there—dare I hope?—some scandal?"

"C'est dommage. No scandal." In fact, of course, the rather self-righteous and priggish John Trumbull, now about thirty, had fathered an illegitimate son in Connecticut five or six years earlier, but in Clérisseau's world, Short knew, that would hardly count. "I hear voices downstairs."

Clérisseau twisted on the window bench. "There's a carriage."

On the stairway landing the voices grew louder; then a door slammed—like a gunshot in the heat—and Short heard nothing at all.

Jefferson's new maître d'hôtel appeared in the hallway, a boneless but intelligent Frenchman named Adrien Petit. Marc had been mysteriously dismissed by letter, rather like Williamos. Petit crossed the carpet, wiping his forehead with a white handkerchief.

"Visitors?"

"Deux personnes, pour Monsieur."

Still in his shirt-sleeves, Short opened the front door to see for himself. At the foot of the steps, just settling back into the seat of their carriage, was the elderly Duc de La Rochefoucauld, one of Jefferson's particular political friends, and beside him a woman, very young, slender, with jet-black hair and a pale white face—Short stopped and blinked. In the cavernous black interior of the carriage the woman's features were indistinct, tremulous; a soft oval of light.

Short hurried forward, fastening his cuffs. The duc held up one hand—gloved, in this heat; French decorum was truly incredible—and greeted Short by name. At the open door of the carriage the glare of sunlight and paint was so strong that it took Short a moment to realize that he had seen the young woman before. "Your daughter?" he was on the verge of asking.

"My wife," the duc said. He added something else, but Short was turning his head to bring his memory and vision into perfect focus. At the nuns' ceremony of "dying to life" she had worn a veil. Then, at Lafayette's house, she had stood in a corner near Madame de Tessé, elegantly dressed, watching him. Today she wore a soft blue cap, a modest blue-and-green redingote à la mode. She stared down into her lap without a trace of smile or greeting.

"My name is William Short," he repeated to her, like an idiot. "William."

The duc was patient. "My wife, *la duchesse.*"

"Madame la Duchesse. Of course. Excuse my state of dress. This heat . . . we Americans can never learn to be formal." Short knew that he was blushing or staring or both. He straightened and faced the duc, losing his perfect focus on the wife. "Monsieur Jefferson has gone to Versailles, but he ought to return by five or six."

"We were merely passing," the duc said, "on our way to my mother's house, and I thought we might just stop and call, without sending ahead." A little shrug. In contrast to his wife's, the duc's hair was as fine and gray as cinders.

The young duchesse finally raised her eyes. "So you see, Monsieur Short, we French can also be informal," she said shyly.

The duc smiled at her, then saluted Short with the incredible glove and signaled his driver. The carriage had actually reached the Grille de Chaillot and passed through a gate before Short turned to see Clérisseau lounging against the rail in front of the door. He grinned down at Short.

"A lovely couple," Clérisseau said. "Like December and May."

In the evening, when Clérisseau had gone away with his notes and his model, John Trumbull joined Short and Jefferson in the garden and promptly set about making one of his numerous social proposals.

"There is *no one*," he said, "I would rather have you meet."

"I think," Jefferson began. He took a few steps along the row of corn and stopped to study a yellowish leaf, all concentration. "I have so much business to take care of, I think I really must say no."

"But consider," Trumbull insisted, following him down the row. "Just an hour to meet them; an hour, no more." Nearby, Short sat down on a wooden bench and crossed his legs. The heat of the August day had vanished miraculously, as it did every night in Paris, and now he wore his coat and even permitted himself a shiver or two, though the sky was still milky white with the long summer sun and Jefferson and Trumbull were lightly dressed in cotton shirts and riding trousers.

"I've neglected everything." Jefferson emerged from a different row, not ten feet from Short's bench. "Ask Mr. Short."

"There is Lester Asquith . . ." Short said.

Jefferson stopped and turned to Trumbull. "An American sailor. He and his crew blew ashore in a storm at Dieppe, and the French promptly clapped them in prison on suspicion of bringing in contraband tobacco for sale. I must write the Comte de Vergennes again, to humbly ask their release."

"Mr. and Mrs. Cosway," Trumbull said. But Jefferson was holding up his left hand—a black paw to Short's vision—and evidently counting on his fingers.

"Lester Asquith first," he said. "Then instructions to Mr. Lamb, who serves badly as ambassador to Algiers for us."

"And a copy to Jay." Short was pleased to interfere with anything that Trumbull proposed. He was also fascinated by Jefferson's continued fury at the Barbary pirates. The Roman naturally counseled patience and stolid diplomacy in all international quarrels; but the taking of American hostages somehow brought out the most fearsome Rebel. Adams was still willing to negotiate; Jefferson wanted to wage holy war.

"And then Ledyard has to be answered," Short added.

Jefferson held up another finger. "John Ledyard," he told Trumbull. "One of Nature's great eccentrics. He wants to march across the Russian Empire, by himself, into Siberia, and down to the western coast of America, or rather, where he surmises the western coast lies. As you know, I have a weak spot for explorers."

"DeMeunier's article," Short said.

A third finger went up. "A little article on the United States," Jefferson said, "for a new edition of the *Encyclopédie*. Some mistakes I ought to correct before it's published."

Short crossed his legs the other way and watched Jefferson's sharp profile against the blue-gray sky. The "little article" was fifty pages long, a tissue of factual errors, and Jefferson had rewritten it twice for the obstinate young Frenchman who was its nominal author.

"And Paul Jones has submitted his accounts for his prize money," Jefferson continued. "At last. And finally"—dropping his hand to his side—"whale oil, my office is awash in whale oil. I must write a treatise for Vergennes on the commercial types of whale oil."

Trumbull had a Yankee pugnacity of manner that Short instinctively resented. "The Cosways are grand friends of David." He lowered himself to sit on the arm of Short's bench, but without looking at Short. "They see him almost every day."

Jefferson crossed, then recrossed his arms. Of all the artists in Paris, Short knew he admired the cool, reserved historical painter Jacques-Louis David most, though foreigners rarely met him.

"In fact," Trumbull drawled—if you closed your eyes, Short thought, and simply listened to his voice, the man was an obvious hypocrite—"this morning we all met at David's studio for coffee. I told them you had finished your architectural model and could turn to painting at last."

"I know next to nothing of painting." Jefferson spoke with a rueful intonation.

"My dear sir, you have an eye, you have an *artist's* eye. And two years in Paris have made you a connoisseur. Look at the things you've bought—those Caravaggios, that little bronze statue of Diana by Houdon. The Cosways can be your tutors in painting."

"William?"

Short shrugged to indicate that he had no opinion. Overhead the sky had grown plumy with stars, and the face of the young Duchesse de La Rochefoucauld had slipped imperceptibly among them.

"Cosway is the most renowned miniaturist in England," Trumbull was saying, to Jefferson, not Short. "He paints everybody's portrait. He travels in the most amazing circle—the Prince of Wales, the Duke of York, *tout Londres*." Jefferson had started to move up the rows of corn again, humming to himself and fingering the dark leaves. James Hemings had declared that he would take the first ripe ears to his culinary school and see what French cooking could do with them.

"And his wife," Trumbull said into the gathering darkness, "—also a painter. An Anglo-Italian. The most beautiful, fair, charming woman. The Cosways propose we meet at the Halle aux Bleds day after tomorrow, at two in the afternoon, to tour it, no more than that."

Jefferson reappeared carrying a bouquet of five or six corn leaves. "Friday?"

"You have a dinner engagement Friday with the old Duchesse

de La Rochefoucauld d'Enville," Short told him. "The duc's mother."

"The Halle aux Bleds," Trumbull said, "has been on your list for months. I know it."

Jefferson nodded thoughtfully. The new Parisian grain market, located not far from the Palais Royal, had been given the grandiose name of the Halle aux Bleds—Hall of Wheat—to honor its innovative architecture. An enormous dome evidently, combined somehow with a series of glass skylights. Jefferson loved skylights, as he said he loved everything to do with the sun. Once or twice he had talked to Short about designing a farmer's market for Richmond to blend with the new capitol building; the Halle was a structure to study.

"The company will be most, most amusing," Trumbull added. "I promise it."

"If Mr. Short went along, to remind me of business. . . ." Jefferson said slowly.

"I was about to ask him," Trumbull said.

Friday, August twelfth, dawned hot and clear. By the time Short finished his breakfast at seven, Jefferson had already been working in their office for two hours, writing letters, running his new copy press. As Short walked in one door, Jefferson was leaving by the other, and before Short had fairly settled into his chair, he heard the sound of his violin upstairs.

"Did Trumbull already eat?" Short rocked a little in his swivel chair and watched James Hemings pour coffee into his cup. Jefferson disapproved of the habit—one takes one's meal at table—but whenever Short had the office to himself, he called for a steady flow of James's coffee.

"Mr. Trumbull came in late," James said. He wiped the silver spout with the white linen napkin he had taken to carrying folded on his forearm, a French affectation. Short nodded and as usual found himself uncertain whether to look directly at James—with his "bright" skin, his curly reddish hair, his uncanny resemblance to Martha Wayles Jefferson—or whether to look rudely away and avoid his eyes.

"Stayed out with the artists," James added. He frowned as he obviously tried to make out the title of one of Short's books. He could read and write English, Short knew, but French? Short's mind made an odd connection. The American sailors taken hostage by the Barbary pirates had been placed in literal chattel slavery, just like southern blacks. Just like James. Was Jefferson's intransigence on hostages somehow connected to *that*?

"Out with the artists," James repeated. "Came back at two in the morning. Mr. Jefferson long gone to bed, after his concert."

They both listened for a moment to the strains of Jefferson's violin.

"These artists," James said, "got the constitution of a plow horse."

"You don't like Mr. Trumbull?"

James allowed himself the smallest, the most discreet of smiles. He refilled Short's cup, then reached in his coat pocket for a sheet of paper. "This is the note when the first string beans come on the market, rue Saint-Honoré. He wanted it before, but Petit just gave it to me."

Short placed the sheet of note paper unread on the desk blotter, and when James had left the room, he stood and transferred it to Jefferson's desk, inserting it in the little cloth-bound volume where Jefferson recorded his first sightings of vegetables and flowers. On the lined pages, in Jefferson's neat, regular hand, the numbers and dates looked like so many inky birds on a fence. Upstairs the violin came to a sudden stop.

Promptly at one-thirty the carriage arrived at the front door, and the three men converged from different corners of the house. Jefferson had dressed almost casually for him, in pale blue coat and thin brown trousers. One hand held his little personal sketchbook—how many different little books did he have?—the other his watch. The old Duchesse de La Rochefoucauld expected them early for dinner, she was not a person to disappoint. Trumbull, last into the carriage, gave an easy drawling command in English to the driver, and they rattled their way onto the Champs-Élysées.

The Halle aux Bleds took up a square block not far north of the Pont Neuf, which they reached by a straight but tedious route along the river; the carriage swayed like a metronome, the day was hot. Short closed his eyes and allowed a series of associations to march Locke-step through his brain: night, watch, time; dinner; old duchesse, young duchesse. Old husband.

He opened his eyes to see that they were going past the gray-green plane trees of the Tuileries Gardens. Would the young duchesse be at the dinner that night?

Trumbull had begun to lecture Jefferson. The original Halle aux Bleds, he announced, had been no more than a two-story circular wall enclosing a central market area: grain stalls, offices, a couple of oversize entrances and exits for farmers' wagons. Ten years ago two architects named Legrand and Molinos had accepted a commission to put a roof on the circular wall. Like all French architects, of course, they stole from the Italians. A Florentine dome was the thing, they decided, not a flat roof; and because the grain merchants, with their vast stalls of dried grain, needed interior light but not fire, a dome that would somehow open to the sky.

Jefferson was visibly impatient, regretting already, Short assumed, that he had left his work for this. Turning away from Trumbull, he penciled an entry in his book and frowned through the window at the labyrinthine old palace of the Louvre, now on their right, where Clérisseau, David, and a hundred other artists had their apartments, not to mention Talleyrand's mistress and her *tolérant* spouse. Then he closed his book and eyes. He was known to abhor the Louvre, with its dank, cramped medieval cells, in almost the same proportions as he loved the wide vistas of Monticello. The truth was, Short thought, Jefferson was bored with France, bored with his life here. If not for the lure of the skylights, he would certainly have stayed home today. Short closed his eyes and tried again to devise a third name for his code: Surveyor; Spartan.

The arcades of the Palais Royal replaced the Louvre; then, as the carriage rolled east into a crowded square, they passed a bizarre stone column at the edge of the Halle, standing free like the turret of a castle and decorated with carved moons and planets and a belt of elaborately shuttered green windows. Dismounting on the rue de Grenville, Jefferson paused to look back at it and murmur in Short's ear, "A long day so far, my friend—don't forget the old duchesse, bring out your watch."

It was almost the last thing Short heard him say for half an hour. The noise of the grain market—a low hivelike rumble from the street—rose to a deafening roar at the entrance.

"Pandemonium!" Trumbull shouted happily. "There they are!"

He pulled Jefferson forward. Short followed, stopped. A wagon the size of a house lurched forward on tilting wooden wheels, dragged by six great dray horses, rumps like the King of England, and pushed by a dozen shirtless workers whose torsos gleamed under a thick silver coating of grain and dust. More workers converged on either side, another wagon, a team of oxen pulling barrels; two merchants shouted orders and pointed in opposite directions, hands snatched Short backward, out of the path of the oxen, and he felt himself passed along a gauntlet of gesticulating men—one woman, mountainous in white apron— until he stood twenty yards away from the wagon. On the other side Jefferson and Trumbull had disappeared into the crowd.

"À droite!" someone shouted. "Attention!"

Short sprang back a step. He pressed his shoulders against the side of a stall. The smell of grain filled his nostrils and burned his eyes. When he looked up, blinking, the whole space of the dome was floating overhead, sixty feet high, hazy, a golden bell of sunlight.

"Monsieur, attention!"

Short pinched the bridge of his nose and squinted upward through the dust, impressed in spite of himself. Score a point for Trumbull. How was it done? The dome appeared constructed in strips of alternating glass and wood, two feet wide at the base, arching in tandem all the way from the top of the circular wall to a small nipplelike center. Below it noise and dust swam in the light, everything moved about in a dazzling light. On the far side of the entering wagons Short could just see Jefferson's red hair between two huge stalls of wheat.

"À droite, monsieur! Prenez garde!"

He stumbled to his right again and stopped by a ten-foot pyramid of burlap sacks. Jefferson was now on the far side of the hall, near the opposite entrance. If he tried to follow the same way, the convoy of wagons rumbling in would hold him up; if he simply kept walking to his right, however, threading the maze of grain stalls and shouting merchants, he would meet them from the other direction. What was Jefferson doing? The red hair dipped in a courtly bow. Blond hair—extraordinarily blond, even in the midst of so much light and gold—bobbed near him. Then Trumbull's dark hair moved in front.

The noise was less overwhelming if you stayed near the base of the circular wall. Short detoured around a basket scale. Grain cascaded out of a wagon, a waterfall of light. He jumped sideways, kicking his feet, and three black Norway rats scampered through his legs, squealing.

He hurried forward over a carpet of grain and dust. On the other side of the market Trumbull was now pointing up to the skylights; beside him stood a small, wiry-limbed man dressed all in purple and red—Cosway? At this distance, with his bad eyes, Short thought, shaking his head, the man looked like a costumed monkey.

Where was Jefferson?

He neared the center of the stalls. Jefferson and a slender young woman—the dazzling blond curls of a moment ago—had detached themselves from Trumbull and stood apart, almost at the second doorway, heads close in conversation.

Now where was *Trumbull?*

By the time Short reached the far entrance, the noise of wagons and merchants had struck an unexpected lull. He quickly circled an island of stacked barrels and almost ran into Jefferson. A moment later, against a backdrop of straw and oats, he found himself bowing, his forehead inches away from those same blond curls, gazing into a clear, exquisitely formed face. Eyes violet or gray. Dress blue. Neck slender and arching, perfect. As she lifted her head he saw the pale white curve of her bust, blue lace, a finger's width of bare décolletage.

"And also Mr. Cosway," Trumbull was saying.

Reluctantly Short turned to his left. Richard Cosway bowed and clicked his heels, stepping backward at the same time, as if, Short thought, to let him take in the whole dandified effect: lavender silk coat, feverishly embroidered from shoulder to tail with red leaves and berries; tight, pipe-stem trousers of shiny black; dress sword with one of those enormous ribboned sword-knots that the English treasured. Lace collar. Silver wig. Brown little face, wrinkles, patches, a quick false smile like the flash of a razor. *Exactly* like a monkey.

"Delighted," Short said.

"Enchanté." Another click of the heels.

"Now we can hear," Trumbull said, beaming at them. The wagons had all come to a halt. The workers and merchants had started to gather for some commercial reason at the other end of the hall, their voices fading. Overhead, a flock of chattering sparrows turned and splashed through the dome of light.

"Now we can *breathe!*" Cosway said, fanning himself with a little leather-bound book.

"No, no—this is the time to look at the dome, study the dome." Trumbull had raised both hands high in artistic benediction. "Look at the joints, all of you, the woodwork, the play of glass and timber!"

Cosway opened his book. "'A modern work, but based on a design by Philibert Delorme,'" the artist read pompously. "'Sixteenth-century author of *Inventions pour bien bâtir.* Twenty-five wooden ribs, twenty-four identical windows. Hemispherical space with a radius of sixty feet. Ninety tons of glass and Normandy oak. Circumference of more than two hundred feet—'"

To Short's amazement Jefferson and Mrs. Cosway had strolled away, to a point just at the edge of the doorway. When Cosway looked up and caught sight of them, he smiled at Short and snapped the book shut.

"My wife and the heat," he said, "the heat and the dust."

Outside, Jefferson had found a stone bench under a tree, and Maria Cosway had sat down on it, in a little blue cloud of crinoline and silk.

"It was too much inside," she told them as they all arrived. "Too close." A shake of the golden curls. A smile, Short had to admit, almost as bright as the curls. She spoke in breathless musical tones, with a charming accent partly English, partly Italian, worlds away from the nasal—Cockney?—of her famous husband. "The air in London is so terrible, so gloomy and wet—we came to Paris for me, really, just to escape the gloom—we call it 'gloomth' in London. But here it's so hot and dusty, I feel like a silly girl, I can't be pleased."

"Oh, Paris *is* hot," Jefferson said, who never complained about the weather. "But outside the city, in little villages like Saint-Germain—"

"We haven't *been*," Maria Cosway interrupted, placing her hand on his sleeve. "Ten whole days, and we haven't been anywhere at all except people's houses and artists' studios, not the simplest excursion."

"Not even to Saint-Cloud or Versailles?"

"Nulle part!"

"My work," Cosway said. He had made his way restlessly behind the bench, guidebook still in one hand, page marked by a long simian finger. "I am a painter, as Trumbull knows, as *Paris* knows. No sooner arrived than the Duc d'Orléans, out of the blue, sends to our hotel. I must paint his children's portraits, his wife's, his friends'—" He turned his tiny brown face from Jefferson. "So Maria languishes days at a time while I pursue the bubble 'art.'" He nodded and made a quick, unnerving bow inside his too-large lavender coat.

"That," Maria said, rising from the bench and pointing her fan, "is a wonderful tower or column—do you see?"

Jefferson had turned with her. Over their backs Short and Trumbull could see the odd three-story column they had passed before. Cosway was already walking forward, thumbing his book, bouncing on his wiry black legs.

"What do you think of them?" Trumbull whispered.

"Beauty and the Beast," Short said. "Venus and her monkey."

Jefferson and Maria Cosway had already pulled ahead of them, walking side by side. The two men hurried to catch up, and then with much lifting of hems and twisting sideways to balance, the whole party advanced between parked wagons and horses, over a dirty curb, over a gutter clogged with golden mud.

"'Constructed in 1572,'" Cosway announced, reading from his book as they gathered around him. A foppish grimace aimed directly at Short. "The architect was the celebrated Jean Bulant, whoever *that* was. Intended first for the grounds of the Hôtel de Soissons, for Catherine de Médicis, who liked to go up the little stairs in the center and consult the stars with her astrologer."

Maria clapped her hands. "Italian—I knew it!"

"My wife is Italian," Cosway said to Jefferson. The two men

were roughly the same age, Short calculated, in their middle forties, but next to each other, the spidery Englishman and the tall, sharp-faced Virginian, they looked like members of different species. "Or rather Anglo-Italian. Née Hadfield, but her father was an English merchant in Rome."

"Florence," Maria said. She was no more than twenty-seven or -eight, Short thought; a good two decades younger than her husband. Automatically he began to compare her to other women—she was far prettier than Madame de Lafayette; smaller, more delicate than the Ace of Spades; but coarse and flirtatious, a mere shopgirl-coquette, if one thought of the shy, dark-haired, exquisite wife of the Duc de La Rochefoucauld.

"Well." Cosway shrugged.

Jefferson was smiling with a boyish animation that Short had never seen on his face before. What had happened? Where had the black mood of impatience and boredom gone? In the space of ten minutes the Roman had vanished, the Rebel had stalked off the stage. Jefferson was bending and pointing out to little Mrs. Cosway the geometric pattern of the windows. With a sense of foreboding, Short reached in his pocket for his watch.

"Sir?" He extended the watch apologetically. "I should remind you of the other appointments today."

Jefferson frowned.

"Mais non, Monsieur Short," Maria said, smiling, pouting, shaking her head. "Jamais—this is my first day out in Paris, away from business. Sir"—her white hand was a feather, a dove, lighting on Jefferson's great one. "Be independent! Declare your independence! The famous author of independence—you see, we know who you are; stay with us, take us all to Saint-Cloud or Versailles in your carriage—for the 'coolth'!"

"The old duchesse," Short began, but Jefferson had turned to Trumbull.

"Do you think—?"

"Why not? Ten days of work, one day of pleasure?"

"Un jour heureux," Maria said. "That's correct in French?"

"Perfect, un jour heureux. A happy day. Mr. Short can carry a message." He stopped, rubbed his chin. With a kind of eerie detachment Short observed his hand bring the watch stiffly back to his pocket like an automaton, deposit it, disappear. Jefferson was the most scrupulous man he had ever known about truth. Two days ago, he had dictated a moralizing letter to his nephew in Virginia: "There is no vice so mean, so pitiful, so contemptible as a lie; he who permits himself to tell a lie once, finds it much easier to do it a second and a third time." What could he possibly tell the old duchesse?

"Dispatches," Maria said firmly.

Jefferson nodded. "A diplomatic dispatch has arrived at the embassy," he told Short. "An urgent letter from John Jay requires my immediate attention. You can stay for the dinner, of course, William, but say that I am unable."

In the corner of his eye Short could see Cosway's wrinkled brown face, Trumbull's smirk.

"Tell the duchesse," Jefferson said with a face of smiling impenetrability, "that it was irresistible."

CHAPTER

Fourteen

Roman; Rebel. What else? Romeo? Machiavel?

In the broad, rational light of morning Short deposited his armload of rolled papers and drawings on the table and looked up, prepared to be wary.

"A marvelous man, absolutely marvelous," Maria Cosway said from the other end of the room, skirt swinging like a bell as she walked. She stopped in front of the empty fireplace and placed her hands on her hips. "All these books, all these *books* —and he's read them all, yes? Every one of them?" Unlike most visitors, Short noticed Maria didn't actually look at the books she was admiring —and there must have been two or three hundred just in the salon alone, not even a proper library setting, but an overflow space for Jefferson's recent purchases.

"Books," she repeated, stopping now under the sunburst painting on the ceiling and looking in fact the other way, toward the great windows and the summer garden below.

"Le Comte de Buffon was in this very room six months ago," Short told her, certain she had never heard of Buffon, "and Mr. Jefferson showed him those volumes of engravings under the

Encyclopédie." He inclined his head in the general direction of the bookcase, where twenty or thirty gilt-edged volumes seemed to march up and down the shelves like little leather soldiers.

"And now you've brought *another* book." As Maria advanced, she came into clearer focus. The golden curls sprang into relief, the deep violet eyes (definitely violet this morning), the tiny waist, full yellow skirt, two exquisite dainty blue slippers poking like mice from under the hem. Her breasts—Short lowered his head and pulled out the long folio volume of *Antiquités de France* that was sitting beneath the papers. A book of extraordinarily detailed engravings that Jefferson had just that week purchased from Clérisseau, as a delicate way of thanking him for the plaster model.

"This is a kind of travel book of the past," he murmured. He disliked Maria's husband enormously—what other words? *Thoroughly, completely, totally;* as one dislikes a bug or a bit of nastiness stuck to one's heel. Too strong, but let it stand. The husband was a fool; the wife was . . . a beautiful coquette, Pope's addle-brained Belinda in *The Rape of the Lock* brought to life; but a Virginian was sworn to politeness the way a Frenchman was sworn to fashion. He opened the book at a marker and showed her the famous Roman aqueduct at Arles, another of Jefferson's interests.

"I'm too tired for books." Maria dropped abruptly into one of the soft chairs next to the table. "Fatiguée, épuisée."

As if on cue the far door of the salon opened, and James Hemings entered, followed by Adrien Petit, who appeared more than usually stimulated by the presence of the Cosways, Maria in the salon, Richard downstairs with Jefferson and Trumbull going over plans, papers, itineraries—Short had no idea. Jefferson and Trumbull had returned long after midnight and risen early, huddling after breakfast in the study until the Cosways' carriage had arrived.

"Dit-on 'épuisée,' Monsieur?" Maria asked Petit, who had come to attention and started to beam at her first words. "C'est vraiment français? Correct French?" James gave a sullen look and slid his tray of teacups and dishes onto the table. James and I, thought Short; immune. Behind them two more servants were bringing hot water, biscuits, a small bright wheel of butter.

"C'est correct, absolument, Madame," Petit assured her. "Mais vous êtes trop jeune, trop charmante d'être 'épuisée,' et de si bonne heure du matin—"

"Sugar." James thumped the bowl onto the table.

"We stayed up—do you know how late we stayed up, Mr. Short?"

"On your *jour heureux*? No."

"First." Maria held up a small, perfect finger. "We left the Halle aux Bleds a little after you did, and we took Mr. Jefferson's carriage all the way to the Parc Saint-Cloud, straight across the river, right into the country."

"For the 'coolth.'"

She paused to give him a smile. "You remember. You're just like him. We went to Saint-Cloud and toured a gallery of paintings and dined at a little inn near that. Then we came back to Paris and went to the Faubourg Montmartre, where we saw fireworks, amazing, wonderful fireworks—like a war!"

Short closed the volume of engravings and accepted the cup James handed him. The fireworks were a specialty of the famous Ruggieri brothers, off the rue Saint-Lazare, who orchestrated what they called "lyric pantomimes" in rockets, colored flares, and exploding candles. Two weeks ago, Short had joined Clérisseau and others for an evening portraying "The Combat of Mars" and "The Forge of Vulcan," with an afterpiece entirely in red rockets, "The Salamander."

"Absolutely wonderful," Maria said. She paused to watch the retreating backs of the servants. "We would never have known about it if not for Mr. Jefferson—the Duc d'Orléans, I can assure you, does not *condescend* to fireworks."

At the end of the salon Petit and James stepped aside to allow Trumbull in, carrying awkwardly under his arm a large canvas wrapped in tissue. Behind him, looking just as ill-matched as Short had remembered, came Cosway and Jefferson. Cosway wore the same lavender-red coat as before, but sky-blue trousers today, ornately buckled shoes, and a wig much too big for his tiny brown face. Monkey or bug? The ornamental sword stuck out from his coat like a sting.

"And after *that*," Maria said, turning her head in a lazy, thoroughly captivating manner toward the three men, "we stopped for a concert."

"A beautiful concert," Trumbull said. He nodded at Short and began to pile biscuits onto a dish for himself. "We should have sent you a dispatch."

"We went to the Krumpholtz house," Jefferson said, either indifferent to Trumbull or not hearing. "Julie Krumpholtz played the harpsichord for us and sang, hours and hours of music."

"In London," Cosway said, likewise serving himself with tea and biscuits, "my wife arranges every week what the press have graciously named Great Concerts. The Prince of Wales comes, Lady Duncan, General Paoli, Lord Sands, Mr. Boswell, the Countess of Aylesbury." At every name a smile—grimace—a sharp, energetic chop of the silver wig. The Roman wouldn't last an hour in the company of such an insect; the Rebel would have turned away in disgust. The third Jefferson, however, the new Romeo . . .

"And she herself composes for the harp," Cosway finished.

"*And* plays it too." Trumbull had Yankee manners, fingers sticky with frosting in his mouth.

Jefferson handed Maria a second cup of tea (where had the first one gone? Short wondered, glancing about). Now he sat down beside her, knees almost touching the fluffed yellow skirt and its plump hint of thigh and hip. He wore the glassy-eyed look of a man utterly captivated, utterly—Short changed his image: the look of a hooked fish. Jefferson bent his red hair solicitously toward her blond. Meanwhile Cosway was speaking pompously again, another spate of aristocratic names; Trumbull, impressively virile, barrel-chested in his tight gray coat and open collar, was simultaneously recounting a story about David the painter and the canvas he was about to unwrap for them. Abruptly Short thought he could take no more. He replaced his cup on the table, waved one hand in a vague, unreadable gesture learned from Clérisseau, and headed for the door. "Urgent dispatches," he murmured over his shoulder to Jefferson, knowing it was feeble, even impudent, smiling to placate the Roman, hurrying to outrun their voices.

An enemy, Maria Cosway decided, watching him leave. In a company of men, however hard she tried to please, there was always one like Short who made her feel useless and foolish. A stupid girl. *Una puttana.*

"So, wake up—what do you think of it, Maria? Be frank, tell me the truth."

Trumbull had pulled the tissue wrapping away from his canvas. He propped the painting against the leg of a chair, just out of the sunlight. He stood behind it with his arms folded like a gladiator and bared his teeth in a grim masculine smile.

"Oh," she said, stalling for time. She broke into admiring, meaningless Italian phrases, not bothering at all with what she said, certain that Trumbull didn't understand a word, nor Richard of course, but she suddenly broke off as she caught sight of Jefferson's curious face. He spoke French badly but doggedly; she had never been in the presence of a man who seemed so entirely, from head to toe, every moment—she searched her head for the English word: *intellectual.*

"Not fair to take refuge in your native language, Maria." Trumbull had been in the army, she thought, and could produce a disagreeable note of command when he wanted.

"I like the colors then," she said, guessing that he had worked hardest on that. "I like the colors very much—they clash, they explode!"

" 'Battle of Bunker's Hill,' " Richard read on the bottom of the frame.

"And the expressions." She rose and pointed toward the head of an American soldier apparently shielding or protecting his black servant. Above him a British officer had fallen back, dying, another American lay under the point of a bayonet, and down the brown hillside to the right a city she took to be Boston grew in sharp angles like a brown crystal. She thought she should be patriotic and resent the obvious British defeat in progress, but she didn't care, she had never cared. "You were there, Mr. Jefferson, no?"

Jefferson shook his head and smiled gently. "I know as little about battles as I do about painting, Mrs. Cosway. I was far from Bunker Hill that day, I'm afraid."

"Jefferson lives in Virginia," Trumbull said rather gruffly, fussing with the slant of the frame, "a good four hundred miles from Boston."

Maria put her chin in her hand in a pose that she knew to be charming. Trumbull called her by her Christian name, in the loose, informal manner of artists these days—she resented it, she thought; she liked the graver dignity of Jefferson. Meanwhile her husband had started to talk, bouncing back and forth in front of the painting, rising on the balls of his feet, little teacup in hand, spouting technical terms, growing critical of the very colors she had liked, the head of the American soldier she had praised, which was anatomically incorrect, he declared; and Trumbull was listening seriously, nodding his head, because, however much he looked (she knew) like a monkey in a wig and silk pants, Richard Cosway was an eminently successful artist and Trumbull was not. And when Richard took it into his head—an extraordinary English phrase; some days, especially in Paris, the *oddity* of English expressions struck her at almost every word—when he took it into his head to analyze a painting, nobody could be as thorough, as detailed, as cruelly precise. She moved her eyes and saw Jefferson, and both of them smiled carefully at Richard's lecture.

Undiscouraged, Trumbull had more paintings to show them—outlines, sketches, an impressive plan for *The Signing of the Declaration of Independence,* which featured Jefferson's own red-haired portrait from life, Trumbull's official reason for coming to France. They lingered in the bright upstairs salon until nearly one, when Richard abruptly announced that he was famished and Jefferson, who seemed to think of everything hours and miles before anyone else, calmly said that his servants had already set out champagne and fruit in the garden below.

A French couple joined them there (how he arranged the timing of their visit baffled her), and Richard, excited by a new audience, decided for the first time in weeks to pay attention to Maria.

"My wife," he said casually during a pause, holding a strawberry over his open mouth but twisting his neck to grin at them each in turn, "my wife is not English, did you know that?"

"She's Anglo-Italian," Trumbull told the French couple, who spoke perfect English. The husband, Éthis de Corny, had fought for the Americans in the Revolution, Jefferson said; the wife, Maria thought, was remarkably pretty and looked at Jefferson too often.

"But we are lucky she's anything at all, you know." Cosway nibbled at the strawberry and rolled his eyes toward the bench where she sat. "She almost became"—breathless, affected

whisper; a little mincing bounce on his toes, like a fool—"a religious *martyr.*"

Her cue. "My husband means," she told the French wife, leaning forward confidentially, "that a bizarre, terrible thing happened
in my family when I was a child. In Italy the newspapers wrote
about it for months." She stopped, barely heard the inevitable
polite questions. She had told—performed—this story so often for
Richard that the words came automatically, even listlessly, in a
smoothly worn track, but this time, watching Jefferson herself,
she put unexpected energy into her voice.

"My father was born in Manchester but moved to Florence to
pursue his business. I was born there, my first language was
Italian, as you hear—but I was the fifth of my parents' children,
and the first to live."

"The first," Cosway repeated.

"The four others had all died as babies, in their cribs at night.
Without being sick. The Italian doctors had no idea why. My
mother, of course, was distraught and hysterical all the time, ready
to die herself. But my father—my father was a wonderful man, my
rescuer. He thought something was too suspicious here. Babies
die, but not four in a row, all in their beds. Each baby had had a
different nurse, he saw to that, and still they died. So when I was
born, he hired a new governess *and* a new nurse, and gave the
governess the secret duty to watch the nurse and everyone else
who came near me."

Jefferson had moved away from Trumbull and found a place on
the opposite bench, beside the Frenchman. His red hair almost
white in the sunlight, his long face framed against the green American corn plants he had showed them—Jefferson had daughters,
she remembered; some of his children had died.

"One day a maidservant who had worked in another part of the
house, the scullery, for years, went into the nursery and, thinking
no one was near, took me in her arms and said, 'Pretty little
creature, I have sent four to heaven, I hope to send you too!' My
governess was hiding in the next room—she *ran* to my father, my
father called the authorities, and the poor wretched girl confessed
—she had a religious mania; she had *smothered* each one with a
pillow case she carried in her dress, and she thought the little
babies went straight to heaven, with no sin. They put her in a

lunatic house. And me, as an act of thanksgiving, they put in a convent."

She sat back and smiled at the company; started to add that sometimes, because of her rescue, she saw strange, impossible . . . signs. But Richard would emphatically *not* want her to say that. She repeated her last words and smiled, particularly at Jefferson.

Afterward, as they stood in front of the door on the rue de Berri, waiting for their carriages, Jefferson asked quietly how long she had stayed in the convent.

"Until I was nineteen, when my father died."

"And then?"

"And then I wanted to take the veil and become a nun, the way so many girls in a convent do."

Jefferson frowned and looked about quickly, as if to check that the arriving carriages had lined up properly; but she saw in the frown the usual disapproval of Englishmen and Americans—to them all Catholics came from the moon. Catholics were worse than pagans. "You have a daughter in a convent," she said.

"Well. But she only goes to school there, she studies French and music—no question at all of taking the veil, as you put it."

Maria let her finger remain on his wrist. To annoy a man was not necessarily a mistake. To show that you could prick under his skin . . . "We must talk about this, about religion and daughters."

"We have so many better subjects," he said elegantly but briskly, handing her up into the carriage and turning away. As she settled into the seat, she watched him walk toward the others with his long, loose-limbed American stride. But two minutes later, from her carriage window above the pavement, she heard him arrange with her husband for yet another excursion that night.

On the fifth day of their friendship, as she liked to call it, Jefferson joined them for a morning at the gallery of the Luxembourg Palace.

"I know less of painting the more I see it," he said, coming to her side as soon as the guards had swept open the doors. She made a point of waiting until all Richard's guests had entered first:

Trumbull, Short, Madame Vigée-Lebrun, a trembling old *gallant*
named d'Hancarville who studied Greek antiquities in an obscurely scandalous way, Richard himself, three other French couples.

"Mr. Cosway obtained the invitations," Maria said, not certain
that *obtained* was the right English word. "For months, you know,
he's talked about nothing except the famous Rubens gallery—
twenty-one paintings that nobody ever sees because the building
is closed—you must stick close to him to learn about painting."

Jefferson smiled. He offered no attempt whatever to join Cosway and the others, now clattering down a dusty corridor ahead of
them. "Mr. Cosway's students are so much more advanced than I
am. It seems a waste of his time."

"Well then." She pulled her cloak tighter about her shoulders
and glanced around with a sense of real alarm—the gallery wing
of the Luxembourg Palace was at least a hundred years old,
boarded up and falling apart, literally. The ceilings bulged, the
walls slanted. Next to them rose a staircase barricaded with old
crates and wood scraps. Its steps were broken off like rotten teeth.

"Well then," she repeated stupidly, and stopped. She talked too
much, she thought. Sometimes it was better to say nothing at all,
especially with someone so quick as Jefferson. And in any case the
old man d'Hancarville had now fallen back and begun to mumble
to them both in rapid, interminable French.

The last guard pulled open the last door more than a century
ago, and they all entered the gallery together. Rubens, her strange
husband's strange obsession, had been commissioned to depict the
life of Marie de Médicis. Huge allegorical canvases, each one at
least twenty feet long and a dozen feet tall, hung mounted high
overhead, on the crumbling gray walls of what must have been
Marie's own palatial ballroom. Richard painted miniatures—fashionable little portraits for gold lockets or watch lids or jewelry
cases, exquisite, precise; *fussy*. The Rubens paintings—Maria
made an involuntary gesture of surprise. Their sheer size overwhelmed everything else, their long sweeping motions of brush
and eye; clouds boiled off the canvas, billowing landscapes and
mountains, great fleshy Dutch bodies that were landscapes in
themselves. In the gigantic painting just to her right Marie de
Médicis lounged backward on a cloud, half-naked, one arm

cocked behind her golden curls, vast royal breasts, an acre of pink and white belly. Nothing in the world like Richard's paintings!

When she had looked once around the room, deciphering the order of the series, she saw that Jefferson, ever systematic, had set off on his own tour, pacing from one painting to another with his guidebook open. She shivered. The gallery was in even worse repair than the rest of the palace. Workmen had propped long beams of rough timber against the walls, between every other painting, like flying buttresses. Directly above her head more boards covered a broken skylight; dust, dark mold, spiderwebs: you peered at everything through a film of filth.

" 'How many pictures of one nymph can we view, all how unlike each other, all how true.' " John Trumbull had almost bumped into her, and now he was quoting verse she didn't recognize at all.

"Pope," Trumbull continued with a patronizing note that sometimes made her dislike him very much. "Alexander Pope. You don't know it? 'To a Lady,' one of the wittiest poems in English."

Jefferson had materialized beside them, out of the gray air. "Our Mr. Trumbull is a graduate of Harvard. He overflows with learning."

"I like that one enormously." Trumbull extended his arm, thumb straight up, to study a portrait of Marie arriving from Italy in a ship, the new bride of Henry IV. Maria tried to follow his moving hand, but her eyes stayed fixed on the queen's swollen breasts. Each one was the size of a wine cask.

"The next painting down," Trumbull said, "is much weaker. The best of the lot is at the end, the allegory of France."

As he moved away, still holding his arm out straight, Jefferson touched her elbow. She found herself doing three things at once: turning to face him with a smile, smoothing her skirt, trying to remember if he had ever actually touched her before. But men, in a room full of paintings like these—

"Trumbull is sometimes too bluff and military, I'm afraid," Jefferson said softly. "I hope you excuse him. He has a great deal on his mind, he worries."

"I'm accustomed to painters," she said, then added, feeling somehow it would be a compliment to Jefferson, "I think he's a very good artist, you know."

Jefferson watched the younger man stop and fold his arms in front of the allegory of France. His own gesture, Maria thought; no wonder he likes him. Both of his young men imitate all his gestures. Short—in the corner of her eye she saw Short approaching them—often stands in a folded-arm posture, head to one side, exactly like Jefferson's.

"In the Revolution," Jefferson said, "Trumbull started out as a very lowly officer. But he literally 'drew himself' to General Washington's attention. He made sketches of the battlefields, the British formations, the artillery placements, such excellent, *useful* sketches that Washington promoted him to his staff as official artist. Now he's decided to record the whole history of the war in paintings— Bunker Hill, Valley Forge, Yorktown, American history in pictures, a wonderful legacy for the future."

"You always think so much about America."

He looked down at her in genuine surprise. "I think about nothing else."

Short had reached them and interrupted with a question about Jefferson's schedule. Poor earnest Short. Jealous of Trumbull, Maria thought; jealous of me. She stepped away from the two men to let them finish their business, but within moments Jefferson had steered them back to her side.

"Mr. Short reminds me that the Comte de Vergennes expects us in an hour. More American thoughts, alas."

One of the traits Maria had cultivated in herself was impulse. Always say what you felt, when you felt it. "Is something wrong with Trumbull's eyes? I never thought of it before, but look how he stands and points, all twisted around. He can't *see!*"

At the far end of the gallery Trumbull had joined Madame Vigée-Lebrun and taken her hand in his, lifting it to trace some design in the painting. Short turned sharply to stare.

Jefferson wore a bland, superior expression—the face of a man who had secrets; for an instant Maria disliked his face very much —then his features relaxed. His quick, deliberate smile softened his eyes. "Of all the painters and artists in Paris, Mrs. Cosway, you are the only one to have *observed.*"

Short had turned back, quizzical.

"Trumbull suffered a boyhood accident," Jefferson explained. "He almost never mentions it—he lost the sight in one eye."

"His left eye," Maria said.

Jefferson nodded.

"Sir—"

"One of the worries I mentioned. He fears going blind." Over his shoulder Jefferson said in a voice too firm for Short to ignore, "If you wait for me at the door, William, I will join you in two minutes."

Maria let herself drift in the gray light, beneath the billowing flesh of the queen.

"Your friend Madame Vigée-Lebrun is an artist too," Jefferson said, drifting beside her. "I find her name in all my catalogues, but never her works."

"Ah, she has no American subjects, that's why. Elisabeth paints portraits of women only, extraordinary portraits—the queen dotes on her—we've known her for years, Richard has, her and her husband." She lifted her chin, showing her throat. "Your protégé there takes an obvious interest, no? Injury or not, he has an eye for a pretty woman."

"Well, artists do."

"And yet." She hesitated, keeping her profile high. In the ecclesiastical gloom of the gallery, voices murmured discreetly, shoes tapped on the marble floor. What was the precise line between impulse and calculation? She made a point of not looking into Jefferson's face. "Anyone can see that she's not happily married."

CHAPTER

Fifteen

C harles-Louis Clérisseau, man of leisure and man of plea-sure—far too much of the former these days, he thought wryly; far too little of the latter—strolled down the crowded Valois arcade of the Palais Royal.

It was midafternoon, sunny again after a morning of low damp clouds, and since he had accomplished nothing at all that forenoon in his solitary, client-free studio, Clérisseau had decided to visit, without spending money if possible, the busiest spot in Paris.

He made his way down the middle of the arcade, pausing occasionally in the crowd to let a squad of workmen bustle through into the center garden. When he was a boy the Palais Royal had been one of the gloomier landmarks in the whole Fau-bourg Saint-Honoré. If you entered from the south, skirting the formidable dark palace of Cardinal Richelieu that gave the place its name, you came, after a few nondescript alleyways and court-yards, to the long plot of grass where Richelieu, to please the king, had built a miniature fort for the young Louis XIV. By the time Clérisseau had seen it, the fort was a crumbling pile of masonry and the entire property had passed into the hands of the fat, popular, amorous Duc d'Orléans, about whom Clérisseau had first heard one of the most curious words in the French language:

"ventripotent." Powerful of stomach. And then, miraculously, the old duc had suddenly ceded everything to his nervous, entrepreneurial son Louis-Philippe, who had promptly turned loose an army of builders and architects —

Clérisseau paused to savor the sophisticated obscenity of a shopkeeper quarreling with a drunken Spaniard. Three covered arcades, two hundred shops and cafés, five thousand milling, idle, pleasure-seeking customers . . . The Spaniard spun away with a volley of oaths, stumbled on his drunken feet, and pulled up short, just inches from Clérisseau's nose. He was a peasant, dressed in the coarse blue wool and clogs of a laborer. It was Clérisseau's private opinion that the most dangerous change in Paris in his lifetime had been the new, promiscuous mingling of classes. He pushed the Spaniard backward with one flat-handed blow and braced his legs to reach for his sword, but the crowd had already surged between them, and the Spaniard's dirty black head was swept away in the natural tide of bodies and noise.

Clérisseau shook his sleeve and dusted, unnecessarily, his shoulder before stepping forward again. Jefferson — of all people the great democrat Jefferson had said the same thing two weeks before. Paris was a fairground, a people's *foire,* out of control; the day the king had allowed a mob of ordinary citizens into Versailles to witness a balloon launch, that was the day, Jefferson said, the king had lost his mystique.

Clérisseau felt suddenly thirsty. In the shops and stalls to his right a *coutelier* was lining up his rows of sharp bright kitchen knives, like so many long silver fish in a school. Beyond him two old men in aprons struggled to lift a saddle to the shelves of M. Duplessis, Bourrelier. A bookshop, a binder, linen stalls, stairways to apartments — Clérisseau walked purposely forward, inhaling the smell of leather and oil, perfume, ripe human flesh; a *fille* pirouetted gaily around him, twirling her parasol, and disappeared up the stairway. Clérisseau slapped at his money pouch and strode on, toward the corner.

The third floor of the Palais was reserved for *belles filles* — he knew that quite expertly; the second floor for clubs and little offices (across the garden on his left he could see the swinging signboard of the Société des Planteurs), but the corners of the arcades were where, by unspoken custom, the cafés and restaurants were found. He stopped in front of Février's, a little stall of oysters on melting ice just beside the curtained doors, and winced at the printed list of prices. Farther on, at the shady corner where the arcade Valois turned left and became the arcade Beaujolais, he stopped again at the Café Mécanique and through the checkered panes of glass saw with a smile the neat, trim figure of William Short, sitting alone at a table.

He was too absorbed (as usual) in what he was reading even to look up.

"May I join you?" Clérisseau inquired.

Short turned his head, blinking. Then he smiled in recognition. "Of course, always. I didn't see you. I didn't know you ever came to this strange place."

"Many times."

Short was busy moving his stacks of letters and papers from the square wooden surface of the table to his lap and the floor, but he paused for a moment to tap the edge with his knuckles. "A wonderful idea, wonderful and strange. 'O brave new world that has such tables in it.'" While Clérisseau watched with an expression of amusement, he waved an arm expansively at the banner hanging on the far wall and read it aloud: "'Sans Serveurs'!" The great novelty of the Café Mécanique, of course, as Short had discovered, was that there were no waiters here whatsoever. The twenty or so individual tables in the room, each with legs as thick as a man's body, were uniformly equipped with a note pad, a pen, and a small wooden lever; when you had written your order on the pad, you pulled the lever (keeping your feet back, as everyone quickly learned), and the table slowly sank into the floor on pneumatic valves. In a matter of moments a cook in the basement had read your order, stacked the required dishes and carafes on the table, and sent it hissing smoothly again upstairs.

"Let me buy you a dish of fresh coffee," Short said, clearing the last of his papers. "I love to see it work."

"Our friend must 'love' it even more." Clérisseau scratched a few words on the pad. Short slid his own dirty cup to the center and worked the lever. "With all the copying machines and three-stage gravitational thermometers you've set up so far, I'm surprised he hasn't installed one of these to replace young Adrien Petit."

"Actually," Short started to remind him. Several of the tables had dumbwaiters concealed in the thick legs, so that additional plates could be sent up to clients without lowering the whole table; more than once Jefferson had mused out loud about the practicality of such a dumbwaiter at Monticello.

Clérisseau listened with only half an ear. Beneath their feet the floor began to vibrate. "Stand back," he said. "*Attention* to your books."

Instinctively they scraped their chairs backward. After a long moment, with a sigh like an expiring kettle, the table rose back between them, a new silver pot of coffee and two clean cups and saucers sitting in the middle, a vase of cut flowers, a bowl of brilliant white sugar lumps. As Clérisseau poured, Short restacked his papers and folded them together. Clérisseau pointed the elegant little finger that supported his cup.

"You have become Parisian entirely, you know, dear Guillaume —a huge beautiful *hôtel* at your disposal, servants, carriages, and yet you bring your work to a café and sit all day by a public window. What's the difficulty? An excess of Trumbulls on rue de Berri?"

Short concentrated on his cup, tasting the soupy liquid. One disadvantage, of course, of the invisible service was that the coffee was practically cold.

"In fact, we have renovations under way at the rue de Berri. The downstairs salon is losing a wall, two new doors are going out to the garden, hammers, plaster, chaos everywhere. With the best will in the world I can't quite blame Trumbull."

Clérisseau shook his head. By unspoken agreement they avoided the subject of Maria Cosway. "If I recall, our Jefferson did the same thing at the rue Taitbout, no? Redesigned one floor, took out a whole retaining wall? Always designing, always constructing."

Short squared his papers uselessly and nodded, conveying (as intended) no clear answer at all.

"Do you know Gibbon?" Clérisseau asked abruptly.

Short pinched the bridge of his nose and made a little face, feeling, as so often, half a step behind Clérisseau's rapid changes of subject. "I know who Edward Gibbon is," he said dryly. "The historian of the fall of the Roman Empire. I've never read a word of him."

Clérisseau indicated the stack of papers and leather-bound books. "Do you know what his neighbor the Duke of Gloucester said when Gibbon presented him with volumes five and six of that great work?" Clérisseau's mock-British accent was perfect. " 'Another damned thick square book. Always scribble, scribble, scribble, eh, Mr. Gibbon?' "

Short laughed uncomfortably, resquared his papers, and then, deciding that even Clérisseau's habitual irony deserved an answer, removed an unbound French journal from the stack. He opened it at his bookmark and turned the journal around for Clérisseau to read.

"I'm preparing an answer to this statement by the Comte de Mirabeau," he said.

Clérisseau pursed his lips. Mirabeau was one of the wild figures of French politics, a mountainously ugly man whose legendary pursuit of female virtue was matched only by his energy in pursuit of radical ideas. Short guessed, rightly, that Clérisseau would read the paragraph he had marked with cautious respect.

"He maintains," Clérisseau said, looking up after a moment, "that there is no country on earth, not even America, where a man can be a fully privileged citizen simply by practicing the social virtues."

"By which he means that you have to swear allegiance to a state religion, as in France or England, or else give up some of your rights. You know that Catholics in England are still double-taxed; theoretically they can't hold office, they can't vote. And in France—"

"So by refusing to make an exception of America, Mirabeau brings down your wrath."

But Short was too seriously engaged with the question to rise to the sardonic tone. Of all Jefferson's accomplishments, he thought, this ranked second only to the Declaration of Independence. All of Europe should know it. "We're sending a copy of this law, in French and English, to Mirabeau. I'm to draft the accompanying letter in French." He handed Clérisseau the printed text that had just arrived, two days ago, from James Madison in Virginia.

Clérisseau read aloud in English: " 'A Bill for Establishing Religious Freedom.' "

"Jefferson introduced it into the Virginia Assembly in 1779," Short said. "But it's taken till now—seven whole years—for the Assembly to pass it."

Clérisseau turned the page over, moving his lips, then read aloud again. " 'The opinions of men are not the object of civil government, nor under its jurisdiction; to suffer the civil magistrate to intrude its powers into the field of opinion and to restrain the profession or propagation of principles on supposition of their ill tendency is a dangerous fallacy, which at once destroys all religious liberty. . . . truth is great and will prevail if left to herself.' "

"Liberty," Short said, and stopped.

"Justice," Richard Cosway said loudly, swaying slightly as he grasped the corner of their table. "Virtue. The red roast beef of old England. How are you, Mr. Short? Monsieur Clérisseau, we met one day at David's studio, if you don't remember. And then again —then again—"

Cosway swayed a bit more dangerously and passed a pale hand over his forehead. The artist wore a coat of hyacinth-colored silk, with strawberries embroidered on it; blue trousers, white boots; and a thin dress sword topped with a golden knot.

"And then again at the studio of Monsieur d'Hancarville, in the Louvre," Clérisseau concluded. "You and your charming wife were paying a visit."

"And my charming wife," Cosway repeated. "I would sit down if I could find a damn'd waiter to bring me a chair."

Short rose hastily to seize an unused chair from another table, while Clérisseau explained the café and stood to offer his own place. By the time Short had returned, they were settled again and Cosway was poking one monkeylike finger into Short's papers.

"Would you like coffee?"

Cosway shook his head. His wig rocked on his head.

"Wine?"

"I've just been to the Camp of Tartars," he told Clérisseau.

"With d'Hancarville?"

"No." He swung his leg over the arm of the chair, slouched, and stared up at Short. "Do you know what d'Hancarville's subject of study is?" Before Short could answer, he shook his head again. "Never guess. By God, it's hot in here. D'Hancarville studies the phallic religion of ancient Greece. Fact. He showed me a locked cabinet full of the most amazing objects. Big as your arm. Made out of bone."

Short felt his dislike for the man rising almost to physical nausea. A drunken, skinny, monkey-faced little fop with the leer and smirk of a schoolboy. He pulled Jefferson's bill for religious freedom toward his lap and pushed the chair back.

"My wife and your ambassador," Cosway said, without the slightest sign of jealousy, "are off somewhere touring the Bois de Boulogne. I painted till noon, then saw old d'Hancarville. The Camp of Tartars is just out there, all those tents on the other side of these arcades. They have a wax model, anatomically correct, of 'la belle Zulima.' Also a Prussian giant and his dwarf wife."

"The Camp des Tartares," said Clérisseau, rising, "is a notorious place for pickpockets and thieves. You should have been warned."

"It is a place," Cosway said, managing to sway even as he sat in the chair. Ostentatiously he tucked the tail of his shirt into the blue trousers. "It is a place," he grinned, "of absolute *liberty*."

In the sunshine outside Cosway appeared less drunk. He walked between the two men to the end of the arcade Beaujolais on rue de Montpensier, where a line of carriages-for-hire was stationed. At the head of the line Clérisseau signaled for a carriage to take Cosway home.

"Rue Coqhéron, is it not?"

"Come with me, Clérisseau, and see what I've been painting." In an obvious afterthought Cosway turned and included Short in the invitation as well. But Short held up one hand and clutched his books with the other. A hasty plea of business, a diplomatic flash of teeth. The last thing he saw was Clérisseau at the carriage window mouthing a word—but what?—while the carriage clattered forward and out of sight.

As Short returned to the Palais he wondered at the peculiar laws that governed marriage. A beautiful (shallow) woman like Maria Cosway, a repellent creature like her husband. He thought of Jefferson and Martha Wayles, like attracting like; the old Duc and the young Duchesse de La Rochefoucauld, December and

May. If he were Cosway—by some act of celestial malice—he would do everything possible to rise above his nature; if, on the other hand, he were Maria Cosway, how could he not be in perpetual flight from such a goat's bed?

But at that moment Maria Cosway was in flight from no one. She was seated on a bench just inside the Pavillon de Bagatelle in the Bois de Boulogne, watching a trio of tame deer walk calmly about, behind the sharply pointed wooden posts of what was labeled, in French and English, an "American stockade." The sight was as baffling to her as it was apparently amusing to Jefferson, who detached himself from the stockade and strolled back to the bench, smiling.

"This represents the gardener's idea of where the 'noble savage' retreats from the dangerous beasts of America."

"And it's not true?"

"The only dangerous beasts I see at Monticello are horses and doctors."

She laughed and, moving the folds of her skirt with one hand, made room for him on the bench. Beyond the stockade, by a little brook and a bridge, other couples strolled through the garden. "You see wild beasts in America, and in Paris you see artists, almost the same thing, no? In the last week you've met David, in his studio. And Madame Vigée-Lebrun and Carle Vernet and the sculptor Pagou and also Houdon—"

"Whom I knew before."

"On business only. And you've met General Kosciusko as well, a bonus of sorts, since you're both politicians." She watched him trace a geometric design in the gravel with his walking stick. Always in slight, contained, *masculine* motion. Kosciusko she had been told was a kind of Polish hero, a revolutionary statesman who had done—something; but *he* had known Jefferson instantly, taking his hand in both of his and bowing low with unmistakable respect. "So now we have brought you into the whole Paris world of painters and artists, without even a stockade to protect you."

As they made their way, like the other couples, toward the bridge, Jefferson pointed out for her and named, in English, every plant and blossom that they passed. Then he came somehow closer —she watched their swinging hands gently approach, veer, brush;

his colored on the back with the soft ginger hairs that also ran stiffly down the nape of his neck, as men's do—and when she was listening again, he had begun a question.

"An education for me, of course, in all the fine arts. But you always let the others do the talking. And yet Trumbull assures me that you are a painter as well. Is it true?"

"Ah," she said. "Trumbull."

"He says you exhibited at the Royal Academy in London."

"Once. Once or twice I showed paintings. But Richard, you know . . ." Leaning, smiling, she brushed the tips of her fingers across his hand and came to a halt in the middle of the path. "Richard forbids me to paint now," she said seriously, "and if someone insists on a portrait, some friend—well, nothing is for sale."

"He *forbids?*"

She had told the story often enough, she knew the effect of her smile, and of Richard's blunt, jealous prohibition; but no one had ever reacted quite as Jefferson did. For a moment she expected his face to harden into anger or outrage—some men did that; other men puffed or blew on their moustaches or raised an eyebrow— the Prince of Wales had laughed. But Jefferson . . . Was she catching the set of his emotions now, or was he entirely a mystery? . . . Jefferson simply changed the subject.

"The Bagatelle up ahead is a building with a curious history."

This time she let her hand rest firmly on his and made no move to resume their stroll, so that he was forced to stop and turn back to her. She said, "We're friends, even in such a short time, are we not?" Through the trees a moving checkerboard of light played across his face; it was like reading a puzzle. "You may hear stories. When our family came back from Italy to England, I was briefly engaged to a musician, a Dr. Parsons, who was quite poor. When I married Richard, some people joked that I had done it for money —Richard is very rich, he was very generous. But it was all for love."

Jefferson was silent. She had no sense at all of what he thought, only the impression of rigid muscles, tension. He rode horses like a soldier; she had seen him swing into the saddle like a boy of twenty. Impulse rose in her throat. "You were married once."

Jefferson pushed away the leaves of a shrub with his stick to allow her to go ahead. Behind her she heard him say in a normal tone of voice, "My wife died four years ago."

"Ah." Side by side now. The Bagatelle was a miniature castle, charmingly laid out with flowers, ponds, varnished bits of terra-cotta that sparkled in the sunlight. John Trumbull had told her that Jefferson was one of the strongest characters he had ever known—a prodigy of learning and will—and the most reserved. He would never say one word beyond his intended effect, beyond what he wanted to say; his self-control was the key to everything else. So, of course, a person of impulse, she thought, watching him, would naturally attempt to turn the key.

"What was she like?"

Jefferson looked sideways, squinting, distressed. "She was musical. Gentle." He hesitated.

"Did she talk about the famous politics with you?"

Carefully, painfully, he smiled at her, a face caught in the hard vise of courtesy. "I did not *forbid* her to talk of politics, you know, but she preferred not. I confess I prefer it when ladies do not."

They had stopped in the center of the path, facing each other. Maria was aware of his height, his flushed skin. In the summer heat her heart pounded so fiercely that her head trembled, her legs in her skirt trembled.

"And when she died, four years ago, were you distraught?" Trumbull had told her he had been like a madman; his friends thought he would die himself or lose his reason.

He spoke with slow formality, as if he had composed his answer long before. "I entered a great stupor of mind," he said. "For many months I was as dead to the world as she was, whose loss occasioned it."

Then he raised his hand briskly to point at the whitewashed walls of the Bagatelle. "The little château here, you know, was built on a wager by the Comte d'Artois—hence the name 'trifle.' His brother the old king bet his wife that it couldn't be finished in sixty days."

The rest of the gardens were tedious. They returned early in Jefferson's phaeton, stopping only at the Pont de Neuilly, where Jefferson made her observe closely the engineering genius of the low elliptical arches that supported the bridge.

As they clattered across the Seine and entered Paris again, he suddenly remarked with a puzzled expression that William Short had been out of spirits ever since the day of the Halle aux Bleds, when he had had to dine in their place with the old Duchesse de La Rochefoucauld and her son and his wife. Short would say nothing about the dinner that night, the company; he was silent as a stone.

Maria smiled and spoke so softly that Jefferson heard not a word. "Poor in-love Mr. Short," she said.

☆　　☆　　☆

Papers and books.

Papers and books lay spread across both desks, across the two large tables on either side of the door, which were usually reserved for mail and parcels; across two of the six upholstered chairs in the study, even across the slats of Jefferson's polygraph copying machine. The heavens had opened and rained books, Short thought, squalls and showers of ink. Above the papers and books rose three new bookcases, already full, constructed of dark French oak from Burgundy and fitted into the walls. He remembered a phrase attributed to the old English curmudgeon Samuel Johnson, recently dead, "the epidemic conspiracy for the destruction of paper."

"Monsieur Jefferson's house," Clérisseau said drolly, "has books the way my own apartment has ants."

"Method in our madness," Short said. Outside the closed door he could hear voices, one mild and even, Jefferson's; the other higher-pitched and, of all things in Jefferson's household, angry. "Do you know François Soulé?"

"The historian. I have seen—but, alas, not bought or, further alas, read—his history of the American Revolution."

"Jefferson bought a copy in London—"

"If I were not an architect"—Clérisseau picked a book at random from the top of Short's desk—"I would, as long as he is here, become a bookseller. And very rich."

"—and he made a memo for Soulé, correcting his facts."

"These are his underlinings?"

"Well, no." Short felt himself oddly embarrassed. In this too he was different from Jefferson. "I made them. That's my copy of

Buffon. Jefferson actually never puts a mark in a book. He writes notes on separate sheets of paper and inserts them at the back."

"In France," Clérisseau began, but stopped as the door opened and Jefferson stepped partly into the room. Just beyond him, standing on the carpet, as tall as a man and showing carrot-red hair under her blue school cap, arms folded, jaw clenched, Patsy Jefferson glowered at her father. In the seventeen months he had known her, Short had never seen Patsy out of temper. Her father's darling, pet; a dutiful, self-effacing girl, but fourteen now and taking on the lineaments of a young woman.

"*I* would like to see the Bagatelle someday," she said, staring at Short without the slightest sign of recognition. "With Mrs. Cosway's *kind* permission."

Jefferson spoke so softly to her that Short and Clérisseau both turned instinctively away, for fear of appearing to eavesdrop. Clérisseau took up the sheet of paper entangled in the copying machine and handed it to Short, who smoothed it on the desk and inserted it into Jefferson's leather portfolio. When he looked up, Patsy was gone. Jefferson was closing the door, entering the study.

"You find us in disorganization," he said genially to Clérisseau, shaking his hand.

"I have decided to combine architecture and commerce," Clérisseau said. Short watched him grin at Jefferson and pull at the ends of his little moustache, like a popeyed cat. "I'll build you a house entirely of books, which I will sell to you first."

Jefferson walked calmly along the three new bookcases. "Well. Sunday evenings. We are always informal. My daughter is home from her school. Mr. Short is in his shirt-sleeves. Do you know," he said to Short, "that my old schoolmaster Maury writes to say his mother has heard Patsy is settled as a nun in a convent?"

By some species of telepathy—or Mesmerism—that Short had never fathomed, James Hemings appeared in the study bearing a tray of glasses and a decanter of red wine. While he laid them out on a cleared table by Jefferson's chair, Jefferson talked easily, serenely to Clérisseau. Short's eye went down the list of corrections on the sheet of paper he still held. Soulé's page numbers, followed by a sentence or two in Jefferson's microscopic handwriting.

Pa. 78. *A grand jury cannot be fewer than 12. nor more than 24. Some authorities say it cannot be fewer than 13. nor more than 23.*

Pa. 158. *Strike out 'et probablement' and insert 'mais veritablement.' I remember the fact well and the leading persons of Connecticut, and particularly their delegates in Congress made no secret that their object was to over-awe New York into its duty.*

Pa. 140. *The fact that the English commenced hostilities at Lexington has been proved beyond question by us; justice requires it should be plainly asserted and left clear of doubt.*

"You have finally become, my dear sir," Clérisseau joked, hefting both volumes of Soulé's *Histoire* in his hands, "European. You dwell in the past."

"The vaunted scene of Europe." Jefferson shook his head, smiling, and gestured to the chair opposite his. From some prick of impulse Short remained at the desk, sorting papers. "It is — seductive. But I don't dwell in the past. No American does."

"You know, you've never told me your impressions," Clérisseau said, "despite all our conversations. You are always on your guard to spare my feelings. But I see, I observe. You throw yourself into our art, our music, even *la cuisine française* — tell me frankly, are you not converted? Are you not *happy*?"

Jefferson turned the stem of his wineglass so that it just caught the glow of the whale-oil lamp behind him. A floating crescent of red. James Hemings was a shadow in shadows; Short scarcely saw him leave the room.

"You wish me to be frank," Jefferson said. "You're curious to know how this new scene has struck a savage from the mountains of America." A quick, unreadable smile in Short's direction. "To be truthful, then, I find the general fate of humanity here most deplorable. I think often of the truth of Voltaire's observation, that every man in this country must be either the hammer or the anvil. Or since it is Sunday evening, I will vary the image: Europe seems to me a true picture of that country to which they say we shall pass hereafter, and where we are to see God and his angels in splendor, and crowds of the damned trampled under their feet."

Clérisseau frowned and crossed his legs. Daringly: "You went to the Bagatelle this afternoon, I think?"

Jefferson leaned forward. "Mrs. Cosway and I did tour that

exquisite château and garden—you know, in your arts, in your music, painting, building, I am almost ready to say it is the one thing which from my heart I envy. In spite of all the authority of the Decalogue, I do covet your art. But—and here is the other side of the coin—last autumn about this time of year I had to attend the king's levee in Fontainebleau. In the afternoon I wanted to see the countryside, so I set out on one of my walks, toward the mountains, and after an hour or so I met a peasant woman on the path. She pointed me in the direction I wanted, and we talked for a time. She told me she was a day laborer at eight sous per day; she had two children to maintain; rent for her cottage was thirty livres a year—that is, she had to work seventy-five days a year to pay it—and that often she could get no work, none at all, for days at a time. Then she was completely without bread, as were her children. Since we had walked together almost a mile, I thanked her for serving as my guide and gave her twenty-four sous. Will you believe, my dear sir, that she burst into tears of gratitude? She could not utter a single word. She had probably never before received such a sum. In such conditions art is truly a bagatelle, a 'trifle,' for an afternoon, when the bulk of mankind in this country live in such perpetual and squalid misery."

Clérisseau had ceased to pull at his moustache. "Well, you said you would be frank."

Jefferson now leaned back so far in his chair that his shoulders slouched and his long legs almost obscured his face. He made a little deprecating gesture with his wineglass. "I think that reading Soulé's history puts me in mind of home. I may confuse frankness and warmth."

Clérisseau glanced over his shoulder. "Our friend Short is uncharacteristically silent. What does he think?"

Short shook his head firmly. What he thought first was that his hand itched to record in his journal every word Jefferson had just spoken; and second, that Jefferson's mind must be composed of a dozen separate locked compartments, as a house is composed of separate rooms. Not a reference to his daughter's deep anger, to the delicate question of Mr. and Mrs. Cosway, to the presence of his mulatto slave, a living symbol of the hammer and anvil, now back and refilling obediently each of their glasses. *Sans serveurs, avec esclaves.* Aloud, he said, "Comparisons, the poet tells us, are always odorous."

Jefferson laughed and shifted comfortably in his chair. "Mr. Short is already further schooled in diplomacy than I am."

"He showed me today, at the Palais Royal, a copy of your bill for religious freedom."

"My friend Madison saw it through the Assembly in Virginia," Jefferson said modestly.

"But you were its author?"

The Roman asserted his presence. Jefferson lifted his sharp profile and nodded once, impressively. "I hope to see it distributed widely in Europe, and widely discussed. I think it might produce considerable good."

"Because we Europeans are so mired in superstition."

Jefferson's eyes were on his books. "If the Almighty had begotten a thousand sons instead of one," he said, addressing neither Clérisseau nor Short, "they would not have sufficed to free these countries from their present ignorance and superstition."

"Mr. Jefferson," Clérisseau said sardonically, looking at Short, "is much given to hyperbole."

☆   ☆   ☆

On the steps of the house, leading down to the rue de Berri, Clérisseau paused and waited for the carriage that was to carry him back to the Louvre. "You ought to have stayed with me this afternoon to see Cosway's paintings," he told Short.

The younger man shrugged. He had come down to wait with him out of politeness. But his mind was full of what Jefferson had said, his mild answer to Clérisseau's sarcasm: The American people were the first and last experiment in true liberty; thus far the intervention of a wide ocean had kept them uncontaminated by European vice; they stood now on a high ground of common sense and happiness. But the only sure foundation for their future was knowledge; education alone would keep the common people free. Gently, he had laid his long fingers on Clérisseau's wrist. Preach, my dear sir, a crusade against ignorance, he had said; in this dangerous world knowledge alone protects us.

"Look at this." Clérisseau's voice still had a sardonic, knowing edge. He held out his palm. In the faint light of the door lamp Short saw a square enameled snuff box half the size of a coffee cup. The outside was covered in thin silver filigree of a typically English design.

"When Cosway is not occupied with his portrait commissions, he told me that he likes to decorate the inside of these boxes, for his friends." Clérisseau flipped the lid with his thumb and held the box high in the light. Short's vision transformed the painted inner lid into a blur of colors. He twisted his head slightly to focus. The lid showed a conventional English pastoral; he could make out a delicately painted tree, a blue-green hillside and a stream, a woman on her hands and knees, wearing nothing but a pink corset, and behind her, advancing, a man with an enormous naked member; in front her red mouth closed around another, its owner's back arched in pleasure.

"It crosses one's mind to ask," Clérisseau said with his usual dry mockery, "do you think our friend inside would recognize the model?"

Short found his tongue. "That is *not* Maria Cosway."

"Ah, well." Clérisseau took one last look, then snapped the lid shut. "As to that, dear Guillaume, neither you nor I could truly say."

CHAPTER

Sixteen

 A LITTLE-KNOWN FACT: THOMAS JEFFER-
son could not endure his mother.

No one acquainted with his history could seriously dispute it. In the impenetrably smooth Virginia manner, of course, which places the golden calf of Courtesy on every domestic altar, you can always find someone to describe Jane Randolph Jefferson as mild, gentle, perpetually sweet of temper, the ideal colonial wife and mother, beloved of her family. But I knew Jefferson all together for more than forty years; in Paris I lived intimately with him for five. I have arranged and sorted his private papers, kept his accounts; in recent months interviewed (subtly, subtly) his oldest friends. In all the thousands of sheets of paper he has preserved and I have seen, his mother appears only three times. In all our thousands of hours of conversation, I never once heard him speak her name.

Reference one. At the start of 1770, when Jefferson was twenty-seven and still living mostly at home with her in Shadwell, he wrote his friend John Page a long letter containing, in the middle, a laconic announcement:

My late loss may perhaps have reached you by this time, I mean the loss of my mother's house by fire, and in it of every paper I had in the world, and almost every book. On a reasonable estimate I calculate the cost of the books to have been 200 sterling. Would to god it had been the money; then it would never have cost me a sigh!

Not a word about *her* loss, *her* cost: only "my mother's house," faintly chilling. When the fire destroyed his books, he had already begun building his own house ten miles away at Monticello, where Jane Jefferson would never live; as soon as a room was habitable he moved in; his mother remained with friends.

More chilling: on March 31, 1776—the great year of the great Declaration—Jefferson entered a single terse sentence in his pocket account book. Reference two: "My mother died about eight o'clock this morning, in the 57th year of her age." And to her brother William, then living in England, he wrote offhand and brusquely a month or two later (reference three), not even using her name: "The death of my mother you have probably not heard of. This happened on the last day of March after an illness of not more than an hour. We supposed it to have been apoplectic." More emotion comes through when he writes about the death of a horse or a slave. (Is this coldness of mother and son a Virginian trait? George Washington's mother denounced her son publicly during the Revolution—*he gives me no money,* she complained to Congress, *he lets me starve.*) Nevertheless, at the beginning of April 1776, a few ˙ys after Jane Randolph Jefferson's death, a few months before the final convulsive separation of colony and mother country, which he had long been demanding, Jefferson fell into another of his strange sunrise-to-sunset "megrim" headaches, bedridden and paralyzed for nearly three weeks of pain, just as he did later when Banastre Tarleton chased him off his mountain, just as he did when his infant daughter died—as if his heart had climbed up and taken revenge on its cool, tyrannical head.

From far-off college days I remember a Greek myth about a

man whom the gods cursed by placing a glass window over his heart: Through it anyone could see at a glance what he was feeling; *he had no secrets.* But Jefferson—why else am I writing these memoirs, if not because Jefferson put up a stone wall instead of a window around his feelings? He was unfailingly courteous; courtesy is opaque, courtesy is not emotion.

An additional fact: Jane Jefferson had been born in England, the meddling, arrogant, imperious country Jefferson absolutely hated; all her life, even in the backwoods of Virginia, she kept a London accent. When Peter Jefferson died, did she become (as mothers sometimes do) a kind of benevolent tyrant over the gawky, fatherless boy? Jefferson never liked authoritative, domineering women. For years after his return to America he used to privately denounce poor Marie-Antoinette as inflexible of will and stupidly obstinate; the real, disastrous power behind the French throne. Had there been no queen, he used to say, there would have been no French Revolution.

☆   ☆   ☆

Martha Wayles Jefferson, no tyrant at all, was a widow when Jefferson first met her. Some five years earlier, at age eighteen, she had married Bathurst Skelton, a college friend of Jefferson, and given birth in due course to a son, John; but Skelton died unexpectedly one August afternoon, as men do in the dying time in Virginia, and nineteen-year-old Martha had moved back with her child to the vast Williamsburg plantation of her father, John Wayles, a barrel-chested, big-tempered man of fifty, who had already outlived three wives and settled finally (as all the countryside knew) on a black concubine named Betty Hemings.

I met Mrs. Jefferson once. Unlike her father, she was petite, an odd but charming sight next to the six-foot-plus Jefferson; auburn hair, much deeper red than Jefferson's sandy color; pale, nearly translucent skin that showed the endless dark veins in her arms and neck, as if she were made of blue twigs under white silk skin. Fragile body, soft, yielding manners—the very opposite, one guesses, of the English-born mother he fled as soon as he was able. Martha Wayles Skelton was known for her skill at the harpsichord; she sang beautifully, she wrote music. She was much courted, as a rich young widow would be. I have heard James

Madison tell more than once how two *other* suitors rode up to
Martha's house one afternoon and were shown by a servant into
the parlor. From the next room they heard the sound of a harpsichord. They looked at each other. Then behind the door two
voices rose in harmony, her's and Jefferson's. The suitors looked
at each other again, picked up their hats, and left.

Marriage was Jefferson's object from the start. He has the
female instinct, if one may say it, always to be building his nest,
pulling together his family under his wing. Almost the first thing
he designed at Monticello—right after the site of the house itself—
was the family cemetery, where (ghoulishly) he had his favorite
sister Jane's exhumed remains brought and reburied. Dabney
Carr, his best friend in the world, married Jefferson's sister
Martha and then, like so many other Virginians, went down two
summers later before the great harvesting fever. Jefferson chose
the burying place himself, on the hillside at Monticello, under an
oak. He hired two laborers to dig the grave, and when they had
finished he neatly calculated in his journal that one man digging at
that steady rate could grub an acre in four days. (Look into *that*
window.)

Now if you set out to make the hundred-mile journey from
Williamsburg to Monticello in the summer, an easy day and a half
on horseback will do it. If you set out in winter, as the newlywed
Jeffersons did in January 1772, married on the first day of the
new year, you must usually battle mud and snow and figure at
least three days of hard travel. For their wedding trip Martha and
Thomas Jefferson left little John Skelton with his grandfather
and rode in a phaeton as far as Tuckahoe, eight miles from Charlottesville. There they visited Colonel Carter, and then—in the
aftermath of a blinding snowstorm—pointed their horses toward
Monticello, where all that existed yet was the little graveyard
down the hill and a one-room brick house somewhat apart from
the cleared spot on which Jefferson meant to build. Foolishly
enough, they had lingered till sunset and so climbed steadily up a
winding mountain track, not even a road, in darkness and
whirling snow almost two feet deep. They arrived very late, soak-
ing wet. The fires were all out, and the servants had retired to their
own shacks near the garden. In the one-room house itself, as
Martha shook the snow out of her hair and clothes, Jefferson

reached gleefully behind a shelf of books (he had books and graves before anything else) and pulled out a bottle of wine he had hidden. They sat down to drink, to startle the black, cold Virginia night with songs, and to begin what Jefferson called, with typical mathematical precision, his "ten years of uncheckered happiness."

As always, of course, he exaggerated. Little John Skelton joined them in April, died suddenly in June. Patsy was born in September; survived. Another daughter, Jane Randolph, died in 1775. Mary survived; an unnamed son died in 1777. Martha failed slowly, under shock after shock of birth and death. Jefferson rose to great heights, fell from his mountain. . . .

A decade earlier he had begun his garden book, a little blank volume in which he first took up his obsessive habit of recording the temperature and weather each day and the dates that flowers bloomed and died. He carried it all the way to Paris with him, where I used to file it with his other records, and sometimes sneak a curious look. I can still remember by heart the strangely poignant entries on the first page: March 20, 1776, *"Purple hyacinth begins to bloom."* April 6, *"Narcissus and Puckoon open."* April 13, Jefferson's thirty-third birthday, *"Puckoon flowers fallen."* Every week in the book a new flower bloomed, another started to fade. Jefferson recorded them all. Monticello, Paris, Philadelphia. As President, in the White House, he would send a servant out to the Georgetown flower market to note the arrival of flowers or plants he didn't see himself.

Which Jefferson kept these records? Not the Rebel. Not the Roman. The cool and unforgiving son? The Father, the Husband?

Flowers die and return. Flowers are born again and again, every year. If your father dies, your children, your mother, your sister, your friend, your wife, perhaps at last you fold your arms across your chest and put up fences, just as Clérisseau said. Fences, defenses. You shift your fear away from people onto plants. You place your faith in visible forms of renewal.

I myself have never married.

CHAPTER

Seventeen

"In the case of General Washington," Richard Cosway said, smirking, "everyone in Europe expects he will be king. Nobody believes for a *moment* that a so-called *democracy* will last. And of course, you know him."

Trumbull stroked his chin solemnly and took his time before answering. "I knew him," he said slowly. "I know him. General Washington never changes. He's always the same. And he won't be king."

"Maria says you were his personal aide-de-camp. . . . I didn't realize that." Cosway bared his teeth at his wife. Maria smiled back sweetly.

"Aide-de-camp, yes; that would about describe it." Trumbull wore a smug, self-satisfied expression, as if the term in fact came nowhere near describing him, and Maria found that she couldn't stand to be with either of them a moment longer. Over Richard's shoulder—Richard's fire-red shoulder, because he had purchased two days ago a new coat of China silk the color of an exploding rocket—over the little rubbery puff of color that was her husband, she could see Jefferson and the printer, old Monsieur Hoffman, still doing something mysterious with copper plates and phials of acid. If she ever had children, she thought, they would be born wearing silk coats and baby white wigs like their father, monkey-people. Monsieur Hoffman had a slight, dancing-master's build, and Jefferson literally towered over him.

"They are discussing politics," she told Jefferson, crossing the room and coming up beside him, "which you would *prefer* a lady not hear."

Jefferson showed her a square copper plate the size of his hand. "Some subjects are not fit for a lady's ear. Tell me what you think of our experiment so far."

Hoffman understood bits of English, and he jumped forward with a little French hop and a bow to show her the tin plate that matched the copper one Jefferson held, both of them having been dipped in fluid and pressed together a quarter of an hour before. It had been Jefferson's impulsive idea, as the four of them had strolled along the Boulevard des Italiens—but knowing him now, she suspected he had planned it all days before—his idea that they come upstairs to Hoffman's shop and witness the new engraving process called polytype.

"The sentences you wrote on the copper plate, with the metal pencil"—Maria frowned (she knew) prettily—"now they're being transferred to the tin plate?"

"Which was hot, made hot, heated," Hoffman declared with a little pantomime of touching his finger against an imaginary plate and a snakelike hiss.

"Then you see," Jefferson explained, "the special ink burns into the soft tin from the copper, reverses the script, and you use *that* plate to print as many copies as you need, of whatever you've written."

"You *cannot*," Hoffman declared, "tell the *original* from the *copy*."

Maria blinked. If the original was written on a copper plate, obviously you could tell; but the Frenchman was racing on ahead of his logic. "Franklin came here, you know, just when I started, and he wrote a souvenir for me." Behind her she felt rather than heard the approach of Trumbull and Richard. "Here."

From the crisscrossed stacks of paper and metal on his table, Hoffman pulled a much-thumbed piece of letter-size parchment on which someone had written in a round, cheerful hand. Trumbull pushed in beside her and read aloud, one eye closed: " 'A

Wit's a Feather, and a chief is a Rod; an honest Man's the noblest work of God. Pope. Passy, April 24, 1783. B.F.' "

Maria shook her head, uncomprehending.

"Another quotation from Alexander Pope." Trumbull tossed the paper back on the worktable. "You really should read more, Maria."

"Franklin," Cosway said, a red blossom at Jefferson's shoulder. "You knew him too?"

"Richard has been hearing from his friends," Trumbull said. At the worktable Hoffman had begun to insert his tin plate in a little roller copying press. "They tell him that Washington's house has been burned down by mobs, Congress has fled Philadelphia in a panic; the whole country, in other words, one long scene of tumult and anarchy from north to south."

"Mr. Cosway's friends," Jefferson said courteously, but keeping his eyes on Hoffman, "have undoubtedly been taking their news from the British papers."

"They *lie*, you think," Cosway said with too much emphasis. "The British press *lie*?"

"A strong word." Jefferson now turned to look down at him, smiling diplomatically. "But assuredly they don't tell the truth."

"Ah."

"For as long as I've been in Europe," Jefferson said, "the British newspapers have been reporting the collapse of the American government. By my count, Washington's house has been burned to the ground four times at least, poor Franklin has been stoned and resurrected a dozen times—I think, to be candid, the Crown wishes to discredit our experiment in democracy and rebellion, so they plant false information in the press."

"They are *jealous*?" Cosway's last word hung in the air for a long moment as he and Jefferson gazed at each other.

Maria turned quickly to Hoffman's table. "He's finished!" she declared, pointing.

Hoffman held up a stiff rectangular paper, slightly larger than a calling card. With a little flourish of wrist and arm he extended it to Jefferson, who took a pen from the worktable, bent over the card for a moment, and then presented it—hesitating—to Cosway.

"He doesn't give me one," Trumbull told Maria in a sardonic aside, "because I'm leaving Paris tomorrow. Why waste paper?" Cosway passed the card to his wife.

> *Mr Jefferson begs the honour of*
> *Mr and Mrs Cosway's Company to dinner*
> *on Saturday the 14th of September.*

"He writes in your name *here*," Hoffman said over her shoulder. "He writes in what date *there*. You see? Now it looks just like he wrote it all himself. I make one hundred copies today, in fifteen minutes. Watch!"

"The great advantage," Jefferson told her as Hoffman turned back to his copying press, "is that you print a supply of blanks, use them, print a new supply as often as you like." Maria looked from the card to his enthusiastic face, then back again. To her eye the printer's dark ink and the ink from Jefferson's pen were so different in shade as to make the card quite ugly. But Jefferson's pleasure was unmistakable.

"You can save hours of copying," he said, "and then you simply store the master plate till you need it again."

"Can you copy drawings, engravings?" Trumbull took the card from her fingers.

Jefferson shook his head. "The details are lost, the quality isn't as fine as an artist would want—excellent for handwriting, less good for designs. In fact, I have an idea for changing the mixture of chemicals in the ink. . . ."

As he spoke, Maria raised her face to catch Richard's eye, but as always Richard had contrived to look elsewhere. His right hand brushed imaginary lint from his left shoulder, his wig slipped backward with the motion, exposing an inch of mottled white skin.

"You don't agree, then, that George Washington will be king?" With a little bounce Richard interrupted Jefferson's disquisition on ink.

Jefferson glanced past her to Trumbull—he has also looked at me today just once, Maria thought; a sign of what?—and moved a step or two away from the *thump-thump* of Hoffman's press. "I think no one will be king in America," he said levelly.

"Now three years ago," Trumbull drawled, "then you would have had a case, *then* we were very near to succumbing."

"To a king?"

"Oh, worse."

"He means," Jefferson said, "a military dictatorship, a coup d'état by the army."

"Ah!" Cosway fairly wriggled in delight. "Just as I said—Washington the sovereign, call him whatever you like."

Jefferson had a mild way of instructing, Maria thought. He savored his words, he made large, expressive gestures with his hands (his large hands), he seemed almost to caress his famous facts. You could see the effect on Short, who would stand by him like a schoolboy, thirstily absorbing every word. Trumbull's gruffness fooled nobody as to his admiration. Even Richard's face softened, his pose relaxed, as Jefferson began to talk. She searched her vocabulary for two hard, precise, contradictory words: he was an *intellectual sensualist*.

"In Europe," Jefferson said, "the general impression is that America won the war in '81 at Yorktown, when Cornwallis surrendered to Washington. But the truth is, the war went on almost two years longer. Cornwallis commanded only a quarter of the British forces—an enormous army still occupied New York and much of New England, and though they never fought another serious battle, Washington had to keep *his* army together as long as the British kept *theirs*."

"No pay," Trumbull said concisely, "no supplies, no food."

"Meanwhile the British dragged out the treaty negotiations in Paris, month after month after month. By spring '83, the army was a powder keg about to blow. The soldiers were in rags, starving, clamoring for Washington to march on Congress in Philadelphia and demand their back pay, two years' worth. The officers wanted even more—they were plotting by the hundreds to rebel and establish Washington as their king."

"Colonel Hamilton wrote him a letter proposing it," Trumbull interposed. " 'Call yourself king, regent—whatever title you like,' the colonel said. I saw the damned thing."

"But every country is ruled by a king." Cosway bared his teeth again in his monkey's smile.

"We believe, oddly," Jefferson said, and Maria lifted her eyes at the combination of idealism and irony in his voice, "that all men are equal. The people choose their government, not the army."

"Washington wouldn't hear of it," Trumbull said, "so the officers decided they would rebel anyway and choose somebody else —General Gates, probably, because he hated Washington. I was there, Newburgh, New York."

"Newburgh," Jefferson said, addressing Maria directly, who felt herself flush at the unexpectedness of it, "was the army's winter camp on the banks of the Hudson River. In early March '83 the soldiers reached such a pitch of anger that the officers called an illegal meeting to organize a march. Washington was horrified. He saw civil war, chaos, the collapse of the whole nation if the army set out on its own."

"What did he do?" Cosway's smile had faded. Behind him Hoffman had finished printing the blank invitations and now stood with them in his hand, watching Jefferson's face.

"He called a meeting of his own. March 15, 1783. The single most important meeting ever held in the history of America."

"You were there?"

"*I* was there," Trumbull said. "They had built a stage out of wood and cannon wagons, and about dusk Washington suddenly strode out on it and started to speak. Half a dozen of us wrote it down, every word. He said he had served all these years without pay himself, just for love of country. The officers' faces didn't soften. He said the country they meant to set a dictator over was in fact their own wives and children and neighbors. How could they fight for freedom, then call for tyranny? Not a face softened. He said democratic government was slow, but eventually it would give them justice. If they marched now, they would destroy their own future and wade into a rising empire of blood." Trumbull paused. "Faces like stone."

"And then . . . ?"

"And then a great thing happened," Trumbull said. "The general had finished his speech, clearly, but nobody was convinced. He hesitated up on the stage, then he said he remembered he had a reassuring letter from someone in Congress, and he pulled it out of his pocket. Now you have to understand—Washington is the most magnificent physical specimen you have ever seen. Six feet tall, built like a gladiator, he used to lead every charge of his army, out front in the middle of rifle fire, cannon fire, pistol fire—he would come back to us, his uniform riddled with holes and cuts, tatters, but himself unharmed, always. Once, they said, in the French and Indian wars his units broke in half and started to fire on each other by mistake, and Washington rode between them on his white horse knocking up their musket barrels with his swords—you never saw such a *man*. But he was fifty-one years old at Newburgh, he was growing old. He pulled out the letter and stared at it and swallowed helplessly. And all the officers in the audience leaned forward, suddenly anxious. He looked up, he looked to his left, square at me. Then he pulled out of his other pocket something only his closest aides had ever seen him wear—a pair of little wire eyeglasses—and he put them on. Then he said, 'Gentlemen, you will permit me to put on my spectacles, for I have not only grown gray but almost blind in the service of my country.' "

"And the officers wept," Jefferson said softly.

As they shook hands with Hoffman and started down the stairs, loaded with samples of printing, Cosway turned back, grin pasted in place once again, and told Jefferson that of course they accepted his invitation for dinner. "Which I can read, you see, without spectacles."

Beside him on the staircase Maria stiffened with embarrassment and looked away. Jefferson and Trumbull had lived so *seriously* compared with them, compared with her. At the street she tried to think of a comment on Trumbull's story, something wise, *true*.

"So General Washington took no advantage of his situation,"

she said; "he was self-sacrificing, yes?" As she spoke she saw Jefferson fumbling with his papers. On the Boulevard des Italiens a carriage careened too close, spraying mud and straw, and everyone scattered, shouting, turning in a whirl of bright skirts and hats. She stumbled backward into the doorway, furious, and swiped with her fan at a stain. Then in her hand she saw the second card that Hoffman had printed.

> *Mr Jefferson begs the honour of Mrs Cosway's Company to dinner on Sunday the 15th of September at the "Désert de Retz."*

CHAPTER

Eighteen

"I think," Jefferson said, settling back into the carriage seat beside her. The coachman, evidently well instructed beforehand, set off down the rue Coqhéron without a signal. In her lap, for reasons she could not explain, Maria Cosway's hands trembled like birds. "I *think*," Jefferson repeated, "that after two years I must have seen every form of wagon and voiture that there is in Paris."

"And made a list of them, I'm sure." In honor of the excursion to the Désert de Retz, Maria had chosen a new straw bonnet with two long trailing blue ribbons, a full skirt of blue silk to match the ribbons, and a bodice of silk and Venetian gauze, finer than lace. Some instinct had led her to prepare secretly a little portmanteau of other things — Richard had walked through her room without even glancing at it — and hand it to the coachman. At no point in her life, she thought, gripping the edge of the bench, had she ever felt so unhappy and anxious.

"Not a formal list," Jefferson said, smiling.

She touched his wrist with the tip of her fan, a gesture all the more daring, she thought, because they seemed so utterly alone in the coach.

"Well," he laughed, "not a *written* list, in any case."

"*Bien.* Let me guess." She held up the fingers of her left hand, swaying slightly with the motion of the wheels, and began to count. "I've been here only a month. But there are remises, cabriolets, phaetons, fiacres, wiskeys, turgotines—" She stopped and frowned, and Jefferson raised his own hand to indicate a little brown carriage going past in the opposite direction, bobbing like a cork. "And *désobligeantes,*" she said, "but I never know why they're called that."

"Ah. Because you cannot seat another person next to you, as we are. It disobliges them."

Maria smiled much more brightly than she had intended.

In another moment their own carriage—Jefferson's phaeton-calèche, with its crimson wheels and blue roof—entered the Place Louis XV, boiling as always with wheels, horses, clouds of dust. The Tuileries appeared on their left, then the equestrian statue of the king on their right, and Jefferson was pointing and saying something about the statue, lost in the noise. Maria nodded but looked past his hand toward the top of the square, where a pair of tall buildings framed the pillars of a handsome new church whose name she suddenly could not remember.

"Now those are the public, commercial voitures," Jefferson explained. "They're not on my list. They go from here to Versailles or Saint-Cloud, and you pay the driver a fee each way."

Maria leaned toward his window to see, grazing his shoulder, inhaling, not the thick cologne that Richard always wore, but Jefferson's lemony soap. The three long *carabas* that stood on the west end of the square all had ornate blue fleurs-de-lys painted across the doors, but otherwise they looked like gigantic mud-stained loaves of bread on wheels. The nearest driver lounged on his seat, shirtless and dirty in the morning sun. He stared goggle-eyed as they rattled past, while his bony horses shifted on their hooves in front of him and a line of waiting passengers snaked along the pavement. She shuddered and sat back in the carriage.

"We have much less elegant ones in America," Jefferson told her, amused. "I've climbed out many a time and helped push a wheel over a ford."

"But not today."

"Today," Jefferson assured her, with a sudden lifting of the chin that made him look still taller, "will be perfect."

The Désert de Retz was a celebrated garden in the *style anglo-chinois*. It lay about four miles from Saint-Germain, twenty miles from Paris. To reach it was an all-day excursion that required them to pass along the right bank of the Seine to Passy, then cross the Pont de Neuilly—Jefferson's favorite bridge—and take the broad, dusty highway for Saint-Germain.

"You've invented a new word," Maria told him as they left the bridge. She had turned to face him in the carriage, holding her lips in a light, half-mocking smile that she knew he liked, but her eyes were on the trees lining the highway. *"Americanism,"* she said. "Mr. Short told me you invented a new word, *Americanism,* but he was very unclear what it meant." Behind Jefferson, in the blink of an eye, the leaves of the trees had transformed themselves into living claws. Snapping, waving, like the hands of a great yellow-green devil in their hundreds and thousands, they swung down toward the carriage window. Maria's heart pounded like a drum. Her scream died in her throat.

"I used it in a letter," Jefferson said, "that William happened to copy. He was quite taken with it, but I only meant it to describe a position of political sympathy with the United States—'Lafayette's Americanism is never in doubt.' Not a very good word," he added doubtfully.

"English is so curious," she said. In another fraction of a second, as always, the metamorphosis had reversed itself, the leaves were retreating into their natural shape, God's shape. She told *no one* about her visions, *never.* Especially not Jefferson, whose mind was so rational and masculine. Not since the day Trumbull had showed his paintings at the Hôtel de Langeac had either of them mentioned her Catholicism. But what else were her visions if not spiritual signs? They had come to her because of the danger she ran, because of the nurse leaning over the cradle, reaching. How else would God speak to an artist?

"Are you all right? Are you well?"

Maria brushed the air with her fan. Life came to a point. Things came to a point. "I'm very well. Very well." She took a breath. "I was only thinking of Mr. Short. Poor in-love Mr. Short pining away for that pretty Duchesse de La Rochefoucauld. Rosalie. Did you see how he followed her from room to room two days ago? So white and pale—I felt sure he would drop to his knees on the spot and declare himself." She fanned the ribbons of her bonnet. "And the duc may be old and preoccupied—the right word, yes?—but he notices."

Whom was she trying to warn? Herself? If he saw the parallel, Jefferson chose to ignore it. His expression was distant, impenetrable. "I had noticed nothing," he said.

"Oh, well." She flushed and beat the air with her fan, making the silky ribbons fly.

Before Saint-Germain they had to pass Marly. Although they had come out two weeks before, in one of Trumbull's groups, to see the château and the king's famous water machine, Jefferson insisted that they stop again and stroll, while the driver rested the horses. These were machines, she knew, after Jefferson's own heart. He had made the whole party walk up the sloping hillside to admire what Louis the Magnificent had wrought—an actual mountain of soil moved, an uphill aqueduct that rose nearly six hundred feet from the Seine to carry river water into a reservoir. From the reservoir—Jefferson had recited each number with an engineer's precision—the water turned fourteen great ironwork wheels that worked two hundred and twenty-five pumps that forced eight thousand tons of water every twenty-four hours into more aqueducts and pipes, which in their turn supplied the jet fountains and waterworks of both Versailles and Marly. He deplored (he said) the king's wastefulness, the outrageous expenditure of money simply to create a fine *joujou* for the Court; but she could see in his eyes, his stooped attention to every detail of the clattering pumps, how much he really liked it. Anything mechanical, she thought, any little *device* held his attention like a magnet. A practical man, rational, unlikely to see visions. And yet at this very moment he was gripping her arm and pointing rapturously with one broad hand at the long, disappearing line of rainbows, inexpressibly beautiful, thrown up by the spray of the whirling pumps.

The Désert de Retz, an hour farther away, had likewise been created by an engineer, but an engineer, Maria thought, trapped in a feverish dream. She had seen buildings in England that were purposely built, from the very start, as ruins—it was all the rage (a bizarre expression, English was such an *angry* language); Horace Walpole's estate at Strawberry Hill, where Richard had once tried to charm a commission or two, contained a striking Gothic chapel, half its roof caved in, one stone wall crumbling to the ground, the whole thing constructed just two years before as a conversation piece in which Walpole and his guests could wander and indulge their sense of fashionable melancholy. As always, however, in matters of fashion, she decided, the French went far beyond the English.

At the entrance to the Désert they paid their fees by a shiny grotto, scooped like a giant black seashell out of a hill, and then, tickets in hand, pushed forward to see what Jefferson dryly announced as "the latest ruin." It was in fact not a simple chapel in the garden as at Strawberry Hill—it was the house of the owner himself, a massive ruined column sixty-five feet in diameter, four stories high, built of limestone and plaster, and Jefferson's dryness of tone was no more than a momentary pose. With barely a word to his coachman he sprang from the carriage, turned with boyish energy to hand her out, then started down one of the winding paths toward the base of the column. As they walked, he gestured broadly, eyes on the high broken roof before them, long legs moving so rapidly that Maria found herself almost trotting to keep up.

Monsieur de Monville, the engineer-owner, had lavished a considerable fortune to achieve the effect he wanted. When they drew up to a grassy space in front of the column, Maria gasped in surprise. Closer, from the carefully designed overlook, the column expanded to fill the sky. Its jagged roof seemed to disappear by strange, irregular steps into the clouds; its windows, set back in the flutings of the column, stood open to reveal an interior of delicate gold and damask furnishings, a spiral staircase, filmy white curtains, everything new, everything in the latest style, in total, brilliant contrast to the gray unadorned stone walls around them.

"The idea," Jefferson said.

"The idea is grand, grandeur." She clapped her hands together. "It makes you see in a new way—so huge, melancholy, such power in stone cut away and humbled. On s'est extasié!"

Jefferson spoke again, softly, and it took her a moment to realize that he was quoting verse.

"Say it again."

She had heard from Trumbull that Jefferson never made

speeches in public if he could help it—his voice became reedy like a boy's, from sheer nerves—but here, suddenly, to her complete amazement he lifted his head toward the column roof and repeated the poem in a strong, mournful chant.

" 'Raise the song of mourning, O bards, over the land of strangers. They have but fallen before us: for one day we must fall. Why dost thou build the hall, son of the winged days? Thou lookest from thy towers today; yet a few years, and the blast of the desert comes; it howls in thy empty court, and whistles round thy half-worn shield. Let the blast of the desert come!' "

"Ossian!" she cried.

"You know Ossian?"

"Ossian is my favorite of all poets." Maria seized his hand between her two hands, forgetting Richard, the garden, the other visitors strolling the paths. "You all talk about Pope, you and Trumbull and Short—Pope! I *hate* Pope!—and Latin and Greek, and I feel so ignorant I could scream. But Ossian—I know every poem by Ossian. The first painting I ever exhibited at the Royal Academy was a scene from Ossian—Darthula showing herself to Caibar, her lover."

Jefferson was smiling down at her. Somehow his other hand now covered hers. They stood facing each other in the cool shadow of the broken column. From the house, she thought, from the garden, to other eyes they would seem to have struck an attitude of two lovers absorbed in each other. But they were, she thought, discussing art.

"You've met the Marquis de Chastellux?"

Maria nodded, conscious against her will of the warmth of his hand; both their hands.

"He came to Monticello, it must have been four years ago, and stayed with us for a week. One night after my wife had retired to bed, he and I sat down by a bowl of punch and talking of this and that came to the subject of poetry. He asked if I had ever read the poems of Ossian—it was a spark of electricity that passed between us. I quoted a verse, he quoted another. I called for the book to be placed by the bowl, and we sat till past midnight reading aloud and quoting."

"Richard calls Ossian a fraud."

Jefferson shook his head. "I have heard people say—in England—that Ossian never existed. They claim the translator Mac-Pherson actually wrote the poems himself as a hoax, but I know no reason to believe it. I corresponded with MacPherson, in fact. Ossian was an ancient Gaelic poet, the Homer of our climate; his every word was sublime. Sublime."

Maria lowered her eyes. Their hands slipped apart like ribbons. "Was your wife also fond of his poems?"

But Jefferson had begun walking along the path, toward the yew hedges that led to the formal gardens.

The hand that created the tower had not hesitated to scatter more ruins across the acres and acres of land surrounding it. As they wandered along the brown gravel paths, laid out in the "natural" English fashion rather than along the geometrical lines of French gardens, Jefferson kept a running count: no fewer than twenty-six buildings of various styles, eras, functions. They paused at a small ruined Gothic church that put Maria in mind of Walpole's estate. (Determined to show herself intellectual and cheerful, she repeated Walpole's famous bon mot: "The world is a tragedy to those who feel, a comedy to those who think.") Jefferson smiled acknowledgment and pointed out to her a Chinese *orangerie* planted incongruously just beyond the church. At the *orangerie* they plucked one of the hard little fruits and proceeded with it, peeling the skin, holding the sticky pulp for each other to taste; at the next ruined structure, a *temple de répose* (according to Jefferson's guidebook), they could sit on a stone bench and look across a lake to an Egyptian obelisk.

"This is," Jefferson said, "a genuinely silly country. I'm fond of it; I am—most of the time—glad to be here. But it is undeniably a frivolous country."

Maria drew her skirt to one side. "What is the 'silliest' thing you have seen?"

Jefferson had finished the orange and was wiping his fingers with one of the white handkerchiefs he carried. He answered slowly, tilting backward on the bench and clasping one knee in the casual pose that Trumbull had told her looked like a human jack-knife, whatever that was.

"When I first arrived in Paris," he said, "I was invited to Dr. Franklin's house in Passy, where he wanted to introduce me to Parisian society. The first woman I met—and I still remember her

name, the Baroness d'Oberkirsch—wore her headdress extrava-
gantly high. She was short, I may say a *very* short woman, so that
her headdress rather than her face looked me straight in the eye
while we talked. At first I saw only a white powdered expanse,
sprayed with starch my nose told me, wrapped in a kind of white
muslin. Suddenly—I was just bending my head to hear better—
out of the headdress sprang five or six fresh flowers, each one held
by a little spring and a vial of water concealed in her hair. The
effect, she told me—I must have looked as if I had seen an appari-
tion—was 'Springtime in the Midst of Snow.' "

Maria laughed, leaned toward him.

"Now you," he said. "The most frivolous, silliest thing."

"Besides Richard's red coat?" she said, and for a long moment,
the beat of a heart, the loud flap back and forth of her silk fan,
both of them were silent. Then Jefferson was wiping her own
fingers delicately with his handkerchief and saying softly, behind
a mask of light and shadow, "Oh, yes, even besides Richard's
coat."

Kindness always won her more than wit. She laughed gratefully
—to her own ear, much too loudly, a coquette's laugh—and
cocked her golden head as if in thought.

"Do you know the *décrotteurs*?" she asked.

Jefferson released her fingers. He shifted on the bench, out of
the sun, so that his long, serious face seemed closer than ever.
"The *décrotteurs*," he said, "are the boys who stand at street corners
and scrape your shoes after you cross the street."

"Because of the mud. The horrible, terrible, *smelling* Paris mud,
it ruins your shoes, your dress, everything."

"Which is why you ladies take carriages or ride in sedan chairs.
Walkers like me come home every day splattered up to our knees."

"The third day in Paris," Maria said, "a storm broke—we
hadn't met you, I had nowhere to go, Richard was far away
painting. I sat at the window and watched the rain. Then an
enormous old lady came out of the door opposite—a duchesse at
least, I'm sure, dressed beautifully, jewels, cape, silk—but she had
to cross the street, she had no carriage. So she simply stood at the
door, waved to a *décrotteur*—a husky boy about twenty—and when
he reached her, she paid him a coin *and hopped on his back*!"

Jefferson threw back his head and laughed.

"Like a sack of feathers!" Maria said. "He carried her all the way down the street and out of sight. The 'silliest' thing I've seen."

Still laughing, Jefferson stood and took her arm. At the last sight in the garden, an ice house shaped like an opaque glass pyramid and filled at this time of year with nothing but damp straw, he bought her tea from an old woman and presented her, from his pocket, a little sketchbook and pencil to use in her art — but only on American subjects, he cautioned, when she came to visit him (with Richard) at Monticello and could draw the Natural Bridge, the Falling Spring, the sublime passage of the Potomac through the western Blue Mountains.

Maria listened, smiling. In her imagination she pictured a scene like Italy, populated with cypresses and animal stockades and tall, glowing churches whose heavy doors slammed shut behind her.

In the carriage she resolved to tell him that she was truly Catholic, that foolish and sinful as it seemed, she still dreamed of being a nun. Hadn't she begun life by almost becoming a martyr? Therefore— But her hands had started to tremble again, like frightened birds, and she shoved them away, into the blue recesses of her skirt. Jefferson took her right hand and stroked it into stillness. You would have needed a heart blinder than stone, she thought, not to know what lay in the air between them.

He studied her fingers and spread them one by one in her lap. "I've sent for my daughter Polly," he said, pretending to measure and count her rings while he talked. Why did he think her hands trembled? She was a married woman, her husband wore absurd silk coats. "But my sister delays and delays and puts me off, and to tell the truth I fear a sea voyage for her almost as much as I do leaving her over there, in Pennsylvania, to grow up without me."

"You are very lonely then?"

When he looked up, Jefferson's smile had become tender, melancholy. "This is not a world to live at random in. Everything is a matter of calculation. The art of life is the art of avoiding pain. Am I happier to leave her an ocean away, safe with another person? Or to risk everything and bring her to me? The Head and the Heart are always locked in combat, you see."

"I am not at all clear," Maria said boldly, "that we are speaking of Polly." But she spoiled the effect of boldness by turning away

quickly toward the green-and-brown blur of the flying landscape,
so that she was not even certain that he had heard her.

At the inn of the Trois Couronnes, a mile or so past Marly,
Jefferson had arranged a dinner for them, the dinner of his engraved invitation—his servant Petit, in fact, had traveled out separately, supervised the table, and then melted away discreetly as
they entered their private dining room.

The windows opened onto a meadow, and beyond the green
band of its horizon a careful eye could just make out the six
pointed rooftops of Louveciennes, a casino built years ago for the
old king's greedy mistress Madame du Barry.

"Say nothing in criticism of its architecture," Jefferson joked,
offering her a glass of the sparkling white wine Petit had poured.
"A king's mistress has royal powers. Do you know that old man
DeLatude who comes to take soup with me sometimes?"

Maria shook her head. Among the many contradictions of Jefferson's character was his habit of talking to workers or peasants
—his lanky aristocratic figure literally stooping to hear them—or
inviting odd, rather disreputable figures into his home.

"DeLatude spent thirty-five years in the Bastille and the dungeons at Vincennes, and that for the sole crime of making four
verses on Madame de Pompadour. I remember the verses:

'Sans ésprit, sans sentiment,
Sans être belle, ni neuve,
En France on peut avoir le premier amant:
Pompadour en est l'épreuve.'

'Without wit, without sentiment, without beauty or youth, in
France one may still have the greatest lover; Pompadour proves
it.' He escaped three times and wrote his memoirs."

"You like a rebel," she said.

He poured more wine into her glass. "Dr. Franklin was once
playing chess with Madame Helvétius, and happening to place her
in checkmate, he reached across the board and snatched her king
away, quite gleefully. 'In France we don't take kings in that way,'
she told him. 'In America,' he replied, laughing, 'we do.'"

At table, with the window to her left, the soft rolling landscape in a golden twilight, she could see past his shoulders to the private staircase that led to the second floor of the inn; her portmanteau had long ago disappeared with the coachman.

"I think," he said, spooning a delicate sauce, pink and rich, to cover the fish on her plate, "that I have now quoted poetry twice in one day—something I must not have done since I was a student at William and Mary College hundreds of years ago." In the candles' light his fair skin had taken on a reddish flush; his hands, she saw with surprise, now trembled as much as hers. "You paint, you sing, you restore a friend's youth. How can there be any contest between Head and Heart?"

Maria seemed to float above herself, a cloud looking down on dolls at play.

"You are a famous statesman," she blurted out, to the last a creature of tremulous impulse, not knowing why she said it.

"What I have become," Jefferson said, and afterward, recalling his tone of voice, the intensity of his face lowering toward hers, she understood he was making a gift of himself, exposing himself; she was certain he had not spoken to anyone else like this, not even his wife, not ever his wife. "What I have become," he said, "the times made me become." Like her, he made no move to taste his food. "As a young man I thought of myself as a poet and scholar. I read and wrote twenty hours a day, I breathed literature. I wanted only to live on my mountaintop surrounded by my family, reading and farming. I gave up the practice of law when I was very young; I had no ambition beyond my books and my home. If the Revolution had not come, and duty, duty—shall I tell you what I think? I think politics has distorted my nature. Politics has made me retire within myself, defensively, all the while I stand publicly open to every gaze. I cannot bear to stand up in public, I cannot bear to be seen as I really am, except by the eye of friendship."

She felt herself moved by every word, every pulse of her heart. She wanted to repay him somehow by explaining that she too had not become what she should have been, her nature too had been distorted by the times—had her father not died, her four baby brothers, had her mother not sold her on the auction block of London society to the highest bidder, to Richard; her visions, her belief were what lay at her core, and unlike him she could not make a gift of them.

"Then you *are* lonely" was all she could say.

Jefferson lifted her hand to his lips.

As they rose from the table, she remembered at last the name of the new church they had passed that morning in Paris: the Church of the Madeleine, named after a sinner.

He drew her toward the stairs.

☆   ☆   ☆

"It's much too late to be working," Clérisseau said from the door.

Short jumped in his chair and dropped his pen. Beside Clérisseau, who was holding his gold watch up to his ear, James Hemings shrugged and made a Parisian moue of resigned annoyance. "I told him you said no visitors."

Clérisseau snapped the watch shut and waved him away with effusive thanks. "He said you were writing, and I said that was preposterous. You Americans are always writing, you and Jefferson. I call it the American disease. Spillers of ink. *Furor scribendi.* I was traveling past, bored, nothing to do, so I appointed myself physician to scribbling Americans. Jefferson, by the way, has the ill manners not to be home yet."

While he talked, Clérisseau strolled about Short's sitting room, inspecting furniture, lifting curtains, running a finger across the marble mantelpiece over the fire. Now he stopped in front of the desk and raised one significant eyebrow at Short. With exquisite timing James reappeared, this time carrying a tray of brandy and glasses.

"A disciple of Hebe, cupbearer to the gods." Clérisseau took the tray in his own hands. "Bless you."

Short cleared a space on his desk and locked away his letters in a drawer. When he sat up again, Clérisseau had filled two snifters to the brim and James was just closing the door behind him.

"Is it true, my dear Guillaume, that in Virginia you give slaves the names of Greek and Roman gods?"

Short held the snifter under his nose and thought about the question. Beware of Frenchmen in ebullient moods. It was true, in fact, that at Monticello Jefferson had a trusted manservant named

Jupiter, and another one named Great George, sometimes called George the Ruler or King George by the family.

"Not true," he said firmly.

"I don't believe you." Clérisseau pulled up a chair beside the desk. "What were you writing?"

"Letters. Dispatches. Business."

Clérisseau twirled his own brandy under his unmistakably French nose, inhaled with his big eyes closed, then opened them and shook his head. "Because it would make a certain ironic sense, of course, to name the most powerless people after the most powerful. I am convinced that you do."

"You yourself have been making the rounds of powerful people tonight. Or at least their tables." Short indicated the wine stains on Clérisseau's ruffled shirt.

"She's not the model for his snuff boxes, you know. *Vous savez.* Our Maria."

"I know."

"But I enjoyed your expression when I said it. Do you know the other rumors? That Monsieur Monkey, her husband, is fond of men as well as women? I have it on the authority of d'Hancarville, our phallic expert. Or that the Prince of Wales seduced Mrs. Cosway—as who could blame him? that halo of golden curls, those ribbons!—seduced her and had a secret passage built between her house and his palace. The monkey was rather proud."

"Clérisseau, it's late." Short's own watch lay face-up on the desk, hunting case open, hands pointing to half past ten. He turned it for the Frenchman to read.

"And finally, in London she tells five hundred intimate friends that she secretly longs to be a nun. She intends one day to enter a convent in Italy. By a secret passage, I suppose."

Short rubbed his hands across his face. Even through his closed windows he could hear the rumble of wagon wheels at the Grille de Chaillot and nearby, in Jefferson's garden, the song of a bird that he had recently learned to identify as the nightingale, unknown in America, the staple of every French love poem.

"Jefferson has spent the day with her, yes?"

Short was impatient. He waved the question away.

"The ways of Paris conduce," Clérisseau said blandly, refilling his snifter. "Is that an English word? Conduce?"

" 'Are conducive to,' " Short said.

"Yes. The ways of Paris are conducive to pleasure between men and women. Even scribbling Americans might notice. There is the king and his mistress to set an example, of course. The Marquis de Lafayette and his squadrons of ladies, Talleyrand and the delightful Madame de Flahaut, whom you certainly must meet—her mother was a royal mistress before her, it's rather by way of being a family career. In Paris we think in terms of scandal, which is entertaining, but not shame, which would be frivolous."

"C'est bien la vie sportive," Short said, managing to his ear a reasonable semblance of Parisian nonchalance.

"And how is our charming friend the Duchesse de La Rochefoucauld?" Clérisseau asked.

Short choked on his brandy.

"If I were about to leave," Clérisseau said, grinning, "instead of staying to finish my drink and greet Jefferson, I would depart with a wonderful exit line. Do you know the great *mot* of Beaumarchais? 'To drink when we are not thirsty and make love in every season—Madame, these are the only things that distinguish us from the animals.' "

He raised his glass.

CHAPTER

Nineteen

J ames Hemings remembered an excellent sentence in one of his books: "Les rues sont l'image du chaos." The streets are the picture of chaos.

Swaying, he gripped the smooth iron shaft of the streetlamp and stared through the crowd at the butcher. If you stayed up by Jefferson's house and the Boulevards, you never saw anything like this. You saw animals, of course, horses and oxen and little herds of fat white French cattle being driven through the streets, shitting and bellowing and knocking down fences and walls; you saw horses racing full speed over the pavement, huge dogs in front of carriages clearing the way, poultry, geese, wagons full of rabbits and ducks in cages. But in the Faubourg Saint-Marcel you saw life the way it was, coming apart in bright red explosions of blood.

"Un joli boeuf," the Frenchman next to him said.

James nodded. In front of the crowd the butcher had now wrestled the steer down to the filthy cobblestone street. The butcher lifted a club the size of a brick and hammered it down in one straight overhead swing, so hard that even thirty feet away, pressed between dozens of chattering Frenchmen, James heard the skull crack and the steer's head bounce against the pavement.

The crowd sighed. The steer writhed on its side and moaned.

With a bound the butcher had straddled its massive neck and pulled out of somewhere a long curving knife that glinted in the sun like a fish before it darted suddenly down toward the outstretched throat. The blood pumped horn-high in brilliant jets.

The butcher jumped back—skating on blood—then hurdled the steer's flank and dropped on his knees by the belly. James saw his back, his head dipping, his red arm plunge. The steer roared and kicked its back legs high in wild convulsions. The crowd pushed forward, murmuring, watching intently as the butcher's hands started to yank the entrails out, pink slithering ropes of skin that a boy caught and coiled in his arms. But James's eyes never left the animal's face. As the butcher sliced and pulled, James fastened his gaze on the brown snout, the great black wondering pupils. Each roar, each feeble shake of the horns drew him closer. The steer twisted his neck, raised his head in anguish. In the corner of his vision James saw the butcher's hands again, then the red heart beating, then the knife.

Chaos to the steer. Order to the butcher.

Every Monday he had the day off, no cooking lessons, no household duty. In the spring months he had wandered the Boulevards until he knew every inch, stopping in like a regular at all the white men's cafés, reading British newspapers at the bar, ending the day (or night) at Denis's three-room bead-curtained brothel with young Marcella, she of the squirming black limbs. But come the hot weather and the long days he had taken to wandering east, far past the Opéra and the Boulevards and all that Jefferson, fancy, silk-swaddled Paris. Faubourg Saint-Marcel, the city's ant-hill, that was where he came now, every Monday, drinking brandy for breakfast and watching animals die.

The Frenchman beside him wanted to parley—"Vous êtes noir? Vous êtes noir?"—but James shook him off, tucked his bottle under his coat, and started to walk. On the Quai de la Feraille they sold birds, men, and flowers—the men were young country drunks hauled staggering up to an army recruiting booth by a bounty-hunter, the birds and flowers were offered to servants and couples passing from the markets or over the bridge to Notre-Dame. James had seen the flower merchants follow a customer half the length of the quai and, if he refused to buy, cover him with mud. The recruiting officers lounged under posters and crooked little fingers at him like a girl.

You'll come back dead, Adrien Petit had warned him; *one of these days you'll walk down an alley in the Faubourg Saint-Marcel, and a Savoyard will drag you back here on a litter, dead as a rock, knifed through the throat.* The Savoyards were the errand boys of Paris. They clustered in groups at street corners, wearing soft caps down over one ear and culottes held up by cloth belts sailor-fashion. They lounged and waited for work, anything from scraping shoes or putting down planks over the mud—Paris was the City of Mud— to carrying letters or parcels right to your door. Rough, loutish boys mostly, but they ran their groups with such severity—no robbery, no drunkenness, no knives—that people entrusted them with the most amazing errands. In James's presence Petit had once handed a Savoyard a package of money for Jefferson's banker and sent the boy off without asking so much as a receipt. Petit was right, they would carry his corpse home piggyback . . . as long as Jefferson paid them.

By nightfall, he had reached the seventh stage of the seventh stage of drunkenness, as his mother used to say. He was slumped in one of the smoky *tripots* next to the Bastille and pushing cards across a table with a crew of broken-toothed, red-eyed soldiers, playing a game he didn't know, by rules that changed with every new bottle. At some point the soldiers disappeared, and he found himself outside on the streets again, weaving along the mossy wall of a building and breathing in sharp foreign smells—French straw, French spices, the cadaverous dead-geranium odor of a nearby church. Jefferson never went to church, but once in a while, remembering the slave houses at Monticello and the Sunday services halfway down the hill, James would go by himself into a Paris church. The trouble was, the French left their corpses in them overnight, before the funeral, so many corpses, so few windows, the churches smelled like wet boneyards, you gagged and choked the minute you entered.

Jefferson.

The man bathed his feet in cold water every morning—to keep off diseases, he said. James knew. Each day he carried the basin upstairs as soon as it was light and put it down by the bed, and

Jefferson was always already awake, dressed except for his shoes, reading or writing something by candle.

"Vien ici, James. Je vais vous donner quelque chose à boire, du café."

James blinked himself—it seemed—to a sitting position. Braced each hand on the arm of a chair, watching a skinny white man with greasy hair pour him a stream of coffee, right out of a pewter pot.

"You're a slave, James."

"I know what I am, you stupid old man. In Paris I'm a free man."

"I mean you're a slave to *that*." The Frenchman pointed to an empty bottle of cognac, emerald-colored and twisted wrong somehow at the neck like the body of a plump green chicken, and James made a point of looking in the other direction, still blinking, forcing the walls to stand still. It was Le Trouveur's little one-room apartment, upstairs, off the rue de Charonne, and James had been there half a dozen times, sober once, drunk the rest, talking earnestly in French with the filthy old man, who carried a five-sided bull's-eye lantern wherever he went, even in his room, and made his living finding things in the street. Le Trouveur, the Finder. In daylight he set up a little stall near the Pont Neuf where people could come and see his display of found objects. At night he took his lantern and crept over the slimy pavement like a big white rat. The streets, James thought, were the image of shit.

"Slave to strong drink," the old man repeated. "Have this."

James raised the cup to his mouth. A year of cooking lessons had given him a nose that could separate ten different smells in a single dish. Have this, the teacher would say, handing him a bare wooden spoon from the bowl, and James could sniff and lick his way through a whole recipe of ingredients—ginger, yeast, saffron, two kinds of dill. The old man's coffee had a strong taste of caramel, like most French coffee; the warm grounds stuck to his teeth like sugar.

"You remember Jean-Claude?"

James nodded. The third man in the room was Le Trouveur's particular friend, another old tramp who made his living off the streets. Why the hell did he come here instead of staying in the

Faubourg Saint-Honoré, where people washed their cups and had carpets instead of straw down on the floor? James opened his eyes and offered a little mock bow to Jean-Claude across the room.

"It's too late for Jean-Claude to go home," Le Trouveur said, earnest as always. "Les espions, vous savez."

James looked at Jean-Claude without interest. One of the stranger things about Paris was that outside the Fauborg Saint-Marcel, the streets were genuinely safe, you could go anywhere (almost anywhere) anytime day or night without fear of bandits or thugs; but from nightfall on the police had spies hard at work, tracking suspicious characters, informers, prostitutes, gamblers, foreigners, occasionally demanding papers, usually content just to have their presence felt. Jefferson hated the spies; he called them the king's black angels.

"Got a load of posters, right?" James forced a little grin. Jean-Claude lived by pulling down posters. Paris was covered with them, of course; batlike, they flapped on every street corner in the city. What the old tramp did was go out by night with *his* lantern and strip a place bare, then sell the posters to butchers and grocers who used them for wrapping or to one of the box-makers on the Quai Tournelle who turned them into crude packages. He also burned them for heat in the winter and used them himself for blankets and shoes. He could read, so he had a little system. Posters that advertised books and medicine he left up; but he took down anything that advertised puppet shows, circuses, theatrical performances, anything he disapproved of. Since posters were theoretically illegal, the police paid no attention whatever to Jean-Claude, who was nevertheless convinced that their spies followed him everywhere. The strongest single drive in human nature, Jefferson had told Short, was the need to feel *important*.

"You remember what I told you, James?"

Le Trouveur sat down beside him and refilled the cup. James squinted at the old man's skylight; overhead was not black, not blue, somewhere in between, meaning he still had time to go outside, walk to the Grille de Chaillot, fall asleep in his own bed.

"You remember? I read it to you right out of the *Mercure de France.* Slavery does not exist in France. You could be a free man, just go and tell him. You have brothers and sisters?"

"I have my sister. Sally."

"She's here?"

"She's coming. *Maybe* she's coming. He sent for his little daughter, and Sally's coming with her, as the maid. If the boat ever leaves."

"How old is Sally?"

"Fourteen. Fifteen." At Monticello the date of a slave's birth was not necessarily recorded in Jefferson's book.

"She could be free; you both could be free."

James sneered. "Free like you? Sniff around the street on all fours, *poor*? Free like him, nothing to worry about but food and money and jail?"

Earnestness was an impenetrable defense. In the gloom of his bleak little room Le Trouveur came up with sheets of paper, some kind of pamphlet. James heard the word *petition*. Le Trouveur pressed the pamphlet into his jacket pocket. It was written by somebody named Condorcet; it told how a slave, even a diplomat's slave, could submit a paper to the courts and be free.

"Free to starve," James spat, struggling to his feet. But he held on to the pamphlet, and outside, in the cool September night, he gripped it fiercely in both hands as he walked, like a club.

☆　　☆　　☆

Like a brighter, silkier club, Jefferson held up Maria Cosway's pink parasol twelve hours later and pointed it into the wind.

"Such a wind, such a wind," she said, using one hand to grip the edge of her straw bonnet, the other to press down her fluttering skirt. "Such a *warm* wind."

"It won't last," Jefferson said, smiling. Every tree in the Tuileries seemed to sway and toss under the wind, like so many huge green balls bouncing. "In half an hour it should all be calm as a baby's cradle."

Maria looked down; looked away; looked at the long, sad river that ran next to the gardens.

At the same moment, a mile farther up the Champs-Élysées, James Hemings dropped into his chair and braced his elbows on the kitchen table. He was used to brandy, he thought glumly. He drank wine or brandy by the bottle six days out of seven, and the only price he ever paid was a bad temper that his mother said he had been born with anyway. But this morning he craved coffee, hot coffee to soothe his brandy-soaked brain, and fresh, cool air to replace the heat of the kitchen.

He grunted at one of the kitchen maids and sat back in his chair while she brought his cup. Then he fumbled in his pocket and brought out a slip of paper.

It was one of Jefferson's peculiarities that he liked to collect recipes. He was known to ask anybody, even one of his elegant French hostesses, to write down the recipe for something they served him, or else he would copy recipes himself from books, adding annotations in English and little unreadable drawings, and then pass them along for James to try.

James rubbed his forehead and unfolded the newest acquisition. They had progressed a long way since the earliest instructions for heating the oven just right, to avoid burning a crust. This recipe—James sipped the scalding coffee and blinked—this recipe, which Jefferson said he was going to send to everybody in Albemarle County, was for a new dessert called ice cream. James smoothed the paper on the table. A cold dessert. You made a mixture of custard and vanilla flavoring and ice and salt in a wooden container, then when it was frozen, you scraped it out with a spatula and put it in tin molds packed with more ice-salt, pounds and pounds of it.

He shook his head, regretted it, looked up.

At the fireplace the old woman who did most of Jefferson's ordinary cooking was down on her knees stoking the fire. To her right the turnspit dog sat on his treadmill watching. She was cooking beef, James noticed, which meant company today, since Jefferson and Short ate practically no meat themselves; which meant that in another hour the kitchen would be a furnace. Which meant that making ice cream there was a near impossibility.

Overhead in Petit's office the floorboards creaked. James fingered a bit of raw meat from the cutting board and chewed it. When the old woman slid farther along the grate, he flicked another bit of meat to the dog. Crazy dog. Sat all day on its dirty blanket till the cook gave the command, then it walked and walked and turned the treadmill that in turn rotated the spit and cooked the meat over the fire. Half a side of good dripping beef close enough to grab and run with, if the dumb black dog ever had the courage. Call the dog James.

He licked his fingers and thought of yesterday's dying steer.

He wanted more coffee. He wanted to sit outside on the steps with his cup of coffee and hold his aching head in his hands and figure out how you roasted meat and made cold ice cream both in the same red-hot kitchen.

"Fait chaud, chaud, chaud." Petit came into the kitchen suddenly, sniffing the air, wiping sweat from his face.

"Dans une heure fait chaud," James said, just to contradict him.

"Hot, hot," Petit said, stopping in front of him. "You were late last night, mon chat."

"I'm here this morning."

"Monsieur will dine at three." Petit pretended to consult his notebook but in fact stared over it at James's sullen face. "Six guests. Madame Cosway. Short. De Corny, three others. Dessert you know about."

The brandy had made him quarrelsome. James stretched to his full height, giving him a head's advantage over the Frenchman, and began to object; it was too hot to make ice cream *and* cook beef. He would make pastry instead, the hell with the guests. They could eat macaroons, or else brandied peaches and cake; he would go ask Jefferson for permission to alter the menu.

Petit only shrugged and turned a page in his notebook. Jefferson was out, he said, walking with Madame Cosway, but not very far away; they had set out for the Cours la Reine ten minutes ago. Spoken sardonically: James was a privileged person. James the black could do as he liked.

James could. Muttering to himself, he stamped up the stairs, slammed a door, and emerged by the wall on the rue de Berri. For half an instant the sharp, hot wind made him think about turning around and going back; then, still muttering, head throbbing, he set off down the Champs-Élysées.

On the map of Paris he kept pinned to his wall, the public gardens of the Cours la Reine stretched along the river from the Tuileries almost to the Grille de Chaillot, but in fact, with their mania for building, the Parisians had started to erect rows of houses at the western end, in sight of Jefferson's door. James pushed between two slow-moving wagons and crossed the dusty road.

Closer to the city you had to pay to enter the Cours—you had to pay to enter *anything* in Paris—but by the customs wall and the Grille, for no good reason that he knew, there were still a few unmanned gates and turnstiles. He bent his head against the wind and followed the first gravel path down through a series of blowing hedges and onto a bare terrace.

He spotted them practically at once, off to the right, by a circular bed of red and white flowers. He squinted and guessed: a quarter of a mile away, but he'd have to take a zigzag path twice as long to reach them, just like a maze.

He rubbed his eyes and thought. Jefferson, of course, would know exactly, down to the inch, how far away they were. On Judgment Day Jefferson would be writing down the temperature of fire and brimstone, counting the number of steps it took to walk up to the Judgment Throne, down to Hell.

Virginia was Hell, James thought.

Jefferson and the woman disappeared behind a bush and came out by a series of waist-high wooden fences. Even at this distance —whatever it was—James could see the pink ribbons on the woman's bonnet blowing back behind her. Jefferson carried a rolled-up parasol in front of him like a stick.

Foutre, James thought, using the foulest French word he knew. He would go back and make the fucking ice cream. Why walk all that way and whine?

But he stood for a moment longer. Jefferson's way of moving today, his way of walking, was like a boy's. At this distance, with her bonnet and curls, and Jefferson with his red hair and lively step, they looked like a young couple. They looked like Jefferson ten years ago and his wife Martha.

At the first fence Jefferson evidently said something. The lady shook her head. Jefferson took a step, extended his right arm toward the fence rail, leaned into the wind, and jumped.

Even where he stood James could hear the knock of his shoe against the wood, then an instant later the snap of Jefferson's wrist as the bone broke and he fell.

James had already run fifty yards down the path toward them before he remembered the exact same sound of the steer's skull hitting the ground.

It sounded, Short thought, as if the man were drunk.

"You get the *other* surgeon too," he said furiously, "and you get him *now*, before I slap you sober!"

Short spun on his heel and opened the door to Jefferson's bedroom. His cheeks still burned with anger. One part of his mind told him that if you spoke to James that way, you guaranteed he would slouch and sulk and do the job nigger-speed if at all; but Jefferson was in actual, visible pain, and his wrist had already swollen the size of a melon, and the idiot French doctor standing by the bed was smiling and scratching his wig and doing *nothing.*

"William—"

"Sir. I've sent for another surgeon. I think the bone is broken." Short approached the bed and stooped to examine Jefferson's wrist, which lay like a detached object on a white silk cushion (the surgeon's sole useful contribution), while Jefferson himself stretched full-length on his bed.

"I must have told you," Jefferson said softly in English, "that whenever I see two or three doctors together, I always look up in the sky for a buzzard."

"Sir, the swelling is even worse."

The surgeon began to rattle in French, a French so pompous and Latinate that Short couldn't stand to hear it. He cut him off with a wave of his hand.

"Sir—"

"Mrs. Cosway is still here?" Jefferson had lifted his head.

"Downstairs."

"You really must take her home, William. And cancel the dinner. And tell Petit to bring up my letter file. Next week, you know, Thursday—"

"Sir"—it was a measure of his anxiety that Short let himself interrupt—"I'll speak to her now. But Petit, the letters, all that can wait; you need to rest."

"I'm thinking of the bust of Lafayette." Jefferson glanced at the doctor, who still stood, thumbs hooked in his vest, studying the swollen wrist. "Does he speak English?"

"Not a word," Short said, straightening and turning to go; and under his breath, *foutre.*

In the downstairs salon, under the painted ceiling, he found Maria Cosway holding open one of the French doors and looking into the garden. Her dress and ribbons today were pink. Her face was paler and more stricken than Jefferson's.

"You really ought to leave," Short said bluntly. "I've canceled dinner."

"And he —?"

"The bone is broken, he's in great, great pain."

"He wanted, you know —" She fluttered her hands in a gesture that Short thought of as purely Italian. "There was a little fence, and too much wind. He was vaulting on one hand, jumping."

He had been showing off like a schoolboy, Short thought, like a damned schoolboy; the least impulsive man in Paris jumping a fence to show off for a girl.

At the street he handed Maria into her carriage and bowed without another word. The new surgeon arrived at virtually the same moment, following James and Petit into the house. As he hurried after them, Short made a mental list: With a crippled right wrist, leaving aside the unthinkable questions of gangrene or permanent deformation, there would still be no playing of the violin for months, if ever; no tinkering with watches and tools, no riding on horseback — he stopped on the stairway landing, watched the surgeon go through the door, and finished the list. Without his wrist Jefferson could not write a word.

CHAPTER

Twenty

Jefferson passed the night in sleeplessness and pain. From time to time, when the swelling appeared to subside, the two surgeons probed the bones with their fingers and consulted each other (Short thought) in thick oleaginous French. Toward morning they attempted to straighten the hand and forearm with wooden splints, but they went about it so clumsily that even their stoic patient cried out in protest. By noon the next day, they had only strapped the wrist in a tight leather bandage, and Jefferson could walk, gingerly, holding his arm to one side like a broken wing.

To Short's amazement, on the day after the accident, Maria Cosway neither came nor wrote. On the evening of the second day, as he sat at his desk in the study contemplating the bust of Lafayette that Jefferson was to present to the city in a week, a Savoyard brought him a small blue envelope tied with a feminine ribbon.

Short stood up, covered the bust with a cloth (let us have no prying eyes), and paced to the center of the carpet.

Like other diplomats, Jefferson kept a journal in which he recorded, with a brief summary of contents, every letter that he sent or received, even the most trivial inquiry or invitation. But this . . . this was, by ribbon alone, no official letter. Short tapped the envelope on the side of the desk. If it were *his* letter or *his* journal, would he want it recorded?

He turned the envelope in his hand. Thought of Maria's pale, strangely unresponsive face in the salon, her spider-legged husband. What could she possibly have to say now?

When he turned the envelope over again, he saw that the ribbon had come untied.

Parigi Mercoledì Sera

I hope you dont always judge by appearances or it would be Much to My disadvantage this day, without my deserving it; it has been the day of contradiction, I meant to have had the pleasure of seeing you Twice, and I have appeard a Monster for not having sent to know how you was, the whole day. I have been More uneasy, Than I can express. This Morning My Husband kill'd My project, I had proposed to him, by burying himself among Pictures and forgetting the hours, though we were Near your House coming to see you, we were obliged to turn back, the time being much past that we were to be at Saint-Cloud to dine with the Duchess of Kingston; Nothing was to hinder us from Coming in the Evening, but Alas! My good intention prov'd only a disturbance to your Neighbours, and just late enough to break the rest of all your servants and perhaps yourself. I came home with the disappointment of not having been able to Make My apologies in propria Persona.

Short folded the letter once but held it clear of the envelope. No one had come to the house last night, late or otherwise. And obviously Cosway had scotched completely the scheme of coming to visit that morning, if the scheme had ever existed. Why should a husband carry his wife to her—? He stopped himself and glanced at the back of the letter. A final paragraph in Italian. Short frowned and translated the first few words. She wrote so badly in English, she said; she was his obliged servant, *obligatissima,* and true, true friend.

Outside the window a horse's hooves clattered on pavement. A water carrier's voice rose in the peculiar singsong rhythm of the streets. Short disliked Maria as he had never disliked a beautiful woman in his life. She was superficial, ignorant, self-deceiving. On the other hand—his mind flickered for an undisciplined moment to the image of Rosalie de La Rochefoucauld—on the other hand, by living with Jefferson, he was hitching a ride on the coattails of history, he was *obligatissimo* to the facts.

With a smile not entirely unconnected to his own word *self-deceiving*, he sat down at the desk and began to copy the letter.

On the twenty-eighth of September, ten full days after the accident, Jefferson's wrist had still failed to heal. Short walked through a rank of French dignitaries, most of them dressed in a dazzling show of wigs and ribbons and brilliantly colored regimental jackets, explaining to them for the sixth, tenth, twentieth time that Jefferson's injury was indeed grave—"très, très pénible"—and regrettably prevented the ambassador's appearing before them.

Secretly, Short thought (he moved to the top of the wooden platform built specially for the occasion and tucked his hat under his arm), secretly he believed that Jefferson's dislike of public speaking had kept him at home quite as much as the broken wrist.

"Monsieur Chort!" the herald announced.

Short took his place next to Lafayette on the crowded platform. ("I am not yet twenty-nine years old," Lafayette whispered to him in French, bending very close and breathing some foul combination of perfume and clove into Short's face.)

"Nor am I," Short said. A military band was marching into the great hall of the Hôtel de Ville, drums rattling. He deliberately looked away from Lafayette, whose enormous teeth were now fixed in a perpetual grin. In fact, it was only three days ago, while he copied down Jefferson's dictated letter of presentation, that he had realized how young Lafayette was, how much (by comparison, for example, with a diplomat's minor secretary) the Frenchman had genuinely accomplished already. Short bowed to Éthis de Corny and allowed himself a moment of conspicuous if false admiration for the bust, still covered at this point by a silken cloth, which he was about to present to the City of Paris on behalf of the State of Virginia.

"My wife, my aunt, my sisters and cousins," Lafayette hissed in his ear, and as he raised his head, Short saw them all, standing in the first row of guests, beaming up at the boy-patriarch like a box of flowers. He had begun to look around (cynically) for Lafayette's two Iroquois retainers as well when the band struck up an anthem. The mayor stepped forward.

It was, Short later admitted, a truly grand occasion, though no one in the room except himself knew how much it owed to Jefferson's tireless diplomatic maneuverings, from the first hint of the idea to the Virginia legislature to the last, nearly comic negotiations on his sickbed with the representatives of the king, including the popeyed *éminence blanche* Rayneval himself. No small thing, after all, to present a statue of a military hero who had helped overthrow a king to the hero's own rather suspicious, certainly unpopular monarch. More practical by far, Jefferson had said ironically, to give Lafayette a tract of land in Virginia, which he might need one day as a refuge from said king.

When the mayor—inexplicably titled prévôt des marchands, provost of merchants—motioned Short forward, Lafayette clapped him on the shoulder and, contrary to all protocol, advanced as well, taking a place directly beside him, grinning and smoothing constantly his bright red general's tunic (like a blazing pineapple, Short thought). In his best French, Short read aloud Jefferson's flowery letter of presentation, the band broke into another anthem and marched around the platform, and Éthis de Corny, Jefferson's friend and Lafayette's former commander, replied on behalf of France, declaring in a voice that rang through the crowded hall that even the ancient republic of Rome would have been honored by such patriots as Washington, Franklin, Adams—he paused—and Jefferson. While the applause broke in wave after wave and the bust was formally unveiled, Short stood with his plumed hat under his arm, hand on the dress sword he had never drawn, and thought that Jefferson's words, Jefferson's irresistible phrases, had begun to color French speech as much as American. Only a fellow writer (though Short had written nothing) could appreciate the real Revolution here; the transformation of ideas through language, that had every mouth repeating "all men are created equal," "the pursuit of happiness," that made disobedience to kings into a civic virtue. Short glanced with sympathy toward Lafayette. Victories in battle were nothing compared to victories in language.

"Une nation libre!" de Corny concluded with a flourish. A free nation!

Afterward, having drunk far more champagne than was diplomatic, Short murmured a remark to de Corny (too loud, too *stupid*) that was to be quoted for weeks across Paris: I am persuaded on this happy day, Short said, toasting the hero's wife, that Madame Lafayette did not receive more pleasure on the night of her marriage.

Early on the morning of October fifth, using only his left hand, Jefferson wrote out a brief note and handed it to James Hemings to deliver.

TH: JEFFERSON   TO MRS. COSWAY

I have passed the night in so much pain that I have not closed my eyes. It is with infinite regret therefore that I must relinquish your charming company for that of the Surgeon whom I have sent for to examine into the cause of this change. I am in hopes it is only the having rattled a little too freely over the pavement yesterday. If you do not leave Paris for Antwerp today I shall still have the pleasure of seeing you again. If you do, god bless you wherever you go. Present me in the most friendly terms to Mr. Cosway, and let me hear of your safe arrival in England. Addio. Addio.

Within an hour James brought back an answer, which Short personally carried up to Jefferson's sickroom.

I am very, very sorry indeed for having been the Cause of your pains in the Night. Why would you go? You repeatedly said it would do you no harm, I felt interested and did not insist. We shall go I believe this Morning, Nothing seems redy, but Mr. Cosway seems More dispos'd than I have seen him all this time. I shall write to you from England.

You will make me very happy, if you would send a line to the poste restante at Antwerp, that I may know how you are.

And then, to the astonishment of everyone, the least impulsive man in Paris came down the stairs, fully dressed, calling loudly for his coachman.

He drove, Short afterward learned, straight to the Cosway residence on rue Coqhéron and, despite the great pain in his wrist (reset moments before by the surgeon), accompanied the two Cosways, their entourage of servants and baggage, and the heavily sighing Monsieur d'Hancarville in a crowded coach as far as the Porte Saint-Denis, where the travelers shifted to a touring carriage.

"The behavior," Clérisseau commented cheerfully, "of a Frenchman, not an American. We have metamorphosed Monsieur Jefferson in record time. In a few years, who knows, he may become as gallant as Franklin."

Short ran his finger over the files of correspondence that, as usual, he was sorting and arranging in Jefferson's system, and debated whether to show it to Clérisseau.

"The picture I like best." Clérisseau paused to raise the back of his hand to his nose and inhale a microscopic bit of snuff. It was a habit he had recently taken up, he said, to honor America. "I like the thought of the four of them crowded together in the carriage. No doubt the monkey-faced little husband sat facing the lover, knee to knee, sword to sword, while the lady blushed behind a mountain of white crinoline and Hancarville, poor Hancarville discoursed mile after mile on the antique prick." Clérisseau made a face at the snuff and wiped his hand on his coat. "No doubt Jefferson told Cosway all men are created equal."

Short tapped the letters into place and closed the file.

"What are you hiding?" Clérisseau demanded.

"A private affair."

"Not if you lift it halfway out of its envelope, slide it back and forth, lift it again, and generally dangle it like a worm before a trout."

Short allowed himself a slow grin. Clérisseau was a trout six feet tall, with an exophthalmic expression (one of Jefferson's words: it meant pop-eyed), and a white wig and a sword. "It's nothing. Jefferson has been writing a treatise on English prosody, but I've had to copy it for him, because of his wrist."

Clérisseau lost interest at once. He sniffed delicately and waved the letter back into the file. "Poetry," he said with well-bred distaste. "Now he passes over the line from gallantry to boredom."

But Clérisseau, Short thought, had no idea what line Jefferson had crossed. Upstairs, in his own room with the door locked, he spread out the file again and examined the last letter, twelve pages not only written laboriously with the left hand but then copied out all over again for the record. Record of what? If ever there were a personal, private letter, this was assuredly it. If ever Thomas Jefferson came close to abandoning his intense reserve, dropping his high fences—he had simply written, Short thought, the strangest love letter he had ever read.

MY DEAR MADAM,

Having performed the last sad office of handing you into your carriage at the Pavillon de Saint-Denis, and seen the wheels get actually into motion, I turned on my heel and walked, more dead than alive, to the opposite door, where my own was awaiting me. Mr. Hancarville was missing. He was sought for, found, and dragged downstairs. We were crammed into the carriage, like recruits for the Bastille, and not having soul enough to give orders to the coachman, he presumed Paris our destination and drove off. . . . At the rue Saint-Denis Mr. Hancarville insisted on descending and traversing a short passage to his lodgings. I was carried home. Seated by my fire side, solitary and sad, the following dialogue took place between my Head and my Heart.

Head. Well, friend, you seem to be in a pretty trim.

Heart. I am indeed the most wretched of all earthly beings. Overwhelmed with grief, every fibre of my frame distended beyond its natural powers to bear, I would willingly meet whatever catastrophe should leave me no more to feel or to fear.

Head. These are the eternal consequences of your warmth and precipitation. This is one of the scrapes into which you are ever leading us.

Short stopped. Although he had read the letter hastily twice before—unable to believe Jefferson would keep a copy, let alone have him file it with everything else, let alone—he inhaled sharply, brought his thoughts under control; started over. How could Jefferson write to his lover in the form of a dialogue? A dialogue. Short squeezed his left eye halfway shut and tried to bring into focus the candle on the other side of the room. Dialogues had been a popular literary form forty years ago, when David Hume and

Bishop Berkeley were writing didactic philosophy; Jefferson the rebel had oddly conservative literary tastes. . . .

The candle remained stubbornly out of focus, a nebulous white globe against a watery background. Short switched eyes. It was typical of Jefferson to make everything, even love, into a debate, a clash of logic, head versus heart. With mild surprise Short realized that he had begun to think of Maria Cosway as Jefferson's lover; with rather more surprise he admitted, against all the rules of French life, that this profoundly disturbed him.

> *Heart.* . . . The Halle aux Bleds might have rotted down before I should have gone to see it. But you, forsooth, who are eternally getting us to sleep with your diagrams and crotchets, must go and examine this wonderful piece of architecture. . . .
>
> *Head.* It would have been happy for you if my diagrams and crotchets had gotten you to sleep on that day, as you are pleased to say they eternally do. . . . Every soul of you and your new friends had an engagement for the day. Yet all these were to be sacrificed that you might dine together. Lying messengers were to be dispatched into every quarter of the city with apologies for your breach of engagement. You particularly had the effrontery to send word to the Duchesse d'Anville that in the moment we were setting out to dine with her, dispatches came to hand which required immediate attention. . . . Well, after dinner to Saint-Cloud, from Saint-Cloud to Ruggieri's, from Ruggieri to Krumpholtz, and if the day had been as long as a Lapland summer day, you would still have contrived means, among you, to have filled it.
>
> *Heart.* Oh! my dear friend, how you have revived me by recalling to my mind the transactions of that day! . . . Go on then, like a kind comforter, and paint to me the day we went to Saint-Germains. How beautiful was every object! the Port de Reuilly, the hills along the Seine, the rainbows of the machine of Marly. . . . Recollect the King's garden, the Désert. How grand the idea excited by the remains of such a column! The spiral staircase too was beautiful. Every moment was filled with something agreeable. The wheels of time moved on with a rapidity of which those of our carriage gave

but a faint idea. And yet in the evening, when one took a retrospect of the day, what a mass of happiness had we travelled over! . . . The day we went to Saint-Germains was a little too warm, I think; was it not?

A phrase tugged at Short's memory. He turned his head sideways and watched the candle flame leap for once into perfect focus. When Martha Wayles Jefferson had lain dying in her bed, hadn't she scribbled a few short lines that Jefferson had finished? —*Time wastes too fast: every letter I trace tells me with what rapidity life follows my pen.* The same word. *Rapidity.* The same Jeffersonian sense of time flying, time lost.

Short put down the remaining sheets of paper, vaguely embarrassed. He remembered what followed in the dialogue. The Head said it was better never to make friends than to lose them and suffer; the Heart claimed suffering was part of life, there was no sublime pleasure without it. In the midst of everything, predictably, Jefferson began to talk of America—Maria should come to America and paint it, perhaps someday (sheer fantasy) she would have to seek asylum from wicked old Europe and he could welcome her—welcome them *both*, husband and wife—to his house.

Of course he would write in dialogue form, Short thought, disgusted with his own obtuseness. The lady was *married*. No matter how warm it had got at Saint-Germain, the Roman would always observe the outward proprieties. But this attraction for married, for *forbidden* women—he glanced at the last page of the dialogue as he folded it away. Jefferson was such a perfect machine of contradictions himself, so perfectly balanced, he had left it unresolved who won the debate, Head or Heart. But Short felt certain that Maria, who could barely write a grammatical sentence in English, would have no idea at all of the subtlety of Jefferson's tribute.

☆ ☆ ☆

In fact, in Antwerp, Maria sat down with the whole dialogue and read it three times through before looking up. Trumbull, lounging in the corner of the room, his right foot on a low table, his teacup resting on his chest, met her violet-blue eyes and smirked. He had delivered the letter to her himself, confidentially, since Jefferson had enclosed it discreetly in a letter to him; Jefferson would send all his letters thus, he had explained, because of the "infidelities" of the French mails.

Trumbull arched his eyebrow in a disagreeable way he had recently cultivated and lifted his teacup from the saucer, as if making a toast.

"Our friend is well?" he asked in French.

Maria smiled brightly. "He has copied the words to a French song for me," she said, "such a long song."

"And which one is it?" Still in French.

" 'Jour Heureux,' " she said, pretending to look at the letter.

"Not so very long," Trumbull said in English, with the faintest possible intonation of mockery.

"I shall go into the other room and write him my thanks," Maria said, but without moving. An English melancholy had descended over her once again, she thought; her face and neck were like stiff sheets of paper cut out with scissors, full of sharp angles and corners; she was an unreal person. In two more days they would be in London. The image of that smoky, gray, stone-faced, fog-smothered city came to her eyes almost like a vision. The wheels of time, Jefferson had written, moved on with a rapidity . . . She had forgotten the rest of the beautiful sentence. The wheels of time were carrying her back to London. In drab, Protestant London there would be no monasteries where men of God prayed at all hours for all those others who did not pray, who were lost and in need of rescue.

"I shall write him my thanks," Maria said after a long pause.

"When," Trumbull asked, uncoiling himself from the chair like —she thought—a snake, "when do you think you will return to Paris?"

"I shall probably return next spring," she said. "To Paris."

Trumbull no longer bothered to hide his smirk. "With Richard?"

"Or without him," she said calmly, but closing her eyes.

CHAPTER

Twenty-One

Memoirs of Jefferson — 7

 I PICTURE TO MYSELF TWO SCENES.
Identical, contradictory.

One, late May 1765, Williamsburg, the House of Burgesses furiously debating what action to take in response to the infamous Stamp Act just passed by Parliament. Thomas Jefferson, then twenty-two years old and still a gangly red-haired student, all collapsible elbows and knees (as his friends remembered him), standing rooted at the doorsill of the lobby intent upon the speeches. Patrick Henry, dressed as usual in preacher's black, with a dour, sour kind of look and an habitual farmer's slouch much like Jefferson's; a member of the Burgesses, almost thirty years old, but coarse-featured and rustic and virtually unknown in Williamsburg, rising to take the floor in front of the most sophisti- cated and polished gentlemen in Virginia.

Nobody ever cared less for that kind of polish. Henry's speech, which started calmly, soon rose to a pitch of furious, terrible invective against the injustice of the Stamp Act and the tyrannical pretensions of the almighty British Parliament, which had assumed for itself the unlawful right of taxation over the king's free-born, liberty-loving colonies. As Patrick Henry paced back and forth and roared defiance, the assembled legislators, still thinking of themselves as loyal British subjects (and thinking too, no doubt, of the formidable royal governor Lord Botetourt, not half a mile down the street in his brick palace), began to mutter or call out to him. He paid them no mind. Mesmerized, Jefferson pushed to the first row of the crowd.

Henry approached the end of his speech. He halted in front of the speaker's bench, then slammed a rough fist down on the railing, under the nose of the king's attorney-general, Jefferson's spectacularly rich, spectacularly fat old cousin Peyton Randolph and, ignoring Randolph's huge red face, launched into his perora-tion. "Caesar had his Brutus. Charles the First his Cromwell. And George the Third"—here the room rocked with noise and protest. "Treason!" screeched Randolph, struggling to his fat feet. On the other side of the floor Jefferson's own professor of law, George Wythe, sprang from his chair: "Treason!" Half a dozen voices joined the cry. Black-clad Patrick Henry simply stood, hands on his hips, in calm defiance. When the cries of treason began to fall away, he raked the room with a look, reared on his heels, and finished thunderously—"and George the Third may profit from their example. *If this be treason, make the most of it!*"

Afterward, defeated nineteen to twenty, shoving past Jefferson in the lobby, Peyton Randolph swore to his followers that he would have given five hundred guineas that day for a single vote. Presumably his lean young cousin did not offer his own opinion then, though he repeated it in awe for weeks after, that Patrick Henry had gifts as an orator beyond anything Jefferson had ever imagined—"He appeared to me," he told his friend John Page, paying a characteristically bookish compliment, "to speak as Ho-mer wrote."

Query: Did this rebellious admiration come from Jefferson's own miserable limitations as a speaker? Or was he merely en-gaged, as always, in some kind of inner debate, choosing sides (for the moment) between the crude upland energies of his own peo-ple, out in the wilderness of Albemarle County, as against the smug, self-oiling political machine of the Tidewater sophisticates? Are politics the mere extension of our childhood? Peyton Randolph was his cousin on his mother's side. Patrick Henry came out of the backwoods frontier world that belonged to his father. The day after his speech, Henry was seen starting for home along the Duke of Gloucester Street, wearing torn buckskin breeches, saddlebags over his arm, leading his horse.

And query: Was Patrick Henry what the mild, rational, self-disciplined Jefferson was not: "sublime"?

Scene Two. Ten years later, March 23, 1775. The old white clapboard Church of St. John, on one of the seven hilltops of Richmond, where the Burgesses, now much less smug and smooth, are gathered illegally to debate the momentous question whether, in this year of crisis, Virginia ought to arm its militia like other colonies and prepare for civil war.

Jefferson, seated as a member of the Burgesses, now a prosperous young lawyer, and author the previous year of a brilliantly hot-headed pamphlet called *A Summary View of the Rights of British America,* which had succeeded in placing his name on a list of "traitors" marked by the British Parliament for hanging. Patrick Henry coming to his feet once again and striding down the aisle to the tiny space in front left cleared for speakers, while up and down, in every pew, the audience, which knows their man by now, stirs in expectation.

It was so unseasonably hot that morning, Jefferson once told me, that all the church windows were flung open (townspeople leaning in to listen) and the air burned when it moved. Henry's face was pale white, but his eyes also burned (if you can credit some of the more melodramatic witnesses) and glowed like coals. As always, he began with the appearance of deliberation. It is a question of freedom or slavery, he said. He has only one lamp by which to guide his feet in this question, and that is experience. Experience tells him that the British ministry will respond to more petitions and more addresses, just as they have already in Boston, with sneers and soldiers. What do we have to oppose them? Shall we try argument? We have been trying that for the last decade. Have we anything new to offer them on the subject of American rights? Nothing. There is no need for Virginians to deceive themselves. The storm is ready to break.

Henry was a legendary master of the orator's pause, the long, daring moment of silence. He liked to stop and draw his body up out of its slouch and wait rigid till his audience had grown unbearably tense. James Madison used to claim that when he had argued a case in patient detail for two hours, Henry would get up slowly, pause and stare at the jury, and undo everything before he had uttered a word. Now he simply broke off in the middle of his speech and glowered at the ceiling. Then: They say America is weak and can never stand firm against Great Britain. We are *not* weak. We are three millions strong.

And more than that—I sat one long afternoon on a porch front in Williamsburg and listened to three old men act out by turns the way Henry had suddenly exploded into his tremendous conclusion. The oldest one of them even wrote it down for me, word for word, with every gesture he remembered.

"Besides, Sir, we shall not fight our battles *alone*. There is a just God who presides over the destinies of nations, and who will raise up friends to fight our battles for us. There is no retreat but in submission and slavery. Our chains are forged. Their clanking may be heard on the plains of Boston. The war is inevitable. And let it come! I repeat, sir, let it *come*!

"Gentlemen may cry peace, peace, but there is no peace. What is it that gentlemen wish? Is life so dear, or peace so sweet, as to be purchased at the price of chains and *slavery*?" Here, the old men said, Henry stood in the attitude of a condemned galley slave, loaded with fetters, awaiting his doom. His shoulders were bowed; his wrists were crossed; his face was twisted into helplessness and agony. After a long, long pause he raised his eyes and his chained hands toward heaven and burst out, "Forbid it, Almighty God!"

Then he turned toward the part of the church where the Loyalists had taken seats together, and he slowly bent his form nearer and nearer the floor and said, "I know not what course others may take," and his hands were still crossed, his face was heartbroken and hopeless. Another pause, longer even than before, so that you could imagine the Loyalists imagining the condition of Virginia under the chains and iron heels of the invading British Army. Suddenly he rose straight and proud—"But as for me"—and his thin body was thrown back, every muscle and tendon seemed to strain against the invisible fetters that bound him, and he hissed the words through clenched teeth. Then the loud, clear, triumphant notes, "Give me liberty," and as each syllable of the word *liberty* echoed through the church, his fetters were shivered; his arms were hurled apart; and the links of his chains were scattered to the winds. When he finished the word *liberty* his hands were open, and his arms elevated and extended, and after a momentary pause, only long enough to permit the ringing echo of "liberty" to cease, he let fall his left hand to his side and squeezed his right hand firmly, as if holding the point of a dagger toward his breast. And he closed the grand appeal with the solemn words, "or give me death!" and suited the action to the word by a blow upon the left breast with the right hand, which seemed to drive the dagger straight to his heart.

Query: How many people in St. John's Church that hot March morning knew that Patrick Henry, loaded down with rhetorical chains, struggling against invisible British coils like Laocoön against the serpents—how many people knew that Henry had a wife who had been insane for years, tied up in a leather strait-jacket and padlocked chains and kept in a basement room of the house, with a trap-door entrance in the hall down which Henry climbed every day to feed her?

How many people thought about what *other* kinds of chains and liberty he meant?

And query: Who can picture—for one instant—Thomas Jefferson in such theatrics?

The privacy of pen and ink was Jefferson's medium. As President he could hardly bear the thought of standing up before an audience; apart from his inaugural address, he sent every message, including the State of the Union, in letter form to Congress. But a little-known fact, a footnote: When Patrick Henry had finished his "Liberty or Death" oration, his audience, as you might expect, lay collapsed, prostrate with emotion around the sweltering church. One man even fell to his knees at the last words, weeping, and raised his hands and shouted, "Let me be buried on this very spot!" But so absolute was Jefferson's dedication to liberty, to the cause, that after all *that* he nonetheless had the courage to rise and walk to the rostrum himself, something he dreaded to his very core, and then he too gave a speech in support of going to war. Nobody heard a word of it. But for twenty minutes he held the floor, arguing for freedom. He told me it cost him a month of headaches afterward.

Did the sublime Henry ever acknowledge Jefferson's greatness?

When he wrote his *Summary View* in 1774, Jefferson was too shy or diffident actually to give it as a speech before the Burgesses as it was intended to be. He set out from Monticello for Williamsburg with two copies of it in his saddlebags, *meaning* to speak. But somewhere along the road he began to suffer one of those attacks of diarrhea (like the headaches) that seemed to come to him in crises. Was he thinking perhaps of the notorious British punishment for treason: hanging, but cutting down the victim while he was still alive and ripping out his intestines, then burning them before his eyes? Or was he thinking (more likely) of the hundreds of eyes that would be staring up at him while he gave his speech? He turned back to Monticello. He sent one copy to Peyton Randolph (now a dedicated rebel), one to Patrick Henry. Randolph thought the speech was so brilliant he had it printed at once. Henry never mentioned it—"he probably left it on a tavern table," Jefferson would say scornfully, later. "Patrick Henry was the laziest man in reading I've ever known."

Hard words from Jefferson. Hardest possible words, given the books that filled every room of his house, on whose backs he always rode. But if Jefferson had chosen sides once at the age of twenty-two, by the time of the Revolution he had seen ten more years of life, and Patrick Henry, the backwoods Homer, had lost his power to charm. What kind of hero, after all, was forever playing his "fiddle" by a campfire and watching the farmers dance? (The fiddle versus the violin.) Or joked his way through his bar examination ("I never studied law six weeks in my life," he told Jefferson, snickering)? Or rose to speak for liberty in front of any audience that would hear him, almost like an actor hired for the part, but rarely stuck around for the long, tedious committee work that followed? Henry was a geyser of rage next to Jefferson, a wild creature of ignorance and passion. When the two finally parted political company, Henry set out to ruin Jefferson with his incessant talk of impeachment and cowardice and flights from Monticello. In his turn, Jefferson stubbornly believed (without any evidence) that the great orator for liberty had plotted in the last year of the Revolution to make himself Dictator of Virginia. Even after the Revolution was over, he wrote Madison (another mumbling, inaudible speaker) that "While Mr. Henry lives, another bad constitution would be formed and saddled forever on us. What we have to do, I think, is devoutly to pray for his death."

Jefferson had no sense at all of the *mysterious* in life; every sense of the *uncontrollable*.

CHAPTER

Twenty-Two

"**P**ère Grasse at our school says that God speaks perfect French as well as Hebrew. What do *you* say, Mr. Short?"

Patsy Jefferson put down the glass of wine that she was permitted to hold, ceremonially, on Sunday afternoons and made an ironic little curtsy as Short entered the parlor. At fourteen, Jefferson's oldest daughter was already as tall as most men, but spindly as a colt. Deliberately she lifted her chin away from her father and looked at the cold November rain outside the window. It was precisely one month since Maria Cosway had departed Paris.

"You may answer in either French or Hebrew, Guillaume," Clérisseau said from the sofa, where he lounged in front of the fire.

At Patsy's side, holding his own wineglass in his left hand, his right hand still cradled in a sling, Jefferson smiled. "If triangles worshiped a god," he told his daughter, "no doubt it would have three sides."

"Montesquieu." Clérisseau stabbed at the coals with a poker and looked up at Patsy. "Your father quotes Montesquieu and hides his skepticism behind his erudition. As a Frenchman I am flattered, as a Catholic I am outraged."

"As a guest," Jefferson responded, "you are hungry. We can

certainly go into the dining room now." And he offered Patsy his left arm.

"Mr. Short," the girl said, ignoring her father's arm, "has been upstairs writing correspondence"—she hesitated a moment, as if to go back and edit her awkward phrase—"*his* wrist being perfectly sound and uninjured. He should lead us in, as a reward."

"Mr. Short," Jefferson said mildly, "is always a favorite of the ladies." Patsy turned her back.

"I shall have wives," Clérisseau muttered to Short as they took their places at the table, "but never daughters."

His words or his tone caught Patsy's ear, and she snapped her red head around to glare.

"I've received yet another package from John Paul Jones," Short said quickly (a diplomat is a man who always has another subject ready). "He sends us medallions this time, you know." Wind racing from the Atlantic up the Seine rattled the window panes, setting the candles flickering. "A new set of bronze medallions commemorating the *Bonhomme Richard* and the *Serapis*. He wants us to hold them for him in our strongbox till he comes back."

"Admiral Jones is now commanding a squadron of Russian ships for the Empress Catherine," Jefferson explained to Clérisseau. "He sends us, alternately, requests for money and valuable personal items to store. You know Short's hydrophobia. I think William trembles at the very thought of anyone sailing in a ship, on the water."

"Very wise." Clérisseau took the decanter from James Hemings's hand and poured for himself. "If it were up to me, the seas would be filled with wine."

"A *commode*," Short said. "This time, along with the medallions, Jones also sent us an enormous porcelain commode 'of superior workmanship and quality,' I quote—from Amsterdam; it took two men just to carry it up the steps. He wrote 'Keep but do not use' on the wrapping."

Jefferson laughed, and Clérisseau arched a Gallic eyebrow. Hands in her lap, studying her wineglass as if it were a viper, the unforgiving Patsy waited for silence. "Perhaps Mrs. Cosway has painted it with her immortal brush, which makes it so valuable," she said bitterly, eyes on her father.

Jefferson's mildness was unruffled.

"Mrs. Cosway," he said, "writes me that she and her husband plan to return to Paris next spring—we can ask her then."

Patsy leaned forward, picked up her wineglass, and drained it.

Afterward, because Jefferson's wrist made any motion painful, Short climbed (warily) into the carriage to accompany her back to the convent school at Panthemont. When their carriage crossed the Pont Royal and began to wind up the rue du Bac, he cleared his throat to break the silence.

"Number forty-six?"

Patsy kept her gaze sullenly on the rain.

"Quarante-six, faites attention."

On her first day at the school—could it really have been two years ago?—Patsy had been assigned the number 46; it was sewn into the collar of her uniforms, tagged onto her belongings, even written across her books and drawings.

"Number forty-six, how is school? How is Miss Tufton and the dull, slow Miss Annesley of Great Britain? I haven't heard about any of your friends lately."

As they passed a streetlamp, Patsy's red hair flared in the dark carriage like a match. "My father says *she* plans to come back in the spring. Did you hear him?"

Short sighed. "She and Mr. Cosway *may* come back. Nothing is ever certain."

"She's married," Patsy said, spinning to face him. "That's certain. And he spends every day he can with her just the same."

"They visit galleries, painters. They talk about painting, everybody in Paris talks about painting."

Patsy folded her arms across her chest in a fence-building gesture, Short decided, exactly like her father's.

On the rue de Grenelle the carriage splashed to a halt in front of the school gates. With a voice barely loud enough to be heard over the rain, Patsy said good-bye to Short and hurried past the concierge's booth. Once inside she shook rain from her hood, stamped her feet (like a horse, she thought, looking glumly at her shoes; tall girl, long feet). Then she climbed the familiar flight of stairs to the dormitory.

All of the girls slept in one cavernous room on the second floor. Four rows of identical beds, twelve to a row. Locked wooden boxes at the foot of each bed held clothes, books, the few (very few) personal items the nuns permitted; no room for John Paul Jones's commode. At one end a tall sinuous crucifix, painted a glossy white and gold, that caught the eye no matter where you turned; at the other end, near Patsy's bed, another door leading to the *salle de bain,* more stairs.

The sister on duty looked up from her little desk, squinted over the candle flame, and acknowledged Patsy with a tiny nod. Two or three girls looked up without curiosity from their beds. On Sundays almost everyone left the school to visit. Even the three English girls were generally hauled out to spend the day with an obliging relative or family friend visiting in Paris. Patsy took off her damp hood and cape and sat on the end of the bed.

Mrs. Maria Cosway. In her mind Patsy sounded each syllable of the name. Mr. Richard Cosway. At home in Virginia wives and husbands were firmly, decisively placed; if men . . . misbehaved, they were unmarried men, the kind you saw lazing on the porches of taverns, or working in dirty shirts out in the sun, exuding an aroma of whiskey and sweat and tobacco as you passed. Or else they were men you sometimes saw strolling out of a slave's house, buttoning their trousers, rubbing their whiskers. But in France —

She stood up abruptly and opened the box at the end of her bed. Nabby Adams had liked to say France changed everyone — look at her mother at the ballet, look at Dr. Franklin cheering balloons. Patsy pulled out the leather portfolio of landscape drawings she was to complete by Tuesday; her worst subject. Nabby Adams was married now — she had written Patsy a special letter signed Mrs. William Stephens Smith — and her husband worked for her father in London just the way, precisely, that William Short worked for *her* father.

"Did you have your *bain* yesterday, Jeff? Or did you get *dispense?*"

Julia Annesley, pastiest and pestiest of the three British girls, had wandered over from her bed to stare at Patsy's things; or else simply to talk — the girls were forbidden to speak in the open rooms outside of classes and only in low voices in the dormitory, but Sunday evenings were lax. During the day the sisters all carried "clacks," two pieces of wood that could be snapped together to bring a girl to attention.

"It was *cold*." Julia peered at the portfolio of drawings. "And the sisters said there couldn't be a fire yet because of the holy water."

Patsy nodded briskly. As a veteran of two winters at Panthemont, she had learned not to think of fire or warmth until the Christmas holidays, if then. The sisters had an inflexible rule: No fires in the fireplaces before ice formed in the chapel's basin of holy water. Meanwhile girls studied in their hoods and capes, teeth chattering, sisters taught in the whitewashed classrooms wearing gray woolen gloves and scarves and puffing smoke with every breath.

"So I didn't have a *bain* yesterday, *à cause de la froideur,*" Julia said, now leaning forward and actually picking up some of the books in Patsy's box. "And also"—she dropped her voice—"because Sister Yvonne was on duty, and I think she's"—Julia swiveled her head to look at the hooded nun bent over her candle like an enormous black crow—"she's too *attentive.*"

"Yes." Patsy had had this conversation many times with Julia. On Saturday the girls were supposed to bathe, one by one, in a large portable tub brought into the *salle de bain.* You wore a *chemise de bain* (with your number tagged on it, of course), and the sister bathing you would reach under the chemise with a sponge and scrub. Sister Yvonne was noted for letting the sponge fall accidentally into the water and continuing to rub with her hands. "Wait for Sister Denise—elle est plus gentille."

" 'Romeo and Juliet,' " Julia read.

Patsy took the book from her hands. It was a small octavo volume bound in red Italian leather with her name "Martha Jefferson" stamped in gold on the lower cover; a gift from her father last Christmas. She tucked it away beneath the drawings and listened with only part of her mind to Julia's bright meaningless chirpings, now turning to the subject of Romeo's love for Juliet, his glorious romantic speeches—the passionate way Père Grasse would read them aloud; if, of course, Père Grasse knew English.

The glass of wine had made Patsy feel first giddy, then sleepy. When Julia wandered away at last to greet another returning girl, Patsy quickly ducked behind one of the dressing screens and changed into her nightdress, then dove for her covers. At the door the Sister was putting out superfluous candles, preparing for evening prayer, which Protestant girls did not have to join in. The crucifix on the wall moved in the flickering shadows like a living person, and the two spots of red on its palms suddenly glowed with reflected light; blood, wax. Mrs. Cosway was Catholic. She was also delicate. If she were punished, she would probably sicken and die. Patsy shifted on the hard mattress and thought of punishment. The sisters were not allowed to strike the girls, though Sister Yvonne sometimes did. In the Hôpital des Vénériens, Patsy had been told by one of the French girls, patients were given a daily spanking before their dose of mercury to punish them for having caught syphilis.

She turned again in the bed. France changed everyone. Mr. Short, it was generally conceded by her friends, was very handsome; he had a "sweet *amour*"—Elizabeth Tufton's word—in Saint-Germain, he might even (but he never smelled of whiskey or sweat) have visited one of those places where . . . She let the thought fade, fall into the maw of sleep. At parties and dinners, Mr. Short stared at the young, pretty Duchesse de La Rochefoucauld, and she was married. And her father watched always with a cold, stern face. A necklace of raindrops slid down the window, white pearls, into the dark. At this very moment Mr. Short was probably visiting at someone's salon in the Louvre, bowing to the young duchesse, kissing her perfumed hand.

☆   ☆   ☆

But at that moment Short was merely, unperfumedly holding his pen over a paper in Jefferson's second-floor study.

"John Stockdale in London," Jefferson said. He hugged himself with his left arm, right arm still in the sling, and stood closer to the fireplace, more sensitive to cold than anyone Short had ever known. "The map surveyed by my father, corrections, terms; also the French translation of *Sanford and Merton* he wants."

Short scribbled two more lines on his list. John Stockdale supplied Jefferson with English books and now had written twice proposing that he publish *Notes on Virginia* for general sale.

"A volume of Homer for Madame de Tott."

"The fair Grecian," Short murmured. Madame de Tessé's protégée Sophie-Ernestine was, Jefferson claimed, Greek in origin, though nobody knew for certain, since she rarely spoke in company and (French-like rather than Greek) never answered a direct question.

"Letters to Madison, John Jay, Ezra Stiles—"

Short finished the list from his notes: "Franklin, Mrs. Trist, General Washington, Calonne, Vaughn about magnets." As always, the sheer range of Jefferson's correspondence exhausted Short.

"I gave you the treaty proposal to copy."

"Yes, sir." Short fumbled in his stack of papers. Until the wrist had healed, he had the additional duty of copying over Jefferson's official papers in a fair hand.

"If John Paul Jones had not taken up with Our Lady of the North," Jefferson said, turning his other side to the fire.

"He is always a favorite with the ladies," Short said, hoping to provoke a question about young Patsy's state of mind. But Jefferson, impenetrable on the subject of his family, had returned to his favorite theme of forming a coalition against the Barbary pirates, six nations that would support Jones and an international fleet of warships. Last year he had proposed another extraordinary venture—the elimination of national passports and political barriers, the free condition of "universal citizen" for travelers—but this had been too visionary even to merit a response from Jay or Vergennes.

"It is almost pointless," Jefferson said, studying the fire. A jet rose suddenly six inches out of the coals, a blue ghost. "France teeters on the edge of bankruptcy, we do no better. The king—"

By the strange form of mental telepathy that existed between them, he looked up an instant before James Hemings entered the room, bearing a tray with a decanter of honey-brown Madeira. While he poured a glass for them each, Jefferson worked the little copy press beside his desk, swiveled his chair back and forth, manipulated with one hand the shackle of a new miniature lock.

"As for Washington's letter," Short began when James had left the room again.

"On the abominable subject of the abominable Society of Cincinnati," Jefferson said.

Short nodded, trying in fact to remember. The Society of Cincinnati, latest scheme of what Jefferson always called the monarchical faction, was intended to perpetuate, through hereditary membership, the officer class of the Continental Army. Washington had been named, automatically, its honorary head, but Jefferson had instantly written to point out the incompatibility of a democracy and an hereditary, de facto aristocracy.

"Washington asks my advice: should he attend their general meeting in Philadelphia? I wrote him yesterday, left-handed scribble. I told him that I have not yet met a person in France who does not consider the whole plan destructive to our government. I said" —Jefferson began to quote himself in a soft, murmuring voice— "I said, 'To know the mass of evil which must flow from an aristocracy, a person must be in France; he must see the finest soil, the finest climate, the most compact state, the most benevolent character of people, and every earthly advantage combined, insufficient to prevent this scourge from rendering existence a curse to twenty-four out of twenty-five parts of the inhabitants of this country.' "

He put down his Madeira and picked up a sheet of paper from his desk. "I told him, the South is already aristocratical in its disposition, as you and I have reason to know. That spirit can always spread." He paused a long moment. "I do not flatter myself with the immortality of our governments, but I shall think little also of their longevity unless this germ of aristocracy be taken out."

His left hand crumpled the sheet of paper into a spiky ball. "Liberty," he said softly. "Liberty, liberty."

The two of them sat in mute contemplation of the crumpled paper. Then Short, feeling obscurely embarrassed, looked down at the topmost name on his list. "Madison writes that a new federal convention will be held next spring, to revise the Articles of Confederation." He raised the idea tentatively. In some part of his mind he was afraid that Jefferson would insist on attending it and therefore leave him alone, without a position in Paris, or afraid he would drag him back to America. For less than an instant, one tick of Jefferson's handsome new mantel clock, he allowed himself to picture the house, the ambassador's office devolving upon William Short. But Jefferson was oddly uninterested in the convention.

"Do you know, William, I have long believed that in New England and in Virginia we have different understandings of the very word, the basic word. *Liberty.*"

Short stirred at his desk; flexed his fingers, cramped from so much writing.

"In New England." Jefferson raised the Madeira almost to his lips; Short noticed the thinness of his left wrist, the increasingly angular cut of his profile. "In New England they think, John Adams thinks, in terms of liberty and *order,* the freedom to do what is right—in Massachusetts you are free to serve God, and you had better; if you don't, the church will tell you. But in Virginia we think of it as freedom *from*—we are free from compulsion, free from churches and tyrannies. We trust a man to make his own mistakes, think as he pleases, go where he wants. My father carved his land out of the wilderness, by himself. In Virginia we have freedom from tyranny. In Virginia the opposite of freedom is slavery."

CHAPTER

Twenty-Three

Memoirs of Jefferson — 8

ON ONE OTHER OCCASION, FIVE YEARS before Patrick Henry's great "Liberty or Death" speech, Jefferson tried to speak out boldly, like an orator. He made an utter, un-Henry-like failure of it.

The scene was a Richmond courtroom, and ironically enough, Jefferson's law professor George Wythe was sitting there as the opposing attorney. Between Wythe and his prize pupil, in the plaintiff's chair, hunched a bright mulatto slave.

Now George Wythe was a book lover and collector even more enthusiastic than Jefferson. He liked nothing better than to sit in the study of the old red brick house in Williamsburg—his wife's house, designed by her architect father—and wave his hand at the shelves and shelves of books he had installed. "They say the law sharpens the mind by narrowing it." He would smile disbelievingly. "But not in this room."

So when Jefferson had come as his apprentice student, fresh from William and Mary College, Wythe laid out a program of reading so broad and stupendous and superhuman that it eventu-

ally took five years, beginning on the top shelf with Plato and
Greek philosophy (Jefferson's sole linguistic weakness) and proceeding down the mahogany tiers through poetry, religion, belles
lettres, Roman rhetoric, history, and (sometimes) law. At what
point Wythe started to utter antislavery remarks nobody knows —
after his wife's death his young black maid bore a mulatto son;
respectable Williamsburg was silent — but certainly he belonged to
that trio of "enlightened" thinkers in the city (Professor William
Small and Governor Fauquier the others) who introduced young
Jefferson to the future by way of the scholarly, progressive past.

And yet . . . I have in my hand as I write an advertisement
Jefferson placed in the *Virginia Gazette*, September 7, 1769, offering a forty-shilling reward for a runaway slave named Sandy, a
mulatto shoemaker and carpenter who stole a horse from Monticello and disappeared into the hot tar of a Virginia night. Jefferson's distaste fairly shakes off the page.

> He is greatly addicted to drink, and when drunk is insolent and
> disorderly, in his conversation he swears much, and in his behavior
> is artful and knavish.

But not eight months later, in April 1770, Jefferson sits down
on the left-hand side of the Richmond courtroom and, if he feels
distaste now, subdues it by sheer will, enlightened principle.

On the other side of the aisle, George Wythe, big hook nose in
profile, child's legs barely reaching the floor, likewise stares
straight ahead at the judge's bench.

Neither of them looks at one Samuel Howell, Jefferson's client
(without fee), a mulatto possessing the nerve, courage, despera-
tion actually to sue his owner Joshua Netherland for his freedom.

The case was thus: Howell's grandmother had been the daughter of a white woman and a black slave — whether or not by rape,
Jefferson would argue, was immaterial; but for the record the
court assumed that no white woman would willingly lie down with
a black and so entered "rape." The daughter was bound to serve
as a slave to her father's master until the age of thirty-one; during
that time *she* gave birth to a daughter, also bound to serve till
thirty-one. And finally that daughter, Howell's mother, gave birth

to him, still unmistakably mulatto, and he too was bound to his master Netherland until the age of thirty-one.

Jefferson had written his brief. He stood up to summarize. In Virginia law, he reminded the court, the status of a slave was determined, not by color, but by the status of the mother. Howell's grandmother had been completely white, pure white. By statute and law her descendants should have been free.

George Wythe folded his tiny hands in his lap and listened while his learned pupil next began to cite, in his reed-thin voice, precedent after precedent, case after case, Greek authorities, Roman authorities, Blackstone, Coke. They might as well have been back in his book-lined study. The jury sagged, the courtroom sagged.

And then suddenly, in the midst of assembling his precedents, Jefferson simply stopped and put down the book he was holding. He fixed his gaze on some point past the judge's shoulder, as if he were about to shake off the legal dust and speak for himself. A year earlier, with sly modesty, he had persuaded his ambitious cousin Richard Bland to introduce in the Burgesses a bill that Jefferson himself had drafted—a declaration that any slaveowner was exempt from all previous restrictions and could, if he chose, emancipate any or all of his slaves, just by registering the fact in a court. Jefferson seconded his own motion but never spoke, and the bill went down to blazing defeat. Poor Bland was denounced from half the godly pulpits in Virginia. Now Jefferson recalled Bland's discredited argument again. The sins of a father, he said to the spot on the wall, ought not be visited on a child to the third generation, and certainly not to a generation without end.

The judge interrupted. What law was the gentleman citing?

"Under the law of nature," Jefferson said loudly—I have copied his very words from his casebook—"*all men are born free,* and every one comes into the world with a perfect right to his own person, which includes the liberty of moving and using it at his own will."

The judge rose and snatched his gavel.

"It was not proved that slave law applied to the first woman's children." Jefferson continued to stare at the blank wall, his hands now fists on the table. "It remains for some future legislature to extend the law of bondage to grandchildren and beyond, *if any legislators can be found wicked enough."*

The gavel hammered, hammered. Samuel Howell slumped in his chair. With a final, furious swing of his arm the judge dismissed the case on the spot, not bothering to call on the defense for a word, a syllable, of rebuttal. "Law of nature," he muttered as he swept past Jefferson toward the door, wig, gown, heels flying. Wythe made a courtly, ironic bow to his student.

Which Jefferson wrote the advertisement for Sandy?

George Wythe had refused six years earlier to sign Patrick Henry's license to practice law, on the grounds that Henry knew next to nothing about anything. But Henry knew how to talk to people and carry his point; Henry had blown through the courtrooms of Virginia like an Old Testament prophet; when Henry spoke, juries swayed like corn in the wind, judges nodded. When Jefferson talked—

One last irony, in such a meditation on orators and freedom. George Wythe died scandalously in 1806, poisoned by his nephew, who crept downstairs early one June morning and dumped arsenic into the coffee pot on the kitchen stove. Wythe succumbed, as did his Negro maid's handsome mulatto son Michael, who was being taught Latin and Greek by Wythe and who had just, to the jealous rage of the nephew, been named co-beneficiary of the old man's will. The Negro maid survived, and the nephew would have been convicted of murder without doubt, except that in Virginia, even in 1806, thanks to the state penal code *written by Wythe and Jefferson themselves,* a black was not permitted to stand up in court and testify against a white. As far as the law was concerned, black was silent: everywhere seen, nowhere heard.

Like his father before him, Wythe bequeathed to Jefferson all of his splendid books.

☆   ☆   ☆

In the bedroom two doors down the hallway from where Short sat writing, Jefferson carried a brass-plated whale-oil lamp to his desk. In every room that he used regularly he had a desk. On the blotting tablet, tied together with a blue ribbon, lay the two short letters that Maria Cosway had so far written.

He took Short's list from his pocket. Still to write: letters to R. and A. Garvey regarding a new copy press. To Wilt, Delmestre & Co. on tariff regulations, to Vergennes on tobacco, to Elizabeth Eppes, Francis Eppes. The last letter on the list was for Eliza House Trist, the comfortable, unpretentious young widow with whom he and Madison and Edmund Randolph had lodged eleven years ago in Philadelphia. A personal letter, not part of the official business of a minister plenipotentiary. Rain drummed its white fingers against the window.

Jefferson dipped his pen in the inkwell; placed his right wrist gingerly on the blotter. Twenty lines of gossip, which Mrs. Trist loved; compliments. For a moment he curled his right hand gently around his throat, as if to guard his voice. Then: *"I often wish myself among my countrymen, dear Madam, as I am burning the candle of life without present pleasure, or future object. A dozen or twenty years ago this scene would have amused me. But I am past the age for changing habits. I take all the fault on myself, as it is impossible to be among people who wish more to make one happy. Yet living from day to day, without a plan for four and twenty hours to come, I form no catalogue of impossible events. Laid up in port, for life, as I thought myself at one time, I am thrown out to sea, and an unknown one to me. By so slender a thread do all our plans of life hang! —My hand denies itself further, every letter admonishing me, by a pain, that it is time to finish. . . .*

Rain became sunshine, dense blue sky.

At eleven the next morning Short looked up curiously when James Hemings announced Mr. and Mrs. Bentalou from South Carolina. Jefferson unfolded himself from his desk and signaled to Short that he should stay.

Mrs. Bentalou, massive in a new bell-shaped jupe and bustle, required an armless chair; James was dispatched to fetch one. Both of them accepted Jefferson's offer of coffee (but no pastry, "Lord, no, not another crumb," Mrs. Bentalou sighed, patting her hips), and James was dispatched again.

Paul Bentalou exported rice from his plantation in South Carolina—or would, if Vergennes and the Farmers-General ever put into practice the theoretical reforms Jefferson had made last year —and at first Short assumed (one eye on his stack of waiting correspondence) that the visit concerned the all-important, all-dreary subject of tariffs.

Bentalou crossed his legs, rubbed the toe of his new silver-buckled shoe. His wife explained between bites (having changed her mind about the pastry, which James cooked himself) that they had spent three days and three fortunes at least in the shops on the rue Saint-Honoré before coming to trouble his Excellency.

"Please, please." Jefferson waved away the title. As always, Short noted, when conversation from strangers touched him personally, he parried with a schoolmasterly fact. "Did you stop at Mademoiselle Bertin's dress shop?" he asked. Mrs. Bentalou nodded and fluffed the jupe; her husband made a noise like a man shot. Mademoiselle Bertin had gained a European fame for the cost and frequency of her fashions, which she announced by mailing to her customers small wax dolls dressed in models of her newest outfits. "Well now, here's a curious thing," Jefferson said. "Her shop is on the north side of the street, as you saw, but she told me once, when I went with a friend"—he paused—"she told me her rent is much higher, and her prices, too, than if she were on the south side of the street. I couldn't think why."

Bentalou was a compact man with a farmer's spade-sized hands. He used them now to shift his legs and pinch the toe of the other shoe.

"I don't know about cities," he apologized.

"But the fact is," Jefferson persisted, "it has to do with the sun—we're both farmers—it has to do with how much sunlight comes in her big glass windows. On the north side of the street you get the winter sun; it keeps the shop warmer, displays the goods better. In Paris, rent's always higher on the north side of a street."

Bentalou rubbed his chin. "We have a problem, your Excellency . . . a consultation."

Jefferson sank back in his chair in the "jackknife" pose that Short could have drawn with his eyes closed: sitting on his bony hip, knees up, left shoulder higher than the right. Despite the sling, the fingers of both hands touched in a steeple.

"We're traveling, you know, for ten months or a year, and we brought our servant with us. . . ."

"Just a boy," Mrs. Bentalou deprecated. "He runs errands, keeps Mr. Bentalou's clothes."

"He is Negro," Jefferson said.

"Two or three days ago," Bentalou said, "in our hotel one of the guests, a Dutchman he was, told us that in this country, legally, a servant is free; you can't keep him if he wants to go. Nobody said that when we arrived at Le Havre, but this Dutchman insisted this was so. So we came to you, as our . . . ambassador. Can we keep our slave?"

Short made himself invisible at his desk.

Jefferson tapped gently the tips of his steeple. For a long moment Short heard only the rustle of Mrs. Bentalou's new crinoline, the asthmatic rasp of her husband's breath.

When he finally answered, Jefferson was lawyerlike, neutral. "The laws of France do give him freedom if he claims it, and in such a case it would be difficult if not impossible to interrupt the course of the law. Slavery is illegal in France, no matter what the status or nationality of the owner may be. Nevertheless, I have known an instance where a person, bringing in a slave, and saying nothing about it, has not been disturbed in his possession."

"Ah." Bentalou sat back in his chair and nodded, not a farmer but a man of the world.

"If the boy is young, he will probably not think of claiming his freedom," Jefferson added.

"It wouldn't be natural, would it?" Mrs. Bentalou probed for reassurance. "Claiming his freedom?"

But the Roman stared at a point hidden in the wall and, though Short would have waited for hours, made no move to disagree.

CHAPTER

Twenty-Four

On January 17, 1787, Jefferson received the first of his visits from the family Valdajou.

"*Rebouteurs*," Adrien Petit explained to Short: "bone-setters. The most renowned bone-setters *dans toute la France.*"

Together Short and Petit stood beside the stairs and watched the bone-setters troop up to the second floor in solemn file, three brothers, one ancient father, all dressed in black wool suits, with hair curled and set in pigtails, followed by four servants likewise in black, each carrying on a cushion a polished wooden box of, presumably, medical implements.

Presumably, because French medicine, Short had learned, liked to keep its methods very much in the guild, secret. The useful and most intimate instrument called a "forceps," now the rage in all fashionable lyings-in, had actually been invented by another family of French doctors some fifty years earlier, so Short's informants claimed, and kept a profitable secret until the last decade. Who knew what bone-crunching devices the Valdajous carried in their boxes? Like the inventor of the forceps, they strictly banished all visitors and friends from the invalid's chamber.

The last servant's heels disappeared at the landing. Petit cocked his head and pursed his lips in the universal French sign for skepticism, stared at Short, and then marched away to his office above the kitchen. After a moment, fingers (if not wrist) sympathetically aching, Short returned to the study and his stacks upon stacks of Jefferson's correspondence.

By four that afternoon, it was already midwinter dark. Lafayette, onstage as always, carried a second candle to the table beside Jefferson's chair, rubbed his hands together briskly like a servant, and glanced around.

"You have books in every room," he said accusingly. "This is the salon, not the library."

"An American custom," Short told him solemnly from the other side of the fireplace. "A *Virginia* custom. As far as books are concerned, Virginians believe all rooms are created equal." In his chair, wrist so thickly bandaged by the Valdajous that it might have been a fat white lapdog, Jefferson smiled and looked faint. Behind him James Hemings continued to sort out his tea tray. Beside Short, who stood, sat a pale young man named John Banister, Jr., knees apart, jaw slack, eyes (Short thought) like a pair of bloodshot buttons.

"Ah well, in that case." Lafayette bowed to the nearest shelf of books, as one American to another; then from a table picked up a metallic instrument shaped like a draughtsman's compass, with an inflatable rubber bulb at one end. For a moment Short's mind turned wildly to the Valdajous.

"That is my hygrometer," Jefferson said. "In between doctors I've been experimenting with a way to measure the moisture in the air, to improve on Monsieur Buffon's calculations."

"Always Buffon," Lafayette said enigmatically. "If poor Buffon said everything was *bigger* in America, you would *love* his calculations." He put down the hygrometer and picked up a padded rectangle two feet long and lined with blue felt trays.

"Seashells." Jefferson shivered though he sat no more than a yard from the fire. "They were found in a Virginia quarry, not far from Charlottesville. One of my neighbors at Monticello gathered them in support of my theory that the ocean once reached far inland, as far as the Shenandoah Mountains, perhaps. This one, for example—"

While Jefferson stretched his good hand to show Lafayette the shell, Short stole a glance at young Banister. Another of Jefferson's charity cases—was he one himself? Short wondered—Banister had come to Europe for a Virginian's version of the Grand Tour, promptly got himself poxed in a Marseilles brothel, and collapsed into near-bankruptcy at the hands of quacks and gamblers. For months his father had been writing Jefferson to ask for help, and at last the prodigal had staggered into Paris and the Hôtel de Langeac, where he now occupied Williamos's old room on the third floor, next to Short's. An unlucky conjunction, Short thought; when (and if) he recovered from his pox, someone would have to take the boy aside and explain about sheepskin condoms and other precautions; not Jefferson, obviously. Short studied the writhing fire; perhaps the Ace of Spades.

"I've brought you a present," Lafayette said, replacing the shell in its tray.

"Not more cheese, I hope." Jefferson made a wan face at Lafayette, now towering over his chair, arms folded together. In the previous summer a group of New Hampshire farmers, stirred by patriotic hindsight, had decided belatedly to honor Lafayette for his services in the Revolution. The result: a five-hundred-pound yellow cheese, shipped across the Atlantic and delivered on September first to his doorstep at the rue de Bourbon. For months Lafayette had been bringing huge slices to the Hôtel de Langeac, on the supposition that Jefferson ought to help to dispose of it.

"No cheese." Lafayette accepted a cup of tea from James Hemings. "Gossip, news. While the *frères* Valdajou have been steering your bones into port, Versailles has been steering the nation into open seas."

"You mean the Assembly of Notables." Jefferson came to life as he always did at the mention of politics, especially rebellion.

"The *not-ables*," Short whispered under his breath, the latest Parisian joke about the extraordinary assembly of dukes, generals, bishops, citizens, and courtiers called by the king, like a miniature parliament, to gather at Versailles and address the increasingly urgent question of King Louis XVI's finances. It would be the first Assembly in a hundred and sixty years.

"I know all about it," Jefferson said. "The papers are full of nothing else. You will recall I even predicted something like it."

Lafayette was wandering, as usual, from object to object in the room. He paused at the mantelpiece over the fire, next to Short, and clicked his big teeth like a horse. "You did, you did. After we met with the Farmers-General, you said the king's budget was so extravagant that sooner or later he would have to call for help, even the king."

Jefferson made a point of addressing young Banister, as if there were an analogy of budgets. "The Assembly of Notables," he explained, "was chosen by the king on the last day of the year."

"December 29," Lafayette corrected, wandering away from the fire. "At his Conseil des Dépêches, a complete surprise to everyone except Calonne and Vergennes."

"For years," Jefferson told Banister, "the king's revenues have fallen far short of his expenditures, especially at Court. The few ministers who tried to rein in his expenses were all summarily dismissed."

"Monsieur Necker," Lafayette said gloomily, now standing before twenty-four leather-bound volumes of the *Encyclopédie*, Franklin's copy, which Jefferson was to ship to him in Philadelphia in the spring. "You put it best, my friend, you said in Europe we've divided ourselves into two classes, the wolves and the sheep."

Jefferson turned in his chair to follow him, and Short observed the ripple of pain across his face. No French room was ever really warm. The cold January air must have cut into Jefferson's poor wrist like a knife.

Opposite him young Banister sat up straighter and made an effort to look interested. "When I was in Marseilles," he told Lafayette, "I saw poor people everywhere, worse off than niggers, but the nobility, they rode in carriages covered with gold."

Lafayette was pulling open one of the great oversize volumes of the *Encyclopédie* (to Jefferson's polite distress) and peering at an illustration. As if Banister had never spoken, he asked over his shoulder, "Do you know — I went to the Palais Royal the other day, to the new gallery of wax models — what did I see?"

Short thought of the anatomically correct Zulima but said nothing.

"Frederick the Great." Lafayette slapped the book closed. "*Already* a wax statue of Frederick, and he only died in August. I saw him last year, you know. I traveled to Prussia, and he sat me down at a banquet next to Lord Cornwallis, of all people in the world. And as I always do" — Lafayette made a quick, insincere gesture of self-deprecation—"I began to praise America. I said in America the ideas of liberty and equality reigned supreme, sublime. I said there would never be nobility or royalty in America, no wolves and sheep like here. Cornwallis sniffed and smirked, of course, and chewed on his bottom lip the way these cannibal Englishmen do, but Frederick—Frederick roused himself from his royal torpor and told me, 'Sir, I knew a young prince who visited a land of liberty and equality and then tried to go home and establish it in his own land. Do you know what happened to him?' 'No, sire; what happened?' 'Sir, he was hanged.'"

Banister snorted, then glanced at Short. A joke? But Lafayette rarely joked.

"This is the state of mind," he told Jefferson, circling now in front of Jefferson's chair, carrying the book with his finger mashed between the pages; "the state of mind Louis must face, *France* must face, if any change is to come."

"Frederick was a formidable wolf," Jefferson said neutrally.

Lafayette put down the book, picked up the hygrometer, and squinted through it at the ceiling, where Jefferson's picture of a sunrise flickered like a second shadow. "Frederick allowed no women to set foot in his palace, did you know that? Men only." He shuddered; like a Frenchman, Short thought. "For love, he would choose his palace guard personally, tall, husky young Germans, the finest physical specimens; then he would summon one of them whenever he felt like it, punch him around a bit schoolboy-fashion, and finally motion him to the sofa behind the screen in his study. He himself was the filthiest old man I've ever seen. He wore a foul crimson dressing gown night and day, covered with tobacco; he had his boots split on the sides so his gouty feet could fit. He always had one of his Italian greyhounds nuzzling under his legs—they were all killed and buried with him—and Voltaire used to claim he seasoned his food with gunpowder."

Lafayette replaced the hygrometer and returned to his point.

"But my news, my dear sir, is that another death is imminent."

"Calonne is ill, I know." Jefferson referred to the king's latest inept minister of finance.

"Not Calonne. Vergennes. I spoke with his physicians two hours ago—hopeless. They give him a week to live, less."

Jefferson sat back in genuine surprise.

"The rising gout," Lafayette said by way of explanation, thumping his hand against his flat stomach. "Comes on like a fire. They say his lips are already black and his flesh smells like pus. He spat half a quart of blood this morning into his soup."

Jefferson addressed young Banister as if in a tutorial. "Vergennes is a great and good minister," he said, "in charge of the king's foreign policy, including trade. If he dies, the Assembly would have to be put off, delayed indefinitely."

"Without a doubt," Lafayette said.

"And the longer the time between the announcement and the Assembly, the greater the chance for dissension and opposition to come together. Already you hear stories—"

"The people"—Lafayette used the insulting French phrase *le peuple*, so utterly different, Short thought, from the expression Jefferson had inserted at the beginning of the Declaration: "one people."

"*Le peuple*," Lafayette said, taking up his tricornered hat from a table, "misunderstand the whole idea of the Assembly—fishwives are petitioning Calonne for divorces, beggars and cripples have Versailles practically under siege; cripples, mountebanks, *filles de joie*—in the Dordogne an abbey of monks wrote asking to be released from their vows!"

"My own news," Jefferson said, coming to his feet slowly as Lafayette started to leave, "is less dramatic. The Family Valdajou prescribe six weeks of the waters at Aix-en-Provence, to heal these bones"—he held up his bandage like a trophy—"and I think I shall leave in a week."

Short put down his teacup sharply, caught off guard. Lafayette, however, in the act of sliding his huge hat under his arm, merely nodded. "Of course. The waters at Aix, a lovely prescription in the dead of winter. If I were not so 'not-able' myself"—he paused to show his teeth; Short thought of a row of tombstones—"I would go with you. But as it happens, my name appears on the king's list."

"As naturally it would." Jefferson made no allusion to the fact —notoriously discussed in the *Mercure de France*—that Lafayette's name had been stricken from the original list of 144 notables, restored, cut, restored again, a process that might have gone on for weeks if his aunt Madame de Tessé had not intervened. It was not only Frederick who disliked the Young Hero's views on equality and freedom.

In the hallway Short waited courteously (shivering) while Lafayette was helped into his blue greatcoat, a beautifully tailored version of Washington's own uniform at Valley Forge.

"Madame Cosway comes again, yes?" Lafayette asked, cocking his head. From the study Jefferson could be heard singing faintly.

Short busied himself with the door. "I know nothing about her plans myself," he murmured.

"When the queen had her first child," Lafayette said, striking off onto one of his tangents of irrelevancy, "I was not in the audience myself. My uncle was. You know, she gives birth in a public room at Versailles, there must be two or three hundred people crowded in to watch, suffocating, terrible. The physician was a Monsieur Vermond, and he could barely fight his way through to the bed. His fee, if the baby was a boy, was to be an annual pension of forty thousand francs."

Short was fascinated in spite of himself. "And if it was a girl?"

Lafayette shrugged. "A single payment of eight thousand francs." He nodded to Petit, who opened the door to a wall of icy black air. "And it *was* a girl, of course."

"The Salic law," Short said, referring to the legal anomaly that made France the only country in Europe where a woman could not reign.

Lafayette pulled up his collar. "Not really. I think in the end it is simply that girls always cost much more." He grasped the door handle and allowed himself a trace of smile. "But she is charming, yes? the little Cosway?"

☆　☆　☆

Number 105 of the Palais Royal arcades housed a celebrated gallery called the *Spectacle des Pygmées français*, a collection of exquisitely crafted objects in miniature.

The day after the bone-setters' visit, Short paused and peered myopically into its window. This month's display was a plaster replica of the entire city of London, three feet square, tilted up on a wooden stand so that the passerby could see at a glance the glossy river Thames (made of a curving green mirror), Westminster Abbey, the Tower of London, a tiny marching regiment of

Beefeater guards, and in the exact center St. Paul's domed cathedral, the size of an egg. On wires, floating above the city, a trio of kilted angels held a Scotch plaid banner that read in English: LONDON, FLOWER OF CITIES ALL.

"What a pleasure for us ladies," said Madame de Tessé behind him. As he turned in surprise she tapped his wrist with her lorgnette. "To encounter by chance Monsieur Short in the arcades. A handsome gentleman who likes to study the shops. Much better than a husband."

Beside her, chin tilted high in the air, stood Madame de Tessé's protégée, the "fair Grecian," scholarly Madame de Tott. And next to her Rosalie de La Rochefoucauld.

"I am myself bored to tears by Anglomania," declared Madame de Tott. Despite her unnervingly clear and piercing eyes, Madame de Tott likewise carried a lorgnette, tiny eyeglasses on a handle, the season's latest fashion, and she used it now to dismiss once and for all the miniature London. Madame de Tessé made a chirping sound of protest that Short scarcely heard. He had seen Rosalie de La Rochefoucauld a dozen times at least since the afternoon she and her husband had called on Jefferson. Each time he had felt the blood rush to his face, his cheeks burn like fanned coals. Each time, recklessly, indifferent to her husband's presence, to Jefferson's frown, he had come closer and closer to making an utter and perfect fool of himself.

"On the other hand," said Madame de Tessé briskly, turning back from the window. "Much as I like English gardens and English woolens, I suppose I should be true to my political principles. Je suis une 'américaine.' The enemy of my friend is my enemy."

"Have you been here at the Palais long?" At the last moment Short remembered to lift his eyes from Rosalie's soft, flawless face and to address the question to all three women.

"Long enough to grow hungry and cold." Madame de Tott trained her lorgnette on Rosalie like a pistol. "Rosalie dear, whenever we encounter Monsieur Short, you always fall very silent. He must think you rude."

"I could never think that," Short said hastily. He felt his face grow even redder. No one in the history of Paris had ever made a more fatuous compliment.

"We have just come from the crystal shop on the other side." Madame de Tessé nodded at the sunlit central garden and the row of shops under the opposite arcade. All four of them began to move away from the window and into the stream of brightly dressed pedestrians strolling before the shops. "But for once we left a boutique empty-handed." She smiled the odd little grimace that smallpox had stamped on her mouth and indicated the packages under Short's arm. "Unlike yourself, Monsieur Short."

Rosalie spoke for the first time. Her voice was so soft that Short found himself bending down till their heads almost touched. "It is the ladies' rule in the Palais Royal," she told him, "that all purchases be explained and displayed."

"Over chocolate, of course," said Madame de Tott, sweeping forward. "Chocolate and cake. Shall we cross to the Grand Vefour?"

Opposite the Grand Vefour restaurant, her bare shoulders goose-bumped in the January cold, an unmistakable *fille publique* lounged on a bench. When Madame de Tessé glared through her lorgnette, the whore grinned and parted her legs. Short was halfway to their table before he recognized the Ace of Spades's young coarse-haired maid.

"You must show us exactly what you have bought," the fair Grecian drawled as he sat down, "according to the rules." Shyly, Rosalie took his nearest package and tugged at the string. With a flourish of bracelets Madame de Tessé reached in and pulled out a set of stoppered glass vials labeled in Gothic script. Madame de Tott pushed aside her chocolate cup and held up, doubtfully, a chemist's balance, complete with weighing pans and brass weights.

"I'm afraid," said Short, "that a friend of Ambassador Jefferson's in Virginia incautiously wrote that chemistry sounded like an interesting subject."

"And Monsieur Jefferson instantly sent you out to buy all the chemicals in Paris and ship them to him." Madame de Tessé nodded, sparrowlike, as she greedily spooned white lumps of sugar into her chocolate. "The man himself. The first time he saw my gardens at Chaville, he promptly brought me fifty packets of seeds from Virginia."

"He leaves this week, does he not?" Madame de Tott had

removed her hat and shaken out her curls. Tall and handsome and stony of expression, she lived apparently on the charity of Madame de Tessé and cultivated a reputation for man-killing scholarship. "Madame" was a courtesy title, since she was unmarried at thirty and was unlikely to be, Short thought. When Jefferson had recently presented her with a set of Homer in Greek, she had promptly repaid him with a lecture on art that corrected (correctly) his misunderstanding of a fashionable painting. Next to her the diminutive Rosalie glowed like a star; Short forced himself not to stare.

"He goes on a trip to Aix, for the waters, and then he plans to tour all the way into Italy. But he's waiting to leave until the Assembly of Notables holds its first meeting."

"Assembly of sheep," snorted Madame de Tessé. "Notable *moutons*. Apart from my nephew Gilbert"—Short was delighted to hear Lafayette called Gilbert—"there's not a true reformer in the lot."

"Monsieur Jefferson makes a long journey," Rosalie said.

Short attempted to meet her eyes. He ignored the two older women and let his fingers brush the silky flame of her sleeve. "Three months at least. And when he returns," he added quickly, "we expect his other daughter to have arrived—he hasn't seen her for three years. She's only eight."

But Madame de Tessé was far from finished with the subject of politics.

"Yet how impossible, wonderfully *strange* it must seem!" She wiped a moustache of chocolate from her lip. "Your country, little unformed America, able to gather its Congresses, declare its rights, throw off a tyrant, snap, snap, snap—and here is France, sinking into bankruptcy, unable even to *assemble* its leaders."

"We've had our setbacks, of course." Short pulled his hand away from Rosalie's and thought of the forthcoming constitutional convention in Philadelphia. But Madame de Tessé was intent on the contrast between the two countries.

"Here a monarchy, paralyzed; a society founded on inequality, repression. There a republic, vigorous; founded on the revolutionary idea that all men are created equal." She dropped her spoon, square little face tense with feeling. "I tease him, you know, 'Monsieur Clever'—his plants, his chemistry—but your Jefferson is a great man. His ideas are enlightened. He believes in freedom, he trusts human beings to make mistakes and still progress. He thought it all out before a shot was fired. Washington gave you the army," she told Short, "but Jefferson gave you the ideas. His ideas *invented* America."

"Were you there, Monsieur?" Rosalie asked, raising her eyes. "When he wrote the Declaration, I mean." Then she blushed and looked toward Madame de Tott. "But what am I saying? He's much too young, he must have been only a boy."

"I've asked him what happened," Short said, "and all the other Virginians who were there—"

"You ought to write it down," Madame de Tott said with a cool tone of mockery, "before the next Revolution."

But Short was addressing Madame de Tessé, whose enthusiasm had transformed her little pockmarked face. "You have to picture to yourself, Madame, the city of Philadelphia first, which would fit into a small corner of Paris. Every building made of red brick, farms practically at your door, no customs walls or gates. Streets paved with pebbles in the middle, frog ponds between houses, Quakers in black suits, Yankees in beaver hats, frowzy buckskinned political delegates everywhere, from every backwoods town and colony, nothing at all like this—" He gestured toward the window, which opened onto the brilliant arcade, a moving toyshop of swords and wigs. The Ace of Spades's *fille* passed on the arm of a soldier.

"The Virginians were the leaders, yes?" Madame de Tessé was certain.

Short nodded. "In 1775, at the Second Continental Congress, the Virginians rode into Philadelphia like Roman centurions," he said, and sat back in his chair, remembering what he had never seen.

Memoirs of Jefferson — 9

THEY CAME ON SPLENDID PRANCING horses, attended by slaves, preceded by rumors; realms and islands were as plates dropped from their pockets. As in previous years the others were already there, waiting, grum-

bling—round-headed, portly John Adams, who looked like a series of cannonballs stacked on top of each other. His cousin Sam
Adams, too, the stout, palsied, slightly mysterious failure in business who had earlier organized with brilliant military precision the
Boston Tea Party, directing his "Mohawks" like a general as they
lifted the 340 chests of tea (each one weighing three hundred
pounds) with block and tackle, then shattered the bottoms and
shoveled the leaves over the side (there was so much tea, it piled
up above the gunwales of the three ships—next day small boats
had to be rowed through the mush to clear paths in the harbor).
John Dickinson, the self-styled "Pennsylvania Farmer," nearest
thing to an American equivocator, likewise waited in his palatial
farmhouse Fairhill (every stone and hinge imported from England), eager to woo the Virginian princes.

Physically they were remarkable. As they climbed down from
their horses and phaetons to go into Mifflin's Tavern, there was
the "orator" Richard Henry Lee, stylish and chilling, who wore a
black silk handkerchief highwayman-fashion around his left hand,
where he had blown away his fingers with a rifle; the two Falstaf-
fian giants Peyton Randolph and Benjamin Harrison, both of
them given to table-buckling feasts and good-humored exaggeration (the four-hundred-pound Harrison said he would have
"walked" to Philadelphia for this Congress); and above all—separate from all, silent where they were hyperbolic—the unapproach-
ably dignified and monumental Colonel George Washington, who
was supposed to have vowed he would raise an army on his own if
Congress would not. When Abigail Adams finally met him—not
ever in her life inclined to hero-worship or hyperbole—she grew
girlish, spoke of Washington's "dignity" and "ease," and even
quoted (to John's disgust) poetry:

Mark his majestic fabric; he's a temple
Sacred by birth, and built by hand divine.

The one delegate nobody noticed, though he arrived a spectacular six weeks late, in a beautiful phaeton with two spare horses,
was Jefferson.

They *knew* of him, of course. His *Summary View* pamphlet had
been passed from hand to hand, wildly praised for the bold bril-

liance of its prose (Dickinson shuddered). And because he was the youngest delegate (at thirty-two) and already celebrated for his pen, they assigned him at once to tedious committee after committee and watched with satisfaction as his reports and letters came flawlessly in, precisely on schedule. But Jefferson the *man*—he never spoke; there is no record at all of his ever speaking in Congress; in committee, Adams said, he was prompt, frank, decisive, but no one else seems to remember. Once or twice he brought out his violin at Philadelphia dinners. Otherwise, from June to October, Jefferson played the role of spectator—silent in a different way from Washington, whose long periods of taciturnity suggested enormous strength marshaled within, a dense mass; the silence of a statue. Jefferson's was the sly silence of reserve, of elusive private guardedness; when someone approached, he folded his arms across his chest like a gate. Visionary, in short, as always; looking past the day's committees and reports and squabbles to a far-off pattern that only he saw emerging.

He had a little box, designed by himself, that unfolded into a compact portable writing desk and served him as the equivalent of an orator's rostrum. "I wonder what in fifty or a hundred years," John Dickinson said to him one day, fretting, swatting at a fly, "will we have accomplished here by our 'revolution'?" Characteristically, Jefferson made no answer at the time. But that night he took out his little desk and wrote a long essay describing what he thought they would have accomplished—a free government, a free people, governing themselves by reason; a revolution that would transform and uplift the condition of men all over the globe; life, liberty, justice, everything achieved by reason: "the world's best hope." He sent it by post, and Dickinson carried it in his pocket and read it to every delegate he met.

CHAPTER

Twenty-Five

Memoirs of Jefferson — 10

LIFE MUST BE LIVED FORWARD, I HAVE read somewhere, even though it can only be understood backward.

I am now, in this rainy summer of 1826, a biblical three score and seven; sixty-seven years old. Casting my mind backward, it is remarkable how little I remember of the past twenty years—a softly turning blur of indistinguishable days and nights, a feeling somehow of gathering speed. Of my years in France with Jefferson, on the other hand, I remember whole days at a time, preserved and hardened in memory as if in amber. Do I, at all, begin to understand?

One memorable day among hundreds: The week before Jefferson set out on his tour of southern France in February 1787, to take the waters at Aix-en-Provence for his still unmended wrist, he and I rode up the highway from Paris to Versailles, battling every foot of the last two miles through an enormous, noisy throng of soldiers, peasants, carriages, and mere foot-slogging *citoyens,* come to Court like us to see the opening day of the long-postponed Assembly of Notables.

I remember with perfect clarity the building where the Assembly was to be held—not the king's palace, but a giant cube of a warehouse across the road, with the unofficial name "Menus Plaisirs," trifling pleasures, because the king ordinarily used it as a storehouse for ballroom costumes, candelabra, furniture, dried flowers, lanterns, theatrical flats, whatever served as ornament for the Court's endless festivities. Jefferson, of course, was fascinated by anything architectural, so we had to stop outside the visitor's door, in the cold February sun, and examine exactly what had been done to such an unpromising barn. Not much, was the answer. The Notables needed a meeting room large enough for two hundred delegates, plus the Court retainers and inevitable crowd of ambassadors and hangers-on who would flock to observe. The palace chapel was briefly considered and rejected; likewise the Hall of Mirrors. Finally, with time running out, the royal architect had simply taken one outside wall of the Menus Plaisirs and to it joined three new temporary walls of thin wood and plaster, making a hollow box three stories high. The doors were little more than boards on hinges; the entrance was unpainted and bare, and except for a series of tinted skylights in the roof, there were no windows at all. The whole thing, Jefferson told me, studying the roof in frowning disapproval, had been built in less than a month.

When we had looked our fill at the exterior, Jefferson presented our tickets to a soldier behind a cordon and we pushed our way through a genuine Babel of other foreign guests, up a set of makeshift stairs, and onto a wooden viewing platform.

The next moment he took me utterly by surprise with a question.

Bending close, cupping his mouth to be heard over the din of voices: "William. You are a man of sensitive observation, great alertness. What singular fact do you notice about this assembly?"

In those days, when I was younger than anyone else in the world, Jefferson's questions always threw me into a momentary fright. I was on trial, exposed. A bad answer would stamp me (for good) as a fool in his eyes.

"What do you see?" he asked, and I looked about, half panic-stricken. Our platform was a vast, jostling crowd of shoulders and faces. We were too far from the front edge for me to make out clearly where the king's party would sit and the delegates conduct their business. I blurted the first thing that came into my head: "I don't see any women!"

My usual good luck. He smiled, nodded, drew me forward through the crowd. A cubic acre of Frenchmen, jammed by the hundreds and hundreds into every space and cranny, and for once in that endlessly stylish, fashionable, chattering nation, not a female in sight.

Jefferson bent close to my ear. "By the king's orders," he said. "He has forbidden all women from attending the ceremony today. I take it as a sign of political seriousness."

Even now I remember the firmness with which he said this, and the confusion with which I heard it. Jefferson belonged to the school of Virginia gentlemen, already old-fashioned when I was young, that treated women with mild, iron-fisted courtesy. He was a benevolent tyrant to his daughters (poor Patsy, who lived in her father's house till her own children were grown), a strict believer in woman's limited sphere. I was present at the Hôtel de Langeac the day he told young Anne Bingham not to wrinkle her pretty forehead with politics. (She wrinkled it with something else.) He once lectured Alexander Hamilton's beautiful, ambitious sister-in-law Angelica Church for half an hour: The tender breasts of ladies were not formed for political convulsion, he said; ladies should be content to soothe and calm their husbands when they returned ruffled from political debates.

"Gratifying seriousness," he repeated now, leading me forward again to the very edge of the platform. I blinked away women and seriousness and examined as best I could the spectacle unfolding some thirty feet below.

It was not, I remember thinking dazedly, the congress of centurions in Philadelphia. An eye-popping show of color greeted us. Below the platform stretched a long open space, brightly lit by the skylights, populated by several hundred milling Notables, each in his most resplendent, luxurious costume. Wigs rose like snowy mountains, Alp after Alp. Entering from one side, a line of bejeweled, bespangled courtiers had begun to wend their way over a blue carpet. Before the ornately gilded throne, at the far end of the hall, bishops and cardinals of the church strolled about in scarlet cassocks and caps; noble gentlemen pulled at their knee-length Burgundy coats, or their silk breeches, or cravats, or else carefully straightened (before a mirror held by a servant) the sweeping plumes of their ceremonial hats.

Jefferson's mood changed in an instant. "Fops, dandies," he said under his breath. I strained to hear him. "Even without women to distract them—how can such a parade of *peacocks* expect to reform?"

"There's Lafayette." I pointed toward the red-headed prince of pineapples walking slowly, hand on sword, toward the raised throne, which was surrounded, as far as I could tell, by a cascading mountain of candy-colored cushions on which, presumably, the royal party would lounge.

Jefferson ignored him. "The minister of police in Paris," he told me, intense, confidential despite the noise, "declares there are more than ninety thousand people in the city without a home, sleeping in the streets or in hovels by the river. Yet here . . ." He waved his hand in disgust.

Before I could reply, trumpets had begun to sound by the door. A master of ceremonies was escorting someone ("the keeper of the seals," Jefferson muttered), and the Assembly was under way. Then soldiers, mace bearers, princes of the blood were filing toward the dais. Louis XVI himself, a blur of blue and gold, was lowering his vast royal bottom to the throne and two lackeys were placing warm bricks under his feet. The tide of spectators surged. For a moment Jefferson's tall profile disappeared, and I was alone in the crowd. The king removed his hat, replaced it, spoke something in a high, slow voice that carried badly, and the keeper of the seals bowed, bowed, bowed and advanced a step, bowed all the way to his knees in abject homage. When I could see him again, Jefferson's arms were folded tightly across his chest. Two spots of red burned on his cheeks.

"From the race of kings," he said as I came close, "good Lord deliver us."

In the carriage returning to Paris, Jefferson held a whale-oil lamp in one hand and read aloud from John Adams's most recent letter, much of it describing a violent uprising in western Massachusetts two months before, a protest against taxes led by a farmer named Daniel Shays.

"Alarming news," I said automatically, watching the lights of Paris approach along the curving river. I tried to think of an incisive political comment. "With such instability, no wonder they plan a new constitutional convention."

But Jefferson shook his head. In the swaying carriage, by the flickering lights, he had never looked so much like an angry hawk. "In fact, I hope they pardon Daniel Shays, whoever he is. The spirit of resistance to government is so valuable in a people that I would wish it to be always kept alive. Better to exercise it in the wrong than not exercise it at all." He stretched his long legs and twisted three-quarters length on the hard carriage bench. "John Adams wants to see them punished, as you hear. Abigail says make a stern example of them." The hawk's smile grew thin, grew faraway serene. "But I like a little rebellion now and then," he said softly. "It's like an electric storm in the atmosphere. It clears the air."

Alas, my mind was never truly formed for politics. As we sat bouncing in the carriage, moving back toward the city I loved best in all the universe, I found myself thinking, not of constitutions and rebellions, but of Jefferson's strong dislike of forward, ambitious women.

Now, so many years later, I find myself wondering how much it explains of his subsequent, cruel treatment of poor Maria Cosway.

CHAPTER

Twenty-Six

"This style, Monsieur," said the shopgirl behind the counter, "is called 'Telltale Moans.'" She held up a length of silky blue lace and draped it across her bosom.

Short cleared his throat, nodded slowly with the solemn air (he hoped) of a connoisseur, and permitted himself to steal a sidelong glance at Rosalie de La Rochefoucauld, whose eyes were lowered modestly but whose lips were turned up in a smile.

"No. No. Perhaps not quite." He plunged his hand at random into the bolts of fabric on the counter and pulled up another spool of lace, rich scarlet (like his face) and decorated with tiny flecks of pink ribbon. "And this one?"

The shopgirl used one hand to spread it across her left breast. "It is called, Monsieur, 'Muffled Sighs.'"

With a muffled sigh of his own, Short let drop the end he was holding. Rosalie had already turned away and begun walking down the counter, toward stacks of dresses, bedsheets—he had no idea. In two steps he caught up to her.

"I am still so surprised to see you," she said, in fact not looking at him, "here, in a ladies' shop. And in Versailles. We all thought you were staying in Saint-Germain."

He touched her elbow with the tops of his fingers and steered her away from the amused stare of the *grisette*. "I was, I am; but I had to come to Versailles on business, and I thought while I was here I might pick up a gift, a something for Miss Jefferson." He listened to the lies flow easily from his tongue—it was simplicity itself to lie in French—and watched Rosalie's soft cheek, the gentle swell of her décolletage as she allowed him to guide her toward the door.

"She is how old, Miss Jefferson?"

"Fifteen."

"And in a convent school?"

"At Panthemont."

Rosalie smiled at the floor. "Somehow I don't believe the good nuns of Panthemont will let her wear 'Muffled Sighs.' "

"Actually." They had reached the door of the shop, and Short gripped her elbow more firmly, stopping them both at the threshold. One part of his mind was noting for the fiftieth time how perfectly they were matched in height—she was much too tall for her elderly, stoop-shouldered husband. The other part was taking a deep breath, consciously, deliberately crossing a line. "To tell the truth, I was riding out from the Hôtel des Affaires Étrangères when I saw you." He swallowed, relaxed his grip. "And I followed you here."

Rosalie had put her hand on the door handle. Now she removed it. Just beyond them, on the busy street, one of the huge public carriages known as a *carabas*, holding at least twenty passengers and pulled by six horses, was passing in front of the shop window.

"I am surprised you could see me so well," she said, so softly that he could barely hear her voice over the noise of the wheels, "since you haven't yet taken my advice about eyeglasses."

"Rosalie."

"Did you know," she said, lifting her head at last as the *carabas* disappeared, "the king is also shortsighted like you, but by royal protocol he's not allowed to wear spectacles?"

"I can recognize you at any distance," Short said. Her hands were trembling, he was sure of it. His own hands were shaking as if they were freezing. He had seen Rosalie de La Rochefoucauld at every gathering of "Américains" at Lafayette's, every diplomatic entertainment Jefferson had arranged, but never once before had he found her alone, without her husband or her female friends or her vast retinue of aged relatives who circled about her like so many dried-up, gray-faced little moons about a radiant white star.

"Rosalie."

"Your Monsieur Jefferson is still away, is he not? On his curative trip to the south? I think he's gone two and a half months. Do you hear from him? Did he make you ambassador in his absence? I never believe the waters at places like Aix can truly heal a person."

Somehow they had arrived on the pavement outside the shop, in the bright glare of the May afternoon, and though she was talking much too rapidly, averting her gaze much too often, nonetheless she was there, he was there, and the brush of her arm and shoulder against his was unmistakable and thrilling.

"Are you staying at Chaville?" he asked, hardly daring to hope. Chaville was the country home of Madame de Tessé, two or three leagues outside Versailles, and a place Rosalie was known to visit often, without her husband the duc.

"You may ask my hostess," Rosalie said, and at the cautioning note in her voice he looked up to see coming toward them, out of the chaotic French traffic, a handsome black phaeton with the glittering family crest of Madame de Tessé on the door and the puckered face of its owner peering at them through the inevitable lorgnette.

"William, the lost secrétaire, enchantée de vous rencontre. And in Versailles. Rosalie, come in." Madame de Tessé signaled her coachman to halt the slow-moving vehicle. Short stepped up to the window and bowed as she poked her wig and head perilously far out.

"I have a letter from Jefferson," she told him in her rushed, emphatic way. "A quite *wonderful* letter that I *insist* you hear."

Short made himself bow again and murmur some words of thanks, but Madame de Tessé rarely paused for little politenesses. "Today, yes? In two hours? Tea? Only ladies are at Chaville this week, I'm afraid. We're having one of my English book readings afterward, but you can hear Jefferson's letter first, and perhaps"—her quick little eyes took in everything—"Rosalie can show you the gardens."

Rosalie sat back in the phaeton, an arm's length away.

"Our group is reading a love novel," Madame de Tessé added as the phaeton began to roll again. "But a tragic one, of course. The hero goes too far and is killed in a duel."

In two hours more, precisely at five, tugging the points of his vest and struggling for composure, Short entered the great nine-windowed parlor at Chaville. Madame de Tessé beckoned him at once toward an empty chair beside her. He had visited the estate before, with Jefferson of course, and even sat in the inner circle by the fire while Madame de Tessé read breathlessly aloud from whatever English book was in fashion. For the life of him, however, he couldn't remember now the name of the aged female cousin shuffling toward him, or the two young girls, scarcely older than Patsy Jefferson, who sat and spread their yellow skirts at Rosalie's feet.

Madame de Tott rose to make him an ironic curtsy. "We are deep into Richardson's *Clarissa*, you know, which is much too sentimental for a man. But by way of a prologue—"

"This is Jefferson's letter." Madame de Tessé held a white envelope high in one hand, with the other waved everyone to their places. "Monsieur Short won't care for our novel, I'm sure, but he's come to hear a perfectly wonderful letter. Your master," she told him, nodding briskly, "writes for the ages. He writes"—she used the latest English word—"like a *genius*. No, I'm wrong. Every word in place, clear, strong. He writes like a *Roman*, yes? Perfect."

Here I am, madam, [he says,] in the old Roman town of Nîmes, gazing whole hours at the ancient Maison Carrée, like a lover at his mistress. The stocking-weavers and silk spinners around it consider me an hypochondriac Englishman, about to write with a pistol the last chapter of his history. This is the second time I have been in love since I left Paris. The first was with a Diana in the Beaujolais, a delicious morsel of sculpture by Michael Angelo Slodtz. This, you will say, was a rule, to fall in love with a fine woman: but with a house! It is out of all precedent! No, Madam, it is not without a precedent in my own history. While at Paris, I was violently smitten with the Hôtel de Salm, and used to go to the Tuileries almost daily to look at it. The chairwoman, inattentive to my passion, never had the complaisance to place a chair there; so that, sitting on the parapet, and twisting my neck round to see the hotel, I generally left with a torticollis.

"What is a torticollis?" demanded Madame de Tott, always the scholar.

"A sore neck." Short accepted a cup of tea from a maid and thought that he had never once seen Jefferson with a sore neck.

"The waters at Aix did nothing for his wrist." Madame de Tessé flipped through the letter. "It's still as bad as ever. But he sees so many antiquities, he hardly cares—you understand why I call him a Roman, Monsieur Short?"

"The very word," Short assured her. "Roman or Rebel."

"No." Madame de Tessé was, as always, decisive. "I've thought much about his character. The man lives with one foot in the past, he rebels by precedent. The most profound revolutionary is the enlightened conservative, is he not? Listen to this passage. 'Were I to attempt to give you news,' he says,

I should tell you stories one thousand years old. I should detail to you the intrigues of the courts of the Caesars, the oppressions of their praetors, their prefects, etc. I am immersed in antiquities from morning to night. For me, the city of Rome is actually existing in all the splendor of its empire. I am filled with alarms for the event of the irruptions daily making on us by the Goths, the Visigoths, Ostrogoths, and Vandals, lest they should reconquer us to our original barbarism. If I am sometimes induced to look forward to the eighteenth century, it is only when recalled to it by the recollection of your goodness and friendship.

"Charming."

"Architecture and friendship, yes, but nothing about the Assembly of Notables?" Madame de Tott arched one black eyebrow. "Nothing about politics? That scarcely sounds like Jefferson, or you, *maman.*"

"In his letters to me"—Short felt obscurely jealous; he put down his cup and came restlessly to his feet, automatically turning in Rosalie's direction before he corrected himself—"which are mostly business, of course, he asks often about the Assembly of

Notables. He says the king has a great opportunity to reform the government and go down in history. He says the Assembly should divide itself into two chambers and meet annually, like a Parliament. And one chamber would be chosen by the provincial administrators rather than the king."

Madame de Tessé had also risen, a look of mischievous delight on her face. "In other words, voted by the people. A democracy."

"Well, filtered through the people. He is a limited kind of democrat. A Roman democrat."

The whole party had by now abandoned their teacups and begun to move toward one of the tall windows that opened like a door into the garden. As he paused to let the ancient cousin pass, Short remembered (with a wry smile of his own) that Jefferson had also written Lafayette a letter on politics, advising the marquis to learn the condition of things by going incognito into the huts of his peasants, sampling their food, testing their very beds. Short treasured the image of Thomas Jefferson of Monticello stooping to enter somebody's hut, lolling on somebody's rat-gnawed pallet of straw.

In the famous (endless) gardens themselves Madame de Tott attached herself unexpectedly to Short and Rosalie and proceeded to speak with her usual bantering irony. "One day," she told Short, leading them to the edge of a thick grove of willows, "you must read us something *you've* written. After all, Jefferson's protégé must write like a genius, too, I think."

"Do you also write?" Rosalie began.

"*My* suggestion," Madame de Tott went on, "would be something in the manner of Mr. Boswell's new book about Samuel Johnson. Give us a *Life of Jefferson*, yes? With dialogue like a novel and personal habits and long intimate description."

"I have sometimes thought—"

But Madame de Tott was in no humor to hear his thought. She glanced left, where Madame de Tessé had fallen back a hundred yards to inspect a new bed of plantings. The others were scattered far and away across the broad expanse of green lawn, gravel paths, and rigid geometrical shrubbery that radiated in spokes from the great château. Short, following her glance, had begun to register, as he nearly always did, how different such a scene, any French scene, was from Virginia—Virginia a dark, wild, gauzy landscape now of memory alone, uninhabited, unshaped by human touch; a cobwebbed landscape of dreams only. But before he could turn back, ever polite, to hear Madame de Tott's next tedious salvo of irony, she had surprised him utterly.

"At the foot of the grove," she whispered to them both, in a voice almost as soft as Rosalie's, "there is a little summer house. It's unlocked this time of year. If you follow the path on the right, afterward . . ."

And without a word more she stretched one thin arm to touch Rosalie's wrist for an instant; smiled with unparalleled sweetness at Short; walked away.

Time stopped. Clouds stopped, wind, voices, sun. The birds in the willow trees went silent, all sounds in the garden ceased. When Short met Rosalie's eyes at last, she too was smiling with unparalleled sweetness.

"I can be there tonight, at ten o'clock," she said. "But only for an hour."

And with that she brushed past him, with fingers like silky fire, and hurried back up the gravel path to greet Madame de Tessé.

At nine o'clock, while the late spring twilight still hung on the tops of the trees, Short tethered his horse at a tavern off the main Paris road and began to walk across the fields.

Madame de Tessé's estate stood close to the road, walled to the outside for perhaps three-quarters of a mile, the length of her formal gardens, and then merely enclosed by a wood rail fence. Short stepped easily over it and set out for the willow grove. Once in the dark trees, with his poor eyesight he could trace the gravel paths with difficulty, sometimes, in the darkest passages, only by the scrape of his boots against stone. But twenty minutes later— still insanely early!—he climbed a little sunken ditch, caught a brief view of the distant chimneys of Chaville, now little more than spots of red, and came to a stop in front of the summer house.

It had been built, he guessed, in someone's idea of the style of a Chinese pagoda. Green dragons and vases painted on plaster walls. Four sharp horns of roof—bright enameled red even in the twilight—swooped skyward from the front double door, which was, as promised, completely unlocked. He called once, out of caution, then pushed the door open and entered. Chairs, tables, other indistinct articles of furniture ghostlike beneath long drooping dust covers of canvas. He poked his head into each of the two rooms. One held a chaise longue and several foil-lined cabinets that evidently served to keep food or drink. Dust was everywhere, rising in puffs at every step.

He listened to his pulse, his heart. By the open door he squinted at his watch, unable to believe he was here, that either woman had really spoken. What would Jefferson say?

Mentally, he kicked himself; he snapped the watch case shut and thrust it into his vest. What matter what Jefferson would say? He of little Maria Cosway, he of another man's wife. Short paced to the first step of the pagoda. Another man's wife. The elderly, benevolent, patriotic Duc de La Rochefoucauld, Jefferson's friend. But Rosalie de La Rochefoucauld was the most beautiful creature Short had ever seen. In his overheated imagination he had already, a thousand times over, met her and confessed it.

He closed his eyes and listened to the blood drum a tattoo in his ears. A crunch of gravel under leather.

When he looked up, Rosalie had just emerged from the willows. She carried a whale-oil lamp and wore a silvery green cowl and a smile still more dazzling and un-shy than before.

"I knew you would be early. You look at your watch more often than any man I know."

"Rosalie —"

"Come inside, help me pull off these awful covers." From her robe she produced a heavy bottle. "I've stolen some champagne from Madame's supply, but I couldn't manage a pair of glasses to drink with."

"I shall drink from your slipper," Short vowed, beginning to believe his eyes; beginning to grin (he thought) from ear to ear like an idiot boy.

"You will not. A ridiculous idea." But Rosalie was smiling as well, and as she brushed past him this time, she paused, lifted her eyes, and ran the fingers of one hand lightly, this time like the touch of white petals, across his cheek. "So handsome," she murmured.

Inside the pagoda she deposited the lamp on a table and shook
herself free of the silvery cowl and robe. "I have one hour. Madame de Tott is keeping watch, making my excuses if someone
asks. But Madame de Tessé runs a very regular household."

"Madame de Tott," Short marveled. He dug the heavy cork
from the bottle with one seesawing thumb. Rosalie returned from
the other room holding two small tumblers. "How Madame de
Tott, of all people, could arrange this—"

Rosalie had taken over everything. She poured the champagne
into each of the glasses, put away the bottle, planted herself before
him, inches away, her left hand on his bare wrist.

"You don't understand France, do you, chèr Guillaume?
French women?"

Short grinned helplessly. She rose on tiptoe and kissed him
once, then drew him sideways toward the chaise longue. "Do you
know about Madame de Tott and her blind lover?"

Sinking, he shook his head more helplessly than before.

"Oh, yes, behind the great walls, *les choses qui se passent.* Charles
Pougens. No—not yet. Listen. Charles Pougens. He was a poor
young painter, and Madame de Tessé and the comte met him in
Rome years ago, when he'd won a prize of some sort and they
were traveling. Then he went blind and, since they have no children, Madame more or less adopted him and brought him to
Paris."

"But—"

"And Madame de Tott and Charles Pougens fell in love, of
course, secretly, and wanted to marry." Short had put down his
champagne untasted and begun to kiss her shoulder, the soft V of
her throat. She stirred, placed one finger across his lips, and
finished her story. "*And* Madame de Tessé found out and forbade
the union (he was so poor) and sent Pougens away, to Geneva
they say."

"Who says?"

"Our laundress has a brother who works in the stables here,
and his wife knows the seamstress for Madame de Tott. They still
correspond, but Madame de Tessé doesn't know. The seamstress
carries the letters in and out in her sewing bag, and the laundress's
brother posts them in Vaucresson."

"I had no idea," Short said with utter truthfulness. Sarcastic

Madame de Tott and her books of Homer, her irony, her little condescending lectures to Jefferson on the art of painting.

"I can't stay." Rosalie's face was disappearing into a veil of shadows. Outside the windows the grove of willows had begun to fade, twilight had metamorphosed into drifting French darkness.

"No. Please." He struggled to regain the initiative, to master her swiftly changing moods. "Since the day I saw you—since the day you came to the Hôtel de Langeac in your carriage."

"In my carriage with my husband."

At every moment she was different. Already there was a new distance in her last words. "Stay with me, Rosalie, Rosalie."

"I'm married, Guillaume."

"But you came here; tonight."

She framed his face between her hands and kissed him quickly. "You are so young; so blind too. Listen. Other women have lovers, but I'm not like them. I have a husband who lives for me alone. He cares for my mother, my grandmother, three aunts, all in the same house. We were married when I was sixteen. I come from a far less worthy family, he gives me safety, protection."

"You love me," Short said with an intensity he had no idea he possessed. *"You do."*

She was transformed, just as everything in France was transformed for him. The shy, delicate woman, too timid and sensitive even to meet his eyes in public, now leaned forward, lips parted, a breath of scent and champagne.

"I only wanted to see you once and tell you," she said after a long moment; pulling back. "While my husband's alive, I cannot be unfaithful to him."

"Come with me, leave him."

"I can't."

"Come to America." Her skin glided under his touch. Her dress slipped from one shoulder.

"No."

Short was trembling now from head to foot. She loved him, she was going away. He reached for her, rose in the chair, twisted the dress farther in a hurricane of rustling silk and crinoline.

"I *do* love you," she whispered, still pulling away, then suddenly returning. "Since the day I saw you first, even before." Her voice was in his ear, on his throat. Her fingers were on the drawstring of his trousers. His heart thumped, stopped. "I can't betray my husband . . . by the last favor."

"Rosalie, je t'adore, adore."

Her fingers pressed harder. She sighed once, moaned. Her head lowered toward his waist. Cool air first, then the crown of her black hair, white cheeks, tongue as soft and melting as honey.

CHAPTER

Twenty-Seven

"He is the most *acquisitive* man I have ever known, surely."
Clérisseau stood at the window and motioned Short to hurry. At
the other end of the room, already hurrying in six directions at
once, Short reached for his coat, Jefferson's papers, squinted at
his watch.

"He has come back with even more *things* than he bought in
England. Put down your letters and come look. Every servant in
the quartier is carrying boxes."

From the window, still struggling himself into the coat, Short
could peer down past Clérisseau's shoulder and see Jefferson's
carriage stopped in front of the door. Servants lined both sides of
the steps, from pavement to threshold, passing trunks and cases
from hand to hand, and in their midst Jefferson, his back to the
house, was directing James and Petit toward an auxiliary wagon,
while all around the carriage and horses more servants and street
urchins danced and chattered like magpies. It was the tenth of
June, four o'clock in the afternoon, the precise day and hour that
Jefferson had planned to return.

"A human magnet," Clérisseau murmured. "If he builds a new
house to hold all that, I'll design it and be rich."

In the downstairs hallway Short presented him with folders of accumulated correspondence; Clérisseau greeted him with an ironic bow and begged to inspect the injured wrist.

"I shall never play the violin again." Ruefully, Jefferson demonstrated the clawlike stiffness of his fingers. Short looked with shock at the withered muscles. "The waters at Aix were useless, worse than useless. But at least I write with tolerable ease now, I can hold the reins of a horse."

"I have brought you, personally, an invitation to the Duchesse de Baronne's masquerade ball tonight," Clérisseau told him. "You can't plead fatigue—it's to welcome you back: Everyone will be there, Lafayette, de Corny." Without a glance at Short. "The noble Duc de La Rochefoucauld. You can wrap up your hand like an Egyptian mummy. You've been away so long, it will be like seeing a ghost."

"If I come, I might better dress as a smuggler," Jefferson said. He was pressing through the busy clutter of bags and boxes being placed on the floor, leading them toward his study. From a leather portmanteau Petit had propped on a chair he seized three little packets, each the size of a brick, tightly wrapped in waxy blue paper of a foreign look.

"Books?" Clérisseau guessed.

"Seeds." Jefferson crossed into the study and began to line the packets precisely along his desk blotter. "Rice seeds. It's against the law to export them from Italy, on pain of death, the border guards told me. But I rode over into Lombardy and stuffed as many as I could in my pockets. I mean to send them to friends in South Carolina to plant there and improve our native stock."

"The Robin Hood of rice," Clérisseau said, taking up his hat and making another ironic bow. "You steal from the poor and give to the free. I leave you larcenous gentlemen to cultivate your garden. For the afternoon only. Tonight, dear Jefferson—'dear heart,' as Lafayette has taken publicly to addressing his wife—I shall see you at the masquerade. I shall be disguised as 'The Friend of Man.'"

As he closed the door, Jefferson extracted a letter from one of the folders and held it up for Short to see. "My daughter Polly is coming," he said. "I almost forgot. My sister wrote *poste restante* at Lyon. She embarked May first, bound for London—she may even have arrived by now. But she was so unwilling to come that they tricked her, poor girl; they all went aboard the ship, her cousins, too, in Philadelphia, as if taking a tour, and delayed and played until she fell asleep. Then they put her in bed and snuck away, and the ship was under sail before she awoke."

The procession of servants with parcels had ended at last. Still behind his desk, head down, Jefferson was now moving from one stack of letters to the next, singing softly as he went. Short attempted to make himself useful by drawing sheets of paper from already opened envelopes. Jefferson's left hand sorted and squared; his clumsy right hand swept the heavier piles to one side.

"I must arrange for transport from London to Paris, or go myself," he said half to himself, half aloud. "She's only nine. And answer these. And fall back into routine at once." He looked up and sighed. "Travel exhausts me, William. I suppose I must go to the ball tonight, you too. But then I need to sit down and write a memorandum of my trip before I bury it under business. And I need, of course, to be brought up to date—the Assembly of Notables, Calonne's performance, Lafayette—"

"Along that line"—Short grinned—"I've prepared a pictorial summary." He took two steps behind the desk and reached over Jefferson's copy press to bring out a large rectangular cartoon that he had cut from the *Journal de Paris* and ordered to be mounted and framed. He tilted it for Jefferson to see: a monkey wearing an oversize crown and carrying a skillet addressed a barnyard of poultry, the Assembly of Notables. The monkey was saying cheerfully, *My dear creatures, I have called you here to deliberate on the sauce in which you will be served.*

Jefferson smiled and put the print aside.

"And Petit will want to make a household report," Short added, hiding his disappointment at Jefferson's reaction; nonreaction. "First, he seems to have dismissed half a dozen servants for thievery—he means to give you every detail. Second, James Hemings has been in another fight. This time with the Prince of Condé's cook, who was giving him private lessons. The cook has a bandaged head and a black eye. James doesn't seem to be damaged at all. He—"

Jefferson surprised him by interrupting. "Have you set aside any letters from Mrs. Cosway?"

After a moment's hesitation Short crossed the room and reached into his own desk for the morocco-bound portfolio where he had placed Maria Cosway's single letter. Jefferson took it without expression and dropped it into his left coat pocket.

"So many days in a rolling carriage alone, so much time for reflection," he said, walking toward the window. In the harsh afternoon light, as Short now saw him, his face was lined, his red hair faded to a sandy brown; Jefferson was what a learned friend of Short's had once described as "prognathous," protruding of jaw. Strained, weary, he looked every one of his forty-four years. "Tonight," Jefferson said. His gaze drifted sideways again in the manner that made his political enemies call him evasive, and suddenly, without warning, Short felt a sensation of ice in his throat. "Tomorrow at the latest. . . ." Jefferson looked away. "Let me sit down with you, William, and have a serious talk about your future."

☆   ☆   ☆

But the future had to wait on the present. The Duchesse de Baronne's masquerade began according to fashion at eleven that night, in the ballroom and lighted gardens of her newly constructed *hôtel* on the rue de Varenne.

"These are called golden 'girandoles,'" said an enormous German woman dressed as a shepherdess. She pointed to the glittering star-shaped decorations attached everywhere to the walls. In the whirl of dancers and noise, Short bowed foolishly.

"They're only made of paper and wax," the shepherdess told Jefferson. Like Short, he bowed. "But they catch the candlelight, don't they, and make the room dance. You're both foreigners."

"American." Short was distracted, glum. He pinched the nose of his domino mask—at such affairs ladies always dressed, men were permitted to wear masks only; not for a moment had he and Jefferson considered a costume. The shepherdess playfully tapped his shoulder with her crook and fairly shouted over the music. "You've done your hair in the style we call 'sleeping dogs.'" Short raised his fingers from his mask to his curled hair. "Very popular style, but too old for you." Her breasts heaved, buttery islands bobbing in a sea of lace. "I believe in dressing young."

She had turned to Jefferson, whose dignity (even in a domino), Short observed, usually had that effect on women. Seizing his opportunity, Short moved away from the entrance, past the musicians, and toward the series of six great crystal punch bowls set out by the garden doors.

Beneath an entire constellation of glittering girandoles he found Lafayette, unmistakable in his tiny black domino, blue silk coat, and elaborately embroidered vest, which showed on the left side an Indian carrying a bow, and on the right side (over his heart) Washington dressed in a yellow toga.

"The Court's chosen color this season," he said, in a mood evidently as glum as Short's, for once speaking French, "is yellow. Even the punch is yellow." He held up his glass. "We go back and forth. When I returned in '82 after the Battle of Yorktown, the new rage was *white*. A decree of the queen. Everybody wore white in every possible combination—before that, thanks to the birth of the royal heir, the color was yellow, *ca-ca dauphin.*" Unbelieving, Short mentally translated: *baby-shit-yellow.*

"Where is Jefferson? Never mind."

In the shifting tide of the crowd Lafayette was replaced by an elderly man who also wore his curls in the sleeping dogs style. Together he and Short backed away slowly from the circle of dancers taking the floor. Short scanned the shepherdesses, princesses, milkmaids, houris before him. Clérisseau was chattering, the two de Cornys were dancing gaily. Rosalie was nowhere in sight—she had been nowhere in sight for him since the memorable night at Chaville exactly one month ago. Not a word, not a note.

"I'm sixty-five years old," the elderly man said emphatically; he gripped Short's arm with an old man's impatience and led him toward a quieter corner of the room. "I first entered society in 1735. Wit was the fashion then, did you know that? All the women thought they were witty, all the priests. Everybody wrote books, conversations became dissertations." With one hand he pushed up his mask to rub his eyes. How could she ignore him now? Could she really be so pure, so devoted to her husband?

"Next," the old man persisted, "this was about the middle of the century, next came Science. Everybody took chemical courses, everybody kept a geometrician instead of a page. The last gasp was Mesmer. Mesmer and Buffon." His fingers scraped lint from Short's sleeve. "Today it's politics. The Assembly of Numbskulls, ambassadors everywhere. All the women are political now, not witty. Last night Madame de Simiane talked for an hour on the question whether Virginian tobacco should be taxed."

"I'm Virginian." It was all Short could think to say.

The old man bared his teeth in a smile or a bark.

In the garden where he retreated, removing his mask, blinking up at the genuine stars above him, Short listened to the distant sound of the music as he walked. He could hear much better than he could see, he decided, closing his eyes; individual notes, violins, harpsichord, oboe—

Jefferson's mild voice broke into his thoughts. "I wrote Mrs. Bingham a letter before I left, deploring the empty bustle of Paris." He fell in beside Short on the dark gravel path. "But I had forgotten the music, how wonderful the music is."

Short made a little motion with his hands, uncertain for the second time in five minutes what to say.

"Polly has arrived safely," Jefferson said, "you will be pleased to know. When I had worked my way to the bottom of the letters you had so carefully filed for me, I found *two* on the same day from Mrs. Adams, announcing my daughter's arrival—she is there, in London."

"Then you will be going at once to bring her here?"

Jefferson guided them to a halt before a low stone bench, flanked on either side by marble cupids. In the moonlit background, larger (blurred) statues peeped from trees or bushes like marmoreal spies. For an instant Short's mind stepped back to Abigail Adams's garden in Auteuil, where mythological statues had guarded John Adams's precious piles of sublime manure.

"In fact," Jefferson was saying, "I plan to send Petit to bring her back."

"Petit?" Short was more than surprised—a girl of nine, a strange servant, the dangerous Channel crossing.

Now it was Jefferson's turn to make a motion with his hands. "So much business has accumulated—the death of Vergennes, you know, the appointment of de Brienne to replace him. Our old friend Malesherbes has joined the king's council, from which I take heart."

Short listened to the roll call of names, the mild voice analyzing and describing the politics of each one. A cynic, Clérisseau liked to tell him, always attributes the worst motive to any action. Either Jefferson knew from his letters that Maria Cosway was arriving in Paris at any moment—hence his reluctance to leave for London —or else he was unwilling to go to London because once there he would have to call on her, and on her husband, and in the company of his daughter. Under the stern Puritanical eye of Abigail Adams.

Jefferson had fairly launched into his subject now. "There is *promise* of reform on both sides," he said. "The Court promises to reduce its expenditures, the ministry promises to establish provincial assemblies to discuss taxation. I would hardly be true to my own principles if I didn't approve of such a move toward representation. But what is chiefly needed is a revolution in public opinion—"

"Sir."

They had strolled a dozen yards from the bench, near a stone wall above which rose, half a mile away, the starlit yellow-gold dome of the Invalides. *Ca-ca dauphin.* The phrase "public opinion" was one Short had never before heard in his life—what did it mean? Another brilliant Jeffersonian invention? Or a political cliché? But he put the idea to one side. He had begun with an utterly different thought.

"Sir, about my future. You referred earlier to my future?"

Jefferson too had removed his mask. The music had stopped. Couples were beginning to stroll after them into the garden. Ahead of the guests, servants carrying lanterns were now lighting torches set in tall iron holders.

"Yes." Jefferson had halted this time before a statue of Laocoön and his sons, who writhed in marble agony, choked by four huge coiling serpents. Short stepped forward instinctively to adjust the focus of his eyes: white marble, streaks of torchlight, black concave background of stone. For a heartbeat he felt as if he were inside his own skull, observing a nightmare.

"You are twenty-eight now, I believe," Jefferson said. "One of the finest minds and characters I have ever known; along with Madison one of the best educated, most serious."

"Sir—"

"But at twenty-eight the world expects that such a mind should have more to show for its training than—" He gestured dismissively toward the crowd of masqueraders spilling into the garden. "Our country needs men like you, educated like you. As much as it would pain me to lose you, William, I want to recommend, as a friend, that you consider returning to Virginia and taking up your place there."

"In the law, you mean?"

"In the law certainly. At the bar of the general court for a short time, then to the bench perhaps; to the Assembly, to Congress. I know that you have no real affection for the law—"

"I have an insuperable aversion to the law." As soon as he had spoken, Short cursed the stupidly defiant tone of his voice. But Jefferson was never offended by defiance. He laughed and stretched his thin, crippled right wrist to stroke the marble serpent that appeared to be squeezing the very life from Laocoön's throat.

"An allegory of your feelings toward the law, perhaps," Jefferson said. "As one who retired early from it myself, I can say little in its favor, as a career. I used to wish old Coke and Blackstone to the devil. But for government it is indispensable."

"I am a terrible speaker as well," Short said abruptly. "At the bar, before a jury; in public."

Jefferson had straightened to look at him, as far as Short could tell in the flickering combination of torchlight and starlight, with genuine surprise. "You speak very well, very well. When I was ill and you presented Lafayette's bust to the city, many people told me afterward how handsomely you had spoken out."

"In French, yes," Short said (he feared) sardonically. "*En français* I am a better and a finer person." Jefferson folded his arms. "But I mean as someone who speaks to persuade, to argue a cause before a judge. My mind goes white, a tabula rasa, I cannot proceed."

"The habit of pleading to a court would soon enable you to

possess yourself of argument, William. You would see the strong sides, the weak sides—habit creates its own strength."

Short was aware of the irony of his excuse. How to put it? *I resemble you in this, who never speak in public if you can avoid it.* They were in fact, in truth as different, as unalike as . . . father and son.

"You speak far more easily than I do," Jefferson said, seemed about to say more; stopped.

Some of the masqueraders had almost reached them on the gravel path. Short spotted the bulk if not the features of the German shepherdess.

"Polly is not alone, by the way," Jefferson said, suddenly returning to the subject of his daughter. "She is accompanied by a servant girl. James Hemings's younger sister Sally."

Voices, masks bore down on them.

"Is there some deficiency," Short said softly, "in my conduct, that you should wish to see me depart?"

Jefferson turned much too quickly to face him. "By no means, William. By no means. The last thing I wish, from my point of view, is to lose your company. What I say is for your interest, not my own. And I insist on nothing—stay as long as you will, as long as you can. I only observe that the sooner the race is begun, the sooner the prize will be obtained. And I say it with a bleeding heart, for nothing will be more dreary than my situation when you and my daughters all have left me."

"Monsieur Jefferson!" called the shepherdess, waving her crook. Behind her a flock of glittering yellow and white. "Now your mask is off, come talk to us about the famous Insurgents."

Jefferson smiled at her and bowed. To Short he said, in the careless tone of an afterthought, moving away, "But if one forms too fixed an attachment in Europe, all freedom is gone." He stopped to brush his sleeve and bow again to the shepherdess. "And if an attachment of a certain sort, perhaps all reputation as well."

In the starlight, in the overturned bowl of his consciousness, Short realized, with deep shock, that Jefferson meant the Duchesse de La Rochefoucauld, just as he had known by a kind of mesmeric telepathy about the Ace of Spades.

"Short, come and join us," Lafayette ordered, raising a torch.

Or—Short took a mechanical step—did he mean by some wild Jeffersonian indirection to accuse himself instead? To refer to Maria Cosway? Or even to both of them, father and son, adulterers in tandem?

At the edge of the path Jefferson was waiting for him. "I haven't seen Sally Hemings," he said, as if to change the subject, "since the day she was born."

CHAPTER

Twenty-Eight

Sally Hemings had grown to be five feet six inches tall, straight as a stick. She wore a faded calico dress, pinned her brown hair up in a braid with a ribbon, plantation-style, and spoke not a single word of French.

"You pick up the tray," James told her in a tone of impatient fraternal disgust. "All right? You don't have to *say* nothing. You carry it into the room and stop in front of each one of them and wait to see what they take."

"Polly too?"

James made a noise she couldn't understand—French. James spoke French like a native. Sally had made fun of him the first day because he talked French so fast and pushed his lips in and out when he did it, in and out, like a fish in a bowl or a pig that wanted to kiss you—wee, wee, wee, this little pig. But his temper was awful, he'd shouted like a sailor. Now he simply turned his back on her and started to shake something out of a cloth bag over his tray of pastry. Sally stepped to one side, ignoring the stare of the old French lady cook, and peered at whatever he was sprinkling.

"Sucre," the old lady said. "Sucre en poudre."

"Powdered sugar." James glanced sideways at Petit, who stood by the cutting table with his arms crossed disapprovingly over his

vest. He handed Sally the tray and pointed one sugary white hand
—white on brown—toward the stairs. "You go to the top. Big
room on the right, ceiling got a sun painted on it, doors to the
garden. Some of them might be in the garden, so you walk around,
just like home."

Sally also looked at Petit, then tossed her head with a flounce.
"Not a *thing* like home," she said.

As she disappeared up the narrow stairs, balancing the tray on
her shoulder, the old lady returned to her stool and gave the coals
a kick. "She's not very black," she told James in a guttural French
right out of the Fauborg Saint-Marcel. "Both of you look almost
white, you look like two big cups of *café crème.*"

James banged a second tray down in front of his oven.

"Quel âge a-t-elle?" the old woman asked.

He squatted beside the oven and frowned. At the top of the
stairs Sally's long legs had reappeared for a moment while she
turned to push the door with her back. Thin feet, shapely ankles.

"Quinze ans," he said. "Fifteen years old. She's only a child."

The old woman followed his eyes and grinned at Petit. Then she
snorted in disbelief. "Ha!"

☆   ☆   ☆

"Only a child," Maria Cosway repeated. She took care to speak in
French so the girl wouldn't understand. Even so, they looked
steadily at each other across the tray of hot pastries until Maria
shook her golden head again and smiled and the girl backed away.
"How old, in fact, is she?"

"Fourteen, fifteen perhaps." Jefferson sat down beside her on
the sofa; a smell of soap, leather—she leaned instinctively toward
him; then, remembering that she had come to Paris as a new
woman, a woman of independence, Maria drew deliberately back
to the arm of the couch. "She's the sister of my black servant,"
Jefferson added, remaining where he was, "the one who cooks the
pastries—and Mrs. Adams used your very words about her: 'quite
a child,' she wrote me, 'so useless as a maid you had better send
her back with the captain.' My sister in Philadelphia chose her."

They watched Sally cross the room. She offered the tray awkwardly to Short and Clérisseau, nearest members of a group of six

or seven other guests—there were nearly twenty altogether—
standing in a half-circle beneath the famous sun painting.

"Well," Maria said. Storklike, Sally was now rubbing the back
of her leg with her foot. "Child or not, you'd better buy her new
clothes, and do something about her hair. Will we be late?"

As she knew he would, Jefferson pulled out his newest watch
and studied the dial. Last year he had briefly carried *two* new
custom-made watches—one he claimed to be testing for his friend
Madison—*and* a pedometer to measure how far he walked.

"We have hours before it closes," he said, and, as she also knew
he would, reached his left hand toward her fingers in a gesture
friendly and possessive at the same time. In the corner of her eye
she saw the white hook of his right wrist—so stiff, withered, and
clawlike that she turned away instantly and started to rise.

"Polly isn't here?" she said at random. With her fan she waved
toward Madame de Corny, who had come to London last season
for a month and never called on her, who (not caring perhaps for
women of independence) had barely spoken to her today.

Madame de Corny was too close to avoid replying. "The most
charming little girl, Polly," she exclaimed. "And you haven't seen
her? Our tall friend here most cleverly arranged for Patsy to stay
at home the first week and take her to the convent school to play
every afternoon. By the end of the week, she wanted to go by
herself."

"Monsieur Clever," Clérisseau said, coming up and bowing.
"Madame de Tessé's pet name for him," he told Maria. "I believe
we should go, yes? The wine and pastries are finished." And
bending down toward her, popeyed and wrinkled as a frog, he
asked loudly, "I don't see Mr. Cosway yet, no?"

Always a rescuer, Jefferson placed his left hand through her
arm. "Mr. Cosway stayed in London, alas," he told Clérisseau.
"Even the opening of the Salon couldn't draw him."

Clérisseau's eyes were huge, his nose was like a snout. "Then,
my dear lady, you are staying where?"

"With Princess Lubomirska," Jefferson answered. "Beyond
the Boulevards."

"Much too far away," Madame de Corny said, and paused,
Maria was sure, long enough to let the ambiguity of the phrase be
heard. Far away from what? But Jefferson had pulled out his

watch again, and the efficient, mind-reading Short was opening the doors, leading the way, and before anyone could say one more word about Richard, about her, about a married woman coming to Paris all by herself to see a Salon of paintings, before she could do anything but smile sweetly (her mask), they were all outside, underneath the golden September sun of Paris, climbing into their carriages. At the corner, as they swayed onto the Champs-Élysées, she saw Sally Hemings standing on the doorstep, still holding her tray; looking, at a distance, less and less like a child.

The Salon, as everyone called it, took its name from the room in the Louvre, the Salon Carré, where the Royal Academy of Painting and Sculpture held an exhibition every other year for precisely one month. Richard had looked up, interested, when Maria first proposed the trip—David would have a new painting, of course; and Madame Vigée-Lebrun, and the silly, effeminate Roland de la Porte, who had flattered Richard so outrageously last year. But then he had simply shaken his head. No Paris. No excursions. No further *talk* of it, please. So that, heart pounding, pursued by her visions like a thief, she had simply gathered her—what? her courage? rebellion?—into a ball and dashed away one morning without permission, over the Channel, over the plains of Normandy, down the long worm-curl of the Seine and into the arms of Paris. Paris only.

"Since you were here," Jefferson said, "they've begun a new bridge at the Place Louis XV."

Maria shaded her eyes, and peered out. In her own mind, the condition of independence was this: She would travel alone, she would mix with friends; she would *not* cause a scandal, *not* yield to . . . the Désert de Retz.

"Over there," Jefferson pointed—miles inside, behind her bright smile, she shuddered at the sight of his wrist—"just beyond the king's statue. In fact, they won't begin construction for another year, but the surveyors are hard at work."

"And the other bridges?" she asked. "They were going to demolish all the charming little dolls' houses on top of the bridges?"

"Ah, Clérisseau is delighted, all the architects are—they've cleared every charming brick and stone from the Pont Notre-Dame and started on the Pont au Change, level right down to the pavement. The views are wonderful."

"They were so quaint and *lively*," Maria said, falling back. The carriage was bouncing east now, along the Seine embankment. On the left, on Jefferson's side, you could see the Tuileries Palace, which Trumbull called a "vile Gothic jumble." "I loved the old bridges," she said. On her side the brown river rocked back and forth, back and forth, like a living thing in a cage.

"Our old friend Saint-James," Jefferson was saying—did he hoard his gossip just for her, she wondered—"Do you remember him? The old gentleman who lived near the Bois? Saint-James has gone bankrupt, to everyone's astonishment, and sold his gardens and taken refuge in the Bastille, where no one visits him. Mademoiselle Bertin's dress shop is also closed—bankrupt."

"A dangerous city," Maria murmured.

Jefferson patted her hand.

In the Grand Galerie of the Louvre their party regathered—the de Cornys, Short, Clérisseau, two or three abbés whose names she had missed, some American merchants in awkward three-pointed hats.

"I appoint myself guide to charming ladies," Clérisseau announced, swooping out of the shadows and inserting his arms, satyrlike, between Maria and Marguerite de Corny: "Virgil to all female spirits." At the top of the stairs he bent comically toward each of them in turn. "This Salon," he declared, "is perfectly to my taste, no criticisms therefore are to be recorded. Everything is antiquity, Roman or Greek. I require only sighs of admiration, the occasional *frisson* of pleasure." He cocked his head at Madame de Corny, whose flattened breasts threatened to bulge entirely out of her dress. "We could begin with *Ulysses Tempted by Circe*, yes?"

"Who transformed men into swine," said Madame de Corny, adjusting her neckline.

"An allegory," Clérisseau said.

"A redundancy," Madame de Corny replied.

In fact, they began with *Priam Asking Achilles for Hector's Body* by Gabriel Doyen, a vast canvas (*vast* was the word of the day in London) in the lurid historical genre that, just as Clérisseau said, dominated every wall. Maria disengaged her arm and stepped back—the painting was truly awful—and while Clérisseau explained it point by point to Madame de Corny, she glanced around, first for Jefferson, then at the room itself. As always, the

French had crowded too many paintings into one place. They ran in uneven lines, five or six rows high, twenty feet or more over the tallest spectator's head, Jefferson's head.

His hand steered her gently to one side, just past the door. "Here are Hubert Robert's antiquity paintings commissioned for Fontainebleau," he said; "they now call him Robert des Ruines." He raised his good hand toward the nearest one, a beautifully colored study of the old Roman Maison Carrée at Nîmes; next to it, the ancient crumbling Pont du Gard at Aix.

"He captures it all perfectly," Jefferson told her. "I saw the originals on the spot, you know, not five months ago."

"Yes, and from there you went into Italy"—Maria affected a pout—"and never wrote me a word of it till you came out again. You might have gone to Rome, even Florence!"

He smiled benevolently, drawing her in his loose-jointed, rambling way down the line of paintings, so utterly different from the stiff-backed European men with their hats under their arms, their noses up in the air.

"I did indeed take a peep into Elysium," he said. "But I only entered it at one door and came out at another. I calculated the hours it would have taken to carry me on to Rome, but they were exactly so many more than I had to spare. In thirty hours from Milan, I could have been at Venice and the Adriatic, but I'm born to lose everything I love, am I not?"

They had drifted almost to the tall windows of the Salon that overlooked the river.

"If you had been with me," Jefferson said, still smiling, "there were so many enchanting scenes we needed you to paint." And without looking at the actual painting on the wall before them, he began to describe a landscape near Milan that she should have captured on canvas, a castle and a village hanging on a cloud, a stream, a mountainside shagged with rocks and olive trees. He had written her something like this in a letter, but to hear it in person, to listen to his voice, see his face, his confident manner . . . Her eye stopped at the withered hand.

"Well." She turned away. "This is a *real* painting, you see, and by a master." She tipped her fan toward the trompe-l'oeil of Roland de la Porte beside the window. It was a rendering of the

Crucifixion in precise relief; chalky white cross, deep violet background, our Savior with head bowed, three bright spots of blood.

"Perfect." Jefferson inspected it as if he would take its measurement. From the corner of the window you could see straight along the river to the Pont Neuf and the gray sloping roof of a church.

"Saint-Germain l'Auxerrois." Jefferson said: "One of the oldest churches, I think. When my friend Adams was here, his son John Quincy was at Froullé's bookshop one day and a bell rang in the street and everybody in the shop fell suddenly to their knees. It was the priest from that church carrying 'le bon dieu' to some dying person."

"Le Porte-Dieu. He carries God," Maria said. "Even the king has to kneel when he passes. They say Louis XV once fell to his knees right in the mud, on the street." Her memory searched for the French words of the famous story: Le roi s'est mis à genoux dans les boues.

"The Adams boy," Jefferson said, amused, "is a New England Calvinist just like his father. He said he was 'revolted.'"

Along the next wall a few samples of sculpture had been arranged in front of the paintings. Here Short and the merchants were admiring Houdon's new bust of General Washington, placed next to the bust of Lafayette that Jefferson had presented to the city. One of the Americans demanded something of Jefferson in the harsh clack-clack of the Yankee accent, the crowd of spectators shifted, and Maria found herself unexpectedly going along the walls with Short, her enemy, her spy.

"You have brightened his spirits wonderfully," Short told her. She could detect no sarcasm in his voice. Ingratiating, rather. All day long, for whatever reason, he had seemed oddly subdued. "When his daughter arrived in July, he was overcome with homesickness, you know. He talked of nothing but Virginia and Monticello and how soon he might be traveling home. Now—"

"This is Madame Vigée-Lebrun's work, no?"

"All these portraits, yes."

Maria pushed herself forward boldly. Madame Lebrun believed that women should dress simply, naturally, without affectation. The painting Maria had fixed on was a portrait of the actress

Madame Raymond, unostentatious, hair falling in natural curls, a shiftlike dress of ivory-colored cotton lawn. Trumbull said that at her dinners Madame Lebrun served nothing but fish and salad, and that she once made her pompous husband strip off his powder and wig and sit down to eat with a wreath of laurel about his head. Short was saying something. Maria moved on. I could do this, she thought. I could paint with power, force, like a man, if only, if only—

"Over there is the queen herself," Short said.

Maria turned quickly, but of course he meant the portrait of the queen, just to the left of the entrance door, in the place of honor. She moved purposefully toward it, folding her fan. Even at a distance it was different from the usual royal flattery, utterly different from Rubens's huge fleshy portraits of Catherine de Médicis in the Luxembourg Palace. Here, when you came close enough, the scene was the Hall of Mirrors at Versailles, but daringly, Maria saw, Madame Lebrun had posed Marie-Antoinette not as a queen or a Greek nymph, but as an ordinary woman, a *mother*. A baby played on her lap, two older children stood at her sides. She wore a hat and a formal velour gown and looked straight toward the painter. But the crib on her left was empty, signifying, Maria guessed, the queen's loss of a child—was it a year ago? She stopped abruptly. Cribs and babies always worked on her imagination; her mind sank backward into memory, drowning, her own crib, her murdered baby brothers, the avenging nurse lowering her gigantic watery face like a moon.

"It meets with a mixed reaction," Short volunteered beside her. "For various reasons the critics are quite divided about its merits."

Maria nodded. She knew all about the scandals whispered around the queen. Richard had repeated every filthy joke he had heard, he had read aloud till she screamed from a little book called *Les Amours de Charlot*, which began with the queen masturbating and went on to love between women, nymphomania, worse. Marie. Maria.

"I like her portraits," Jefferson said, doubtfully, appearing at her other side. "She captures expressions very well. But her palette can be too somber, too dark for my taste."

"You had thought of commissioning her," Short said.

"Perhaps. For Monticello." Jefferson was somehow drawing

her leftward, toward the next painting. "I dream of installing a little gallery at Monticello to remind me how I have passed among heroes. But now look at the next—surely this is the finest thing in the room, superb, sublime!"

"David," said Short.

"The Death of Socrates."

Maria allowed herself to be brought within inches of the new canvas, which was large, dark, austerely masculine. On a bed, left hand raised to calm his weeping students, Socrates reached for a bowl of fatal hemlock. Behind him a bare stone wall, an arched passageway leading to barred windows. The only woman was Socrates's wife, insignificant, resembling a man. Maria opened her fan and dropped back a step. Ordinarily no one was more enthusiastic than she was for the works of David, but this cold, calculated painting—what about it so appealed to Jefferson? She let her eyes go back to Marie-Antoinette.

"Sublime," Jefferson repeated. "If it were not already taken I would purchase it."

"You like the colors?" Maria could see the artist's intent: the tragic force of the students' love was meant to burst in colors against the severe, classical lines of the composition; David was indeed sublime, Madame Lebrun merely domestic. But today the effect made her shiver.

"I like the colors," Jefferson said. "Yes. I like the way Socrates breathes greatness, soul." He had extended his hands, the good and the injured, to frame the painting.

"And the theme?"

"I see this as a register of conflict," Jefferson said. "On the one hand, law, rigor, the state; on the other hand, emotion, love of life. Public duty and private desire. Sacrifice."

Short saw the two of them look at each other as if exchanging a private code, a secret appeal. "Head and Heart," Maria said softly, finishing Jefferson's thought. But as Short watched she carefully stepped aside from his touch.

"They see almost nothing of each other," Clérisseau declared. He paced half the length of the rug and made a kind of pirouette around the three massive wooden boxes. "All of Paris wonders why, after six weeks, the flame seems to have died out."

Short was irritably searching his desk for the right envelope. "All of Paris wonders nothing of the sort."

Clérisseau circled the boxes warily. "All right; true, correct. No one in Paris actually cares. The spectacle of a married woman and her perhaps *amant* is hardly new. Or shocking. Or interesting. Especially if the woman travels about in a perpetual caravan of female attendants and is never seen so much as to get into a carriage alone with him. Discretion is the better part of nothing."

Short found that even the letters on the envelope blurred in the slantwise light of the room. If or when he returned to Virginia, would his eyes improve? Clérisseau stopped in midpace and read over his shoulder: "Madame Townsend. Monsieur Grand. Monsieur Daubenton."

"Daubenton."

"And," Clérisseau said, taking the letter, opening the seal for him with a snap of his thumb, and handing it back, "especially nothing if the *amant* takes a room in the monastery at Mont Valérien and spends two or three days a week in dreary, masculine retreat when he could be with his beautiful lover. Can you explain —think of me as a visitor to the strange American planet—can you explain *that* behavior?"

Short started to speak, then shook his head.

"He rented his room when?" Clérisseau asked. "September fifth? Hardly a week after she had arrived? 'Love's first moment after noon,' the poet says, 'is night.' Yes?"

Short could only shake his head again, unfolding the letter at the same time. He had devoted many hours himself to just that question. Jefferson was a man who always seemed to need two houses, one for open, public living, so to speak, as at Monticello; the other for retreat, solitude, as at Poplar Forest or now at the hermitage on the French mountain. All month he had disappeared regularly on Fridays and returned on Mondays, carrying great batches of correspondence and diplomatic ledgers. The monks enforced a rule of absolute silence in their gardens, but Jefferson said the paying guests were allowed to speak, quietly, during meals. As for Maria Cosway's bristling caravan of attendants— Short refolded the envelope.

"I like the child Polly," Clérisseau said. "She has a fragile air, and she already speaks French. But why has her aunt in Philadelphia shipped her these three herculean boxes?"

"She hasn't. The Hercules in this case is a General John Sullivan of New Hampshire, and the letter says they're to be delivered before they spoil to Buffon's assistant at the Jardin du Roi."

"A gift from Jefferson?"

" 'Objects of natural history.' That's all it says."

Clérisseau sniffed once. "Another potshot in the Wars of Truth."

"If you want to come along," Short said, ringing for Petit, "the mystery will soon be lifted."

Clérisseau sniffed again and picked up his hat. "*This* mystery. Not the other."

In the carriage, to Short's surprise, they discussed politics. Clérisseau, far less conservative than his habitual irony suggested, declared bluntly that the disturbances of the summer would go on and on until—"until the king divorces the queen?" Short asked. Like everyone else, Short was amazed by the violence of the popular revulsion against Marie-Antoinette.

Clérisseau shook his head. "You know the riots this summer?" Short nodded. In August, after the Assembly of Notables, the king had exiled the remaining unruly and liberal *Parlement* to a provincial village. Riots of protest had broken out across Paris. Mobs escorted favored nobles to their carriages, pelting others with mud and stones. They looted bakeries, shops, toll gates. Intransigent, the king had decreed yet another set of taxes to pay his crushing debts.

"Jefferson is right. Nothing will truly change until the fundamental *injustice* of our system changes." Clérisseau smoothed the fabric of his handsome emerald coat. "A parable. At dinner some years ago in Versailles, as one of the king's little games, each of the guests was required to tell a true story about a thief. When Voltaire's turn came, he simply smiled his wily little foxy smile and said, 'Once upon a time there was a man who was a member of the Farmers-General—I forget the rest.' "

The Jardin du Roi lay to the east of the Latin Quarter, in the Faubourg Saint-Victor, facing the river. "Almost out of the city and into the country," Jefferson liked to say, and he had come a number of times from the Grille de Chaillot to see the collections of plants and wander among the botanical curiosities that Buffon had put together. But Buffon himself, though he was granted a handsome house rent-free on the southwest corner of the gardens, rarely appeared in Paris anymore. Deputies did all the work while the master, in his Burgundy retreat, wrote volume after volume of his endless, inexhaustible *Histoire naturelle.*

A man after Jefferson's own heart, Short thought as they pulled off the main road and entered the gardens. A public house and a private life; a team of printers at his disposal. More and more Short found himself thinking of Madame de Tott's suggestion — when he was not thinking of Madame de Tott's complicity. Why shouldn't he write a life of Jefferson one day? Who knew him better? Who had lived with him longer? He would gather reminiscences, facts, and letters from Jefferson's boyhood friends in Virginia. He would write down what Franklin had told him; John Adams — the carriage bounced uphill past a brackish pond crowded with lily pads and weeds; he craned to look back at the following wagon with its load of boxes.

Why *not* write such a book? He might well begin with the death of Jefferson's father — the early death of a father is always a cataclysmic, shaping event for a son, and no one had ever told him exactly how Peter Jefferson had died. Was it in summer? On a lingering sickbed like Jefferson's wife? Did the father's death account for the constant, stoic self-control of the son? Enthusiasm crept into Short's mind. He would sift, examine, develop. Penetrate Jefferson's defenses, disclose the springs of his character: explain once and for all why he guarded his feelings so closely; why his feelings were all the stronger for being walled in and guarded.

At the official house and office they were greeted by Buffon's forty-year-old secretary and alter-ego, Louis Daubenton.

"Le Comte de Buffon, alas, is not well, he is not here to receive you," Daubenton told them. He raised one black eyebrow at the three immense boxes Petit was unloading onto the steps.

"I understand," Clérisseau said cheerfully, brushing dust from his coat, "that even when he's here, he never speaks to his guests until they sit down at the table." He pushed the door with his foot and peered in.

"This is Monsieur Clérisseau," Short explained.

Daubenton was a tall, many-boned man with a flat wig and a nose that split his face like a hatchet. He bowed to Clérisseau. "Charles-Louis Clérisseau, author of *Les Monuments de Nîmes*. Honored. A great book."

"My own opinion as well," Clérisseau said. "If only the purchasers of great books had agreed. Monsieur Short is also a writer, of diplomatic fiction; formerly a poet. Now, sir, here are three crates from Monsieur Jefferson to Monsieur Buffon"— Short handed over a letter, Petit and a Savoyard began dragging the first box up the steps—"but no one knows what's in them, and Jefferson, like Buffon, is away on retreat."

"I don't read English." Daubenton was frowning at the letter.

"I'm sure Jefferson would call it American," Clérisseau said. "Shall we use this room for the unveiling?"

Daubenton looked at Short, shrugged, then followed him into a first-floor chamber whose walls were lined with glass-topped cabinets of minerals and, between each cabinet, stacks of dirty brown folios, which on Clérisseau's inspection all turned out to be copies of Buffon's *Histoire*, volume three.

"A library of a thousand books," Clérisseau said, opening one at random, "nine hundred of which he has written himself."

"Monsieur Jefferson sent us once before a panther skin, from Philadelphia," Daubenton reminded Short suspiciously. "You brought it yourself."

"Well, these come from a General Sullivan, who lives in New Hampshire," Short said, "and it can't possibly be another panther skin." They stood back as the Savoyards deposited the third box on the floor. Side by side, they made a platform six feet in length, ten feet wide, braided across the middle with thick hemp rope. At Short's nod, Petit produced a hammer and clawed a rope loose; in a matter of minutes the room was filled with flying straw, boards, the squeal of ripping nails.

"Horns!" Clérisseau cried.

He bent over the first box and pulled out a set of knobby gray antlers that belonged, Short thought, taking them as they came down the line of hands, to a small New England deer or caribou.

"More horns!"

Clérisseau had unceremoniously shed his wig and elegant green coat and now stood over the open box in his shirt-sleeves. Beside him one of the Savoyards, streaky-faced, grinning through gapped teeth, was scooping out straw with both hands.

"A direct hit!" Clérisseau wrestled another set of deer antlers out of the packing. "A broadside shot. Books at twenty paces, horns across the Atlantic—Jefferson really knows no limits!"

Daubenton handed Short a third set of antlers and a handwritten tag, attached with a cord.

" 'This is the roebuck, of Massachusetts,' " Short read. " 'About three years old. All of these specimens come from either New Hampshire or Massachusetts.' " He looked up to see Clérisseau beginning the next box. "You have several sets of elk horns," he told Daubenton. "Caribou horns, a number of deer hides and deer skeletons, the 'spiked horn buck.' Jefferson has sent them all for the Comte de Buffon to study and exhibit."

"And greetings from Brobdingnag!" Clérisseau shouted over the sound of more boards tearing. From the middle box he was in the act of drawing out an amazingly large animal skin, most of whose hair had fallen off or was just now coming away in coppery puffs. Short held his nose. With the instinctive flourish of a true-born Parisian, Clérisseau raised the floppy skin to his shoulders, grasped the neck with one hand, and transformed it into a swirling cape.

"On the Boulevards," he said with a courtier's mince, "I shall dress in the latest fashion *d'Amérique.*"

" 'sieur." His attending Savoyard was staggering under the weight of a new set of horns. Clérisseau's face broke into a delighted grin. One hand still gripped the front of the skin at his collar—legs and hoofs dangling down each shoulder—the other lifted the new horns onto his head. He swayed, took a step. Daubenton had put on his glasses and stood beside him, staring. Through the haze of straw and dust Short saw Clérisseau dance into the open, trailing the brown cape, wearing the towering, unmistakable flat-boned horns of a New Hampshire moose.

" 'Moose'!" Clérisseau shouted, reading the card Short held up. He turned in circles before the glass-topped cabinets, whirling like a popeyed pot-bellied Dionysus. "I've fallen in love with American words—moose! Moose! À la mode de moose!"

CHAPTER

Twenty-Nine

Memoirs of Jefferson — 11

AMONG THE LOYALISTS AT THE SECOND
Continental Congress, it was considered a sinister
habit of Sam Adams's that he liked to organize unruly young men
and teach them, of all amazing things, how to sing psalms together.

"Harmony," he would say slyly, making one of his strange
palsied gestures. "Psalm singing brings many different voices into
harmony. Harmony is what we aim at."

Seduction. Sedition and seduction were what Sam Adams
aimed at, the Tories fumed, just as he "harmonized" his three
dozen so-called "Indians" into the infamous, ill-named Boston Tea
Party. But by the spring of 1776 even the stubbornest of Tories
would have admitted that their complaints were largely drowned
out by the clamor for independence that Adams had so tirelessly —
I choose the metaphor — orchestrated.

Jefferson slipped into Philadelphia late as always (he has always "slipped" onto a public stage), just in time to be greeted by
rumors, flattery, the first buzzing flies of a Pennsylvania summer,

and the unceasing attention of Sam and John Adams, who immediately saw a use for him.

Or rather for his pen. Because on June 7 the stylish, stiff-
necked Richard Henry Lee, "Virginia's Cicero," with his bony
face and his thin, chilling smile, had walked to the front of the
room and placed on the president's table a resolution that every
member of Congress had known would come, sooner or later:

> *Friday, June 7, 1776.* The delegates from Virginia move in obedience
> to instructions from their constituents that the Congress should
> declare that these United colonies are & of right ought to be free &
> independent states.

The debate, anticipated for months, raged on for days, inconclusive, bitter, the great states of New York and Pennsylvania still
hanging back, South Carolina and Maryland not yet matured
(Jefferson said) for "falling from the parent stem." Midway
through June, a committee was appointed to write a declaration,
in case the resolution finally passed. The whole of Congress assumed that Richard Lee would head it.

But Thomas Jefferson was the favorite of the two Adamses
("he is the greatest rubber off of dust I have ever seen," John
Adams repeated busily everywhere), not least because Lee was
distrusted by all northerners as "radical," a kind of oratorical
highwayman bound to no one, while the grave, studious Jefferson, mute always in the presence of his elders, looked like a safe, a
harmonious, Virginian. Not least, as well, in John Adams's mind,
because Jefferson wrote with the crisp, elevated felicity of a prag-
matic angel, and if there was one flaw Adams would admit to, it
was that his own prose style, pungent as it was, had too much the
smell of earth.

Was it John Adams who put the very pen in Jefferson's hand?
Probably. The other committee members were no writers either,
except for Franklin, who wouldn't do it (and who would have
ruined it with a joke if he had).

In any case Jefferson went back to his sparse rooms on Market
Street and sat down alone before the little folding travel desk. Sat
down with a head still aching from the long, intolerable April-to-
May attack that had followed the death of his mother. With a head

still reverberating—I am guessing now, nobody has been inside
that head—still reverberating with anger at his mother for that
last unforgivable parental desertion; at his long-dead father, too,
no doubt. "Falling from the parent stem" is, after all, strange
phraseology for a political revolution. But then, a child's feelings,
though they go underground soon enough, are like stars and never
burn out. Break with a parent, willingly or not, and prepare for a
deep, melancholy sense of unmendable loss. If you read the Declaration of Independence closely, in its first drafts, you will find it a
family document.

You will find it a family document, for example, in the opening
paragraph of "grievances," which the Rebel must have written
with extraordinary speed on the first piece of paper that came to
hand (the reverse side of the sheet is covered with pencil drawings
of a horse stall he admired in the stables of Governor John Penn):
*"The king has sent over not only soldiers of our own common blood but
Scotch and foreign mercenaries to destroy us, invade us and deluge us in
blood. This is too much to be borne even by relations. Enough then be it to
say, we are now done with them."* Then: *"unfeeling brethren! . . . we
might have been a great and happy people together."* And at the bottom
of the page, with many scratchings over and revisions, this: *"we
acquiesce in the necessity which pronounces our everlasting adieu."* Then
crossed out and substituted the exact phrase from *Tristram Shandy*
that he would use six years later on his wife's deathbed, when he
would once again collapse like a man singled out by the gods and
destroyed: *"the necessity which denounces our eternal separation."*

Surprisingly enough, for someone so essentially rational and
private, he left these last lines in the final draft he laid before
Congress on June 28. By then, Pennsylvania was ready to vote on
Lee's resolution, New York would probably vote—the Declaration was shoved to one side, the angry debate resumed. Dickinson
rose to protest, John Adams rose (bounced) to refute. On July 2,
American independence was abruptly voted and the Congress,
with scarcely a moment's pause, snatched up Jefferson's document and began to read.

Began to read and *slash*, Jefferson must have thought. Adams
stubbornly defended every word his young protégé had written,
but Congress was filled with too many orators and critics. Out
came some oversharp phrases and adverbs in the beginning. Out

came a fine sentence accusing the king of inciting insurrections. Out came the climactic paragraph describing the treachery of our unfeeling English "brethren," which had left John Dickinson shaking his poor old egglike head till John Adams believed it would fall off and crack. And out, finally, out came the whole long section denouncing George III for encouraging the slave trade (this was urged by South Carolina and Georgia, but Jefferson noted sarcastically in his journal that the northerners felt a little "tender" about it as well, since they had been pretty considerable carriers of slaves to others). To the author's mind this was the unkindest cut of all. Jefferson had labored on the passage over and over, on the very steps of the meeting hall John Adams had told him it was the best part of the whole composition, "a noble, vehement philippic." It reconciled with reality the great assertion of the preamble, that all men were created equal, it joined Jefferson's youthful campaign against slavery and his anger against the parent stem. Independence made no sense without an attack on slavery. To see it crossed out by a clerk's indifferent pen—

What did he think? In the state house no one could really tell. He sat in the back row, on an old cane chair, fanning away the flies in silence. Few people knew that on the morning of June 28, when he first had to submit the Declaration, his mind was already deeply troubled, not by the document itself (no one was a more confident *writer*) but by the terrifying prospect that he would have to walk to the front of the room, turn and face the Congress, and then read *aloud* what he had written—Jefferson, who never exposed himself by public speaking. He had spent most of the previous night nervously marking up his copy with intricate little slashes and dots intended to tell him just where to pause as he read, and for exactly how long, like a clockwork Patrick Henry. (Afterward the baffled printer would mistake his little marks for commas and periods, so that the first printed copy of the Declaration of Independence was in fact the most ill-punctuated composition in American history.) Now Congress, which had chosen him because he was a writer, was simply hacking away his most deeply felt passages, and he could do nothing but sit and smile in courteous silence.

Next to him Franklin watched with his usual droll expression. Not much about human nature escaped Franklin. He leaned over and tugged Jefferson's sleeve. "When I was a young printer," he said, "I knew a hatter who made a new sign for his shop. He wrote it on a signboard: 'John Thompson, Hatter, makes and sells hats.' But his friends came by—you understand friends. One said the word 'hatter' was redundant and struck it out. Another said 'makes' was unnecessary. Somebody else said, '*sells* hats? Who expects you to give them away?' When they were finished, his sign was reduced to plain 'John Thompson' with the picture of a hat."

CHAPTER

Thirty

O n November 3, Jefferson gave an evening party for men only.

"Monsieur Short," said Lafayette with impenetrable courtesy, coming up to him beside the fireplace, "I believe you know the Duc de La Rochefoucauld?"

The duc bowed and did not smile. "We have met a dozen times at least, have we not, Monsieur Short? Our noble friend has grown so thoroughly American as to introduce old acquaintances to one another." A smile arrived at last, like winter, on the duc's gray lips. "Though I believe it is my wife who has the advantage of knowing you well."

Short was certain that his face had turned to sheets of flame. He smiled, bowed, accepted wine from James Hemings's tray, and listened to his voice murmur perfectly truthless, perfectly civil nothings in reply. Out of the background Clérisseau suddenly appeared, grinning broadly and bringing Jefferson with him.

"I have been speaking to our host," said Clérisseau, not hesitating to interrupt, "about horns."

Short held his smile in a vise.

"Monsieur Short, the most attentive man in Paris, kindly let me go with him last week to the Jardin du Roi and present that old scoundrel Buffon with twenty sets of horns and a hundred dozen animal pelts from Maine. Now our Thomas says he had no idea they were coming."

"In fact, they cost me forty-seven pounds sterling," Jefferson said wryly, "and nearly lost me the friendship of John Adams in London. I had merely written General Sullivan many months ago and asked him to be on the watch for the skins and horns of a New Hampshire moose, if one came on the market, so that I could prove to Buffon how large our animals really grow."

"And instead?" Lafayette was genuinely curious.

"Instead, as a former general, Sullivan made the acquisition of a moose the object of a regular military campaign. His troops sallied forth in the middle of March—much snow—a herd attacked—one killed—a road cut twenty miles through the wilderness—the carcass drawn on a cart to his house to be cleaned and packed and then shipped on to me. When he arrived in London two months ago, he presented a bill, without explanation, to Abigail Adams, who gave it to her son-in-law, who paid it, aghast, and asked John Adams for reimbursement."

Short watched Jefferson bend down and stoke the coals in the fireplace. The Duc de La Rochefoucauld was sixty-five years old if he was a day. Rosalie was twenty-four. Short had seen her alone exactly once since Chaville—a whispered protest in the anteroom of a party, a hurried kiss, not given, not resisted. In the fairy tale the two children pushed the wicked troll into the fire.

"The *size* of the bill rather stunned them," Jefferson said, straightening, "as it did me. And on top of that, I had already put Mr. Smith, the son-in-law, to immense trouble ordering a harpsichord to be made for me in London."

Lafayette looked around the drawing room possessively. "Not here."

"Not yet. It's being shipped down the Seine from Le Havre." With a regretful smile Jefferson held up his withered right hand. "My days of playing music are finished, I'm afraid. It will be for Patsy and Polly."

The Duc de La Rochefoucauld took his seat unceremoniously

in one of the new blue upholstered chairs arranged before the fireplace. "I understand," he said, "that Madame Cosway plans to hold an exhibition of her paintings in the Palais Royal."

As if on cue, Sally Hemings came into the room to replace her brother, carrying with her a silver tray and two more decanters of wine. She had recently been given money to buy new clothes and have her long hair dressed, and Short saw the duc look up at her with something like distracted masculine interest. Then he let his eyes slide past Short's and repeated his question.

This time Jefferson made an almost imperceptible shrug, which Short interpreted silently: He was not privy to Mrs. Cosway's plans, he had organized his little gathering of men as a perfectly independent occasion.

"More new rooms!" Clérisseau returned from the doorway, where he had been squinting into the stairwell. He let Sally Hemings pass with an appreciative glance. "It's ungracious of me, an architect, to say so, but how do you put up with so much *building* all the time? You've been in two houses in Paris and you've tried to remodel them both—nails, hammers, *racket!*"

"My passion is tearing down and putting up," Jefferson said placidly. "I cannot let it alone."

"Is it true you went a whole winter in Virginia without a roof?" This was the Abbé Morellet, who had the smooth pink cheeks of a roasting pig and held a glass of wine in each trotter.

Jefferson smiled and shook his head. He took the nearer of Sally Hemings's decanters and began to move from guest to guest, filling their glasses. The dinner had been typical of him, Short thought; mostly vegetables (including Indian corn from his garden), very little meat, an excellent Château Haut-Brion. The Roman ordinarily followed a strict rule of no more than three glasses of wine a day, but in the past few weeks the rule had been less and less observed. When Maria Cosway had last come to the Grille de Chaillot, which was two weeks ago now, attended by the triple-chinned Princess Lubomirska and an entourage of chattering Poles, Jefferson had served champagne and duck and Maria had neither eaten nor drunk.

"You must tell us," said the duc from his chair—Short turned his back and took a step away, which he recognized as idiotically symbolic. What did the duc really know? Or care? More to the point, what did Jefferson know?

"You must be perfectly honest," the duc said. "When you return to America, will you rebuild your famous Monticello? Will you make it a *maison française*?"

It was a shrewd question. The duc was a shrewd man. Rosalie would not marry a fool. Would not love a fool.

"I have plans in fact," Jefferson said with mock pride, "to rebuild it completely *à la française*. You know the Hôtel de Salm?"

"Aha!" Clérisseau beamed.

"You wrote my aunt," Lafayette said through a mouthful of cheese. "You said you had fallen in love with it, '*smitten.*'"

"I have spent many an afternoon in the Tuileries Garden watching it go up," Jefferson admitted. "And most of all I admire the great dome that crowns the house, a wonderful play of horizontal lines against rising curves."

"Like the Halle aux Bleds," said the duc.

"Exactly. The same combination of Palladian form and modern engineering." Short handed Jefferson the sheets of ruled paper he knew were wanted and watched as he and Clérisseau began to sketch for the rest a diagram of the intricate beams that supported the dome of the Halle. The Roman could metamorphose into the Enthusiast in a split second if one of his dozen—his two dozen—special interests were mentioned. As Jefferson, now in a chair by the duc, started to draw skylights and stairs he had seen somewhere else, Short edged across the carpet to Lafayette.

"He is a man of such brilliance," Lafayette murmured. "Purity." With his habitual curiosity—or desire to be seen?—Lafayette pulled the curtains apart and looked out on the Champs-Élysées. "Like Washington," he added as an afterthought.

"A Madame Townsend has been to see him," Short said confidentially. "She brought a letter from John Paul Jones and wanted to borrow money. She *hinted* strongly that she was a daughter of Louis XV and highly placed to aid America."

Lafayette was more interested in the dry moat that separated Jefferson's house from the pavement of the Champs-Élysées and the torchlit customs gate, thronged as usual at this hour with wagons, merchants, lounging soldiers. "Well, it's easy to check."

He stretched his neck and ran a hand over his bristly red hair. "There's a man in Versailles who has the official list of the old king's bastards—I can give you his name—but offhand I don't remember a Townsend."

"Jefferson surmises she was Jones's mistress."

The Prince of Pineapples chuckled. "Dr. Franklin used to say that part of the American mission was to keep Admiral Jones's mistresses happy. John Adams's face would go black each time he said it." He dropped the curtain and looked back at Jefferson, now folding his sketches and slipping them into his pocket. "Architecture bores me. My dear friend"—he turned his back on Short and began to walk briskly toward Jefferson—"here it is November. Have you not received the new constitution? Have you heard nothing?"

Jefferson had not. Politics displaced the Halle aux Bleds. The convention in Philadelphia was over, Jefferson reported, copies of the proposed new constitution were en route—rumored even to be in London already—but for some unfathomable reason Madison had sent nothing yet, though two packet boats had come and gone. No document, no letter. Short glanced at his watch. He privately guessed that Madison had delayed sending the new constitution because he was afraid of Jefferson's reaction. What political horror could the assembly of demigods have dreamed up?

He lifted the curtain, peered; streaks of nothing. Clérisseau said he should go back to Virginia and make his fortune. Clérisseau said Jefferson was not a man ever to give up an idea, once he had conceived it. Short opened the lid of his watch again, the spidery hands jumped. Five twenty-three, Paris. Bleak, cold, Rosalie-less Paris. Clérisseau said that Maria Cosway had lost interest in Jefferson either because she was ambitious as an artist, trying to establish herself alone, or else because she was a deplorably prudish married woman—that is to say, English. In any case, he had added in a world-weary tone, quoting Horace, *Post coitum omne animal triste est*. After love every animal is sad.

But three miles away, listening to the Princess Lubomirska describe in the most mournful voice and in the most tedious detail in the world the young queen's newest outrage, Maria had not lost interest. If she closed her eyes, she could see him. If she blocked out the princess's monotonous voice, she could hear Jefferson naming the trees in the Désert de Retz, explaining the intricate mathematical structure of bridges, the two hundred types of Parisian carriages. A woman might or might not be independent. But a vow was a vow before God, marriage was marriage.

"They say, of course, that the child isn't the king's at all, the father was a Swedish count in the embassy. At night, you can hear her *moans* all over the palace."

Maria blinked and smiled. Should she tell the princess that she felt a complete, total sympathy with the good, maligned, misunderstood Christian queen? "Shocking," she murmured. "Terrible." Last spring Richard had taken a trip to Wales in the company of a woman, an actress—she shivered and smiled at the princess—and written back obscene letters, comparing the actress in bed to her.

The princess was complacent. "The king will send her away," she said, "or else the throne will collapse."

"Maria, martyr," Maria said, and it was the princess's turn to blink.

CHAPTER

Thirty-One

There were twenty reasons, Short decided, why Jefferson and Maria Cosway would never be happy lovers.

To his left, as the crowds spilled out of the theater lobby and onto the rainy Place Condé, Jefferson and Patsy stood side by side, father and daughter unmistakably, while Maria and her inevitable Polish duenna looked up at them both with wary interest. Then Maria reached forward, laughing merrily, and placed her small white hand on Jefferson's great freckled one, and Patsy scowled as if her face would break apart into chunks of granite.

Short stopped to allow another surge of theatergoers to roll past. If he had a sheet of paper he could write down the reasons on the spot.

Reason one: Maria was far too flirtatious and independent (now tilting her pretty chin, calling brightly to the de Cornys), especially without the restraining presence of her little monkey husband. Jefferson liked women who were submissive, feminine, yielding; women who were at once (Short considered his paradox) decorative and invisible.

Reason two: Patsy Jefferson, who now clung fiercely to her father's arm, hated her; and Jefferson's ties to Patsy were the unshakable Virginia ones of blood.

Short made another effort to reach them through the crowd. Wigs and bonnets sailed past him like snow-covered galleons. He raised both hands to Patsy in a gesture of frustration.

And finally, how could he put it? For all her bare-shouldered, high-bosomed beauty, her blond tresses and pearl-like teeth, Maria struck him as in reality . . . not sensual; not a woman who would—his mind veered to the image of Rosalie, Rosalie's lips. Maria was not a woman who would *please;* pleasure. Whereas Jefferson, whatever else he might be, was a man of passions, a man of flesh like other men. What a man wanted, Maria might not willingly surrender.

Short found an opening in the crowd and squeezed his way across the lobby.

"I've got the carriage, sir."

Jefferson was by far the tallest man in the room. Next to him, on a high shelf built into the wall, was one of the busts of theatrical "notables" that the directors of the Comédie Française had commissioned from Houdon to look down upon their patrons. In this case it was Voltaire, whose sharp aristocratic features looked uncannily like Jefferson's beside him, at the same level. Short raised his voice to be heard over the crowd and the rain. "But we need to go around the portico, to the other side."

"Will you come with us?" Jefferson had bowed close to Maria's ear, but Short and Patsy could hear every word. "The carriage holds four and we are only three."

Maria gestured helplessly at her Polish chaperone, who in turn spoke rapidly and cheerfully in a language Short didn't know. To Jefferson the chaperone added in orotund English: "She will. I have zo many friends here from the Pologne. I see you at home at the princess's, *ma chère.*"

On the portico they waited again, dodging splashes from horses and cabs, until Petit himself drove up in Jefferson's *équipage* and the four of them clambered inside.

"We will give you mulled wine and toast to dry you off," Jefferson said decisively. The carriage lurched, stopped, jumped into the pack.

"Ah, no. I should go straight to the princess's house," Maria protested.

But Jefferson slid open the coachman's window and gave his order just the same.

"I have come three times in the last week to your house," Maria said as he settled back. They were side by side; facing Short and (Short glanced to his right) the Great Stone Face of Patsy. "Three whole times, and you were not at home."

"And I," Jefferson said, smiling but firm, "have come at least that often to the Princess Lubomirska, only to find you are away, painting, exhibiting . . ." His voice trailed away.

"You need to square your accounts," Short said (stupidly), jumping in to fill the silence. Beside him Patsy's folded arms communicated an unbreachable disdain.

"Do you hear from anyone?" Maria asked. "Our London friends? John Trumbull?"

Jefferson had momentarily occupied himself with a loose strap on the door. Rain drummed against the roof. The carriage struck a curbstone and rocked. Short said the first thing that came into his head. "We heard from Trumbull yesterday. He's found three splendid English painters, so our commissions are coming along just fine."

In the furious pause that followed, before he fully understood his slip, Short could see Maria's face suddenly drained of all color, Jefferson's mouth clamp in a thin, icy line.

"Commissions? You have commissions in London?" When excitement took over her voice, Maria had the clipped accent of a Cockney. She swung to stare up at Jefferson.

"I made—I asked Trumbull to order some paintings for me in London, for my private collection."

"Not me? I am a painter."

"I thought he would be able," Jefferson began. Short looked down, up, away; wished himself in Virginia, Chaville, the moon. "He knows my taste, he can advise the framers, shippers."

"But not *me*!"

Worse than Short's blunder was Jefferson's tone: teasing, unserious. "You are too charming and pretty to waste your head on such a little business."

Maria started to reply, closed her mouth. As the lights of the Pont Neuf appeared in the rain, she fixed her gaze straight ahead. Patsy and Jefferson refolded their arms. A moment later, Maria braced herself against the swaying carriage, slid open the coachman's window, and changed the order.

At the Princess Lubomirska's, Jefferson climbed out of the carriage with her, and they stood together, speaking intensely in the falling rain. Patsy glowered at her shoes, then turned her head sharply in the other direction. Through the half-open door Short heard tones, but not words. When Jefferson rejoined them, he wore the air of calm, unruffled benevolence he always assumed at times of stress. "Mrs. Cosway leaves for England in five days, she tells me."

"I had no idea," Short said, ambiguously.

"So I have asked her to come to a farewell party the night before, in her honor." Jefferson wiped his forehead, now plastered with wet red hair and milky powder.

"She won't come," Patsy said with undisguised satisfaction.

☆   ☆   ☆

But in fact, on the appointed Thursday she arrived breathless, stunningly dressed, precisely ninety minutes late.

When she made her entrance, Jefferson was seated at the far end of his book-lined salon, on a crimson couch, beside the ancient, faintly bewhiskered Countess Potocki.

At the sight of Maria he rose like a shot and started toward her.

The countess turned calmly to Short. "I will have another glass of water," she said, "if you please. The water of the Seine is thought to be lightly purgative." Short glanced at his watch. The countess leaned forward to tap his knee sharply with her finger. "On dit qu'elle sort de la cuisse d'un ange," she said, and translated into perfect English: "They say it's the piss of an angel."

At the other end of the room Jefferson had already reached Maria's side. He pressed her hand to his lips. "So you really leave tomorrow?"

"In the early, early morning, by the carriage to Honfleur." Not a word of reproach for her lateness. Good. She took a step deftly around him and saw that he had, in truth, arranged a brilliant party for her. There were thirty guests at least, all staring toward her with bright expectation. The walls glistened with new paper; new chairs, a crimson sofa, musicians in one corner.

"Stay longer."

She smiled, shaking her curls, and as if she were onstage, an actress, she began to cross the room briskly, formally, greeting the guests as they bowed and curtsied. Beside her, splendid, handsome in a sky-blue coat and dark brown breeches, Jefferson hurried to keep up with her, bowing like a page, reminding her of names.

At the crimson sofa she stopped and turned graciously to Short and the little countess, drawing them into her circle, then turned in the other direction to include de Corny, his flat-breasted wife, all of them petals, she thought, around the central blossom that was her presence, *her* performance.

"You've installed the new *tables aux fleurs*," she told Jefferson gaily, and she indicated with a tilt of her head the cut flowers that appeared to grow, improbably, out of the small tabletop by the sofa. A calculated actress's pout. "I haven't been to this house in so long."

"And we know you leave tomorrow." Madame de Corny, a Jefferson ally, was cat-faced and polite.

"In the too-early morning, yes," Maria repeated; "yes, by horrible, horrible carriage to Honfleur." To her surprise Jefferson had bent over the tabletop and begun to do something mysterious with it. Through the nearest window she could see snow.

"He loves his flowers," said the little Countess Potocki from her perch on the sofa. *"Un homme sensuel."*

"In Virginia, Madame," Jefferson said, straightening and presenting a primrose blossom first to the countess, next, with a bow, to Maria, "I have orange and acacia plants in my house constantly, in a greenhouse just off my bedroom. Their scent is the first thing that greets me in the morning."

"You need a wife," the old lady said. "This is one of those tables, yes? You have a tank of water lined with tin, built right into the wood."

"For you." Jefferson bowed and presented Madame de Corny a blossom. "You?" Her husband smiled and took his flower with a solemn, military click of the heels. "At Monticello," Jefferson said, "I intend to install these tabletops everywhere."

Maria felt her moment slipping away, changing. Always Monticello. It was *she* who was about to depart. "You haven't informed me," she said in a sharper tone. The de Cornys looked at each other. "Do you have any messages for Mr. Trumbull in London? I can certainly carry your messages." She flushed and twisted the yellow blossom in front of her dress; looked down at her breasts.

"No messages, thank you. He arrives in Paris on the tenth for a short visit, he writes me. Not even a week away."

"Then we shall practically pass on the Channel." In the manner of parties, the others were backing away, leaving them face to face.

"In my bedroom at Monticello," Jefferson said—it was impossible to read his bland expression—"I want to install an alcove bed like the ones we saw at the Désert de Retz. Do you remember?"

She felt her cheeks grow even warmer. To talk to her of his bedroom . . .

"I believe I even proposed a return excursion to the Désert," Jefferson persisted, "but you were too busy this time."

"It might have been a disappointment, things always are. If my inclination had been my law—"

"Your domestic entourage," Jefferson said, as explanation or rebuke—his eyes were a thousand miles away; no one could be more polite, no one more remote—"has been so numerous *et si imposante* that one could not approach quite at one's ease."

"I know." Suddenly miserable.

"When you come again, you must be nearer, and move more extempore."

"You like flowers," the Countess Potocki declared, hobbling up between them. She held a red lorgnette to her eyes and showed big yellow teeth nearly the size of Lafayette's.

"I think of them as a parable," Jefferson said, bowing to her again, either droll or serious, impossible to tell. "The flowers come forth like the belles of the day, have their brief reign of beauty and splendor, and retire like them to the more interesting office of reproducing their like."

Maria opened her mouth to speak, but the countess was not to be dislodged. "You went to Rome, I understand. Last spring. Now we are Polish, of course, my family is, but a branch is installed at Rome."

"Ah, Milan was the spot at which I turned my back on Rome and Naples. It was a moment of conflict between duty, which urged me to return, and inclination urging me forward."

Maria felt it all going wrong. In the mirror, for the beat of a heart, she saw herself disappear, vanish like a ghost behind a bright, false smile. "Mr. Jefferson," she heard her voice tell the countess, "*always* chooses his duty."

Jefferson's face flickered, as if in pain.

At dinner, where she sat as guest of honor, though Jefferson knew she hated the subject, Lafayette lectured the table for two eternities on politics.

"In the Netherlands," he announced, "the rebels have adopted an *American* slogan — 'Liberty or Death.' "

"He raced to the border last summer," Clérisseau murmured in Maria's ear, "and demanded to be made general of the liberated Dutch. They sent him packing."

"And now" — Lafayette had raised his glass without looking; Sally Hemings filled it — "America again, always; we have a new American constitution that takes us into a new world."

Jefferson was shaking his head; Clérisseau was whispering something else in her ear, an English quotation she had heard before about a brave new world. When she filtered his voice away, Lafayette was leaning intensely across the table, listening to Jefferson, who was — the very opposite of intense — sitting back in his usual informal, casual manner, fingers lightly gripping the stem of his glass, head propped on his right fist.

"I only received a copy of that new constitution two weeks ago, from Mr. Adams in London," he said.

Lafayette seized on his tone. "You don't like it? You don't approve?"

Jefferson studied the glass. "There are very good articles in it, and very bad; I can't say which preponderate. I confess there are things in it which stagger all my disposition to approve. For one thing, I dislike very much the fact that the President can be reelected — he can become, for all practical purposes, an officer for life."

"A king," Lafayette said.

Jefferson sank deeper into his familiar jackknife slouch. "More important still, I dislike the omission of a bill of rights."

"A bill of rights to do what?" From the center of the table de Corny had now stretched forward, against all rules of French etiquette, to enter the conversation. Farther down, between Short and Adrienne Lafayette, the old countess was nodding vigorously, Madame de Corny had forgotten her food. Parisian women, Maria thought; an Assembly of Bores, politics. Jefferson had engineered this. She pushed her plate to one side with a clatter.

"Do you hear any news of art?" she asked, too loudly. "The portraits you commissioned in London? Painters here?"

Jefferson hesitated. "None at all," he said. "No news of painters at all." He smiled quickly, then turned back to de Corny. "A bill of rights would guarantee religious freedom. Freedom of the press, trial by jury, habeus corpus, protection against standing armies." He glanced past her, to Lafayette. "It isn't enough to say, as Adams does, that all these rights are reserved implicitly to the people. It is altogether more prudent, more practical, to state the people's rights in the beginning, without sophisms. A bill of rights is what the people are entitled to against every government on earth, and what no government should refuse them."

"The British press make much of your late rebellions in Massachusetts," de Corny said, still leaning forward, both elbows on the cloth, pinching the bridge of his nose with two fingers; Short's gesture, Maria thought, balling up her napkin. Would they never shut up? She felt more in sympathy with Short every day. All Paris knew why the Rochefoucaulds were not at the party. She took a deep breath. De Corny droned on. "They insist America is in anarchy and needs the strong arm of a king."

"Like their own," Jefferson said, never once looking her way. "George *rex*. The English have spun so many lies about America for so long, they now probably believe them. We have had very little in the way of rebellion and anarchy, if the facts be known. Calculate. One rebellion in thirteen states in the course of eleven years is but one per state in a century and a half. What country ever before existed a century and a half without rebellion? And, to be frank, of what significance are a few lives lost in a century or two? I am an old gardener. The tree of liberty should be refreshed from time to time with the blood of patriots and tyrants."

Against her will Maria shuddered. So serene, so *bloody*. Jefferson's two hands, the one strong, healthy, open; the other crooked and weak. Symbols of—what?

"You hate kings that much?" The old countess was wrinkling her brow, offended. "We have kings in France."

"I hope"—Jefferson smiled diplomatically—"America may be spared them."

"But a country needs a king. The people need to be guided."

"Have we found angels in the form of kings to govern us?" Jefferson's smile never wavered. "I think in America we have embarked on the world's last, best hope—to govern ourselves, freely, by the light of reason alone."

"England will settle the new constitution," Lafayette said, clicking his teeth like castanets, drinking his wine. "America is still under England's sway. I speak as a patriot and admirer—but your language, your trade, all your history and laws—hopeless."

Jefferson nodded. His eyes followed James Hemings and the procession of maids behind de Corny's chair, carrying plates. "America is indeed chained to England by circumstances," he agreed. "You may say we enact the old Roman fable of the living and the dead bodies bound together. We embrace what we loathe."

Maria rose abruptly from her chair, spilling her wine, and rushed from the table.

In the hallway, scarcely seeing what she did, she fumbled with the outside door, a key, then stepped back to let the footman pass. The snow had turned to rain. A servant appeared for an instant—a white spot of a face—then vanished. From the dining room Clérisseau's voice came and went, and then Jefferson was behind her, holding the soft lambswool cloak—Richard's present—she had arrived in. "My dear friend," he murmured. Did he ever apologize? "You're upset. I've made a mistake—too many people, we've been dull on politics." Then bending closer: "I will come to breakfast tomorrow before you leave."

She shook her head but kept her eyes fixed on the door. "I'm merely confused, distracted." Taking a deep breath, she turned to look up at him. "You are all brilliant, wonderful." Then formally, coldly, to pierce him, "I hope our correspondence will be more frequent and punctual than our meetings have been."

Jefferson nodded and stood close to fasten the cloak at her throat. Behind her the door blew open again and the wind gusted. He was a public man, with ambitions; a jealous daughter; a hand like a claw.

"I will arrive at seven," he said, adjusting the cloak. James Hemings was holding the front door ajar. Jefferson's lips were warm, polite on her outstretched fingers. "And then escort you all the way to the Porte Saint-Denis, just as before." From behind his back, surprising her yet again, with the gentlest possible smile he held out a second delicate primrose.

"Just as before," she repeated, seeing the flower through tears.

The next morning, as Short watched from his bedroom window, Jefferson left the Hôtel de Langeac at half past six.

An hour later, from the second-floor study, Short saw him return. He opened his watch in surprise, then squinted down at the street. Jefferson's face, as best he could tell, was calm and impassive. But his shoulders were high and loose, like those of a man relieved of a burden.

At midmorning, without having reappeared, Jefferson departed again, this time for his room at the hermitage. In the office Short filed letters and balanced their ledgers. Petit, passing the open door, brought in the miscellaneous papers he had found in Jefferson's room and laid them carefully on the letter table. When he had gone, Short got up slowly, walked to the table, and since it was his usual task, began to leaf through the stack. The last letter was an unsigned note, in an envelope, written in a tiny, feminine script.

Friday night, December 7

I cannot breakfast with you to morrow; to bid you adieu once is suffi-ciently painful, for I leave you with very melancholy ideas. You have given my dear Sir all your commissions to Mr. Trumbull, and I have the reflection that I cannot be useful to you; who have rendered me so many civilities.

It had begun to rain softly again. Short stood for a long moment, reading the letter, pondering the strange, cool, not un-Jeffersonian word *civilities*. Then, without thinking, he turned over the envelope and ran his thumb along the seal. On the inner flap, so faint as to be almost invisible, was a pen-and-ink drawing of a small unhappy female face, imprisoned inside a pillar, like a caryatid on a temple. He held it up to the light. From the drawing room downstairs came the thin, distant notes of the harpsichord, one of the girls, Patsy or Polly, playing a waltz.

PART

REBELLION TO TYRANTS IS OBEDIENCE TO GOD

Three

CHAPTER

Thirty-Two

"He will never, *ever* promote your interests while you remain *here*."

Having delivered his opinion, Gouverneur Morris sat back in his chair—not with an air of self-satisfaction, Short thought; a better word to describe Morris would be *composure*. Or *complacency, self-assurance, arrogance, charm*—Short gave it up. Morris had arrived in Paris two months ago, on February 17, 1789 to be Jeffersonian and precise, and Short still had no idea how to take his measure.

"If he wants you to resume the law, and in Virginia"—Morris shivered delicately, as one might shiver in disgust at a rat—"then he has made up his mind, and it won't do to cross him. You hate the law?"

Short nodded. It was pointless to correct Morris, who misunderstood Jefferson willfully and completely.

"But not Virginia?" Morris shook his head in wonder.

In fact, Short wanted to say, Virginia too; but Morris had begun to wag his empty glass significantly at the nearest garçon.

"A cold well easily runs dry," Morris said. He tilted his big, handsome head toward the window, where pedestrians were clattering by, bundled and gloved and hatted like white-faced bears. "I read today that the winter of 1788–89 has been the coldest winter in French history."

"In my history, certainly."

"But you found a warm enough little bolt-hole, yes? I like this very much." While the boy refilled his glass with wine, Morris looked approvingly from one side of the room to the other. The Café du Parnasse, Short had warned him, lacked some of the *ton* of the Palais Royal, but it was precisely the kind of Parisian café Short had come to like best: on the Right Bank just beyond the Pont Neuf, with a view of the river; coffee from the Isles; an informal but prosperous clientèle who watched the street and played endless games of dominos while the owner, a stocky Champagnois named Charpentier, wandered among the tables in his round wig, his muslin cravat. Short squinted: Today, to battle the cold, Charpentier also wore a bright red vest and a blue wool coat, so that he looked like the flag of France. In the corner near the fire his black-eyed daughter sat buttering bread for her new fiancé.

"Well, I thought you would like it better at least than the Club des Colons," Short said.

Morris made a face. The Club des Colons, just above the Café du Grand Véfour at the Palais Royal, was a gathering place for young Parisian liberals. Short had made the mistake of taking the aristocratic, distinctly unliberal Morris there for their first meeting.

"Your trip," Morris said. "As I understand it you left Paris last fall."

"September."

"And you made the Grand Tour with two other young Virginia bucks with the nautical names of Shippen and Lee."

"And Jefferson's friends Mr. and Mrs. Paradise."

Morris made another face, but this time Short couldn't be sure whether it was because of the wine he had just tasted or the mention of Jefferson's name.

"Two quacking ducks. I met them in New York." Morris had, as far as Short could tell, met everyone in the world. "The old man dithers on about the pronunciation of modern Greek and the old woman opens and closes windows hysterically all day long. Am I right?"

Short smiled. It was as concise and accurate a description of the Paradises as could be imagined. "The lady," he said, "was widely thought here to have an infatuation"—*for*? *on*? he had forgotten English after speaking French so long—"for Jefferson."

"Humph. I'm going to write an essay one day about the way names start us off on the great career of lying. You, for example, are not Short. An hysterical, window-slamming old lady is not Paradise."

"You are not a guv'nor." Short gave it Morris's own clipped pronunciation.

"Nor a senator nor President. But so. You took your Grand Tour, to acquaint yourself with Europe." Morris adjusted himself in his chair and glanced over his shoulder at the round-wigged host; drained his glass. "I will surmise that you took it to bolster your credentials for a diplomatic post, yes? Instead of returning to the knobby red soil of Virginia and practicing law, you decided to make yourself acquainted with all the great European Courts, so that Congress, when it finally establishes its diplomatic service, will think at once of Mr. Short."

"I would rather stay in Paris than anywhere else, including the rest of Europe."

"And," Morris said, "you hoped that a little breathing space would ease whatever tension—oh, the tiniest, the most invisible of tensions—there was between you and Ambassador Jefferson." He flourished his empty glass at the garçon and stared through the window at a gust of snow now obscuring everything on the street. By the Pont Neuf a team of horses burst out of the swirl like a fist through a sheet of paper. "Good God," Morris said, "and this is the middle of April."

"You remind me of Colonel Humphreys, who used to hate the Paris weather."

"I have met Humphreys," Morris said. "A saturnine son of a bitch."

"But there is no tension between Jefferson and me."

"And I further surmise," Morris said, ignoring this, "that you, who are a very intelligent though hero-worshipful young man, looked far enough downstream to see that when Thomas Jefferson returns to his slaves and swamps, someone will need to replace him here, in Paris. And who better than Mr. Short, who already knows the work inside and out?"

"I am content as I am," Short murmured.

"And I finally surmise," Morris continued, "in fact, I don't surmise, I know it—you went on your trip in part because some people regard you as too attentive to a certain married lady and Jefferson thought it would cool your blood, if not hers."

Short felt his ears and cheeks burn, not cool. Morris had a formidable, bantering way of speech that he thoroughly enjoyed until he himself became its target. "Those are unfounded, slanderous rumors," he said as stiffly as he could, "which I resent."

Morris smiled. He inspected the newly refilled glass and swallowed a gulp of red wine. He looked at the fireplace and the young couple beside it, the girl now feeding her fiancé bits of bread with her fingers.

"I am a cad," Morris said, "even to repeat them." He straightened his powerful body in the chair and extended his left leg until the stump of the amputation was visible above the wooden peg he used for walking. "Did you ever hear how I lost my leg?"

Despite himself, Short gazed in fascination at the wooden peg. The French believed, to a man, that Morris had lost his leg heroically in the Revolution, fighting at his patron George Washington's side. In fact, as Short knew very well, Morris had lost it in Philadelphia one early morning in 1780 when a jealous husband had returned home unexpectedly and Morris had overturned his carriage galloping away. According to gossip, it was far from his first (or last) such adventure. "I am almost tempted to wish he had lost *something else*," John Jay had written to Washington.

"I have never heard the story," Short lied.

Morris was thirty-seven years old, scarcely seven years older than Short, but he had an assured bearing—a sophisticated Horatian levity—that made him seem much older. Levity rather than gravity, Short thought; a delightful man, but certainly not a great one. Morris swung his stump around with one hand and allowed his teeth to flash in an ironic grin. "You will make a splendid diplomat, Mr. Short," he said.

☆　　　☆　　　☆

For her part, ironic or not, Patsy Jefferson liked Morris's banter almost as much as Short did. And it was no disadvantage, more-over—she decided to be brutally honest with herself—that Gou-verneur Morris was one of the handsomest men she had ever seen. She stopped at the door of the carriage and waited while her father and Morris came down the steps together. Her father, lanky, loose-jointed as ever, wearing clothes altogether too casual for the street; Morris, powerfully built, like a soldier, beautifully dressed in fawn trousers and green coat, hopping down the steps on his wooden leg with an air of unconcern, brave nonchalance that made her heart go out to him.

"Your little sister," Morris said, pausing in front of her, "is the first young lady of my acquaintance *eager* to return to school."

In the carriage Polly slid farther away from the door and made herself into a ball.

"She loves Sister Amélie and the other nuns," Patsy told him. It was a lie; Polly hated the school.

"I like old Sam Johnson's remark to the abbess of a convent," Morris said, turning to her father. " 'Madame, let us be honest. You are here, not from the love of virtue, but the fear of vice.' "

The two men laughed, her father shaded his eyes against the sun—sun at last in Paris!—and when they said nothing more to her, Patsy climbed into the carriage and sat down by Polly. Sally Hemings peered inside with a puzzled frown, then closed the door.

"I had this carriage specially built for me in London," Patsy's father told Morris. He put his head through the window and blew a kiss to each of them. Withdrawing: "John Trumbull made all the arrangements, down to choosing the harness."

"I know John Trumbull," Morris said as the carriage began to roll.

Patsy looked at Polly, who had begun to bite at her nails again. Automatically she pulled her sister's hand from her mouth and, at the same time, glanced at the little round outside mirror Trumbull had added as one of the carriage's special features. In the glass Morris and her father had been joined by Short, all three of them undoubtedly talking politics, riots, French craziness. Patsy watched the sycamore trees dip in and out of the mirror. On the other hand, despite his charm, Gouverneur Morris was definitely, to her ear, not truly nice to her father. He used a droll, ironic tone of voice—and people were never ironic with Papa, only Cléris-seau, who was French—and there was something, a hint, of condescension or dislike; disrespect. And whatever else you felt or happened to think, Papa was never a person to be used with disrespect, either.

"Have you told him yet?" Polly asked from her corner.

"Shush. *Tais-toi*."

Polly shrugged and made herself into a tighter ball. Polly disliked the school, her classmates, and Paris, and every Sunday afternoon when they returned to Panthemont she retreated into glum eleven-year-old sulks, worse than tears. They bounced and rattled down the green Avenue des Tuileries, among the sun-dappled trees, and swung over toward the river. Polly took her nails out of her mouth and began to read from the folded-up sheet of music that Mr. Hopkinson had sent them all from Philadelphia, where she used to live.

> *No comfort the wild woods afford,*
> *No shelter the trav'ler can see—*
> *Far off are his bed and his board*
> *And his home where he wishes to be.*
> *His hearth's cheerful blaze still engages his mind,*
> *Whilst thro' the sharp hawthorn still blows the cold wind.*

When they had played the song on their new harpsichord for Papa, Polly had burst out crying. Even now her eyes were dry but red.

"Do you miss Philadelphia that much, Polly?"

"I miss Aunt Eppes. And my cousins. And I *hate* Paris." She folded the sheet of music carefully and tucked it into her school bag. "When are you going to tell him?"

At the Pont Royal they crossed to the Left Bank and made the familiar turn onto the rue de Grenelle. In the school itself Polly went off, clutching her music, to her dormitory room, and Patsy proceeded to the smaller rooms on the third floor where the oldest girls lived. Julia Annesley, who was English and very short and who had gone riding with them twice in the Bois on her father's invitation, was waiting by their door.

"Did you say anything?"

"No."

"You won't."

Patsy walked past her, down the hall, and into the gloomy little reading room that they were permitted to use for extra assignments or, once in a great while, tea. One of the nuns had tried to stock the shelves with books and magazines from foreign countries, but they were always disappearing and in any case nothing from Protestant countries (except America) was allowed at all; several times her history sister had asked Papa for a copy of his *Notes on Virginia,* but somehow it had never been delivered.

There were three desks, three chairs, three bookcases. Trinities. Patsy sat down at the desk nearest the window. Because it was spring, the sun now stayed overhead until six or seven in the evening—Papa would have recorded it exactly—and the little gardens below seemed to have turned green overnight. Patsy adjusted her quill, her inkwell, the sheet of fine vellum paper. Mrs. Cosway—the thought came completely unbidden into her mind—was Catholic.

"Patsy, *ma chère,* have you spoken to him yet?"

Patsy looked up to see the thin, beautifully complexioned face of Madame de Mézières studying her from the door.

"No, Madame. We had visitors. My sister was unwell. She cried a good deal. And my father was worried about his congé and the calling of the Estates-General and, and—politics. Those dreadful riots in Aix and Marseilles."

Madame de Mézières came into the room and used her thumb to tamp down one of the unlit candles on the desk. She wore a tailored gown of deep purple and red, lace sleeves and collar, and a plain gold crucifix on a black moiré ribbon; because she was the director of the whole school, she was excused from the usual gray wimple and hood that the other nuns wore.

"It is always so serene and peaceful here, is it not?" she said.

"Always. When I see the frivolous life—at the Théâtre des Italiens there was a woman with *two* men, and her dress was cut low enough to show everything, she nearly popped out"—Patsy stopped, blushing, aware that she was talking too fast and, no doubt, about subjects she ought not even mention.

"Flippant, frivolous," Madame de Mézières agreed. "But Father Edgeworth asked me distinctly this morning if you had acted."

Patsy looked down at the blank sheet of paper on her desk. Father Edgeworth had come to the school six months ago from Ireland and was even more handsome than Gouverneur Morris.

"You *are* seventeen years old," Madame de Mézières said, less gently. "You need to take your own situation in hand. Your father leaves for America in three months."

"Or more." Patsy knew she had her father's liking for accuracy of dates. "He has *asked* for leave, but Congress hasn't replied yet, because of the new constitution, and he probably can't go to America until the summer, and then only for five months. So he would be back by January certainly. To cross takes only four weeks in summer."

Madame de Mézières, as everyone understood, never permitted herself to dispute anything with her girls. She simply smiled the sharp, tight-lipped, unsmiling smile that meant she was about to give an order. "If you finish your letter to him tonight," she said, "even though it is Sunday, Father Edgeworth and I will see that it goes into the post."

Patsy nodded and took up her quill. When Madame de Mézières had closed the door, she dipped it into the brass inkwell, then stopped. The inkwell had DEO GRATIAS engraved on both sides, joined by two silver-painted crosses in relief. From the chapel downstairs came the high, peaceful sounds of the choir. She closed her eyes. Mr. Short was always writing. What would Mr. Short say?

Slowly, with little tears of joy and terror running down her cheeks, she opened her eyes and began to write.

CHAPTER

Thirty-Three

"At the Constitutional Convention," Morris said, "we took up at one point the question of whether the President should be capable of being impeached."

"For misconduct?" Jefferson asked.

Short stopped on the muddy gravel path and waited for the two men to catch up to him.

"For misconduct or any other reason. The question was simply, should there be a clause declaring him capable of being impeached by the Senate." Morris stumped up beside them and balanced expertly on the wooden leg. Short forced himself not to stare. Morris wiped his brow with a silk handkerchief and squinted down the Champs-Élysées as if he were about to start a race.

"In the convention I was given to strong and frequent statement of my views," Morris said dryly, putting away the handkerchief. Jefferson looked sideways at Short. According to Madison's letters, Morris had never stopped talking. "On this occasion I demanded in my strongest terms that the President *not* be impeachable, for the sake of having a strong executive. At which point our venerable friend Dr. Franklin, who was sitting quietly in the first row with his hands folded over his cane, cocked his head at me and said in his mild way, 'Well, the President would either be impeachable or he'd be assassinated.' I looked down at him and said at once, 'My opinion has changed.' "

Jefferson laughed loudly, pleased at any story about Franklin, and Morris grinned and looked about with enormous self-deprecating charm.

"You know, in 1784 before I left for here," Jefferson said. They resumed walking along the path, Morris fanning his cheeks with his big tricorn hat. "In '84 some pioneers on the other side of the Blue Ridge Mountains wanted to form a new state and call it simply Franklin State. They proposed that in his honor taxes would be paid only in deerhide or whiskey."

Morris hobbled a step behind them. "Well, it's '89 now, but there will be a new state there one day, many new states."

"Many." Jefferson was now lingering by a white-blossomed shrub—when the snows stopped, everything had bloomed at once—and he paused to snap off a leaf while he talked. "Meanwhile, as we put together a nation, our hosts are hard at work taking one apart."

"Lafayette is late." Short held up his watch.

"Has he reached a decision as to the orders?" Morris had amazed Short by the speed with which he absorbed the French political situation. Lafayette was a delegate to the great, repeatedly postponed Estates-General, the new assembly that was to address the linked questions of the king's seemingly endless debts and the continuing bread riots in the provinces. For weeks he had been agonizing over whether the three orders—nobles, clergy, commoners—should vote as blocs or as individuals. The latter choice, as Morris had instantly understood—and denounced— was tantamount to pure, unprecedented democracy.

"Lafayette inclines to the individual vote," Jefferson said. "All of the liberals do. I do."

"Sheer folly," Morris said firmly. Short prepared himself to observe how Jefferson, whose cheeks had gone dull red, would respond to such blunt contradiction. But before he could speak Morris was looking past him and was raising his hat: "Et voici enfin notre général. Bonjour, mon ami. Vous êtes tellement en retard, nous avons déjà marché quelques ligues sur la route."

Morris's French was so easy and fluent that the hurrying Lafayette answered distractedly in the same language, forgetting for once his sworn allegiance to all things American. He was *en désha-billé*, he explained, puffing and flapping the skirts of his corduroy coat, because of politics, because of meetings, declarations, speeches, petitions, *everything*. He could only stay a moment— "Tell me, my dear friend," he begged Jefferson. "What should I do?" He ran one hand over his high, sloping brow, making red bristles of hair stand up like a brush. The great teeth flashed like cannons. "Should I speak at the first meeting? This is the question. La Rochefoucauld says no, wait, de Corny says speak. And should I speak often? Sparingly? How to decide?"

Morris had an answer before Jefferson. *"Not* at the first meeting."

"Which will be all ceremony," Jefferson murmured.

"The King, the Keeper of the Seals, Necker—" Morris knew the sequence exactly. "By the time they're through, no one would listen to you. Wait."

"Yes, yes." Lafayette crossed in front of them both, laying a hand on Short's shoulder by way of greeting, farewell, benediction.

"Speak only on important occasions," Morris said. The four of them were now proceeding slowly down the gravel path, treading their shadows, lifting their faces one at a time to the chilly sky.

"Be patient, dignified," Jefferson said.

"But Mirabeau will speak for hours—everybody fears it, the man is mad." Lafayette wrung his hands and used the odd new English word that had just appeared for the first time in Madison's *Federalist*. "He has no *responsibility*."

Short glanced left at the speeding carriages and horses of the Champs-Élysées, let his mind drift. They could talk politics, repeat themselves, inflame themselves for hours, everyone in Paris could. As what the journals now openly called *la révolution* lurched and stumbled forward like a great shaggy beast—he pulled at his collar and let the thought lurch to a stop. Paradoxically, in the midst of a revolution, Short found that his own mind recoiled more and more from politics. He heard Washington's name pronounced in quick succession by Lafayette, Morris; "constitution," "human rights." Below them, off to one side of the snowy blossoms, small boys were pushing wooden boats across a pool of filthy water. In Williamsburg, when he was a boy, the men had played cards with ivory chips shaped like fish and they kept them in leather indentations on the table, called "ponds." Why had he thought of that?

"Dr. Franklin," Morris was saying beside him, reverting to what Short privately described as Tales of the Constitution, "used to urge us to compromise on everything. He said when he was a young printer in Boston he went to see Cotton Mather once and he had to stop outside the study door, because it was so low and crooked. Mather watched him for a moment and then pointed one hand at the floor—'Bend! Bend!'"

With a guffaw and a Gallic flurry of handshakes Lafayette departed as hurriedly as he had come, and Jefferson proposed that the remaining three of them continue to the Palais Royal, where a new machine for automatically drawing one's portrait had just been put on display. Frowning, Short pulled out his watch again—suddenly, sharply aware, in the very act, of who had first noticed his habit, and when. His face reddened.

"You have a social engagement," Jefferson said in a tone as neutral as November ice.

The part of Gouverneur Morris that understood French life so well merely grinned and appeared, in the glare of the afternoon sun, to wink.

☆　　☆　　☆

"You look at your watch," Rosalie de La Rochefoucauld said, touching his hand with two fingers and gently closing the case, "first, because you want to be precise, like him. He is your hero. And second, because he has in effect ordered you to go home. You think about how little time you have left here."

"I am almost thirty," Short said.

"My husband is sixty-five." Rosalie's fingers remained on the watch lid, exquisitely brushing his skin. "He says that for him every day goes by like a whizzing arrow."

Short put away the watch, brusquely. He had little interest in hearing the duc's brilliant metaphorical sayings. This was the fourth time (to be precise) he and Rosalie had met alone since Chaville, or almost alone—he looked up quickly from the bench to see whether anyone else had yet arrived at Madame de Tessé's town house—and he felt that every moment came and went with the speed . . . of a whizzing arrow.

"Where is the duc now?" The watch sat in his pocket like a red-hot egg. It was five forty-five. Madame de Tott had agreed to signal from the window when the first carriage appeared. "With his soldiers again?"

Rosalie nodded and leaned closer to pick at a spot of lint on his sleeve, close enough to allow him a breath, a lover's stolen inhalation of the perfume she wore, the scent of lemon verbena that reminded him of childhood days, his sister and his mother crushing the leaves between their fingers and laughing. "He took his regiment to Versailles to patrol around the Menus Plaisirs, because somebody wrote a letter threatening to burn it down."

Short made a little grimace of understanding. The Estates-General was to be held in the same building as the Assembly of Notables two years ago, but since there would be almost three times as many delegates this time, the whole structure was being demolished and rebuilt, although not without threats, speeches, little local riots between democrats and monarchists. Lafayette had moaned for days over the decision to build separate meeting rooms for the clergy and the nobility, so that each order would be cut off from the others.

"You also look at your watch because people will arrive in ten minutes."

"Five." He looked at his watch again; in his mind he stood up and heaved it like a flaming bomb into Madame de Tessé's garden.

"And when they do . . ." Rosalie's hair was dark, her throat milk white, exposed by her dress down to the point, the line, the miraculous finger's width that divided her breasts; his hands curled and ached.

"We must transform ourselves into creatures of discretion." Miserably, he finished her sentence. He started to say more, discovered that his mind was an absolute blank, empty of thought.

She had lowered her eyes to her hands in her lap. "The last time we met I could hardly speak to anyone for hours later," she confessed, so softly that he could scarcely hear. "I made myself stand by the window, with the light at my back, so no one could see my face."

Short nodded. They had become more artful than politicians,

masters of the eliding glance, the unseen, subtle pressure of a handshake, the furtive brush of skin as they passed. Three days ago they had arranged to walk together, publicly, in the Cours la Reine. (The very spot where Jefferson had snapped his lovesick wrist, a sardonic inner voice broke in.)

"I don't care what people see," Short said recklessly. "I kept your note."

Rosalie blushed, shook her head, studied her lap. He touched the back of her hand with the tip of one finger and, leaving it there, began to quote: " 'Je t'adore, mon chèr, chèr ami. Je ne t'abandonnerai jamais.' "

She jumped to her feet, looking at the house and shaking out her skirt at the same time. "Arrivé!"

In the window the tall, conspiratorial figure of Madame de Tott could be seen waving a hand. Without another word Rosalie was gone, a flash of blue muslin, black hair, the ghost of a breath of lemon verbena. Short reached for his hat, lying beside the stone bench, patted his left pocket—opposite the watch—and felt for the key. In another moment he was walking briskly in the opposite direction, through Madame de Tessé's elegant roses and white columbine, toward the rear gate, where the gardeners and servants entered.

In the alley he paused to scrape dirt from his shoes, then proceeded along the stone wall of the garden until he reached the rue de Varenne. At the corner of the wall and the street he took out the iron key, dropped it in the vase Madame de Tott had shown him, and looked up to see, peering out of his carriage window, the handsome, smiling, completely intelligent face of Gouverneur Morris.

☆　　☆　　☆

At precisely the same moment Jefferson also looked down at his watch.

In the diagonal beam of the new skylight the hands showed just a moment before six. James Hemings handed him his black hat with silver trim. Sally Hemings started to open the door, but Petit, lips pursed as always, cheeks faintly rouged, stepped in front of her and followed Jefferson down the outside stairs and across the cobblestone sidewalk to his waiting carriage. When Jefferson had climbed in, Petit closed the door, looked up to the slouching driver, and clapped his hands twice.

On the rue du Faubourg Saint-Honoré Jefferson took out an envelope and from it slipped a twice-folded letter.

MY DEAR , DEAREST PAPA ,

You are the best father. I have made it my study to please you in everything. My happiness can never be compleat without your love and approval, and I hope that I can have them both now as I take a great, wonderful step forward into life. You know how happy I have been in the convent. I believe I have a calling to become a nun, and Father Edgeworth and Madame de Mézières agree, so that, with your loving approval, I wish to make my abjuration of the world and take the ceremony of the laying on of the veil, which you remember we witnessed once with Mr. Adams and which was so beautiful—

There was more—two pages more—but Jefferson refolded the letter and replaced it in his pocket. The carriage skidded over wet pavement, sending a spray of mud and straw from the wheels. On the edge of the street a trio of beggars scattered, shouting, a squadron of red-plumed soldiers appeared; the carriage jolted through a logjam of wheels, leather, horses, and bounced free again before the great Gothic jumble of the Tuileries Palace, where more soldiers lounged in front of barricades and a ragged tide of pedestrians and carts flowed around them, downhill toward the Seine.

At the rue de Grenelle the driver turned right; at Panthemont braked to a noisy halt.

From her window Patsy had seen the carriage coming for half the length of the street. Before her father could even step down to the pavement, she was pushing through the wicket of the huge wooden door and taking his arm. How would he be? Once near Gum Spring in Virginia they were crossing the James River and the two ferrymen started to quarrel—drunkards—and the boat swung headfirst into the current and toward the rapids, and her father rose up with a face of absolute fury and *roared* (the only time in his life) that they had better row for shore before he pitched them over the side like sacks.

"Patsy." He took her hand and covered it with his own. "Patsy.

You have the blue eyes of your mother and the foolish red hair of your father." His smile was never more gentle. Inside the school he patted her hand again, then walked away in the direction of Madame de Mézières's office.

In the corridor, conscious only of flitting shadows, whispers, Patsy waited with her hands clasped in prayer. A servant walked by, then a dog, shaking its ears. Patsy was taller than Mrs. Cosway, than Madame de Corny, than Madame de Tott, but she felt like a small child sitting on a floor, surrounded by giants. When her father emerged from the office, he was still smiling, but the sensation she suddenly felt was fear, climbing her throat like a bird.

"I have paid all your bills at the school," her father said, "and Polly's too."

"But—"

"The servants will pack your trunks and bring them tomorrow. Polly is on her way."

"Papa—"

"And we will never speak of this again."

"I want to stay," Patsy protested feebly, willing the blue eyes of her mother *not* to cry.

"I have bought you a wagonload of new linen and dresses. And tomorrow we will go down the rue Saint-Honoré, just the two of us, and buy all the lawn and cambrics you can carry."

She clenched her fists until the nails pierced the skin.

"You see," he said gently, bending close until his face filled her whole field of vision, as in truth it always had. "You see, I am one of those parents who mean to rule exclusively by love."

She burst into scalding tears.

CHAPTER

Thirty-Four

Memoirs of Jefferson — 12

THREE VEHEMENT PUBLIC QUARRELS.
For so ostensibly peaceable and benevolent a man as Jefferson, whose unofficial motto was always to "take things by the smooth handle," it seems a very high number indeed. (I omit those lesser, rather poisonous or smoldering grudges with Patrick Henry and John Marshall.)

The first, as all the world knows, was with that disdainful, aristocratic master of numbers (and motives) Alexander Hamilton. Conventional wisdom has it that Jefferson and Hamilton quarreled because they were such natural and mighty opposites. Hamilton was the bastard son of a West Indies shopkeeper, a dedicated monarchist and roué (whose conquests included his own sister-in-law), brilliant in oratory, brilliant in the army (no ignoble flight across Carter's Mountain for him), absolutely savage and joyous in political combat: it would be hard to think of a person less like the Sage of Monticello. Down to their very difference in heights — Hamilton could not have been five feet, seven inches when he strutted—and their taste in clothes (Hamilton the fop incarnate), the two of them, everyone prophesied in retrospect, seemed born for confrontation.

In the beginning, of course, it hardly seemed that way at all. There was a scene I never saw—I was still in France—but heard described: Jefferson the new secretary of state meeting Hamilton the new secretary of treasury outside Washington's door on Broadway in the muggy New York spring of 1790; the two of them strolling arm-in-arm up and down that placid street for an hour, talking over the ways they might jointly resolve the Constitution's first political crisis. The issue (then, now, forever) was money; specifically, whether or not the new government ought to pay back the states' revolutionary debts at full value, thereby enriching the wealthy speculators of New York and Philadelphia (Hamilton's people, as it turned out) at the expense of the poor and agrarian. Jefferson was disposed to compromise, and as always, his course of action had something to do with buildings and land. Swing your influence to establishing a new capital city along the Potomac, he told Hamilton; and you can fund your debts as you will.

But even as they shook hands (and brought the District of Columbia into being), signs of discord could be seen. Hamilton was arrogant, monarchical, devoted to the forms of the British government. At the Constitutional Convention he had shocked poor James Madison by proposing a president-for-life. Jefferson was shocked even more by his love of power and contempt for the people ("Your people, sir, is a great beast," Hamilton truly did say, smiling over his wine). One day when Jefferson was unpacking in his offices the crates I had sent him from Paris, Hamilton strolled in on some sort of errand and saw three small portraits on the wall.

"Who are they?" he asked.

"They are my trinity of the three greatest men the world has ever produced," Jefferson told him. "I had them commissioned by John Trumbull in London. Sir Francis Bacon, Sir Isaac Newton, and John Locke."

Hamilton stared at the trio a moment longer. Then he said, "The greatest man that ever lived was Julius Caesar."

A few weeks later, his eyes opened about banks and debts,

Jefferson wrote James Madison that Alexander Hamilton's only philosophy was preparing the boots and spurs for the rich to ride on the backs of the poor.

I saw Hamilton but a few times myself; Aaron Burr put a bullet through his heart long before I could know him. But even at a distance one thing was always clear to me—without President Washington there probably would have been no quarrel; with him, Jefferson and Hamilton were like rival sons, scrambling for the father-attentions of that great, cadaverous, remote, violent-tempered Colossus, who had no child of his own (but burst into tears once telling of his love for Lafayette). Childless father; fatherless sons. In their heart of hearts, brothers. I always liked it that Hamilton was also called out by the newspapers on charges of adultery (admitted); and that the woman's name was, of all things, Maria.

"But Hamilton had no sense of *place*," John Adams told me once when I advanced my theory. The year was 1820, six years before he died, and the place (in that case) was Braintree, Massachusetts, that flint-gray, bone-hard section of New England coast where he and Abigail had retreated home many years earlier, licking their political wounds after his tumultuous presidency. I had come to pay my respects at his ancestral farm, the tag end of a useless two-day business trip to Boston. We sat all morning in the plain little front parlor. (He was allowed exclusive use of it till noon, he said, when Abigail would sweep in with her train of leaping grandchildren.)

"The core about Jefferson," Adams said, "is ground, soil; *land*. You think about it. Monticello. Virginia (awful state—I never saw it). That whole *vast* Louisiana Territory he couldn't wait to grab. But Hamilton didn't care a hoot where he lived. New York, West Indies, London, all the same to him. The man had no roots, no land loyalty."

Adams had changed a great deal in thirty-five years, but not his salt-plain habit of speaking.

"I don't like your theory," he told me. "But it's just as well Washington never had any children. Half the royal families of Europe would have tried to marry them, and we might have been right on our way to a monarchy, after all. Which was Jefferson's greatest fear. Never mine."

"You correspond with Jefferson now." I ventured onto dangerous ground.

"I do. But I didn't speak or write to the man for a dozen years,
Mrs. Adams either." Adams puffed on his pipe like Old King Cole
and eyed me over the hump of his belly. When he was first elected
vice president, I had been told, and was presiding over the Senate,
he went into agonies over the proper titles for everybody. He
seriously wanted to call Washington "His Highness the President
of the United States and Protector of their Liberties." Behind his
back the senators called Adams himself "His Rotundity."

"When Jefferson took the election of 1800 from me," Adams
said, "I was too mad to talk to him. Didn't even wait to give him
the keys of the mansion. Left at four in the morning so I wouldn't
see him."

"I was in Europe."

"I wasn't. I was right there, a one-term President, while Jefferson and Burr tied for votes and ended up in the House of Representatives for the election. Thirty-six ballots they called, from
Wednesday in a snow storm to Tuesday in the rain. Old Joseph
Nicholson of Maryland was sleeping in the coatroom, burning up
of a fever. Whenever there was a new ballot, his wife would wake
him up, put a pencil in his hand, and he would scribble 'Jefferson,'
then fall back in a faint. They said if Burr won, the country would
be sold off to the banks, and if Jefferson won, the people would
have to hide their Bibles under their beds. *Hamilton* finally decided
that much as he hated Jefferson, he didn't think the man could be
corrupted (which nobody in his right mind ever said about Burr).
So he threw the last ballot to Jefferson."

Adams disappeared behind a huge puff of smoke, emerged
slowly like a pink moon in a cloud. "Maybe you *are* right, Short."

The third quarrel was with, inevitably, Washington. Adams and
Jefferson had parted company over politics, and they had done it
in a noisy, pamphlet-flinging kind of way; and when they were
past politics and both of them retired, they took up (warily at first)
their comfortable old-shoe friendship again. But Jefferson's break
with Washington was more . . . Jeffersonian. A slow freeze. A
buildup of ice. Words behind backs. Washington's great sin was
that he failed to see Hamilton's plans as sinister and therefore
refused to denounce the Federalists. When Jefferson resigned as

secretary of state in 1793, the two simply ceased to be colleagues; then allies; then friends. Once in my hearing in Paris, Jefferson lectured little nine-year-old Polly in a way I approved of then; shudder at now: "I hope you never suffer yourself to be angry. The way to be loved is never, never to quarrel or be angry with anybody."

"*You* never quarreled with him, did you?" John Adams demanded of me through his cloud of smoke.

CHAPTER

Thirty-Five

Toward the end of April 1789, John Paul Jones, with his usual mysterious efficiency, had managed to purchase eight plaster copies of his own Houdon-carved bust, which he intended to present as needed to admirers and friends; and since he was afloat somewhere on the Baltic Sea, he had naturally ordered them delivered to Jefferson's house.

James Hemings scowled at the eight neatly stacked crates—left in the basement kitchen because Jefferson had now started rebuilding the study—and squeezed awkwardly between them; then he grabbed his sister's arm and hurried her up the outside stairs.

On the street he made her walk quickly, keeping in front of the oncoming river of wagons and horses. At the rue de Surene somebody's lackey shouted in French to clear the way, and a gilded carriage came tilting, speeding into sight, two huge sheepdogs bounding at full gallop ahead of the horses, a servant running on each side, people jumping, flying—the nearest dog bounced against a peddler, a blurred cannonball, knocking him flat. Sally screamed and pinned herself and James to a wall till the barking-rattling-cursing procession whizzed by in a high fan of water and straw and spinning wheels.

"You not scared of dogs?" he said scornfully, shaking her off.

"When they got teeth I am." She showed her own white teeth in a nervous grin.

James snorted. He looked at her as she straightened her dress at the hips, tugged at her front, looked right back at him. Without waiting he turned on his heel and pushed forward again through the crowd, and she caught up just past the Place Vendôme, where Jefferson's banker lived, the man who watched Sally when she served the wine just like a flat-eared cat watching a bird. But then, men usually looked at Sally like that.

"Where's Petit?" She was pressing close enough behind him that he could smell both her French perfume and the tart brown soap Jefferson made them all use.

"I told you twice, Petit takes his day off on the Left Bank, by Saint-Germain."

"Because of me," Sally said. "He wouldn't come with you because of me."

James knew the other servants disliked him; they said he was arrogant and quick-tempered and always angry with his sister. Well. He stopped to peer in a tinsmith's shop. Dozens of gleaming pans and flat cooking dishes had been stacked, à la mode de Palais Royal, with their prices written on little cards beside them. "Petit," he said, making an effort to speak slowly and not snap, "I told you, is an *efféminé*. He don't like any woman except the old bitch who works in the kitchen."

"And she's got a moustache." Sally giggled.

"And Petit likes to go to a club on the rue Buci where men all dress up like women and dance."

In the windowpanes of the tinsmith's shop six separate Sallys clapped hand to mouth to stop from laughing. "Did he ever take *you?*" White teeth, bright as the tin.

James glared at the window and set out again, faster, certain that whenever he stopped, there she would be, just like a shadow, just like a burn on the back of his neck. As a matter of fact—what he would never in his life admit—Petit *had* taken him once, very drunk, both of them very drunk, and James had slumped on a bench in a dark, slate-bottomed *cave* drinking brandy while the *efféminés* danced and dipped and swirled in and out of the candle-light, cackling like witches at a ball, and when he got drunk enough, he had danced too because they were actually beautiful-looking women, and then he had passed out and never gone back.

"You making me scared," Sally said. "People riot yesterday in the Saint-Antoine."

"Riots every day," James told her, picking up his pace. And there were. The winter had been so fierce and cold—the river frozen solid for weeks, wagons camped on the ice—that most of the tradesmen had had no work since November. Ships and boats didn't move, builders shut down, masons, carpenters, tanners, skinners, the *flotteurs* who pushed the timber rafts, everything east of the Louvre pulsed and rumbled with anger. Now he *loved* Paris, he thought, now Paris was just like him.

"Réveillon," Sally said.

"You ask Le Trouveur. He tell you all about it. Whole point is for you to meet Le Trouveur."

"I already know. Réveillon owns a factory in the Saint-Antoine, and he wants to drop the pay to fifteen sous a day and they tried to burn his house down last night, that's what I know."

But Le Trouveur, when they reached his door, had fled the quartier, and the neighbors were milling dangerously in the narrow street. James stood indecisively, gripping Sally's wrist. Crowd on its way to a mob, he thought. He turned; turned. Sheer force of numbers began to drag them forward with a deep, tidal pull toward the rue de Charonne, where nobles were said to be passing on their way to the races.

"I want to go home!" Sally cried.

He snarled and shoved her away—the last he saw of her was her brown hair bobbing through the crowd like a cork—and elbowed his way down an alley, over a flattened wood fence. On the rue de Charonne a dozen carriages and coaches had come to a halt, surrounded by blue-shirted workmen. Somebody shouted slogans. A huge pregnant woman stood on a box making a fiery speech. In the first carriage James recognized Jefferson's friend the Duc d'Orléans. He had climbed up beside his driver and spread his arms to the crowd.

New voices snapped like whips: "Vive le duc! Vive le père d'Orléans!"

Closer, scrambling, James could see that the carriages were blocked by soldiers and barricades. On the other side of the barricades stood a big three-story house, iron gates, dozens of straw figures dangling from ropes, a makeshift sign painted in blood red: MAISON RÉVEILLON.

The duc had started to make himself heard. In furious, rhythmical counterpoint the pregnant woman pumped her fists — "Estates-General" — "Bread!" — "Patience!" — "Liberté!" The duc was looking back along the line of carriages. From one pocket of his splendid red coat he drew a fat purse, waved it over his head, then flung a dozen coins into the air.

Instantly the crowd surged, the other carriages rocked on their wheels. The noble occupants were lowering their windows. More purses appeared. Gold and silver coins sailed overhead like wingless birds, birds' heads. The crowd pushed and roared with every toss, and James's ears rang with the noise. To his right, where he stumbled away in self-defense, the soldiers were now lifting the barricades in front of the horses.

A shout rose and died in James's throat. The barricades came apart and the soldiers saluted the duc's carriage, the brilliant harnesses and plumes of the horses as they clattered through, but in the wake of the last wheels, too numerous and wild to be stopped, the still-furious center of the mob rushed forward like a wave. The barricades splintered, soldiers scattered. The iron gates of Réveillon's house tilted, twisted, then disappeared under a flood of bodies.

For an instant James resisted, clinging to a lamppost with both hands, a man in a rapids. Then he gave it up, shot forward, rising to the crest of the mob. Objects flew past — faces, arms, a torn brick wall, limbs from an uprooted tree. When he reached the door, Réveillon's house was already starting to burn. A running man thrust an armload of bottles toward him; fragments of chairs, sofas, the wings of a huge mahogany table all passed from hand to hand, toward a great bonfire building in the first courtyard of the house. Wine from Réveillon's cellar went from mouth to mouth. James drank greedily from one bottle, staggered with the force of the angry crowd as it shifted, drank again from another bottle, wiped his teeth and struggled for air. The sky was black with smoke; with amazing speed the house had begun to come apart in loud, nerve-shattering cracks and then — half-drunk, dazed, whirling — James understood that the cracks were muskets. The soldiers had re-formed their ranks, lined up across the street, and begun to fire at random.

Pandemonium struck with the first bullets. Through the stinging smoke, through the breached walls, the crowd was running in blind, frenzied panic. James lurched for the rue de Charonne, saw sparks of gunfire and dropped to the ground. Crawled, clawed toward the sidewalk, over glass, boards, a bloody leg, a trampled body unrecognizable, male or female. He staggered to his feet and pressed forward, arms outstretched, driving toward a doorway shelter. From the rooftops of the houses, tiles and stones were flying. The soldiers had marched into the center of the street in a compact square, deadly muskets turned in four directions. At every new shower of tiles and stones some lifted their barrels and fired, others charged a few feet forward, jabbing wildly with red bayonets at whatever moved, yielded, bled, or cried out.

The street had become a maze. Through choking billows of smoke James recognized Le Trouveur's building, the door where he had begun. With a desperate lunge he covered the last few yards of pavement, dodging, tumbling, coming to a halt by the tiny stairs in the rear. Moments later, curled into a ball by an upstairs window, he looked down at the scene. His ears went dead. No sound reached him. Soldiers and mob seemed to dance in eerie, crablike motions, backward and forward across a stage grown dark and slippery with corpses. Where the fires burned or the muskets flashed, the streets were the blood red image of hell.

☆   ☆   ☆

"What the country needs," said Madame de Tessé with an emphatic, sparrowlike nod of her head, "is democracy. The people would never riot if they had a voice in the government."

"The people would never riot"—Gouverneur Morris bowed slightly toward her—"if they had bread. What this country needs is a government suited to its particular history and nature, and that is not a democracy. You are not ready for a democracy."

"You want to retain the monarchy." Madame de Tessé faced Morris with the belligerent, hard-eyed stare of a bantam rooster. Short considered his simile, rejected it, and cleared his throat. If he could think of a witty, distracting remark, he would interpose himself between them.

"I would, for this kingdom," Morris said coolly, "retain a limited monarchy and a parliament chosen from the educated propertied classes. The peasants in the field and the squalid, drifting laborers of the cities have no experience whatever in making a government work."

"Hmmph." Madame de Tessé glanced at her other guests. Jefferson was by the fire, talking to her protégée. Clérisseau had cornered two or three of the ladies. A knot of men with hats under their arms stood beside the nearest mullioned window, grimly studying the gray sky. "That is your theory, I suppose."

"Ah, my dear learned lady," Morris said in the smoothest possible French. "Ma chère madame érudite. I subscribe to Dr. Johnson's definition, 'Theory is speculation by those unversed in practice.' I have no theory."

"But you were, I am told, very busy at making the new American Constitution."

"He was a delegate from New York," Short put in. "A colleague of Colonel Hamilton's." (Feeble; he ran a finger around his collar and looked back at Jefferson, who had started, slowly, in their direction.)

"More than that, surely." Madame de Tessé continued to stare.

"I was in fact the humble penman of the Constitution," Morris admitted. "When the convention had agreed on all the articles, I was assigned as a committee of one to write the actual document. Which I did."

"So you are the author of the Constitution." A flat, uninflected statement. Morris bowed again. "Which explains why you don't hesitate to differ with your minister to this country. Jefferson wrote the Declaration of Independence, you wrote the Constitution—neither of you is in awe of the other."

"Mr. Jefferson," said Morris, grinning as Jefferson somehow appeared among them with perfect timing, "is a person of whom I should always be in awe."

Jefferson acknowledged the compliment with mock gravity.

"Today we are discussing theories of government," Madame de Tessé told him. "Monsieur Morris is so alarmed by our riots that he wishes to see the king act with a firm hand."

"The king has been very moderate to this point," Jefferson said. "But in any case it looks to me like a case in which the king and the parliaments are quarreling over the oyster, while the shell will be left, as always, to the people."

"Monsieur Morris does not share your enthusiasm for reform."

"Oh, my dear lady"—by comparison with Morris, Jefferson's French was stilted and cold, the strange Scottish burr more pronounced than ever—"I hold an office that prevents my taking sides in your political battles. Mr. Morris is a free, private citizen."

"The monarchical author of a republican constitution." Madame de Tessé smiled to show that she still observed the French rule of disagreement without positive abuse.

"I have come to admire Mr. Morris's Constitution very much," said Jefferson, with an attempt at a distracting pun that took Short by surprise. Morris's splendid athletic figure was much talked about in Paris. Houdon was so impressed that he had asked him, wooden leg and all, to stand as the model for his full-length sculpture of General Washington. More than one Parisian lady, according to rumor, had shared Houdon's impression.

"You are not disturbed by the riots?"

Jefferson smiled at Madame de Tott, inclined his head very slightly toward Short. "I like the remark by one of the members of the Third Estate—was it Launay?—that there is no form of disorder that is not preferable to the funereal tranquillity arising from absolute power."

Madame de Tessé beamed and looked up defiantly at Morris, who was in the act of taking a glass of wine from a servant's tray. He stumped sideways an awkward step. His big face, unwigged, twice the width of Jefferson's narrow one, flushed crimson with anger. "And in my turn I like the word *funereal*. Abstract, Latinate, unconnected to reality. It is my understanding that in the riots that destroyed Monsieur Réveillon's house and factory, some three hundred citizens met with a final, funereal tranquillity. In plain language, Madame, they were murdered."

"Surely not three hundred," Jefferson demurred.

"Three hundred or three, it was unnecessary. It was—undemocratic."

Madame de Tott had stationed herself protectively next to Jefferson. "Your two servants were caught in the middle, were they not?"

Jefferson nodded, to Short's eye as calm and unruffled as if

Morris had never spoken. Diplomacy was deafness. "James and Sally Hemings," he said. "They had gone to the Faubourg Saint-Antoine for some reason—a visit—when the riots broke out. Sally came back unharmed, right away; James was considerably bruised and shaken. He said he hid most of the night in a building near Réveillon's house."

"These are brother and sister, your servants?"

Before Jefferson could reply, Morris had thrust himself in the center of the little group. The flush of anger had been replaced by a smiling pallor that looked like ice beneath powder. "Let us call things by their right names, by all means," he said. "These are not Mr. Jefferson's 'servants.' They are his slaves."

For a single unguarded instant Jefferson's head snapped back as if he had been struck. In the long, palpable silence that followed, the only sound that could be heard was Morris's wooden leg grinding hard into the waxy floor.

"One concession to theory I did make, my dear friend," Morris finally said, addressing Madame de Tessé. "At the Constitutional Convention I supported with every fiber of my being the elimination of slavery. I regard it as the curse of heaven on my country."

"On any country, surely." Madame de Tessé rallied faintly. "Surely."

"And in July 1784," Morris said, "five years ago, together with John Jay and Aaron Burr, old friends of our friend Mr. Jefferson here, I founded the New York Manumission Society for the abolition of slavery. This was practice, not theory. If I had slaves, I would free them. I am unable, for the life of me, to see how men can profess to be republicans and reformers and yet profit from the tears and blood of their fellow men."

Morris drained his glass. His voice had kept all its usual smoothness and urbanity, but there was no mistaking his passion. And Jefferson's? Short's mind was echoing with arguments on Jefferson's behalf. He too despised slavery. He too had acted boldly, years ago. In the Declaration he had denounced the "ebony trade" in terms so strong that Congress had instantly struck them out.

"A Frenchman has recently established a society to promote worldwide emancipation," Morris said.

"Brissot de Warville." The Roman remained as calm as if whale oil or tobacco duties were the subject. "He asked me to join, but of course I could not."

Morris was less than Roman. "Of course," he drawled sarcastically.

But Jefferson held his gaze. When he replied, it was with an offhand eloquence that made Short long to reach for pen and paper. "Nobody wishes more ardently to see an abolition not only of the trade," he told them, "but of the condition of slavery. The whole commerce between master and slave is a perpetual exercise in despotism on the one hand, and degradation on the other. But I am here in France as a public servant, and those whom I serve have not yet spoken against it. For me to join, without serving the cause here, might render me less able to serve it beyond the water."

Morris took another glass, arched one eyebrow in a diabolical hook. "To the causes beyond the water," he said, raising the glass close to Jefferson's white face.

☆   ☆   ☆

Outside, on the path to the stables, Morris gripped Short good-humoredly by the elbow. "Come with me to the Louvre tonight."

Short pulled free. "You were unfair back there. You know he can't speak freely for himself, even here."

"Ah, my dear young-old, tall-short *ami*." Morris's breath was pungent with red wine, his nose flecked with broken veins. "I could have done much worse than *that*. I could have reminded our red-haired hypocrite of one Virginian, close by, who had nobly freed his slaves—in practice, not theory."

"Me?"

"You."

Short felt the back of his neck burn, as if the pale monk's head of a sun above them had focused on him alone. "They were merely inherited, not even a dozen. My brother and I—"

"I could also have said"—Morris was raising his big hand, signaling the nearest groom, and carriages were starting to roll over the gravel, so that he bent close again, all blue-white eyes and cracked nose, and repeated himself with deliberate, malicious clarity—"I could have also told Ambassador Jefferson what he certainly does not know, that at least one American public servant in

France, in Jefferson's very home, has been bold enough to pay his forty-eight-franc dues and join Brissot de Warville's society *contre la traite de nègres.*"

The carriage wheels crunched to a halt inches from Short's foot. A horse stamped, sending up a spray of gravel that he did not feel, though he watched his hand brush it away; he heard his voice ask in French, "How do you know that?"

"Because it's true. Come to the Louvre and meet my friend the Comtesse de Flahaut." Morris bounced on his good leg, twisted his shoulders awkwardly, jumped and somehow arrived on the bench of his carriage, looking down at Short. "You will like her," he said, breathing hard. "She is the mistress of the Bishop of Autun, although she thinks she keeps it a secret from me. She writes lurid novels, also secretly, and pretends to be optimistic and political, when she is in fact tragic and principled, but you would insult her cruelly if you said so. She reminds me, in other words" —Morris swung the door of the carriage wider—"of you."

☆   ☆   ☆

In the carriage Short tried again. "If you knew the extent to which debts have shackled him . . ." The word was idiotically chosen. Shackled. Morris arched his brow again. "He inherited his father-in-law's enormous debts," Short continued passionately; he knew this well because, in the dim, shapeless past that was Virginia he had done his earliest legal work on John Wayles's complex estate. "And when the Revolution wiped out our paper money credit, he had to pay the debt all over again, twice in effect. If he were to free his slaves, he would be ruined financially, he would have nothing left to give his daughters."

"On whom he dotes."

Short thought of the nearly grown Patsy, more Jefferson's partner than daughter since she had left the convent; the frail Polly, the sole member of the household who had been given the free run of Jefferson's books. He had walked in two days ago to find Polly cheerfully writing her name in the margins of a Dutch folio while Jefferson printed a letter for her on his copy press. "Yes. On whom he dotes."

"Choose blood," Morris said ambiguously.

"And in any case, you don't know Virginia, you don't know

blacks. To free them without provision is like abandoning children. They steal, they beg, they idle. Their money disappears, they become slaves all over again."

Behind Morris's shoulder were passing houses, uniformed soldiers, cheeselike wedges of gray sky. Morris grinned his amiable, charming grin. "Choose freedom," he said.

In another moment they had reached the Pont Neuf and begun the clamorous trip across it, through butchers' stalls, tents, carts, swarms of beggars, squads of soldiers. When Short had first come to Paris (a lifetime ago!), the bridge had been dominated by singers and hawkers and roaring pitchmen—as your carriage squeezed between them, you could have leaned out and purchased anything in the world: dogs, pistols, flowers, glass eyes, wooden legs (he glanced at Morris), fruit, jewelry, false teeth, candy. An open-air dentist worked at one end, giants and puppets cavorted at the other. Now politics— *"la révolution"*—had changed even the bridge. Gone were most of the boutiques and stalls, replaced by unsmiling soldiers, ranting speechmakers. The hawkers specialized in pamphlets and obscene songs about the queen; the beggars cackled political slogans as they pounded your carriage door, snapped at the horses' bridles, peered in the window boldly to see who you were.

Morris stared grimly out until they reached the far side of the bridge, turned left past the Café du Parnasse, and started to follow the quai along the broad, grime-streaked facade of the Old Louvre.

In another minute they turned right, through a stone vault, and into a courtyard that looked like the home of a republic of artists. On strings or flat against damp walls hung brightly colored canvases, prints, black-and-white engravings by the hundreds, the work of the resident painters. Above them, clinging precariously to flat stone, the painters had added wooden balconies to the windows of their little apartments; then flowerpots and makeshift charcoal stoves. In the very center of the courtyard, like a gypsy encampment, rose a conglomeration of crooked shanties, hen coops, dog houses, tented laundries, and soap-making vats. In one corner kerchiefed women stood with their arms folded, washtubs at their feet. Near the entrance children squatted, half naked, by dirty puddles, laughing and shouting as if the old Pont Neuf had somehow been transported inside, safe behind the king's walls.

"She lives through there." Morris pointed toward another, lower vault, and the carriage rattled across the paving stones and into a smaller, more elegant courtyard, where the carriage stopped, and then Morris led him across yet another little square. Through a grille Short glimpsed traffic and the two stiff rows of chimneys that always made the Palais Royal look like a sow on her back.

"And up here."

Stumping loudly with his wooden leg, Morris mounted the stairs, coat flapping, paused at a landing, squinted down a window. At the third landing he straightened his coat with a sharp tug and knocked once, loud as a shot.

The next two hours passed for Short as a dream. Jefferson's circle of friends—apart from Saint-Germain, *Short's* circle too—was limited to political liberals, *"les américains,"* and visiting merchants. On his own, by force of charm alone, Morris had somehow found his way into a different Paris. The lady novelist Adèle de Flahaut, as beautiful, easily, as Short imagined, bore no resemblance at all to the brisk, modest matrons of the Hôtel de Langeac, whose chief role was to ornament and admire. When he followed Morris into the drawing room, the maid continued on ahead, pulling open a second set of doors, and then a third. Abruptly they entered Madame de Flahaut's boudoir itself, where their hostess stood before a mirror, dressed in a diaphanous pink shift, extending her hands like a Delphic priestess while another maid powdered her lovely arms.

Morris greeted her with relaxed urbanity, sat down on a shabby couch beside the mirror. Short was introduced, seated, ignored in rapid fashion. Over her shoulder Adèle spoke in languorous, extremely colloquial French to Morris. The two maids, heads together, draped and redraped the gauzy shift.

Blinking to focus, Short saw just to his left a Chinese screen and behind it one corner of a brass tub. He bent. The tub was filled with warm milk and water, and when he looked up again his nose told him that the priestess three feet away had just emerged from it.

" 'Belinda sees no charm that's not her own,' " Morris quoted cheerfully from the couch.

"Parlez français," Adèle told the mirror.

" '*Cois tibi paene videre est,*' " he said, " '*ut nudam.*' "

"I speak Latin," she informed him, "and you cannot see through my dress." In the mirror her heavy-lidded eyes shifted to Short. "Can you, Monsieur Chort?"

In the parlor they were joined briefly by a bandy-legged older man in English lounging coat and twill jodhpurs. He nodded at Short, mumbled to Morris, and wandered into another room.

"The Baron de Flahaut has his apartment downstairs," Morris explained. He drew Short to one of the Louis XV chairs beside the fireplace, and both of them watched as Adèle, now fully clothed in a green-and-white gown, herself exited through a different door. "They live here on his pension and whatever salary he makes as director of the king's gardens."

"Buffon's old post."

"Buffon's old post, but hardly Buffon."

Short looked around the room. The walls were hung with engravings of country scenes, the fireplace was stuffed with cheap wood, not coal, crackling and spitting as it burned; mirrors between engravings, fine chairs worn at the back and arms and leaking cotton; a long threadbare rug of no distinct color, rumpled across a stone floor. Jeffersonian, Short registered the fact automatically: no books.

"*Nil admirari,*" Morris murmured.

When Adèle returned, she was followed by a handsome blond woman obviously her sister, a tall, hawk-nosed Frenchman dressed in ruffled court finery, and last—most striking of all—a man of medium height, middle age, with a thin, mocking expression and a ponderous club foot encased in black leather that thumped more loudly than Morris's leg and swept back and forth like a pendulum under the folds of his cape. As Short got to his feet, even with his poor eyesight he had no trouble recognizing the former Abbé of Saint-Denis, now the Bishop of Autun, Charles-Maurice de Talleyrand, the most worldly and libertine of all French reformers; if he were only a believer, Mirabeau had joked, Talleyrand might be the conscience of the Revolution.

No introductions this time, not even from Morris. The three

new arrivals took their places around the fierce little fire and began to eat and drink whatever the procession of maids carried to them.

"We have come from Versailles," began Talleyrand, and Morris, peeling an orange, nodded.

"Have some of this conserve," the sister urged, passing a jar of green jelly to Morris. "Cela vous purgera trois fois."

Morris smiled and handed it to Short. By the fireplace Adèle had taken up another Delphic pose, equidistant between Talleyrand and Morris, arms along the mantel but inclining her head to Morris. In spite of himself, Short stared at her heavy-lidded eyes, the smooth face full of complex, sensual defects.

Talleyrand was now questioning Morris. "You saw the opening of our theatrical season?"

"He means the Estates-General," Adèle said.

Morris was grave. "Madame de Tessé gave me an extra ticket. She hoped it would make me less a royalist and more a democrat to observe the excesses of power."

"You're no royalist," said the hawk-nosed man. It was his one and only contribution to the evening.

"Nor democrat either. But I confess—is that the right word, my dear bishop? Confess?" Talleyrand raised two crooked fingers and made a sign. "Thank you," Morris said. "I do confess, in all the pageantry your king and queen made a brilliant showing. I sat at the back of the Menus Plaisirs, where I could see everything, even your ecclesiastical ermine, sir, and hear nothing. The king appeared to read his speech well. Necker read well. The applause of the Third Estate—well, should I admit that at times tears came to my eyes? But the poor queen was so altogether alone and unpopular."

"By all means, admit it," drawled Talleyrand. His eyes came around, indifferently, to Short.

"The King of England," Adèle informed them, her finger now deep in the jar of conserves, "has gone mad again, you know. This time he claims to be George Washington. They say his doctors follow him everywhere but don't dare speak unless he speaks to them first, because *that* would violate royal protocol." She placed the finger in her mouth. "The only book they allow him to read, I'm told, is, of all things, *King Lear*."

"Which in English literature," Talleyrand said, "curiously enough exists with two different endings, Shakespeare's and the revised, happy version of some modern hack. Do we know the king's choice?"

The conversational banter flew. Morris stretched his leg and his stump, rolled his eyes, joined in with a fluent, insinuating French that made Short feel suddenly a hundred years old. He took brandy from a maid. Talleyrand brought out a fat gold *tabatière* from the folds of his cape and offered him snuff. Morris told how Houdon had made him pose for Washington's statue and asked his advice about the bust he was now making of Jefferson, at Jefferson's request.

"Jefferson leaves soon for America, does he not?" asked Talleyrand.

"He has written for permission, but heard nothing."

"And will he return?" The sister, whose name was Julie, had joined Adèle at the fireplace.

"He will return, of course," said Talleyrand without bothering to look up at her. "Poor Lafayette will need him to spell *Rights of Man* or whatever childish declaration our fevered marquis decides will save the nation." Adèle shifted her skirts by the firescreen, and the bishop reached up, as casually as if he were plucking a fruit, and kissed the inside of her wrist.

Morris stretched his wooden leg. Another six inches, Short thought, fascinated, and the wooden leg would meet club foot. He raised his eyes to find Adèle's fixed on him.

"I think," said Morris seriously, "you underestimate our red-haired minister. To my mind, it is unthinkable that General—or rather President Washington—will form a new government without Jefferson. He is too aloof, reserved, I grant you, to be a great politician. But he is a man of infinite subtlety."

"I saw Jefferson once," Adèle said. She smiled at Morris but spoke to Talleyrand. "From your carriage, at the Tuileries. I distrusted his face, *hated* it. He is obviously a man *faux et emporté.*"

Flushing, bewildered, Short translated her phrase: *a man false and passionate.* But he had no chance to object—no chance even to absorb Morris's remark, which could mean only that Jefferson, once gone, would not return to France as minister. The bishop was rising to his feet. In a corner Julie was whispering to her sister.

At the stairs Talleyrand lingered to say good night to Adèle, and Morris, Short in tow, bowed and walked on. In the courtyard his carriage was already waiting—Short had the sensation of being surrounded by hundreds of invisible wires, each one manipulating a hidden part of the scene. Morris sat back on the bench and folded his arms across his waistcoat while the horses backed and clattered.

"Emporté," he said softly. " 'Passionate.' A nice word for the ever-amiable, ever-distant Mister Jefferson."

Prudence collapsed in a rush. "He said nothing to *me,*" Short blurted, "about not returning. I assume that he returns in five months."

Morris looked at him coolly. "You're worried about your future, yes? If he remains at home, you think you might replace him here."

Short made an involuntary, deprecating gesture; took refuge in consulting his watch, whose face, in the bouncing darkness, he could not see. The carriage joined the river of wheels on the rue Saint-Honoré.

"I would not," Morris said carefully, "place my trust in Jefferson. He would not recommend you."

"He would."

"He thinks all young Americans should flee the temptations of fleshpot Europe," Morris said, "as you well know." He gripped the leather strap by his window and leaned close enough for Short to smell wine, sweat, the faintest possible scent of milk and water. "You have become far too French for him, my dear fellow. Let us face it. You are one of his 'sons,' but the most wayward, alas. Madison and Monroe busy themselves day and night with politics, they advance the great cause of the father. Meanwhile, you neglect everything for the sake of your pleasures." Morris tapped Short's knee with one finger. "He thinks you have formed a scandalous attachment."

Before Short could do more than bristle, Morris had leaned back again; his grin flashed in and out of a streetlamp. "I name no names," he said.

"Jefferson would not—" What was the word he needed? *Deceive? Betray?*

But in his peremptory way Morris had decided to change the subject completely. "The Bishop of Autun has offered to take me to an impotence trial," he said cheerfully. "Do you know the custom? When a French woman wishes a divorce, the Church in its militant wisdom grants it only if the husband can no longer perform his conjugal duties. Sometimes he agrees. Sometimes, for reasons of property or pride, he elects to demonstrate—shall we say his 'competence'—before witnesses? The bishop will take me as his guest, he says. He claims the rate of failure is remarkably high. *Quod est demonstrandum.*"

Short could only shake his head.

"The bishop means me to understand his invitation allegorically," Morris said, sounding in his irony precisely like the bishop. "That is, I am to stay away from Madame de Flahaut."

"She is very beautiful." Short watched the Champs-Élysées appear on his left, a dark mass of trees and gravel. When had Morris given instructions to the coachman? More wires.

"Her nose is too big," Morris said. "Her sister Julie left her husband when she was twenty-five, did you know that? And traveled for months with the Cardinal de Rohan, dressed in the clothes of a boy acolyte. Jefferson may be right about the corruptions of old Europe on youths like you and me."

The carriage was wheeling through a crowd of other carriages, en route to the theaters. Beggars and soldiers had suddenly popped up, gopherlike, on opposite sides of a corner.

"Not, of course," Morris added slyly, "that the celebrated friend of the celebrated Mrs. Cosway should be the first to cast stones." He sniffed in mock alarm. "I seem to speak in nothing but biblical terms after I see the demonic bishop."

Short could only shake his head again and pinch the bridge of his nose. Morris was watching with lynx eyes. "Jefferson has fooled you," he said flatly. "He won't openly denounce your 'attachment,' you know—that would be despotic, and Jefferson is the apostle of freedom. But he will do what he thinks best for you, not what you want. He will maneuver you round and round till you go home. Little gestures, little coldnesses, favors. Look at his poor browbeaten daughters, caught like fish in his nets. Look at poor Maria Cosway. What a subtle old domestic tyrant he is. He professes freedom, our Jefferson, but he keeps slaves."

Morris placed his whole hand on Short's knee this time. "Shall I tell you another allegory, mon chèr Chort? Religious, too, curse the bishop. There was a priest a hundred years ago at a village near Mézières, much beloved by his parishioners for his saintliness. He consoled them, comforted them, led them daily to God; an exemplary Catholic priest. When he died, he left a will and some letters to Voltaire confessing that for the last thirty years he had secretly been an atheist and had never believed a word he preached."

He gave Short's knee a final push. "Here is Jefferson's house," he said.

CHAPTER

Thirty-Six

In the late afternoon of Sunday, July 12, Jefferson was returning home in his new English carriage from a visit to the Palais Royal, where he and his daughters had been taking tea.

To avoid the soldiers and wagons now permanently jamming the rue Saint-Honoré, they crossed below the Louvre and rolled west along the river until they reached the Place Louis XV. For Jefferson this was nearly the most familiar of Parisian landmarks. Those mornings when he did not ride through the Bois de Boulogne he customarily gave over to a walk from the Grille de Chaillot to the life-size equestrian statue in the center of the Place, exactly 820 double steps, he had calculated, from his own front door.

With a gesture as automatic as Short's he opened his watch, but ignored it and stared straight ahead at the Place. Around the statue, drawn up in battle formation, stood more than a hundred German cavalry, part of the king's hated mercenary guard. Behind them foot soldiers—Swiss, also belonging to the king—flags up and bayonets glinting in the sun.

The carriage swerved, jolted to a halt.

Scattered through the square were piles of stones, large and small, intended for the new bridge under construction, and behind the stones, damned up like a flood, hundreds and hundreds of grim, blue-shirted citizens were massed and waiting. Jefferson cranked down his window and called to the driver. They rolled another few yards and stopped. Where the Place was usually alive with carriages and horses and noise, there was now only a weird, unearthly silence and a wide empty space. A German horse stamped its hoof against pavement. An officer's voice carried like the crack of a whip.

Jefferson ordered the driver to go forward.

They clattered noisily into the center of the Place. The gray-green equestrian statue slid by their window, the tense white faces of the cavalry, plumes, boots, a blue and red German flag.

Ten yards past the statue a German officer, horse prancing, sword vertical in a gesture of command, pulled into their path. Patsy sat up straight and cocked her head, as if listening to the voices now coming from somewhere behind their carriage. Beside her father Polly began to cry.

Jefferson stretched his arm to pull Polly toward him.

The officer bent from his saddle and peered inside, but only for a moment—the noise of the huge crowd was sweeping closer in a rising growl, the horse was edging sideways. Jefferson spoke in French, the officer pointed his sword toward a lane between piles of stones, leading directly into the Champs-Élysées, then shouted something unintelligible to the driver, who shook the reins wildly and yelled. The carriage shot forward and they galloped through a parted sea of angry faces. To the rear, seconds after they passed, the crowd was surging into their wake, heaving stones and bricks at the cavalry, which was backing, wheeling, turning.

Patsy stuck her head out the window and looked back on a tumultuous roaring mass. The mob had surrounded the soldiers, stones flew in geysers. A man's body dropped from a roof like a falling sack. Before the trees and dust cut off her view, she saw the German flag dip and fall, the first puffs of smoke, and then, catching up, came the sharp slap of air against ear that was the sound of muskets fired in battle.

☆   ☆   ☆

"The king," Lafayette groaned, pacing straight toward the window as if he would crash through it. "The king, the king, the king."

"The whole riot," Jefferson said mildly, "was set off by the king's dismissal of Necker. That and the use of foreign troops to guard French soil."

"I know it, I know it." Lafayette turned sharply at the last moment and stopped in front of Patsy. "I know it. Sheer madness to dismiss him. The only minister in the cabinet whom the people *liked*." He pulled the curtain and looked out, then shook his head at Patsy with a puzzled frown. "I cannot get used to the fact that the Grille de Chaillot is gone."

Patsy leaned to follow his gaze. Three weeks ago she and Polly had stood at the same window and watched while a combination of mob and soldiers had dismantled the customs barrier and most of the stone wall of the Grille de Chaillot. Since then, with the soldiers gone, their house had been burglarized twice and her father's favorite ormolu clock stolen. Now they had bars and bells on the windows and a private guard in the garden.

"Here is your Declaration of Rights again," her father said. He held out a paper, and Lafayette bounced halfway across the carpet to take it. "I've ventured a few suggestions, as you asked."

"We look to you, *I* look to you," Lafayette muttered. With another turn of his heels he was back almost to Patsy's perch by the window and holding the paper up to the light. "You've changed the first sentence, the list of essential rights?"

Patsy rose and looked over Lafayette's shoulder, quickly translating as she read. Where Lafayette, in his large looping handwriting (exactly like Polly's), had written *"Declaration of Rights — Every man is born with some inalienable rights, such as the right to property, the care of his honor and his life, the free disposition of his person"* — around these words her father had placed thin, square brackets and drawn a line, eliminating both property and honor from the list of inalienable rights.

" 'Honor,' " her father said with a stiff motion of his bad wrist, "is the main principle on which monarchical government rests — it creates those charades and ceremonials that keep the aristocracy obligated to the Crown. I take the idea, in fact, from Montesquieu."

"Montesquieu," Lafayette repeated and stared blankly at Patsy, as if trying to remember a face.

Behind him William Short slipped into the room and took a seat at his desk. Patsy smoothed her skirt against her legs. She had not seen Short in almost a week, thanks to the mobs and riots. But where Lafayette had been racing with his troops from Versailles to Paris or back, or coming constantly to see her father, pleading for help, Short had been away attending to the Duc and Duchesse de La Rochefoucauld, whose country house in La Roche-Guyon he seemed to think was exposed to the wildest kinds of threats and attacks. He looked completely, totally exhausted, Patsy decided, worse than she had ever seen him. Good. It served him right.

"And as for 'property,' " her father said. Short propped his head on his fist and looked up at him. "I had originally written 'life, liberty, and property' in the Declaration of Independence, you know."

Lafayette, who could have known no such thing, nodded.

"But I revised it to 'life, liberty, and the pursuit of happiness.' "

Lafayette studied his text for such a revision.

"Indeed"—her father was now in the full tide of reminiscence, a mood she always loved to see in him, even when she had no knowledge at all of the people or places—"I think we did retain 'property' in the Virginia Declaration of Rights in 1776, but I have always regarded property as a means to human happiness, not an end in itself. My old law teacher George Wythe used to distinguish between natural and civil rights, and property belonged to the second." He saw Lafayette's worried expression and broke off.

"I will study the changes and take them to my committee," Lafayette said. He put away the sheet of paper and reached for his three-cornered general's hat (uncharacteristically stained with dust and mud, Patsy noted), which he had dropped on a chair as he entered.

"You've erected a superb edifice," her father said, walking with him toward the door. "The essential principles are sound, the reforms well in hand. Have courage."

"If you had been injured, or your daughters—"

"Now I will own one apprehension," her father said with great serenity. "Not that one, because we have been walking the streets otherwise in perfect safety. But the refusal of the National Assembly to accept trial by jury as a right, this troubles me. Trial by jury is the only anchor by which a government can be held to its principles. Individually or in groups, judges can be biased, or bought; but twelve honest men, chosen at random—"

For once Lafayette interrupted. "Today there have been riots not one league from here at the monastery of Saint-Lazare, all afternoon. I must beg you to stay in."

"Are they demanding bread?" Patsy asked. Now that she was out of Panthemont, Patsy went everywhere in the city, observed everything. She had walked down the rue Saint-Honoré with Sally Hemings earlier that day. They had seen bakers' shops boarded up or looted and smashed to splinters. Bands of armed men stood at corners selling stolen flour from wagons.

"Bread, always bread," Lafayette sighed. One of his multiple duties, she had read in the *Journal de Paris,* was escorting shipments of grain into the city. He patted her absentmindedly on the shoulder and spoke to her father. "Paris has less than three days' supply of bread—but in the last few hours the mobs have grown much more organized. They're marching from Saint-Lazare to every armory they can find. The leaders want to be armed against the king's guard."

"Short and I warned you weeks ago about the effect of foreign troops on the mobs."

"You did, you did. You were both so practical." Lafayette grinned suddenly, feebly. "So *Anglo-Saxon.* You must despise our Latin wildness. How did you find our friends in the country? Safe? Well?"

Short had now joined them at the study door. He had found the duc and the duchesse well but anxious, he told Lafayette. The peasants in their district were loyal so far. On the other hand, rioters roamed the countryside everywhere, especially in Normandy, torching the houses of the nobility. As he talked on with his typical good-natured earnestness, Patsy wondered whether to believe a word of it. As far as she was concerned, Short and Rosalie de La Rochefoucauld were behaving disgracefully. Everyone could see it. Her father disapproved sternly, that she knew; he never invited the duc and duchesse to his house anymore if Short would be there, and when they met at other people's parties, he watched Short with narrowed eyes.

Not, she told herself, making an effort to be scrupulously honest, that the two of them actually *did* anything; they only talked and looked in a certain obvious way, and walked up and down a room for hours together, heads almost touching. She listened to Short say something clever about the riots. The duc was old enough to be Rosalie's grandfather. When she was married, Patsy had already decided, if she couldn't live in Paris, she would live with her husband in her father's house at Monticello.

Short asked a question she didn't hear, and smiled at her. Had he and Rosalie, she wondered, ever *really*—?

"The duc is changing his politics." Lafayette shook his head; his huge teeth were as big as flagstones.

"In fact," Short said, "the duc begins to think the mobs pose a greater danger than the king. I told him he sounded like John Adams."

Her father's hand was on the study door. He laughed and pulled it back. "Mr. Short refers to an old debate between Adams and me. Our little Shays's Rebellion out in western Massachusetts had a great and sobering effect on him, you remember. In politics, we used to say, Mr. Adams fears the *many*, I fear the *one*."

Her father was pulling open the door. In the hallway facing them stood James Hemings, hands on hips, scowling. As usual, her father walked past him without a glance. "You know, Adams once told me he had read through all of Plato and learned only one thing," he said to Lafayette. "That sneezing is a cure for hiccups. Did you ever hear what Franklin said about Adams?"

Lafayette shook his head. Slowly James Hemings began to unfasten the door, newly barred against burglars.

"He said Adams was 'always an honest man, often a wise one, but sometimes, in some things, absolutely out of his senses.' "

Lafayette gave only a distracted laugh. As James Hemings drew the door open with a grunt, he clapped the hat on his head and looked out to the street, where three soldiers waited on horses. Beyond them, over the dark green trees of the Champs-Élysées, low clouds walled off a sullen sky.

"Tomorrow," Lafayette said, "the mob intends to march to the Invalides for powder and guns, but they won't find any powder there."

In French, to Patsy's utter amazement, James Hemings asked

the Marquis de Lafayette: "Where do they keep their powder then?"

Lafayette appeared unsurprised. His left hand was steadying his scabbard, while his right hand shifted to the hilt of his sword. "They keep it in the Bastille," he said.

The next morning, Gouverneur Morris noted in his journal that the wind was still from the southwest, something unusual in his experience of Paris, and that the streets were covered with puddles and mud, something entirely familiar. Showers had fallen during the night; leaning from his *hôtel* window he could see the same heavy black clouds of yesterday, now lowered almost to the treetops and chimneys.

When he went for his accustomed early morning walk, the streets were already thronged with angry crowds, "moblets," he wrote, enjoying the play with words. Moblets of soldiers in uniform, moblets of chattering laborers now often called *sans-culottes*, wearing the revolutionary cockade of red and blue in their hats; moblets of boys, muddy Savoyards, hysterical, speech-making women.

He returned to the *hôtel* for his carriage but found that the driver and groom had both disappeared. When he had finally hired another, he set off for his banker's to discuss the complex tobacco loan that had originally brought him to Paris, but twice his carriage was stopped and searched for firearms, and at their offices the French bankers were plainly too nervous to carry on business. As he reconstructed it later, about the time he had taken his chair and spread out his papers — noon, or a little after — Éthis de Corny was leading a ragtag army of citizens up to the very mouths of the cannons guarding the Invalides, where they demanded powder, bullets, and the thirty thousand muskets stored deep in the arsenal. Behind the cannons stood gunners holding lighted candles. Four hundred yards away, mounted but not stirring, a detachment of the king's Swiss and German guards waited for orders. Inside the Invalides a few crippled pensioners worked halfheartedly to remove firing pins or triggers from the guns. By the time de Corny's men marched scornfully past the cannons, the pensioners had disarmed all of twenty muskets.

But the guns were no good without powder. In answer to de Corny's question, the governor of the Invalides replied that his powder, some 250 pounds of it, had been transferred a week ago to the Bastille.

Morris was dining in his *hôtel* when the mobs passed by again, now heading directly (though he could not know it) for the huge eight-towered fortress that dominated the eastern edge of Paris, not far from the burned-out shell of Réveillon's house. Morris had never seen the Bastille. He had heard of it only as a prison notable for its endless underground dungeons and its one celebrated inmate, the curious and learned Marquis de Sade, who liked to stand at his window and shout long-winded obscenities at passing strangers. Morris finished his meal—"a very bad one," he wrote— closed his journal, and proceeded on foot to the Louvre. There he joined Adèle de Flahaut and (for once) her elderly husband, both of them peering out of their own windows like the Marquis de Sade and listening to the distant thunder of gunfire and explosions that had become the punctuation of every Parisian dialogue.

At tea, while the old baron paced and listened, Morris amused Adèle with stories of his house in New York—Morrisania—on which he lavished all his money and care. "I am like Jefferson in that," he told her. "I've fallen in love with my house, a relationship much more dangerous than the love of women."

"Don't be like Jefferson."

"I will be like Hamlet then." He placed the tip of his finger on the smooth ball of flesh beneath her right thumb. " 'Every man has both business and desire.' "

They were speaking in English, which the baron did not understand. Adèle shifted in the chair to incline slightly in Morris's direction. "I have heard—don't ask from whom—that you also write poetry impromptu, to charm the women."

"That would be most romantic of me, if it were true."

The musket fire grew louder. The baron had come close to their chairs and now stopped, head tilted toward the window. Adèle silently handed Morris the wooden escritoire she had been holding; a sheet of paper, and a pen, which she carefully dipped first in a brass inkwell shaped like a lion's claw. Morris dipped the pen a second time as if for inspiration, then quickly scratched out two quatrains.

In fever, on your Lap I write,
Expect then but a feeble Lay,
And yet in every Proverb's Spite
Tho' 'tis in Verse, believe I pray.

No Lover I. Alas! too old
To raise in you a mutual Flame.
Then take a Passion rather cold
And call it by fair Friendship's Name.

When he handed the paper back to Adèle, her husband looked down for the first time. "Now the shots come from the Hôtel de Ville," he said in French, "or else the Place de Grève. What have you written, Monsieur?"

"He writes," Adèle said, ignoring the pinched, gray expression on her husband's face, "that he is too old to be a lover."

Across the city later that day, Jefferson and Short, waiting at de Corny's house, learned that the Bastille had been taken in a great blast of cannon fire, musket fire, blood. A hundred citizens were dead. Thirty or more Swiss guards had been hanged indiscriminately by the mob. The wretched commander of the prison had been dragged through the streets to the Hôtel de Ville, spat upon, kicked, pummeled every step of the way. When a member of the crowd—a pastry cook—approached him for some reason, the commander lashed out with a wobbly kick. Instantly a dozen knives were plunged into his chest, the body was rolled over and over through the mud to a gutter, and two pistols were fired directly into the skull. Then the pastry cook took a pocketknife from his apron and painstakingly sawed away the commander's head, which was jammed onto a soldier's pike and thrust up to the roaring crowd.

For two more days the mobs roamed the streets almost at will. In Versailles the king made a conciliatory speech. In Paris he rode in procession, escorted by Lafayette, to the Hôtel de Ville, where he received (no one knew why) the keys to the city and placed on his royal hat the blue-and-red cockade that made him too a "sans-culotte."

Jefferson watched the procession from a borrowed apartment on the rue Saint-Honoré. He told Short, when the king's carriage passed, followed by thousands of citizens armed with pikes and swords and pruning hooks and scythes, that liberty had been bought at a low price. Below them the crowd was chanting over and over, "La-fayette! La-fayette!" and when the marquis saw them, he rose in his saddle, turned his horse in a gallant, prancing circle, and waved his cockaded hat at Patsy and Polly.

Two days later Morris dined at a *table d'hôte* in the Palais Royal. At just before five in the afternoon he was walking alone in the arcades, waiting for his carriage. On the street in front of him yet another crowd began to pass, waving the inevitable scythes and pruning hooks and muskets and carrying in triumph the severed head and shredded torso of a nobleman whom he recognized, though the jaw and mouth were stuffed with clumps of filthy straw and mud. In his journal Morris wrote in the mesmerizing present tense, in a tone as close as he ever came to outrage:

The Head on a Pike, the Body dragged naked on the Earth. Afterwards this horrible Exhibition is carried thro the different Streets. His Crime is to have accepted a Place in the Ministry. This mutilated Form of an old Man of seventy five is shewn to his son-in-law, and afterwards he also is put to Death and cut to Pieces, the Populace carrying about the mangled Fragments with a Savage Joy. *Gracious God what a People!*

CHAPTER

Thirty-Seven

"Has anyone told you the anecdote about the Duc de La Rochefoucauld's witty reply to the king?" Clérisseau grinned expectantly at Short, with only the faintest trace of malice.

"Many people," Short said untruthfully.

"It is a legend already, is it not, my dear?" Clérisseau turned his grin toward Rosalie de La Rochefoucauld, who stood at least three feet away from them in the dark shade of a sycamore. Without waiting for an answer Clérisseau turned back to Short. "On the night the Bastille fell—was it really only a month ago?— the duc rode out to Versailles and demanded to see the king in his private apartments. Naturally the guards resisted—it was nearly midnight, the king was asleep; but the duc pushed his way through all the same, right up to the royal bedside.

" 'Sire, I have just come from the city,' the duc said.

" 'Is it a revolt?' said the king.

" 'No, sire, it is a revolution.' "

Clérisseau chuckled. "Perfectly French, that story. When I was a boy learning my grammar, we were always taught that there are three main qualities of the French language. The first is clarity. After that is clarity. And the third is also clarity. I do not think," he added after a moment, "the king has quite understood it yet."

"We have been strolling about in the gardens." Rosalie emerged from the shadow of the sycamore. "To escape the heat."

"And our friend has been reading aloud from diplomatic dispatches, I presume. Very romantic, very charming." Clérisseau let his round eye draw their eyes, in the French manner, toward the sheets of paper Short held in his hand. Short looked down gloomily. He had counted on half an hour alone with Rosalie before anyone else arrived. But Clérisseau was now living temporarily in the old Duchesse d'Enville's town house and had immediately followed them—tactlessly or deliberately—into the gardens.

"No." Rosalie placed herself between the two men and began to walk. Today, for escaping the heat, she wore a white linen dress with billowy muslin skirt and a neckline scooped low enough to show, almost, the two pink coins of her nipples. "Monsieur Short has taken Madame de Tott's suggestion and written a little history of the great Declaration of Independence. He was just reading parts of it to me. It's very brilliant."

"Have you given us, à la Jefferson, the temperature and the weather each hour and day of the great event?" Clérisseau took Rosalie's arm with his right hand, Short's arm with his left, and beamed on Rosalie's décolletage.

Short folded the papers in half. In fact, he *had* written that the temperature on July 4, 1776 was 68° at 6 A.M., 76° at 1 P.M., information he had copied from Jefferson's own memorandum book. He had also written, not brilliantly at all, an account of how Jefferson's original version had been "mutilated" (Jefferson's word) by the Continental Congress. And then how John Dickinson had walked nobly out of the hall so his delegation could vote for independence without him, and old Joseph Hewes of North Carolina jumped up as if out of a trance and stretched out his arms and shouted, "It is done! by God, it is done!" And he had ended with a long, stupid, truly pompous meditation on how "All men are created equal" was the most important sentence ever written in the history of political thought. He folded the paper again. His prose was not witty in the least.

"Someone is here at last." Rosalie smiled and turned to wave at Madame de Corny, descending the steps of the house fifty yards away. Clérisseau clapped his hands and started toward her.

"You look beautiful," Short whispered to Rosalie.

She took a step along the gravel path, toward the nearest flower bed. "I don't. It's so hard to think of one's personal life now. These politics and riots—"

"You three were wise to come out of the house." As she approached, Madame de Corny made an exaggerated fanning motion with the silver lorgnette she carried. "So hot in there. And your grandmother"—she nodded to Rosalie—"so old-fashioned. She won't hear of leaving the doors open to the garden."

"We were just discussing the Declaration of Independence," Rosalie said.

"Comparing a good revolution to a bad." Clérisseau stooped to pick up a fallen rose from the gravel and grunted with the effort as he straightened again. "Though as an architect, of course, I approve of the destruction of buildings, since they must all be replaced by new ones."

"You've lost your liberalism," Short said.

"The bloom is undoubtedly gone," Clérisseau agreed. He frowned comically at the rose, then tossed it away. "But as for the Declaration of Independence, you know I saw John Trumbull's sketch for his giant painting of it when he was here. He had Jefferson, Franklin, Adams all lined up like choirboys in front of a desk, pens in hand. The first historical painting I ever saw without corpses or horses."

"You've changed all your opinions," Madame de Corny scolded. "You're just like the Duc de La Rochefoucauld."

"There was never a signing," Short said with pedantic gruffness. "The Continental Congress passed the resolution for independence on July second, and *that* should be the day we celebrate. They approved the wording of the Declaration on July fourth, but nobody signed anything until August second, and then they just trickled into the clerk's office when they felt like it. The whole so-called signing took more than a week."

"Ah." In the bright afternoon sunlight Madame de Corny's smile was tentative and puzzled. Clérisseau played with his coat buttons and said nothing. After a moment, Rosalie took the other woman by the arm and steered her toward the shade, saying something over her shoulder that Short missed completely. His hands, he saw with surprise, were still folding and refolding the pages of his manuscript.

"Lady talk, of course," Clérisseau commented. "And the younger lady looks particularly enchanting today, does she not?" Short made no reply. He added, "Your employer was very kind to send me the gift of that silver coffeepot. I've written him a note."

"He's still awaiting his official permission to leave." Short folded the papers one last time and stuffed them into his pocket. In his mind's eye he could see the painting Trumbull would finally make of the signing—destined, he was now morosely certain, to set a great historical lie in motion. "But he's prepared to sail the moment it arrives. The house is filled with packers and trunks."

"Hence his absence today. The ambassador who cannot wait to be home."

Short watched the two ladies strolling tête-à-tête down the lane of trees that bordered the old Duchesse d'Enville's garden. The house itself belonged to Rosalie's husband the duc, but in some twist of French custom his mother continued in every real sense to possess it. Short studied the Palladian facade, the carefully raked gravel paths, the mossy pond at the wall that separated the estate from the rue des Petits Augustins. Nothing he saw reminded him of home. Home was a fictitious painting, scraps of folded paper.

"He will return when?"

"He plans a six-month leave."

"And you serve in his place?"

"I will be chargé d'affaires."

"I sometimes think of emigrating to America myself." Clérisseau began to walk again, drawing Short along.

"Ah, don't do that," Short said jokingly. "Stay in France. I would."

It was Clérisseau's turn to be suddenly gruff. "Of course, you would. You're a foreigner. To you it's all an art gallery and a distraction. You're not a victim—of *this*." He flapped his baggy sleeve toward the ancient stone wall, the massive trees, the distant flat spires of Saint-Sulpice, meaning to indicate, Short knew, the mad, ceaseless upheaval going on all over Paris, all over France. "Yesterday *they*"—Clérisseau used the French word *cohue*, the nobility's contemptuous name for the mob—"they threw stones at the Duc de La Rochefoucauld's carriage; they nearly killed him, one of their true friends."

Short looked up quickly in Rosalie's direction, decided the

news made no difference. Since the day of the Bastille the mobs changed heroes constantly, for no clear reason. Even Lafayette, the man of the hour in July, was being hissed in August.

"By contrast, I see America as a vast open space." Clérisseau dropped his left arm and rubbed it hard with his hand. "A last glorious chance to let human nature mature in freedom. I see thousands and hundreds of thousands of Europeans like me flowing into it, filling it up, marching to the edge of the continent. Fleeing this insanity."

"You see it the way Jefferson does." Short could hear the irony in his voice but could do nothing about it. In fact, he himself now saw the future of American history as nothing but tragic, the great unstoppable flow of immigrants coming long before anyone had learned what to do with freedom, how to claim it without blood and violence and revolution. A Jeffersonian phrase came back to him: *It was the nature of human nature.*

"Jefferson would be a great man," Clérisseau said, "if he did not own slaves."

"He is free to free them," Short said slowly. How had their roles become reversed? he wondered idly. Clérisseau now the voice of optimism, himself more cuttingly ironic with every sentence. Europe changed everyone. Revolution changed everyone.

"My dear old American William," Clérisseau said, and brought them to a halt by the mossy pond. Closer, it turned out to be choked with weeds and oily green mud; a dead goldfish floated on its side like a rag. "You've never really seen us as we are. Your particular friend"—he nodded toward the distant Rosalie and held up a palm to stop Short's protest—"let me be frank. She is French. You're not. She is the niece of her husband—did you know that?—and the granddaughter of the old duchesse, her mother-in-law. You haven't the requisite insincerity for our games. You don't enjoy her, you won't have her. She will no more leave her husband than"—Clérisseau's big-nosed, saucer-eyed face broke into a familiar grin—"than I will leave all this for the buffalo plains of Virginia."

On August 25 Lafayette sent them a frantic note, begging that Jefferson would break every engagement and give a dinner next day for himself and seven other members of the National Assembly, who desperately needed to agree together before everything plunged—here Lafayette's pen skittered dramatically to the edge of the page—into civil war.

Promptly at three on the twenty-sixth, Short ushered them into the dining room, bowed, and started to leave; but Lafayette, clutching at everything American, grabbed his elbow, someone else drew up another chair. At the head of the table Jefferson smiled and signaled to James Hemings. In another moment Short found himself taking a place at what Lafayette grandly announced as a "Symposium unparalleled" of statesmen.

It was a symposium that began slowly and badly. Jefferson had decided to serve the meal Virginia fashion, which meant that no wine would be poured until after the table was cleared of food. The French statesmen twirled the stems of their empty glasses, glanced at the clock. Meanwhile, Lafayette, clearly nervous, described at greater and greater length, as if he had forgotten the purpose of the meeting, the horrors he had encountered at the siege of Yorktown, when the British fought back so fiercely that the allies nearly broke. "We used to clean the wounds in the trenches, you know," he suddenly told Short in English, "by urinating into them." One of the Frenchmen looked up and raised an eyebrow. "Pisser dans les blessures," Lafayette obligingly translated, and the Frenchman put down his glass.

"The gallant French soldiers of today," Jefferson began, evidently intending some compliment that would open the discussion. At the door James Hemings now hovered with his tray of bottles.

Lafayette ignored his cue. "Nothing compared to Yorktown. My friend, you know Alexander Hamilton?"

Jefferson nodded. "He is to be secretary of the treasury in Washington's new government."

"I'm surprised to hear it." Lafayette picked up a last forkful of food and left it suspended. "At the beginning of '81 Hamilton was Washington's aide-de-camp, a post he always hated, and they quarreled more than once. I was present in February, in New York, when Washington called Hamilton on some errand, and Hamilton delayed until, when he finally appeared, the general rose in a towering fury—'Sir, you have kept me waiting at the head of the stairs these ten minutes. You treat me, sir, with disrespect'—'I am not conscious of it, sir,' says Hamilton cooly, 'but since you have thought it necessary to tell me so, we part.' And he left. This was the man I had serving under me the day the British—" He saw James Hemings at last and broke off. "I'm sorry," the Prince of Pineapples said with a dignity that surprised Short. "It is a fault in a soldier to dwell in the past."

"Aux armes," said one of the Frenchmen sardonically.

When the wine had been poured and the cloth taken away, Lafayette stood, raising his glass, clearing his throat. The question to be resolved, he said, and looked up and down the table, was whether in a new French constitution the king would have an absolute veto over the Assembly, as some members wanted, or no veto at all, as others did. This was the sticking point, the symbolic wall between those who favored monarchy and those who favored republicanism. "I need not remind you of the state of things. Without agreement among us, the leaders, the Assembly will fall into utter chaos, the nation will explode again in geysers of blood. I have my own opinion." He extended his glass toward a sour-faced man in a huge white wig, sitting at Jefferson's right hand. "Monsieur Mounier has his."

Jefferson motioned to Short, and the two of them pushed their chairs back, as a gesture of invisibility. The Americans were to be silent observers only. The Frenchmen hardly noticed. Mounier, having lifted his white wig with both hands and pulled it down again like a bowl, was now also standing and speaking in rapid French; the others were likewise speaking or raising their hands. Lafayette sank back into his chair, waving his glass as if he had launched a ship.

At half past six, after more than three hours at the table, the symposium declared a brief recess. Most of the members wandered into the garden, where Jefferson's yellowing Indian corn still stood in plowed furrows. Short started to follow, reached the hall, then came to an abrupt halt. James Hemings was standing before a mirror, arms straight, fists at his side, mouthing words silently. Short hesitated; cleared his throat. In the glass James's eyes flashed yellow. In another moment, glaring as he passed, he had vanished down the corridor.

Short frowned and pinched the bridge of his nose with two

fingers. At the door to the study he looked in and discovered two of the Frenchmen deep in conversation with Jefferson.

"Come in, please." Jefferson saw him at once. "Our guests asked to see my paintings, but most of them are already packed." He indicated the maze of trunks and shipping boxes that covered the floor. "This one," he said, holding up a picture of Herodias with the head of John the Baptist, "I intend to hang over the parlor fireplace at Monticello." He propped it against a chair leg and then from an open box by the desk pulled out three small paintings in thin gilt frames. "And these are for my library."

"Fran-cis Bacon." The sardonic Frenchman squinted to read a label.

"Bacon, Newton, and Locke," Jefferson said. He arranged the paintings on the cluttered copy-press table for them to admire. "The three greatest men who ever lived. In my opinion," he added politely. "I had my friend John Trumbull commission them to be copied in London. My original idea was to place them all together in one frame, so." He quickly sketched on the copy press a large square containing three ovals. "But Trumbull said the effect would be awkward, so I mean to hang them separately."

"They are"—the Frenchman squinted again—"all atheists, are they not? Your three greatest men?"

Jefferson shook his head briskly and straightened the nearest portrait—a very bad one, Short thought, of John Locke, who had emerged from the painter's brush looking like a blue-haired horse.

"Locke wrote an essay against 'enthusiasm,'" Jefferson conceded, "which you know is the English term for religious fanaticism. But he was a Christian, certainly. Bacon and Newton too. Newton spent the last twenty years of his life calculating the exact date of the Day of Judgment. The three of them together laid, I believe, the foundation for all modern physical and moral science."

"But you yourself," the Frenchman persisted. His voice was disapproving and suspicious. "You are known to be an atheist, yes? There was a joke you made about the Church. When the commoners walked out of Versailles and met at the Church of Saint-Louis, you said, 'This is the first time that churches have been made good use of.'"

Jefferson folded his arms across his chest; his eyes slid to Short.

"Well, as to my own beliefs, of course," he said carefully, "I keep them private; you must judge of my religion by my actions."

"Should an atheist be tolerated"—the Frenchman gestured toward the dining room—"in our new constitution? This is another question."

Short had never known anyone so reluctant to reveal his feelings—*some* feelings; unpolitical feelings. Jefferson turned away almost rudely and began to wrap Isaac Newton in a sheet of waxy green paper. "To my mind," he said, using his bad wrist to hold down the paper, "it is an easy question. The legitimate powers of government extend only to such acts as actually injure others. Not to matters of conscience."

"But to protect the truth—"

Jefferson's eyes remained on the vanished Newton. "We arrive at truth," he said, "by trial and error, reason and experiment. That was Bacon's contribution in my little trinity. Do you gentlemen recall that in France the potato was once forbidden as an article of food, because it wasn't mentioned in Aristotle? Or that Galileo was sent to the Inquisition for calling the earth a sphere? It is only error that needs the protection of government."

Lafayette poked his anxious face through the doorway, blinking.

"In fact," Jefferson said, but so softly that only Short could hear, "I am no atheist."

☆   ☆   ☆

At ten o'clock the symposium at last pushed back its chairs and adjourned. In the hallway Short made himself busy gathering coats and directing grooms and coachmen. When he turned to say good night to the first of the statesmen, he saw, not French wigs and ruffles, but James Hemings again, dressed now in a plain cotton jacket, standing rigidly with his hand on the door to Jefferson's study.

"Excellent pastries, James, excellent meal today." Short stared at the mulatto's scowling face. No servant *ever* went into Jefferson's study uninvited. "Beautifully cooked."

"Mr. Jefferson through yet?" Sullen, angry.

From the dining room French voices rose and skipped, followed by Lafayette's bray. When Short looked again, James Hemings was gone.

"It has been," Jefferson said, entering the hallway, "a dialogue as fine as any in antiquity, anything by Xenophon or Plato. A feast of logic and chaste eloquence."

"We have agreed," Lafayette told Short, as if he had not been present for all six hours of debate, "on a suspensive veto, capable of being overturned by a two-thirds vote."

"Have you further wise thoughts for us, Monsieur?" The disapproving Frenchman had planted himself squarely before Jefferson. He cocked his head like a belligerent terrier.

Jefferson composed his face into a grave neutrality. "No. No, you have seen everything to perfection, you have penetrated to the mother principle that governments are republican only in proportion as they embody the will of their people."

"The American Revolution is our Bible," the Frenchman said.

"Then you will convert me yet," Jefferson said, suddenly grinning; and laughing, Short pulled open the door.

☆   ☆   ☆

Forty minutes later, not laughing but scowling, gripping too hard the brass handle behind his back, James Hemings closed the study door with a bang.

At his desk Jefferson put down his pen and looked up. Looked mild. Looked calm. As he always, always did.

"I received your note," Jefferson said, rising from the desk and making a vague, polite gesture of welcome. "As the guests were leaving." His long arm went completely out of the circle of light cast by the whale-oil lamp; as he stepped around the desk, his face floated in the shadows like a ghost.

James bumped his way between boxes and stopped at an open black leather trunk that had just arrived the day before, specially built for Jefferson in London.

"Is it about the packing?" Jefferson was invariably polite to everybody, black or white; James had never seen him really lose his temper, though he had often seen him turn ice-cold in an instant, *le roi de glace.*

"If it's about the packing," Jefferson said, and he walked idly toward the same black trunk, "as you know, I haven't received permission to leave yet. I haven't even booked our passage to Virginia. So there should be plenty of time to finish"—the right hand appeared in the light—"all this."

"Not about the packing." James licked the inside of his front teeth, probing quickly with his tongue for brandy. Two glasses were the limit, his sister had said, and kept the bottle squeezed tight in her lap, right between her thighs.

"Not about the packing," he repeated.

Jefferson ran his hand along the smooth lid of the trunk and said nothing.

"I can read, you know," James said. More brandy would have stopped his hands from trembling. "Sir."

"You have been able to read for many years, I think. My wife saw to it you learned."

"And here, I can read French too." James looked at the blank square on the wall where the portrait of Washington had hung. "A little."

"Something you have read upsets you."

James had rehearsed his speech for three weeks while he cooked, while he carried armfuls of clothes to boxes, while he skulked up and down the ruined, smoking rue Saint-Antoine, in and out of mobs and soldiers, looking for Le Trouveur. Now, of course, every single word had gone. His eyes shifted to the books glinting on the dark shelves. He took a deep, brandy-laced breath.

"In the French law," he said, "nobody can be a slave. Under the law I'm a free man as long as I stay here. Sally too. Virginia law don't matter one bit here."

Jefferson floated almost entirely into shadow; outside the study window the clop of passing horses echoed on the pavement, soldiers going somewhere; free.

"That's what I read. And I know a man, a Frenchman, who can make a petition, and if I give it to the government, I am free."

Jefferson had moved all the way to the other window, next to Short's desk. From where he stood by the black trunk, James could see the faint crescent of red in the lamplight that would be his hair. It was too dark to tell, but James knew for a certainty that his arms were folded across his chest and his face and his eyes looked like ice.

But when he finally spoke, Jefferson's voice was as mild as it had been at the start. "This time of year, this time of night," he said, "it would still be hot at Monticello. You and I would be in our shirt-sleeves instead of these heavy French coats." He paused. The last of the horses passed by and faded into the distance. "When we arrive, it will be early November probably, still time to see the leaves turning color and bring in the last vegetables from the garden. I'm looking forward to being home," Jefferson said. "Virginia is home." His sleeve rustled in the shadows. "If you file your petition, James, you can never go home."

"I can get a piece of paper that says I'm free."

"It will do you no good in Virginia. In Virginia you will be a slave again, but you will have a family, a home. Here you will have nothing."

"I can get along."

Jefferson was back in the light, shaking his head. "James. You've been in nothing but fights and trouble and drunken brawls ever since you got here. Last year I paid your French teacher extra money because you lost your temper and ripped his coat to pieces. I've paid for your quarrels at the cooking school and stopped the owner who wanted to sue you. I've taken care of you. And your sister."

James looked down and saw that he too had folded his arms across his chest.

"Your sister's no more than a child."

"She wants to be free."

For a long moment the two men were silent. In the flickering shadows they seemed to be posing, standing face to face, mirror images of each other. Jefferson started to speak again—"In this revolution and unrest," he said, "your chance of finding employment"—then, as if giving up the argument, he simply stopped.

James felt the brandy fading out of his blood; the tips of his fingers and toes were ice-cold. He shifted on his feet. Jefferson moved slowly to the desk and sat down.

"Let me think on this," he said at last.

Now the whale-oil lamp was just to Jefferson's left, so that while half his face was sharply illuminated, half was still in shadow. James Hemings had known Jefferson all his life. Auto-

CHAPTER

Thirty-Eight

"I n London," said Gouverneur Morris, settling back into the carriage seat, "I made the acquaintance of the divine, enchanting, splendidly golden-haired Maria Cosway." He snapped the window shade and peered out. "You were extremely good to meet me at the gate, my dear Short. But Paris looks serene tonight. Not a mob in sight."

"You called on her?" Short crossed his legs and spoke (he told himself) with Parisian serenity. But his mind had jumped with apprehension—Morris and Maria Cosway?

"I carried a letter to her from Jefferson. I entered into the bosom of her household. She told me, in all innocence, that she was in love with me, as she is in love with all American men. For some days I was afraid that her husband, in his own special way, would repeat the compliment."

"And you saw her often?"

"We had many a tête-à-tête. One day she told me a very funny story about your leader."

"I would not take seriously any story," Short began, shaping his face into a judicious frown.

Morris glanced back from the window, amused. "Evidently they met for the first time at the Halle aux Bleds."

"Trumbull introduced them."

"Yes, the blind painter, and subsequently—this is the story— Maria tried to introduce Jefferson to her particular English friend in Paris, the celebrated Miss Perdita Robinson, and Jefferson quite mysteriously, quite stubbornly, refused."

Short focused on a wine-yellow streetlamp, refined his frown, and said nothing.

"Because you see, as it turned out, Perdita Robinson, once the mistress of the Prince of Wales, had come to Paris with her new lover, and if Jefferson met her, he would also, perforce, meet the lover."

The streetlamp bounced away like a burning ball.

"Whose name," Morris continued gleefully, "was Colonel Banastre Tarleton, late of his British Majesty's army in America. Now Perdita, as you may know, is occasionally an author, and she was here helping the good colonel to write his memoirs of his American campaign, about which poor Maria was at the time completely ignorant."

"Colonel Tarleton was in Virginia."

"Colonel Tarleton was in Virginia and, according to himself, chased Governor Jefferson off the top of his hill like a scared rabbit."

"There are two versions to that story," Short said stiffly.

"As there are two versions to every story I have ever heard about Jefferson. But what I liked was the amazing coincidence of rabbit and hound turning up ten years later, on the arms of two such charmers. Imagine the scene if they *had* met—Jefferson frigid as a monk, Tarleton suave and bloody British. 'How is your fine house at Monticello, sir?' They both have red hair."

"You saw Tarleton?"

"No. But I did see the new book Perdita has written and Maria has illustrated. I quite liked the title: *The Progress of Female Virtue and Female Dissipation.*"

In spite of himself Short smiled.

"I shall give a copy to the Bishop of Autun," Morris decided.

In another moment the carriage swayed to a halt on the crowded rue de Richelieu, opposite Morris's *hôtel*, and Morris began to lower himself, wooden leg first, to the pavement. Half-way down he looked back over his shoulder. "After eleven hours in the Chantilly coach, I intend to have a steaming hot bath and then a bottle, possibly two, of good Burgundy, which you cannot buy or steal this year in London, *à cause de la révolution*. Can I repay you for the ride with a little supper? Say nine o'clock?"

"Your club?"

"The elegant Club Valois."

At half past nine, diplomatically late, Short pushed through the crowd of *filles de nuit* and their masculine admirers and climbed the stairs to the second floor of the Palais Royal. The Club Valois occupied a set of rooms next to the Chess Club of Paris and looked down on the long, beautiful, still twilit gardens between the arcades. From his table Morris looked down on the *filles de nuit*, turning their skirts in a languorous parade of color.

"That is the very tree," he told Short, pointing past the women, "where Desmoulins made his speech."

"The cockade speech." Short sat down and watched Morris pour, with steady hand, from an already half-empty bottle of Clos de Vougeot. Two days before the Bastille was taken, a student named Camille Desmoulins had jumped on a table before the Café de Foy and worked the crowds to a fever pitch. At the climactic moment of his speech he had first pointed a pistol at his head—a sign of his readiness for martyrdom—then snatched a handful of leaves from a chestnut tree and proclaimed them the green cockade, the color of hope. For weeks after that every citizen without a cockade in his hat or his hair had run the risk of revolutionary justice.

"But all that"—Morris moved his big head restlessly—"everything like that is over. The Polish general over there"—he nodded discreetly toward the leathery dark recesses of the club—"tells me Paris has been quiet for weeks. The king has even been given a suspensive veto by the National Assembly."

"Jefferson helped arrange it. At a dinner at his house."

"Paugh," Morris said. "Not a word about Jefferson, not a word about this misguided revolution of nothing."

But in fact, through a five-course supper and three bottles of wine ("small ones," Morris murmured; "the British use bigger bottles"), they had talked of little else. When the table was cleared they were talking of Lafayette—"his passion to shine," Morris grumbled; " 'his canine appetite for popularity,' " Short quoted

Jefferson—and when they finally emerged into the garden down-stairs, they were talking of the ominous calm that had gripped the city; the lull, they agreed, before a greater storm.

"Come and stroll," Morris said, beginning to stump along the path. He moved ahead briskly three steps, faltered, and caught at the arm of one of the *filles*, who steadied him, giggled, whispered in his ear. By the famous tree they found a bench, and Short helped him sit down.

" 'For this relief, much thanks,' " Morris said, leaning back. "As the preacher said in the brothel." His head rested on the tree trunk and his white wig tilted askew. In the light of the Japanese lanterns hanging from the nearest arcade, they could see the *filles*, revolution or no revolution, hard at work plying their trade, and the same perpetual, inexhaustible stream of men flowing out of the cafés and restaurants that lined the eastern side of the garden.

"I'm told," Morris said, breathing heavily, "that the revolution-aries have taken to shaving the heads of debauched women."

Short nodded; useless, he thought, in the darkness. "They do, some of them. The women are 'impure.' "

"Ah, like the queen."

"Jefferson says without the queen there would be no revolu-tion. Marie-Antoinette bullies the king and provokes the people."

Morris ignored the reference to Jefferson. He watched a beau-tiful young woman pass through the nimbus of lanterns, followed by a nobleman in a mulberry-colored coat. "But I'm also told that when they have their executions, amorous couples in the crowd" —he worked his hands in an expressive gesture.

Short's eyes tracked the blurred figure of the prostitute and the nobleman till they disappeared in shadows. "I've heard that too." His mind spun suddenly, back to his first days in Paris, while the vague, muzzy outlines of the trees and lanterns metamorphosed into rocking faces. Where was the Ace of Spades now? John Adams? Her little servant, who had shown up that day when he and Rosalie—? In the distance a girl was now running, they heard a muffled shout. In his whole life, he thought, abruptly sad, noth-ing had ever been as sensual and exciting as those first months in Paris. He could inhale now, this moment, anytime, and bring back the first smells of the outdoor markets, the mixed aromas of green mud and perfume, horses, the cut flowers on every table and every bosom.

"Give the whores a suspensive veto," Morris muttered.

Short nodded without actually hearing. The first months in Paris he had never been so conscious of women before—so many arms, wrists, turning necks, rising breasts, so much pressure of flesh against silk, as if the women of Paris had been pumped like balloons every morning into their clothes. Everywhere he had looked he was conscious of flesh, the very buildings were creamy and white, swollen, ripe. He had rubbed his way through the streets as he might rub his way through a harem. When he returned to Jefferson's house each day, he was sweating like a sultan.

"I will tell you something in confidence," Morris whispered. The big man was obviously drunk, but in a Morrisian way, every word under strict constitutional control.

"No." He was thirty years old, Short thought, pinching the bridge of his nose, and no further along in life than when he had landed five years ago. No career, no wife. He blinked at Morris's thick face and moving lips. No friend.

"One day," Morris said, "when I had drunk rather too much, I asked Madame de Flahaut to compare the Bishop of Autun and myself in the Cyprian rites. She reverted to a learned language, I was impressed to see. The bishop, she said, was *suaviter in modo*, while I was *fortiter in re*."

"I cannot imagine," Short began, not imagining what he could not imagine.

"*I* cannot imagine Jefferson doing this," Morris said. "Sitting on a bench at midnight and companionably watching the whores. You are a son of man, my dear Short. Jefferson is a son—"

"It is not his nature."

"Ice is his nature. But you don't think so."

"My view is complex," Short said pompously, thinking that it truly was. *In vino veritas*. In the manuscript he had started he would lay out once and for all the shifting, multifaceted history of his view. "I began, certainly, as a hero-worshiper. I was a boy—"

But Morris had come back from London accustomed, like the English, to interrupt. "He is much too hard in his judgments of people," he rumbled. "He does not form just estimates of character. He assigns too many people to the humble rank of fool, but the gradations in life are really infinite. He is a democrat in theory only."

"He departs in a week." Short was struggling to his feet. He had heard enough. He was tired of Morris; he was afraid of Morris.

"And when he arrives in Virginia, he will be secretary of state."

Short stopped where he was. He concentrated on the swaying lanterns, the light breeze that had sprung up, carrying Parisian smells.

"I had a letter in London." Morris had also come to his feet. Short stiffened.

"*Jefferson* had a letter, rather. From Madison." Morris had taken his arm in kindly, avuncular fashion and was now leading him, with his awkward stump-step rhythm, toward the arcades and the carriage gate. "Jefferson had a letter from Madison in August informing him of Washington's nomination. You didn't see it?"

Did he shake his head? Short had no idea. In broken stages he saw his hand waving the question away. Morris was speaking again, but Short's mind was spinning forward, this time away from Paris and the past, toward Paris and the future.

"He's known for weeks," Morris said with disgust. "Too secretive to tell you."

Short was slowing his steps, adjusting. "If he is to be secretary of state"—they had reached the Galerie d'Orléans, which led to the rue de Richelieu and Morris's *hôtel*—"then he will not be returning to Paris."

"He would begin at once."

"But he may not accept—"

Morris laughed out loud and steered them through an archway that echoed to shoe and stump like the bottom of a cave. At its far end, carriage lanterns floated in watery darkness. "Not accept," Morris repeated scornfully. "He talks about retirement to his farm, he *does* retire when he sulks, but he's as ambitious as Lafayette. I know politicians. He'll take secretary of state, and he'll be scheming every moment to be president after that. Jefferson plays for the long view. It wouldn't surprise me in the least if he had dropped the charming Mrs. Cosway just to avoid a scandal later on."

They had reached the rue de Richelieu, twenty steps from Morris's *hôtel,* and servants were descending the steps, holding little bull's-eye lamps.

"Ask him if he's coming back," Morris challenged.

Short's hand passed through squares of light. "He's been confined to his bed with a headache for two weeks, and now he's packing in a frenzy to leave—"

"I told you he'd never look after your interests, not over here. You think he'll appoint you Minister to France in his place, yes? Here's what Jefferson will tell you, my friend. A tactful compliment first. 'You speak perfect French, you're excellent at business, people like you—oh yes, dear William, you'd be ideal as a diplomat.' Then the shrug, the cool apology." Morris mimicked Jefferson's voice. "'But I'm only a humble public servant, of course, without opinions of my own. And alas, you're not very well known to Washington or Hamilton or Congress, who may have other plans, to which I am not yet privy.' Besides"—Morris resumed his normal tones—"let us be honest. Jefferson thinks you've become more French than the French. He wants nothing more than to get you back to the healing, wholesome moral climate of America."

"The secretary of state can name whom he wants." Short's voice was small, full of foreboding.

"And he will," Morris said, dropping his arm, "and it won't be you." In the yellow light his teeth flashed like a wolf's. "It will be me."

☆   ☆   ☆

On the sixteenth of September, as Short sat in his shirt-sleeves on the third floor and filed letters, he heard the gong sound in the downstairs hallway.

When he peered over the banister, he could see the tops of three heads—Jefferson's, red as a carrot in the morning light; Petit's pigtail; and the oversize white wig of Madame de Tessé. By the time he reached the hallway, they had been joined by two husky footmen, who had just tilted upright in one corner a narrow wooden crate.

"Not for the voyage to America," Madame de Tessé said, twinkling. Short bowed to her protégée Madame de Tott, now materializing in another corner. "For your *return*, Monsieur."

Jefferson made polite murmurings and stepped forward, over discarded slats, to see what the workmen were uncovering.

"The idea came on me," said Madame de Tessé, "when I saw the bust Houdon did of you in this year's Salon."

"Houdon has been very busy forming American faces," Jefferson said, smiling at Madame de Tott and placing one hand flat on the back of his neck. "Dr. Franklin started it, but then there was Washington, Lafayette, Paul Jones."

"Who multiplied himself like a rabbit," said Madame de Tessé. "He ordered a dozen copies of his own bust, I know."

Ever the precise record-keeper, Jefferson shook his head. Short thought the past two weeks of painful illness, worse than the long "seasoning" of his first year, had cost him weight but given him dignity. The habitually mild expression had an edge to it, the long chin thrust harder still in profile. "Eight copies only," Jefferson said. "He's asked me to distribute them to friends in America."

"Mistresses," sniffed Madame de Tessé.

"Ah, look." To be helpful Short had positioned himself beside one of the footmen. As the last cotton wrapping came loose, he snapped it back with a flourish.

"My friend! Madame!" Jefferson came to attention like a soldier, spread his arms like a Frenchman. "This is too much, this is far too kind!"

"To put under Houdon's bust," she said delightedly. The tall wig dipped perilously forward. Madame de Tott raised her lorgnette.

"This is . . . beautiful," Jefferson said, and Short nodded in vigorous agreement. The kneeling footmen were pulling away the last scraps of paper and cotton from a marble pedestal five feet high, snow white, with a smooth circular top. Around the edge of the top ran a series of alternately smiling and weeping cherubs, and beneath them, in a broad spiraling band down the column, a set of carvings that Short recognized as the twelve signs of the zodiac.

"I ordered an inscription," said Madame de Tessé.

Jefferson stepped over the wrappings and bent to read.

" '*Summo rerum moderati / cui tandem / Libertas Americae . . .*' " He translated aloud. " 'To the Supreme Ruler of the Universe, under whose watchful care the liberties of North America were finally achieved.' "

Madame de Tott finished the translation. " 'And under whose tutelage the name of Thomas Jefferson will descend forever blessed to posterity.' "

Jefferson took Madame de Tessé's tiny hands in his. Tears glinted in the corners of her eyes; the little pockmarked cheeks were tremulous beneath the absurd wig.

"My dear friend," Jefferson said with the slow, stiff formality he adopted when moved, "I am never so conscious of my littleness as when praises are bestowed on me which I do not merit. I feel like a thief, running away with the property of others. My conscience binds me to make a small alteration in the last line."

Short glanced at the pedestal. *Nomen Thomas Jefferson.*

"Let it be changed to say '*Nomen de Noailles, comitissa de Tessé.*' "

In her flat voice scholarly Madame de Tott retranslated. " 'The name of the Countess of Tessé will descend to posterity.' "

"You are a true, devoted friend of Liberty," Jefferson said, still holding her hands.

At the door to the dining room James Hemings appeared, arms loaded with folded sheets.

"When you return to Paris," said Madame de Tessé, "I will see that the bust is installed on it properly."

"We shall place it here in the hall." Jefferson's voice was gentleness itself. He moved out of James Hemings's path without appearing to see him and indicated, over the customary Jeffersonian litter of trunks and boxes, the cleared table in the dining room. "Every other room has been metamorphosed into a packing shop for the voyage. But come in here and take a glass of wine with me this morning."

Madame de Tott, the fair Grecian, said something quite loudly in Greek, with a lilting musical accent completely different from her usual dry tone. Jefferson looked around with an amused twist to his mouth.

"What did she say?" Madame de Tessé arched her right eyebrow to the edge of the wig.

"She quoted the end of the second book of the *Odyssey*," Jefferson said, "when Telemachus makes a sacrifice of wine and oxen before he embarks on a long sea voyage."

"What prodigies I know," said Madame de Tessé comfortably.

"Alas, we have run short of oxen."

"I defer the pleasure. When you return from America"—she craned her head to include Short in the remark—"you will find us all prodigies, I hope; democratic prodigies."

"Those who still have their heads left on their shoulders," Short said, far more sharply than he intended.

"Monsieur Short," said Madame de Tessé. She stopped on the threshold of the dining room and frowned with displeasure. "You've grown as antirevolutionary as Monsieur Morris."

"It's only the mention of sea voyages that makes him anxious," said Madame de Tott, a step behind her.

"Ah yes, I remember." Madame de Tessé's frown relaxed; she nodded with maternal tolerance. "Monsieur Short hates the water. He won't sail if he can help it, will he?" But at her side Jefferson's frown remained sternly in place.

An hour later, when the ladies had departed, he entered Short's room without ceremony, with only a peremptory rap on the open door, and reached Short's desk in three long strides.

"The tone of your remarks about the revolution," he said before Short had gotten to his feet, "has for some time given me pain."

"Sir?"

Jefferson glanced around the room, then turned and stepped back to close the door. "Your remark this morning to Madame de Tessé."

"I meant," Short began, not quite truthfully, "only a jest."

"This revolution is a great event, a very great event in the history of liberty. This country has already begun steps to abolish its aristocratic titles, to establish a free and republican government. I am a friend to it."

Short had come around to the front of his desk. As always when he was frightened, a part of his mind took refuge in exact, obsessive observation. Jefferson wore his usual costume of blue coat and gray trousers, his neck wrapped in a blue scarf; anger had dug long lines across his brow and his chin—prognathous—stabbed to a hard marble cleft.

"You think, like Gouverneur Morris, like Clérisseau, that the violence of the revolution invalidates the revolution. Where there is such excess, you think, such bloodshed, there is no freedom. I think otherwise. Many guilty people have fallen in the last six months without a trial, and some innocent people too. These I deplore as much as anyone, and shall deplore to the day of my death. But I deplore them as I should have done had they fallen in battle. To make a revolution here it was necessary to use the arm of the people, and that is a blind instrument."

"Very blind." Short spoke firmly, but his mind came up with no other words. Feebly he repeated himself. "Blind indeed."

Jefferson had meanwhile turned his back and walked toward the single window in the room, which looked out at the decaying garden. "Was ever such a prize won with so little innocent blood?"

What could Short answer? He saw blood one way—crimson smears on pavement, cold rags of flesh. Jefferson saw everything —how? Abstractly? In a blind vision?

"Some of those martyrs," Jefferson said, "I knew personally, and I have been wounded, in spirit, by their loss. But rather than let the revolution fail, I would have seen half the earth desolated. Were there but an Adam and an Eve left in every country"—he spun on his heel and looked back at Short—"and left *free*, it would be better than it is now."

In the distant, recording part of his brain Short was remembering: *Mr. Jefferson is much given to hyperbole.* But he said nothing and was conscious, shamefully, that he had lowered his eyes and face in something like abasement. All his life, he thought, the one great thing he had envied in other men was not wealth or learning or physical strength, but passion.

At the door Jefferson stopped and cleared his throat. Virginia reasserted itself, courtesy reasserted itself. "If I speak too warmly, William," he said, paused, started over. "The preparations for our trip have made me impatient, too much so. Finding a ship, booking a passage for so many people . . ." He waved his stiff right hand at one of the packing boxes that had invaded Short's neatly organized room. "The confusion."

Short felt the back of his legs touch his desk. Suddenly, almost against his will, he could think of nothing except Gouverneur

Morris's cruel prophecy. "Have you made your bookings yet for the return to Paris?"

The stiff hand disappeared into the blue coat. The smile was Roman, a thin crease of dignity and frost. "That will be much easier to arrange in Virginia."

"But you will be back in the spring?"

"I will be back, of course," Jefferson said, with his other hand on the door.

"It is only," Short began. "It only occurs to me to ask—" And then he stopped. Morris's voice rang in his head. The urge was overwhelming to ask Jefferson directly, confront him even—*If you don't return, will you recommend me? Will you fix me in this place? Give me what I want?* His heart thumped like a cannon under his ribs. What if he asked? And what if Jefferson answered?

At the door Jefferson waited, his hand still on the handle. Slowly his expression softened. "You were going to ask?" he said.

Short saw him as if at a great distance, in the hazy shadow of memory and fear. Even to ask would be to mistrust. He had known Jefferson's quiet, fatherly voice all his life, he thought, longer by far than he had known Morris. Jefferson would never deceive him.

With the bittersweet sensation of having made an irreversible choice, he shook his head. "No."

☆ ☆ ☆

On the morning of Jefferson's departure Short awoke early, much earlier than anyone else in the house. When he lit his candle and opened his gold watch, the spidery hands pointed to ten minutes before five.

He dressed quickly and crossed the room to pull back the shutters. Pointless. The garden and street were completely dark; not even a flickering *réverbère* along the Champs-Élysées. His candle's tongue made the only sound.

No lights. He felt the cold smooth glass of the window against his forehead. The year that he was six, his father had taken him one night up the side of Loft Mountain in Albemarle County, to watch a ceremony of Indian signal fires. The two of them had sat on the cold, smooth wagon bench listening to animals and night birds while his younger brother dozed behind them on a burlap sack. The Indians had set piles of wood every two miles apart straight up and down the Shenandoah range, and at midnight, far to the north, they lit the first one. Then the next hilltop south lit its fire in relay, and the next, and the next. From where he stood, held upright by his father on the wagon, it had looked to Short as if a great red bird of flame were flying from hill to hill.

He yawned and rubbed his cheek and watched a single lantern appear somewhere along the banks of the Seine. He had no desire whatsoever, he thought, to return to Virginia.

On the stairway going down to the kitchen he could hear stirrings from another part of the house. Then a door opened and a voice carried softly down the stairs. Jefferson, singing.

In the kitchen itself a footman was asleep on a stool. Petit stood in front of the fireplace warming a piece of bread. When he saw Short he tilted his head to indicate the silver coffee service on the table.

"James has just taken him his breakfast and his bowl of cold water for his feet."

"We're all up early."

Petit shook his head sorrowfully. "He wants to leave in two hours, but I told him the servants would never load the carriage properly by then."

"Not all those trunks, and the girls, and the extra horse."

Petit pursed his lips and spoke with Gallic melodrama into the fire. "He is *le roi des maîtres.*"

The king of masters. An undemocratic sentiment; unrevolutionary. Don't let the master hear. Short picked up the coffee service and, on this morning of mornings, carried it himself to his room.

By now, as he closed the door with his foot, the sun was casting pink and gray lines of light into the eastern sky. Rooftops, church steeples, fresh lanterns; moving lights on a river barge. A paradox: Europe, older by two thousand years, seemed young and new in comparison with the endless dark, mossy, tangled, impenetrable forests of the New World. Yes? No? He would find some way to work the idea into his manuscript.

His manuscript. Petit's acid black coffee burned his tongue, churned his stomach. Short glanced with dislike from the window back across the room to the desk, where sheets of paper lay in faint white squares on the blotter. *The Life of Thomas Jefferson, in the*

Manner of Mr. Boswell. Unfinished, unreadable. Last night he had labored for three hours trying to write the story of Jefferson's governorship in the Revolutionary War, and in the end everything he had written was contradictory or inconclusive. Colonel Tarleton either chased Jefferson like a rabbit over Carter's Mountain, or else Jefferson waited bravely until the last minute and rode away, and though he had worked until his head ached, Short still had no idea which version was true. He had wadded up his paper and thrown it away.

When they had departed this morning he would return and try his hand at something else: Jefferson and Mrs. Walker; Jefferson and his rival Patrick Henry. He poured a second cup of coffee from the silver spout, watching the liquid black stream turn silver itself in the rising dawn. Everything was metamorphic, ambiguous. Every day he learned a new incongruous fact. Morris, grinning wickedly, had informed him that Patrick Henry's mad wife had actually been John Paul Jones's lover first—what use could he make of that? He raised the coffee cup to his lips. The truth was, he had begun too soon; he could work for years and years and still reach no conclusion about Jefferson, Jefferson's life, or the distant, fire-signaling country to which Jefferson, far more than he, belonged. Better to wait, he thought. Better to wait two decades before he tried again. Better, when they had departed this morning, to ride in the opposite direction, toward Rosalie.

By nine-fifteen, Jefferson's carriage was fully loaded and waiting outside the front door on the rue de Berri. The servants were assembled on the pavement, and Jefferson, who had wanted to drive away quietly with no farewells, was walking stiffly from group to group, murmuring a few words in French.

"When you see me next," Patsy told Short, "I shall be seventeen years old."

"She wants to be married," Polly said as she climbed into the carriage. She poked her head out the window and added, "I don't."

"Say au revoir for me—to everyone."

"I will only say à bientôt."

"When we are both old and married," Patsy said, "we shall speak French to each other, at Monticello." Her long, narrow face assumed a Jeffersonian solemnity. And then, contrary, he was sure, to all her resolutions, she suddenly embraced him in a rush and planted a loud, tearful kiss on his cheek.

In another moment the girls were joined in the carriage by Sally Hemings, resplendent in a new green traveling robe, grinning from ear to ear at the prospect of going home; James Hemings, no less resplendent (but scowling) in a blue-and-gold coat and new boots, climbed a mountain of trunks and settled onto the bench beside the driver.

Beside Short, Madame de Tessé waited with a handkerchief pressed to the corner of one eye. "I have such *prémonitions,*" she whispered over and over, until both of them looked with relief at the gay, roguish figure of Gouverneur Morris stumping up the Champs-Élysées.

"I've been at the National Assembly, listening to Necker and Mirabeau," he announced cheerfully, "but thought I would stop by for *le grand départ.*" Jefferson bowed to the last servant in his personal gauntlet, pressed a coin in the man's hand, and joined them.

"A few letters, my friend," Morris said, handing him a set of envelopes, "which I beg you to deliver as convenient. One is to General Washington."

"I heard you mention Necker."

"An extinct volcano of a man. No longer a power. You may quote me on the other side."

Jefferson smiled and placed the letters in the outer pocket of his blue jacket. "You make it sound as if I'm about to cross the Avernus rather than the Atlantic."

"Your classical allusion would turn Virginia into Hades." Morris winked at Short. "Much my own view, of course."

Jefferson appeared not to have heard. "I will send you shiploads of new plants for Chaville," he told Madame de Tessé, "in meager return for the pedestal." He bent to take her hand, kissed it gallantly, then straightened his tall frame as if to look around once more.

"*Dieu vous protège,*" whispered Madame de Tessé.

"You will be late reaching Le Havre," Short said.

The Roman grasped his hand and covered it with both of his. In the glare of the French sunlight Jefferson's strong features some-how slipped in and out of focus. Symbolic, Short thought ironically; of something. He clung to the solid grip of Jefferson's hands. Then Petit appeared, leading Jefferson's horse, and Jefferson turned to wipe its neck with a handkerchief.

There would be no whip today. He swung easily into the saddle, and they all followed the carriage into the Champs-Élysées, even the servants, where, standing dangerously in the midst of passing wagons and coaches, they waved their hats and handkerchiefs over their heads. From one side of the carriage Sally Hemings leaned out and waved back; from the other side the two girls did the same. Dolphinlike the carriage rose over a hump of light in the road and dropped out of sight. At the last moment, so far away that Short could hardly be sure, Jefferson's horse broke into a gallop.

EPILOGUE

Memoirs of Jefferson — 13

THE MORNING JEFFERSON WAS INAUGU-
rated as President for the first time, March 4, 1801, he
walked down Pennsylvania Avenue with a group of friends from
his boardinghouse and entered the still domeless new Capitol
building under construction (he had a hand, and more, in choosing the design) to give his speech.

Inaudible, of course, beyond the first two rows. When people
read it later, they learned that he had extended the olive branch to
his enemies — "We are all Republicans, we are all Federalists" —
and even called on the "Infinite Power" to guide him, a mild shock
for the New England delegations, which habitually referred to
him as "Atheist Tom."

After he finished his speech — I was in Europe still, but I heard
the story a hundred times — he walked back to Conrad's boardinghouse and found that all the comfortable places at the head of the
table, by the fireplace, were already taken. Nobody offered the
new President his seat, until a Mrs. John Brown, wife of a senator
from Kentucky, shyly stood up. Jefferson refused, with exquisite

Virginia politeness (and shrewd Republican simplicity) and took his usual chair at the very foot of the table.

He was to keep up this pose—not pose but fact—of Republican simplicity all eight years of his presidency. The President's House was barnlike and unfinished most of the time he lived there. The roof leaked, the East Room had no paint or furniture (Abigail Adams had used it for her laundry), and the master of the house, though he entertained constantly, generally received daytime visitors in his old slippers and threadbare red waistcoat, just as if he were at home in Monticello. In private, when he was under no obligation to extend the olive branch, he liked to sit with a bottle of his good French wine and describe his election as the "Revolution of 1800."

That was in the beginning. That was when he pushed success after success through the Congress—sent off his gunboats to beat down the Barbary pirates (something he had dreamed of doing since Paris); sent off his agents, secretly, to make the Louisiana Purchase (the most acquisitive man in the world, Clérisseau had said; in 1812 Jefferson wanted to march into Canada and annex it too). Sent off his secretary Meriwether Lewis to explore Louisiana pretty much as the king had sent Peter Jefferson fifty years before, to survey the Fairfax Line. For a time, among the common people, Jefferson was as popular, almost, as George Washington.

Did I bring him bad luck? Does a part of me like to think so?

I returned to America in the summer of 1802, not rich and not married, in the pursuit of happiness. At almost the same moment a frustrated office-seeker and journalist, one James Callender, reported in the Richmond *Recorder* the "fact" that Jefferson kept a slave concubine at Monticello, a "black Venus" named Sally Hemings, who had so far borne him five mulatto children.

I still have copies—filed away in my office, for whatever motives—of some of the virulent, unspeakable effusions that followed. The New England newspapers, always staunchly anti-Jefferson, could hardly restrain their glee. The President kept a "Congo harem," they wrote in Massachusetts; he rushed back from Washington at every chance to sink between Sally's "mahogany thighs." A thirteen-year-old New York boy named William Cullen Bryant won applause with a poem called "The Embargo"

("Go wretch, resign the presidential chair"). The Philadelphia *Port Folio* published a poem to the tune of "Yankee Doodle":

> Of all the damsels on the green,
>   On mountain or in valley,
> A lass so luscious ne'er was seen,
>   As Monticellian Sally.
>
> Yankee doodle, who's the noodle?
>   What wife were half so handy?
> To breed a flock of slaves for stock,
>   A blackamoor's the dandy!

Did I believe it?

Is one's answer the key, the ultimate clue to Jefferson's character?

In the early autumn twilight of a September afternoon, in the not-so-distant year of 1819, long after Jefferson had surrendered the presidency to the next Virginian in line, I walked up the steps of the east portico at Monticello and the servant who opened the door and took my hand and greeted me in French (I recognized her instantly) was Sally Hemings.

Patsy was next, tumbling on Sally Hemings's heels, trailing grandchildren, speaking French, too, reminding me with Jeffersonian tenaciousness of memory that she and I had promised each other in Paris that one day we would speak French in Monticello, but who could have guessed it would take us twenty-five years?

She led me into the entrance hall, where I stood, flabbergasted first at the *clutter* (not for nothing had I fled the South forever), then, as I sorted it out, the nature of the clutter.

Where anyone else would have had a coatrack, a bench, and a table of hospitable flowers, Jefferson had created, higgledy-piggledy, a private museum. There was a ceiling-high weekly calendar and clock on my left, constructed out of old cannon balls, pulleys, and ropes. There were moth-eaten buffalo heads on the walls, framed maps (Peter Jefferson's map of Virginia among them), paintings of various subjects, curios. One table held a scientific collection (I suppose) of rocks and fossils, neatly labeled.

Another had horns and antlers from every cornute creature on the planet (I thought of Clérisseau *à la mode de moose*). In front of the fireplace reclined a life-sized marble statue of Ariadne with a serpent coiled around her naked arm. Indian bows and arrows and painted skins covered every other available space.

Sally Hemings took my hat and cloak. Patsy introduced me to her husband, Mr. Randolph. I craned my head to look up at the balcony that circled the second floor, where dozens (it seemed) of wide-eyed children stared down like owls on a perch. And then from the door on my left, the library, Jefferson entered.

He was seventy-six years old by then, growing deaf, growing (that fine red hair) quite gray, but otherwise unbowed by time. He wore his presidential slippers, his old red waistcoat (likewise growing gray), and octagonal reading spectacles, which he promptly took off and held as he conducted me on a guided tour of the hall. The fossil table was much depleted, he explained, since he had recently sent a shipment to the Museum of Natural History in Paris; claiming yet again, as if Buffon had not been in his grave these thirty years, the preeminent size of American mammals over European. The Indian artifacts reflected his latest interest; in his spare time he was making a dictionary of tribal languages.

"And these?" At the end of the tour I indicated two marble busts on pedestals that flanked the main door. One was a larger-than-life bust of Jefferson himself; the other I could not place.

"Hamilton," Jefferson said with a laugh, finally putting on his glasses. "Opposed in death as in life."

In the morning he took me through the library, book by book, then showed me his adjoining study (the *sanctum sanctorum*, Patsy told me; not even a servant could enter without her father's permission). He had furnished it with more bookcases, of course, a desk and a swiveling chair that he had designed himself, and a telescope on a tripod, aimed at Carter's Mountain.

In the parlor he had jammed the walls with three full tiers of paintings purchased during his Paris years. By the French doors stood a harpsichord that I recognized from the Hôtel de Langeac. The dining room held a dumbwaiter built into the walls (he explained, as if I could not guess) so that his guests could speak their minds on any subject without the inhibiting presence of servants.

In the afternoon I saw the ex-President on his hands and knees playing with two grandchildren by the fishpond.

At dinner, while the dumbwaiters hummed and turned, he described his plans for the new university he had at last persuaded the Virginia legislature to establish at Charlottesville, and for which he was designing both the buildings and the curriculum. "If a nation expects to be ignorant and free," he said with all the old Roman firmness, "it expects what never was and never will be."

Did I believe he kept a "Congo harem"?

On the second afternoon I strolled with one of the other guests, a French woman, wife of a former British diplomat, who asked with Gallic thoroughness about every fact and scrap of my life with Jefferson. No, I had not succeeded him as Minister to Paris. Gouverneur Morris had. (The teeth of memory are still very sharp.) Yes, I had stayed through the worst of the revolution, and had lost many friends to the Terror. Who? I named Lafayette, exiled and imprisoned; certain French *américains;* the Duc de La Rochefoucauld, who was dragged from his carriage and stoned to death by rioters while his family watched in horror, and whose young widow had thereafter remained true to his memory, never leaving France, though her friends, some of her friends, one of them, had importuned her with passion.

We had by that time reached the edge of the west lawn, from which we looked down on the slave shacks that lined the lower patio beside the lawn. Directly in front of us three middle-aged black men dressed in gray cotton work clothes stood in a circle, leaning on their rakes. What was my profession now? Madame Thornton asked. Was I also a plantation owner? I scarcely heard the questions. I had visited Jefferson twice or three times in Washington when he was President; once briefly in Monticello when I first returned from France, but the house had no second-story roof then, the daughters lived in other places, I had no stomach for southern realities—I had fled in a day to Philadelphia. And after that I had simply stayed away from Virginia.

What in fact did I do? Madame Thornton repeated her question. I lived on my investments, I told her modestly (money had in fact rained on me for forty days and forty nights from the Philadelphia skies). Thanks to the two magic words *real estate.* And I had just begun a term as an officer of the American Colonization Society, whose goal was the emancipation of Negro slaves and their return to Africa, in a new country of their own.

"You are an abolitionist then?"

"My ideas were formed under our host," I said carefully, gesturing toward the white dome of the house (there was no denying Jefferson's liking for breastlike domes). "Who predicted in a book long ago that black and white could never live together permanently here." It was amazing how well my mind retained Jefferson's very phrases. "Slavery will eventually 'divide us into parties, and produce convulsions which will probably never end but in the extermination of the one or the other race.'"

She was far from shy or indirect, Madame Thornton. She stood, hands on hips, with that pugnacious, sparrowlike tilt of her head that I had seen in other French ladies. "The mulatto servant at dinner last night," she said, "looked exactly like Mr. Jefferson, down to his red hair and freckles."

"His nephew Peter Carr," I said, clearing my throat. I fumbled for the glasses I too used for reading. "Is the acknowledged father."

"By the *family* acknowledged." She switched to French, the language of moral precision. "That housemaid with the big smile is his mistress, yes?"

I put my hand to my mouth and, with great originality, cleared my throat again; a diplomat forever.

"The source of that story was an alcoholic Scotsman named James Callender, Madame. It is a fact that Callender left England after writing an attack on George III and being charged with sedition. In America he set up as an anti-Federalist and went after Hamilton first, whose private life perhaps was not spotless. He subsequently wrote that John Adams was a British spy. That Washington personally robbed the army treasury. That Adams (again) imported for his pleasures not one, but two young mistresses from Europe, one French and one German, then tired of the German and sent her back." I did not add that Adams thought this outrageous charge, which secretly flattered him, had cost him Pennsylvania in his first election, where the Pennsylvania Dutch could never forgive his supposed preference for a French girl over a German.

"The man was encouraged by Jefferson, for a short time only. But after Jefferson rejected his tactics and refused to pay him money, Callender turned on him too and published those . . . reports. As it happens, I have known Sally Hemings since she was fourteen years old and a household servant in Paris, which is where, incidentally, Callender says the affair began."

Madame Thornton had begun to stroll again, leading us away from Mulberry Row toward a painted wooden bench and a bed of bright autumnal flowers.

"That is a lawyer's answer, my dear Chort," she said, reverting to English. "It comes from the head, not the heart." She mocked my pompousness. " 'It is a fact that—Subsequently he wrote that.' Why doesn't Jefferson merely free his slaves? Or deny these charges?"

"He did deny them once." We sat on the bench, facing the splendid house with its dome and its Palladian facade and little roofed pavilion where Jefferson and his wife had spent their wedding night. Stacks of bricks lay to one side of the pavilion, and a wheelbarrow full of trowels and mortar. Like every other house Jefferson had lived in, Monticello was perpetually unfinished. "He did deny the charges in a letter to a friend. I have seen it. But he refused to allow the letter to be published. He is a very private man."

The tall, angular profile of our host was just visible now, passing from one room to another. My mind took an odd turn. Jefferson loved windows, he needed sunlight daily, he had told me once; but wherever he lived, invariably he put up shutters or blinds on all the windows, as if to let in light but keep himself hidden. While I watched he vanished into the shadows of his study. A second odd association. At dinner yesterday, pouring my wine, he had said that Maria Cosway's husband had died and she was now in Italy, a nun.

"And as for freeing them, Mr. Jefferson believes it is right to wait till they can earn their own livings, with a skill. He has set some free already." James Hemings for one, who had left Monticello and looked me up in Philadelphia; then returned to Monticello, left again, finally committed suicide in a drunken stupor. I would not tell Madame Thornton. Nor would I tell her that Jefferson's wealth, such as it was, now consisted almost entirely of slaves. If he freed more, he would soon have nothing, leave nothing for his grandchildren to inherit. My own view (brutally correct, as it turned out) was that he would die a bankrupt.

Madame Thornton was now sitting on the edge of the bench, looking up at me quite curiously.

"I notice that you always answer what Mr. Jefferson thinks. You never speak for yourself," she said.

I took a deep breath and looked up into the cloudless blue Virginian sky.

"Then I don't believe a word of it," I said, speaking for myself, freely, from the heart.

"Because he is your hero," she said simply.

Yes.

Note

There was really a William Short. I have brought him back early from his Italian trip and altered a few other minor dates; I have also returned Lafayette to Paris on one occasion when he was away and have moved Vergennes's office around at Versailles. And as Clérisseau rightly suspected, I have transferred one famous Parisian anecdote from Franklin to Jefferson. Otherwise, *Jefferson* keeps to the generally agreed-upon facts as I have found them in Short's papers (now in the Library of Congress) and numerous other contemporary letters and diaries, above all in the vast annotated edition of Jefferson's writings published by Princeton University Press under the editorship of Julian Boyd.

I am grateful to the research staff at Monticello for many kindnesses, particularly to Lucia Stanton, who allowed me to study the proofsheets of her forthcoming edition (with James A. Bear, Jr.) of Jefferson's account books. Jack McLaughlin, author of *Jefferson and Monticello,* and Douglas Wilson, editor of Jefferson's *Commonplace Book,* have been generous correspondents. For information about Jefferson's most celebrated work I have drawn on Jay Fliegelman's *Declaring Independence: Jefferson, Natural Language, and the Culture of Performance.*

I thank Diana Dulaney for computing my words into prose and

Janet Biehl for scrupulously checking my history. I likewise thank the staff at the Bibliothèque Historique de la Ville de Paris, whose beautiful rooms date back to the years when Jefferson knew Paris. And finally, I am most deeply grateful to Steve Rubin, who first suggested this project, to Virginia Barber, who knows only encouraging words, and to Kate Miciak, who is a wonderful, wonderful editor.